Suzanne Wright lives in England with her husband and two children. When she's not spending time with her family, she's writing, reading or doing her version of housework – sweeping the house with a look.

She's worked in a pharmaceutical company, at a Disney Store, at a primary school as a voluntary teaching assistant, at the RSPCA and has a First Class Honours degree in Psychology and Identity Studies.

As to her interests, she enjoys reading, writing, reading, writing (sort of eat, sleep, write, repeat), spending time with her family, movie nights with her sisters and playing with her two Bengal kittens.

To connect with Suzanne online:

Website: http://www.suzannewright.co.uk
Facebook: https://www.facebook.com/suzannewrightfanpage

Also by Suzanne Wright:

The Dark in You

Burn
Blaze
Ashes
Embers
Shadows
Omens
Fallen
Reaper
Hunted
Viper
Legion

The Devil's Cradle

The Wicked In Me
The Nightmare in Him
The Monsters We Are

SUZANNE WRIGHT
LEGION
A Dark in You novel

PIATKUS

PIATKUS

First published in Great Britain in 2025 by Piatkus

1 3 5 7 9 10 8 6 4 2

Copyright © Suzanne Wright, 2025

The moral right of the author has been asserted.

*All characters and events in this publication, other than those
clearly in the public domain, are fictitious and any resemblance
to real persons, living or dead, is purely coincidental.*

All rights reserved.
No part of this publication may be reproduced, stored in a
retrieval system, or transmitted, in any form or by any means, without
the prior permission in writing of the publisher, nor be otherwise circulated
in any form of binding or cover other than that in which it is published
and without a similar condition including this condition being
imposed on the subsequent purchaser.

A CIP catalogue record for this book
is available from the British Library.

ISBN: 978-0-349-44038-5

Typeset in Goudy by M Rules

Printed and bound in Great Britain by
Clays Ltd, Elcograf S.p.A.

Papers used by Piatkus are from well-managed forests
and other responsible sources.

Piatkus
An imprint of
Little, Brown Book Group
Carmelite House
50 Victoria Embankment
London EC4Y 0DZ

The authorised representative
in the EEA is
Hachette Ireland
8 Castlecourt Centre
Dublin 15, D15 XTP3, Ireland
(email: info@hbgi.ie)

An Hachette UK Company
www.hachette.co.uk

www.littlebrown.co.uk

For Ivy

CHAPTER ONE

Turning away from the canvas propped up against the breakroom wall, Tobe smiled at her, his blue eyes twinkling. "It's amazing. Moody. Striking. An absolutely *perfect* replica. Take a fucking bow."

Naomi Chamberlain felt her lips curve up. "I already did. Twice." She shrugged at the three imps in front of her, adding, "I'm humble that way."

Chugging down more of her coffee, she cast the landscape painting a quick look. The artist of the original was on the level of Monet and Picasso, but Naomi had always had a knack for re-creating any drawing or painting she laid eyes on—even as a child.

"No art appraiser would ever guess that this wasn't an original," Ciaran declared. "Not that any will ever see it. This is for a client's personal collection."

"I don't know why he collects fakes," said Lachlan, scratching at his salt-and-pepper hair. "Most people hire us to steal originals."

"He has no genuine art in his collection, only fakes," Tobe told the older imp. "He keeps it all in a vault in his basement."

Alarm bells going off in her head, Naomi tipped it to the side. "And how would you know?"

Lachlan leaned into Tobe, his tall figure towering over him by a few inches. "Don't answer that," he muttered.

She narrowed her eyes. "You didn't break into it, did you?"

"Don't answer that either," Lachlan told him.

Tobe shot her a disbelieving look, managing to appear offended by her question. He folded his toned arms over his equally defined chest. "Do you honestly think that I'd consider breaking into not only the home but the vault of a human honest-to-God mobster?"

"Yep, totally," she replied, under no illusions about him.

Tobe could be described as many things—including a thief, liar, card shark, embezzler, seller of counterfeit art, and master of breaking and entering... which didn't make him much different from most imps in their lair.

"Tell me you at least didn't steal anything from the guy," she pressed.

Lachlan leaned into Tobe again. "*Definitely* don't answer that."

Naomi sighed, and her inner demon rolled its eyes. Honestly, having imps in your life could give anyone an ulcer. She was a siren like her mother, but most of their lair were imps. They tended to disregard all laws, not to mention their own safety. The latter particularly drove her crazy when it came to Tobe—as psi-mates, they were very close.

All their kind had a predestined psi-mate. An anchor in the storm that was a demon's existence due to their struggle to maintain supremacy over their psychopathic inner entity. Forming a mental link with your anchor ended that struggle, though a person's inner entity still surfaced as and when it pleased for what were usually brief pockets of time.

"Once the client coughs up the cash, I'll get it to you," Tobe said to her.

She nodded and took another mouthful of her coffee. As the aforementioned client was a repeat customer, she wasn't worried that the deal would go bad—they'd always gone smoothly in the past.

"I'll be doing the handover on the same day I take the abstract painting to that annoying harbinger who keeps pushing to meet *his artist*. Like you're his own personal pet painter," Tobe added, scraping an agitated hand through his deep-brown hair.

The harbinger was truly becoming a pain in the padded ass. "If he does it again, tell him I'm done and that he'll need to find another painter." Naomi preferred to remain anonymous. Stefan Brandt wasn't the first client to request that she meet them face to face, but unlike him, the others had accepted her refusal with grace.

Imps came in handy if you needed to operate in the shadows. Take Tobe, for example. He acted as a middleman for people looking for commissioned art from ghost artists. Kind of like a ghost writer, Naomi produced and sold work that others could take personal credit for. Then there were clients who wanted replicas of classic pieces, or fake "lost paintings" by famous artists that then often ended up in art galleries and museums.

She also acted as hostess part-time here at her stepfather's pizzeria. It meant people didn't question how she made money, because she'd only trusted a few with the knowledge that she was a ghost artist.

Naomi wasn't a fan of the spotlight. Being a siren, she was a sexual magnet of sorts, and had attracted attention all her life. So much whistling, ogling, staring, and heckling. She was constantly hit on, constantly oversexualized, constantly underestimated.

People outside her lair often assumed that she was dumb, superficial, and up for a good time. They didn't expect her to have talents, or be a hard worker, or have any real *substance*. And there seemed to be this societal attitude that since she was beautiful, she had no right to complain about anything. It rankled with her inner entity something fierce.

"Naomi?"

She blinked, refocusing on Tobe. "What?"

"I lost you again, huh?"

It would be fair to say that she had a habit of mentally drifting. Her brain would follow rabbit trails, and she'd end up zoning out. "What did I miss?"

"I asked what time Belinsky's supposed to show up for his sit-down with Jolene."

The mention of the male Prime made her pulse stutter. Luka Belinsky might be the boss of an underground demonic crime syndicate, but he was also sex on a stick. "Any minute now, unless he plans on being fashionably late."

"Do we think he'll step in and help with the Iain situation?" asked Ciaran, setting his hands on his trim hips.

Naomi shrugged. She didn't know the guy; had only met him on the three occasions he'd eaten at the pizzeria over the past couple of months. Each time, he'd watched her in a way that made her feel hunted—the sheer boldness of it intrigued her entity. But despite the sparks of sexual tension that bounced between them, he'd never made a move on her or given her any indication that he would.

Lachlan rubbed at his bristly jaw. "It's hard to say. Belinsky is a cold son of a bitch. Mean as a snake and as ruthless as they come." Respect coated every word.

"So I've heard." Luka's reputation certainly proceeded him. "But you don't successfully manage a lair that doubles as an overly large crime family by being 'nice'," Naomi pointed out.

The criminal underworld was a dark place. The *demonic* criminal underbelly was a thousand times uglier. Nonetheless, Luka kept his alliances strong, ensured his businesses thrived, persistently held back enemies, and maintained peace with other lairs. That would require a certain mercilessness.

"I know his anchor a little," said Ciaran. "Ella spoke to me about him a couple of times; said that though he has a twisted kind of code that can change by the minute—a code he won't always listen to—he's not a bad guy. Don't know how accurate that is, but I know he's very protective of her and her daughter."

"It's well known that he runs a tight ship and doesn't let his demons get away with any bullshit," Tobe added, "so my gut says he's unlikely to ignore the fact that Iain won't leave you alone. Hopefully he'll have a word with him and that'll be that."

Lachlan pulled a face, doubt gleaming in his dark-blue gaze. "I'm not sure it'll be that simple for Iain to let go. He's in the firm grip of a full-on obsession."

Which could be blamed on the good ole siren song. Its notes weren't audible; they were more like predatory vibes that sought to bewitch their prey. Naomi had no control over that. It was just as much a part of her as the blood in her veins.

When it came to dating, she was careful to choose men who were mentally tough and had their shit together. They were less likely to fall victim to a siren song. But it wasn't always a guarantee—case in point.

"You know, we could just kill Iain," Lachlan threw out with a casual shrug. "I'd make it quick."

Tobe gave a mocking snort. "No you wouldn't."

"No, I wouldn't." Lachlan pursed his lips, his brows sliding together. "Don't know why I even said that."

"I do," claimed Tobe. "You're a fucking liar."

Lachlan looked appropriately offended. "I resent that implication."

"It was a statement, not an implication."

"I only edit the truth when it's necessary."

Tobe frowned. "How was it necessary to tell me that you only edit the truth when it's necessary? Because *that* was a lie, too."

Lachlan turned to fully face him, studying him closely. "You're not really bothered about that, are you? You're still mad at me for stealing your uncle's watch. That's what this is about."

Tobe's mouth tightened. "Well, it was disrespectful."

"How? He's dead, what could he possibly do with it?"

"My aunt wanted him to be buried with it. You took it off his wrist while he was in his damn casket. A casket you *dug up*. You also took his shoes."

"My own were muddy from all the digging."

Unable to bite back a smile, Naomi exchanged an amused look with Ciaran ... which was right when her stepfather's mind bumped against hers. *A black town car just pulled up outside*, Alfie telepathed. *Pretty sure it's Belinsky.*

Her belly did a slow roll. Knowing that Jolene wanted her to greet him at the hostess station, she replied, *I'll be right out.*

Refocusing on the imps in front of her, she said, "Luka seems to have arrived, so I'm gonna get moving. I'll leave you three to get the painting ready to be transported."

After rinsing her empty cup, Naomi placed it on the drainer and then exited the breakroom. By nature, she wasn't a person who was easily rattled—especially by something as simple as sexual tension. But there wasn't anything simple about the tension that existed between her and Luka. It was too visceral, too oppressive. Hence the butterflies in her stomach.

Doing her best to quash said butterflies, she strode down the narrow hallway. On reaching the dark wooden door that led to the dimly lit main eating area, she pushed it open. Immediately, the scents of spices, tomatoes, cheese, peppers, and garlic swirled around her.

The place was full, but not rowdy. Its color palette of taupe, yellow, and burgundy complemented the informal Italian feel to the place. The murmuring of voices, sizzling of food, and scraping of cutlery on plates overlaid the soft background music.

She gave a quick wave to her stepfather, Alfie, who was prepping food in the open kitchen along with several other chefs. Waiters went back and forth carrying trays or electronic notepads. Some patrons sat at the ornate tables. Others were tucked into booths or stood at the bar.

Weaving her way through the tables, Naomi plucked a bit of lint from her black dress. It was elegant, but enhanced "the girls", clung to her curves, and stopped just above her knees.

Arriving at the hostess station, she smiled at the petite redheaded waitress there. "Thanks for covering for me."

"No problem," said Donna absently, her attention on the window – or whatever lay beyond it.

Naomi tracked her gaze ... and saw a veritable sexual cocktail of supreme masculinity striding toward the pizzeria. Luka moved with the fluid, powerful grace of a tiger, carrying an unmistakable air of nobility; of a person who was to be obeyed, served, and feared. Like he owned the freaking world.

Donna swiftly scarpered. Unsurprising. By virtue of being a legion—a rare breed of demon that hosted three inner entities—he naturally unnerved people. What amped up their fear was that the guy radiated an unchecked danger that seeped out like ooze, touching even those at a fair distance from him.

One of his bodyguards shoved open the door, briefly scanned the venue, and then nodded at Luka. The Prime breezed inside, his default stony expression firmly in place. Naomi's inner demon went ahead and eye-banged him.

Who wouldn't?

Naomi was average height, but Luka was so tall that he made her feel petite. He was also lean and broad-shouldered. His piercing eyes—a striking velvety black—were as dark as his short hair and layer of stubble.

In his tailored suit, not a wrinkle in sight or a hair out of place, he looked groomed, elegant, and—despite his distinct reptilian coldness—oh so very fuckable.

There was something almost scandalizing about possessing such staggeringly lethal sex appeal. It was indecent. An outrage. Totally unfair. It crawled over your defenses and seeped into any fracture it could find.

Luka's gaze fixed on Naomi, and yeah, her pulse lost its shit. He prowled toward her, his focus holding a rapacious edge. The faintest shimmer of power steamed the air around him—a drugging thing for her demon.

The first time they'd come face to face, her primitive hindbrain had woken up and warned, *Careful*. Nonetheless, her hormones had become ridiculously light-headed. They were doing the same thing right now.

Luka came to a stop in front of her station, his eyes still locked on her face. A very familiar static awareness laced with sexual chemistry buzzed to life and pricked at her skin like blunt needles.

How annoying. She flashed him her courteous hostess smile. "Mr. Belinsky," she greeted. "Welcome back to Sizzle and Slice Pizzeria."

"Luka," he corrected with the bare hint of a Russian accent. "I'm scheduled to meet Jolene here." There was a distinct sexy roughness to his voice, as though his vocal cords had once been damaged.

"She let me know you'd be coming." Naomi flicked a look at his guards—two identical rough-looking muscle-bound brothers with buzz cuts and sharp gray gazes. "Will all three of you be eating?"

"No. Just myself."

She nabbed two menus. "Follow me, I'll take you to Jolene. She's waiting for you in the private dining room."

Luka trailed behind the waitress, still recovering from a brutal punch of need to his gut. Each time he laid eyes on the creature in front of him, sheer want ripped through him. A visceral reaction he had no way of fighting. Partly because she was a siren, but also because she was a fucking vision.

Long, thick lashes framed her hooded gray-green eyes. Blonde streaks ran through the silky cinnamon-brown hair she'd loosely curled at the ends. She was slender but curvy. Her breasts were high and round, her legs long and shapely. She smelled like pure sexual heaven, and her voice—all smoke and sin—was an enticement all on its own.

Sensuality seemed woven into her very being. It could be seen in her eyes, her smile, the sinuous way she moved.

She hadn't only snagged Luka's interest, she'd snagged that of his entities. The trio were as conscienceless, remorseless, and malevolent as all inner demons. That said, they were each different in their own way and had named themselves when Luka was an infant.

Chronically broody, Dagon was a skilled liar and manipulator. The ever-narcissistic Abraxas was preoccupied with beauty and sought to charm women. Belial was probably a little insane, really—the only joy the mercurial sadist found in life came from hurting, degrading, and shaming others.

And currently, they were all focused on the woman in front of them.

It was a typical scenario around Little Miss Naomi Chamberlain—he'd learned her name from the background check he'd done on her. It had revealed nothing of note. She lived a simple, quiet life. She spent most of her free time alone at home, only venturing out when going to work, shopping, visiting her parents, or meeting up with her psi-mate.

If Luka didn't know any better, he'd think it all bullshit. The picture the dossier painted was just a little too pretty for a demon—especially one who'd grown up around imps.

"The place is as busy as ever," he observed aloud.

She glanced at him over her shoulder before pushing open a door. "It's fast become a staple in this area of Vegas. Not a shocker. As I told you once before, you won't find better pizza elsewhere."

She *had* told him that, Luka recalled as he followed her through the door and along a hallway. *'That's a bold claim,'* he'd replied back then, to which she'd said, *'And a fact. I'll be surprised if you don't become a return customer. It's rare that people don't come again.'*

He'd returned twice, but it wasn't merely for the good food. It was for her. He would have made a move on first meeting her, but he'd not long ago walked away from a fling. He liked to leave a short period between such arrangements. So he'd waited. Watched her. Bided his time.

Arriving at another door, she paused. "Here we are."

Reaching out to the twins on their telepathic channel, Luka said, *Wait here.* They only nodded in response.

He didn't anticipate any issues cropping up. Jolene Wallis was unpredictable with a splash of crazy, but they had a tentative alliance—one they'd formed when his anchor and her daughter began spending time with several of Jolene's imps, including the woman's granddaughters.

He followed Naomi into the private dining room. It was cozy and stylish, featuring only a table and six chairs.

Decked out in a simple blouse, pencil skirt, and high heels, Jolene rose from the table, a smile on her face that somehow seemed both welcoming and shrewd. "Luka, always a pleasure."

"Jolene," he greeted smoothly as Dagon observed her intently, always recognizing a fellow master manipulator.

Jolene waved Luka into the chair opposite her own as she lowered herself back into it.

"Your waitress will be with you in a few moments to take your orders," Naomi announced, laying the two menus in the center of the table.

Jolene cast her a smile. "Thank you, Naomi."

"Enjoy your meal," Naomi said before breezing out of the room.

Luka's entities all grumbled their annoyance, only placated by the knowledge that he would speak to her again before he left the pizzeria.

His skin still tingled slightly from how the notes of her song had played over him, searching and exploring; looking for some weakness to exploit so it could drag him under its spell. It had failed, but that wasn't to say he didn't still intend to have her in his bed.

He skimmed his gaze around the room. "Just how many hidden bugs and cameras are in here?"

"Maybe none. Maybe many." Jolene waved away his concern and nabbed a menu. "I don't plan on asking personal questions. I only hope for us to come to an agreement about something."

Luka felt his eyes narrow. "If you're intending to request that I grant your lair admittance to Infernal, my answer will be a resounding no." Imps as a species were barred from his illegal gambling club due to their habit of cheating and stealing.

"Nothing like that," she assured him. "I seek only your cooperation."

He grabbed the other menu. "Cooperation on what, exactly?"

At that moment, a young waitress entered the room. Luka and Jolene gave their orders for drinks and food, and the girl left.

He snapped his menu shut and lowered it to the table. "So?" he prompted, ignoring Abraxas' put-out sigh—it didn't want to talk to Jolene, it wanted to track down the pretty siren.

"Iain Forrester," Jolene threw out. "He's one of your demons, correct?"

It hadn't really been a question. "You know he is."

"He's also being a major pain in the ass. It can't be allowed to continue."

Luka fought a frown. "Expand on that."

"He dated one of my demons. They were together a little over four weeks—nothing serious, just light and fun. Although it's been three months since they parted ways, he won't let it go. Won't let *her* go. He bombards her with texts, turns up at her house, and sends her gifts."

Luka couldn't wrestle back a frown this time, because that didn't sound like Iain.

"She's tried different ways to make him admit defeat and leave her be. She's yelled at him. Ignored him. Threatened him. Even set his hair on fire at one point. He just keeps coming back. Like the clap."

"You want me to intervene," Luka guessed.

"Actually, I want to fish out his gullet with a rusty spoon, but I'm pretty sure you'd have an issue with that. I'd prefer that we weren't at odds. So yes, Luka, I'm going to need you to intervene. As a psi-demon, he can feed from people's emotions and drain them dry; I won't risk him turning that gift on her. You make a bad enemy, but so do I," Jolene warned, her face hardening. "If there's one thing imps are good at, it's making themselves a problem for others."

Understatement of the century.

"I can see that Iain's behavior has surprised you. He might not have been stalkerish in the past, but I'll bet he has a history of being clingy and overly possessive when in relationships."

Some of the whispers he'd heard about the demon in question flitted to the forefront of Luka's mind. "I might have heard something to that effect."

"Traits like that can often be problematic for male demons who get involved with sirens—their allure draws out the intensity of those characteristics."

That was when the penny dropped. "Naomi. She's his ex."

"Yes."

Agitation spiked through Luka and his demons. He straightened in his seat. "Why wasn't I informed of Iain's behavior before now?"

"Naomi didn't report it to me initially because she kept expecting his obsession to wear off. But it hasn't, and none of her attempts made him back off. Just about done with his shit, she finally came to me. And now I'm coming to you. There's little point in us having an alliance if we can't count on each other at such times."

Luka gritted his teeth. If you were around a particular siren often enough, you could become desensitized to their song . . . unless you fell victim to it. He wouldn't have expected Iain to do the latter. "I want to talk to her."

"I suspected you would, which is why I asked you to meet me

at her place of work." Jolene's eyes went out of focus—a telltale sign that she was using telepathy. Moments later, her gaze sharpened on him once more. "She'll be with us soon."

The waitress arrived first. She set drinks on their table and assured them that their food would soon follow. It was as she was leaving the room that Naomi returned. Her gaze found Luka's, and, that easily, lust smoothed its way up his spine.

Abraxas grinned, pleased she was back. It adored women. Well, it adored the validation of their attention.

"What d'ya need?" she asked, her gaze bouncing from Luka to her Prime.

"To talk to you," he told her. "Alone."

Jolene stilled. "I called you here—"

"And we spoke. Now I want to talk to Naomi."

"You can do that while I'm present."

"You know I won't hurt her, so there's no need for you to object to my speaking with her alone."

"Why request that?"

"There may be things she'd prefer not to mention in front of you—mostly because it's well known that you blow up entire buildings when in a rage. I want all the facts. She can always call out to you telepathically if she feels the need to."

Sensing that Jolene might argue regardless, Naomi smoothly edged forward and said, "It's fine. I don't mind talking to him alone."

Her lips thinning, Jolene stared at Luka thoughtfully for long moments. "All right," she said eventually. "If you're sure, Naomi."

"I'm sure." Naomi found Luka intimidating, yes, but she didn't fear him. Nor did her demon. The fact was that she was no easy target. Her Prime knew that well.

Jolene rose from her seat, shot Luka a look of warning, and then swanned out of the room.

Naomi took the seat she had vacated and met his gaze steadily. He was still, but not the slightest bit tense. On the contrary, he was at ease, comfortable. And so very *watchful*. His eyes were fixed on her face, unwaveringly intense, as if intent on not missing a thing. It rubbed at her nerves, because Naomi didn't like scrutiny as a rule.

She waited for him to speak, entirely too conscious of the chemistry buzzing in the air between them. It only added to her discomfort.

"You don't need to fear me," he assured her, clearly mistaking the source of her unease.

"Hmm, pretty sure I'd be a fool not to."

His lips twitched minutely. "I mean you no harm. I'd just like for us to talk." Leaning back in his seat, as if to seem no threat, he went on, "I want specifics regarding Iain. How often does he contact you?"

"Daily. Usually by text, though he sends them via spoofing websites using different phone numbers."

"And what do those messages say?"

"The classics, really. 'I miss you', 'I love you', 'We're not over', 'You're meant to be mine.' That sort of thing." It was *beyond* tiring.

"Jolene said he comes by your house."

"At least once a week." It pissed off her demon something fierce. "In the beginning, I would open the door and tell him to leave. Now I just ignore that he's there."

"He also sends you gifts, yes?"

She nodded. "Mostly flowers. Sometimes chocolates. The occasional plush bear. Clichéd stuff. He leaves them on my doorstep while I'm at work."

Something dark moved behind Luka's eyes. "How often?"

"Two or three times a month. In sum, he's been a busy boy."

"And this has been going on for three months now?" he double-checked.

"Yup."

"And yet he hasn't been beaten to a pulp by any of your relatives. Odd. Imps aren't the type to overlook such things."

No, they definitely weren't. "I managed to convince them to stay out of this."

"Really?" Luka asked, skepticism coloring his words.

"Okay, correction, I managed to talk them out of attacking him. But they've retaliated in other ways, as have I." Messed with his finances, slashed his tires, had him declared dead in several states. "Nothing helped."

Luka drummed his fingers on the table. "I wouldn't have pegged him for someone who would be swept under by a siren song."

"Me neither, or I wouldn't have agreed to date him." Sometimes people who came across as tough and confident were hiding a fragile ego—even from themselves. Not the demon in front of her, though. Luka Belinsky was *not* a guy who'd get caught up in a siren song. Too powerful. Too steady. Too much his own man.

"Look, I know it's not his fault that he's in the throes of a siren-induced obsession," she continued. "But much as he can't control how it's messing with his mind, he *can* control how he reacts to that. An obsession doesn't steal your will or dictate your actions. He could stop if he wanted. He just won't."

"Has he at any point threatened you?"

Naomi's nape tingled at the overly casual question—a hint of danger was threaded through it. "No, but I can sense he's becoming impatient with me. He truly feels that I'm being unreasonable. It only seems like a matter of time before this gets ugly."

Luka's eyelids lowered slightly. "You sound as though you have experience with things becoming ugly. Other men in your past were violent?"

Her skin pebbled at his dark tone. Her demon, on the other hand, wanted to roll around in all that menace. It had a weakness for danger and power. Oh, and diamonds. "There were threats. Only one guy followed through with it—he tried to scar my cheeks and forehead with a knife so that I'd forever be marked as his."

Luka muttered a Russian curse. *Asshole*, she knew—one of her demonic abilities was to understand and speak every possible language. "What happened to him?" he asked.

"Many things," she replied vaguely. "He did apologize after the obsession lost its hold on him. He was in fact deeply ashamed of his words and actions. Iain may feel equally ashamed when he's back to his usual self. The sooner that happens, the better, because things can escalate to a point where someone gets hurt." And that someone would *never* be her.

Right then, the door swung open and Jolene walked in with a tray balanced on her hand. "I caught Donna heading here, so I thought I'd bring our food myself."

Probably a good thing, given how nervous Donna felt around Luka.

"I hope you two are done talking. I don't want our pizza getting cold."

"Naomi has brought me up to speed on everything," Luka replied. "I will speak with Iain and ensure that he doesn't bother her again."

Jolene grinned, satisfied. "Just what I wanted to hear."

"Thank you," Naomi said to him as she stood, grateful for the excuse to escape being the focal point of his attention. "I'll let the two of you enjoy your meal." She walked out of the room and began making her way back to the hostess station.

As she reached it, Donna approached and asked, "Well, how'd it go?"

"Luka has agreed to step in," Naomi told her.

Relief washed over the waitress's elfin face. "Good. Maybe he'll have better luck getting through to Iain."

"Let's hope so."

The front door opened once more, and a cute couple entered. Focusing on them, Naomi gave them her warmest smile. Over the next hour, she greeted several patrons and showed them to tables or booths.

She was tidying the pile of menus when her skin prickled as the weight of someone's attention settled over her. She instinctively looked over her shoulder, her stomach clenching as she saw Luka striding down the aisle with his guards in tow.

His gaze flitted over her face. "I'll speak with Iain tomorrow morning. Be assured that he will stay away from you in future."

She gave a slow nod.

He paused, his eyes dark and hot on hers. "I'll be back." With that, he and his guards were gone.

Donna rematerialized at her side. "I don't think he meant that he'll be back for pizza. I think he meant that he'll be back for *you*."

"He'll want to let me know how his conversation with Iain goes," Naomi pointed out.

"Maybe so, but I doubt that's *all* he wants. It's obvious that he's into you."

Just because he was attracted to Naomi didn't mean that he intended to do anything about it. And really, it was probably better that he didn't. Because she could sense that he was a perceptive son of a bitch; the kind of man who'd ferret out all a girl's secrets if he put his mind to it. And she had plenty to guard—one in particular was a doozy.

Setting the matter aside, she went back to work. At the end of her shift, she helped Alfie close the place down, said her goodbyes, then slipped on her jacket and left.

The pizzeria was only a five-minute walk from her home, so she arrived soon enough. Her house was small but cozy—living alone, she didn't need a lot of space.

Inside, she kicked off her heels and tucked them under the bench in the hall. She then removed her jacket and hung it on one of the hooks high above the bench.

Intent on making herself a cup of green tea, she walked into the living room. The first floor was open-plan, the living room separated from the kitchen and dining area by partial glass walls, creating zones.

Naomi froze as she reached for the light switch, her instincts screaming at her.

She wasn't alone.

CHAPTER TWO

A man stepped out of the shadows. And another. And another. Very soon, Naomi was surrounded by seven bald, clean-shaven, sword-wielding men. They all wore black clothes that were plain aside from the emblem on the breast pocket. A silver shield over which a red crucifix was embroidered.

Crucifix?

Angry at its home being invaded, her entity slunk forward to study them. Though they seemed human, there was a certain *air* to them. It was preternatural. Light. Spiritual.

Clerics, she concluded.

Descendants of the Nephilim.

Born with the innate ability to channel divine power, clerics—also referred to as Eliouds—regularly embarked on holy quests.

One idly angled his sword in a way that allowed the light to dance along the blade. The steel gleamed as if it had been given an infusion of magick. A glance at the other swords confirmed that they too weren't simple weapons.

While clerics somewhat loathed demons, they generally didn't target them without very good reason. Why a holy quest could bring them *here*, Naomi had no clue.

She did know that she wouldn't be letting any of them come near her with those bespelled blades. Nor would she be engaging in any fencing—she was quite frankly shit at it.

"To what do I owe the pleasure?" she asked as the molten power that lived inside her naturally rose, gathering beneath her skin. The room temperature would steadily rise along with it.

The cleric directly in front of her tilted his head slightly, his green gaze narrowing. "You seem surprised to see us here, yet not afraid. I suppose you believe that he will crawl out of the depths of hell to save you."

Naomi could only stare at him, dumbfounded. "I'm sorry, what?"

"God will permit no interference from him or anyone else," he added, ignoring her question. "Tonight can only go one way."

"The dark one's plans must be thwarted," another cleric threw in.

The dark one? Naomi sighed. "You guys escaped from the funny farm, didn't you?" Really, it made perfect sense. "Drop your weapons," she ordered, injecting compulsive power into her voice. But, uh, they didn't.

Green Eyes flicked up a brow. "We are aware that you are a siren. Did you think we would not magickly shield our minds from compulsion before coming here?"

Well, she'd hoped that they hadn't. "You appear to know plenty about me. It seems only fair for that to be a two-way thing. You're not going to introduce yourselves?"

He tightened his hand around the hilt of his sword. "You do not need to know who we are. All that matters is what brought us here."

"The need to thwart the dark one's plans, right?" *Eye-roll.* "And who is he, exactly?"

"Oh, he has been given many monikers. The Great Pretender. The Bringer of Light. The Morning Star. The Father of Lies."

Naomi blinked slowly. "Wait, you're talking about the devil?" *Unreal.* Lucifer wasn't actually some pure evil, all-powerful beast of a being. More of a mercurial, childlike, asocial stoner.

"If it were possible, we would kill him to prevent what is to come. But he is out of our reach, and so it is you we must end. We cannot allow the prophecy to come to fruition." The cleric spoke in a very old language before adding, "That translates to: 'For she who bears the mark will birth the child of the devil.'"

Oh, dear Lord, these guys were ridiculous.

"The air is becoming hot," a younger cleric noted, his cheeks flushing. "What are you doing?"

"Inwardly laughing at how pathetic you all are, if I'm honest," replied Naomi. "You can't truly believe that I'm going to squeeze out the devil's kid."

"We *know* that you will." The cleric to her left lifted his sword. "We cannot allow the Antichrist to walk this earth, and so you must die."

"Or"—the burning force within her bubbled, hissed, and snapped—"we have a little fun instead." And then her power burst out of her in red-violet flames that engulfed her from head to toe.

The clerics squinted, flinching back at the sheer brightness of the flames, shock rippling over their faces—all of which she saw clearly, the fire no obstruction to her vision.

They recovered fast, their lips rattling as they chanted low, the words coming quickly as glowing streams of pure-white magick arrowed at her.

Some hits landed, but the flames surrounding her dulled their impact, so they were more like stinging pokes than blazing-hot stabs. Still, they carried enough of a burn that she hissed.

"Not nice." She slashed out her arm, tossing a rope of red-violet fire that quickly morphed into the shape of a snake. It looped around Green Eyes' neck and bit into his face. He screamed as the roasting-hot lethal venom entered his system.

Another cleric came at her from the left, swinging his sword. Hot pain blazed along her side as the steel sliced into her flesh. She bared her teeth at him, not placated by how the flames engulfing her body had melted the tip of his weapon—especially when she felt something foreign trying to push its way into her: a pulsing barb of insidious magick.

The fire that lived inside her rushed upward, incinerating the barb, cauterizing her wound, and neatly knitting her skin back together.

He blinked, his lips parting.

"Well, that was stupid." Naomi pyroported behind him, grabbed his head, and gave it a vicious twist. *Crack.* He and his weapon dropped to the floor with a thud.

Yelling out their rage, two others charged at her. She slammed up her hands and released flickering blasts of red-violet fire, lighting up both clerics like they were Roman candles. They screamed and staggered, their blades hitting the floor with a clang, their skin sizzling and blackening as her acidic power scorched them.

Magick crackled as ropes of it traveled through the air toward her again.

She flung out her arm once more, emitting a glimmering wave of red-violet fire that sliced through the streams, making the magick *wink* out of existence. Glaring at her attacker, she tossed out another red-violet fiery serpent, watching as it wrapped around his head before burying its fangs into the top of his scalp. *Yeah, that had to hurt.*

A fifth cleric charged her with a battle cry. Naomi snatched a fallen weapon and hurled it at the bastard. The sword speared him, stabbing right through his heart. He stumbled to a stop and dropped to his knees, the life beginning to bleed from his gaze.

Twirling rivulets of magick hit her from the side, stabbing at her so hard so she almost jerked. Naomi locked onto her assailant and retaliated with a shimmering wave of fire that curled around him like a giant serpent; engulfing in flames that began to eat him alive.

She turned her focus back to the last cleric alive—Green Eyes. He was on his knees, his skin pale, his gaze cloudy, his face creased with pain from the snake venom.

She took a moment to toss a red-violet ball of incinerating flames at the other clerics, and watched as fire rushed over every inch of the bodies. It would go to work quickly and swallow its victims, consuming all trace of them until nothing was left—not even ash.

Leaving the flames to do their job, she moved toward Green Eyes.

Resentment briefly blazed in his gaze. "What are you?"

"To put it simply, I'm a person you should have left well alone." Taking his sword from the floor, Naomi squatted in front of him. "You see, you mistranslated that little sentence of whatever prophecy you quoted." Thanks to her gift, she had understood the language perfectly. "It does say that I will bear a mark—and I do, yes. As for the rest? You're off base. I'm not going to birth the child of the devil." She inched her face closer to his. "I *am* the child of the devil."

She deftly swung the sword and lopped off his head.

*

After she'd relayed the incident to a select few in her living room a short time later, Tobe set his hands on his hips. "Unreal. This is fucking unreal. All your life you've hidden your connection to Lou ... and a bunch of clerics just went and unearthed it. Yeah, they mistook its source, but still."

As far as the preternatural world was aware, Lou's children lived in hell. Naomi was the exception, but hiding the truth of her parentage kept her safe. She might otherwise be used by demons or celestials to either gain Lou's cooperation or punish him.

It wasn't distrust that kept her from sharing the truth with the rest of her lair. She didn't believe they were a threat to her. It was simply that the best way to keep something secret was to ensure a minimal amount of people were aware of it. And it wasn't as if her lair *needed* to know, was it?

Her mom had entrusted Jolene with the information, and then later Alfie. Naturally, Jolene had felt comfortable sharing it with her psi-mate, Beck. Once Naomi formed the anchor bond with Tobe, she'd revealed her secret to him. Jolene's twin grandchildren, Ciaran and Khloë, only knew because they'd overheard Naomi talking to Tobe about it a year ago. She wasn't worried that they'd blab—the twins would never endanger anyone in their lair.

She gently nudged a sword with her foot—the weapons were the only evidence left of her intruders, since she'd burned every corpse. "The clerics clearly didn't know the truth of Lou's nature, or they wouldn't have thought he could be responsible for the conception of the Antichrist."

Most non-demons *didn't* know the facts. Satan, a hell-dwelling monster of sorts, was the true anthesis of God; *his* offspring would be considered the Antichrist. Lou was a fallen celestial being—singular in some ways, but not as powerful as Satan.

"That tells us that these particular Eliouds aren't in contact with celestials," said Alfie from the sofa, his burly build stiff with angry tension. "They would otherwise have realized they'd mistranslated the prophecy."

"The Uppers rarely bother with Eliouds," her mother, Tia, pointed out, sitting beside him. "They don't like *any* non-celestial species to have holy blood."

Sad as it seemed—not to mention a complete overreaction, in Naomi's opinion—the upper realm had sought to wipe out not only the Nephilim but all their children eons ago. Some of those children, however, had been hidden too well for the celestials to find.

At this point in time, Nephilim blood was so diluted that the only preternatural trait being passed through generations of Eliouds was the ability to channel divine power. But those people would live human lives, oblivious to their heritage, unless located by monkhoods and taught how to access that ability.

While some had become clerics and formed holy sects like the one that had targeted Naomi, it was possible that not *all* had done so; that some Eliouds had decided to instead ignore their ancestry and blend with humans. But no one knew for sure.

"It amazes me that clerics would worship God, given that the upper realm once targeted the Nephilim and their descendants for death," Naomi mused. "I mean, I know they can't utilize their ability to channel divine power *unless* they have the utmost faith in God. It's a literal necessity. But if I were them, I'd personally rather forfeit that ability than serve a being who had so many of my people slaughtered."

"I think they initially did it in the hope that the Uppers would leave them alone," said Jolene, standing near the fireplace with Beck. "Sort of 'Look what good boys we are—founding monkhoods, devoting ourselves to God, serving him in all ways—there's no need to kill us.' But at some point over the generations, clerics began to maintain that God let them be because he'd chosen them to do his work." She snorted derisively. "I suspect the only reason the Uppers haven't targeted them for death is that the Nephilim blood in them is so very weak."

Beck sighed. "A lot of religious fanatics pick and choose what they believe and twist the facts to suit them."

Amen. No pun intended.

"I'll use the description you have of the emblem on their tunics to find out what I can about these guys, Nome," Khloë piped up from the armchair.

"Why bother?" asked Alfie. "They're dead."

"There could be more of them," Khloë pointed out. "Plus, I'm curious to know more about the prophecy they quoted. It'll be interesting to hear it in full. The language the main cleric spoke isn't one that I recognize, though."

"It's a very ancient dialect that has its roots in Egypt," Naomi told her. "The part that they thought stated 'For she who bears the mark will birth the child of the devil' is actually 'For she who bears the mark is the progeny of the devil.' The meaning of a lot of ancient writings gets lost in translation. That appears to have been the case here."

"Did they describe the mark?" asked Khloë.

"No. It has to be somewhere in the prophecy, though."

"Plenty of old forecasts talk of the Antichrist bearing a mark—it's even in the Bible. So that doesn't give us a lead on which prophecy it might be," said Ciaran, perched on the arm of his twin's chair.

"I'll pull up as many as I can find that go back as far as the language the cleric spoke," said Khloë. "It'll then be a matter of elimination."

"If it was foretold by ancient clerics, there'll be at least *some* truth in it," said Jolene. "The first generation of Eliouds were direct sons of the Nephilim; they experienced premonitions, healed the sick, and wielded holy magick."

Naomi prodded the birthmark on her shoulder, which faintly resembled a flame. "I never thought to cover my birthmark, because I never thought it would mean anything to anyone. Nothing about it screams *I am the offspring of Lucifer*."

"The prophecy must contain a description of it," said Beck.

"Maybe I should conceal it with makeup from now on," Naomi mused. "Just in case any other clerics stumble upon the prophecy and get dumb ideas."

"Better to be safe than sorry," said Alfie. "What I don't understand is how these particular clerics tracked you using the birthmark. It isn't in a highly visible place. You don't wear a lot of tanks."

"People take photos and upload them to the web all the time," said Tobe. "Other people are often in the background, oblivious." He cut his gaze to Naomi. "It could be that you showed up on someone's picture; that the photo was taken from an angle that gave a glimpse of your birthmark. The clerics might have scoured the internet in search of some such clue. There's technology that can search the web for faces. Why not for birthmarks as well?"

"I hate to say it, but Tobe's probably right," said Khloë.

Tobe frowned. "Why do you hate to say it?"

"Because *I* was going to suggest it first. I don't like that you beat me to it."

"Kind of childish, don't you think?"

"Not at all, no."

Plucking at his wiry beard, Beck skimmed his gaze over everyone. "Do we contact Lou about this?"

"I don't see any point," said Naomi. "I'm fine, and the clerics are dead. Plus, Lou can sometimes ... overreact. Hence why I haven't told him about Iain either."

The last time someone had wronged Naomi, Lou had thrown him off a building—and then opened a portal to hell so that the asshole would drop right down into it when he fell. Her good ole dad was kind of a nut.

"Speaking of the Iain situation," began Jolene, "what did Luka say when you spoke to him alone? He didn't go into specifics when I questioned him."

"He just wanted more details," Naomi replied. "I briefed him on all that Iain's been up to. I thought he might defend him—I mean, Iain is one of his demons after all. But Luka made no excuses for him; didn't pile the blame on me as others have done when their loved ones or associates got snared by a siren song. He assured me he'd deal with it and that Iain won't come near me again."

"Good," grunted Tobe. "Iain would be a fucking idiot to go against Belinsky. Which, unfortunately, isn't to say that he won't. People under the influence of a siren song aren't always rational. But if he's likely to listen to anyone, it'll be his Prime."

"That, at least, is one bit of good news," said Alfie. "The clerics went and shit all over it, though. You sure that it's best to keep it from Lou, Naomi? Your dad will whine like a two-year-old if he finds out about it from someone else."

"Without a doubt," agreed Naomi. "But I don't see any reason *why* he'd hear of it." It wasn't as if she saw him daily, and earthly business didn't much interest him.

As dads went, Lou was ... atypical. He cared for her and was part of her life, but in the way of a protective uncle. He was too emotionally immature to be what you'd call fatherly.

That said, he visited her every few months. He never forgot her birthday. If anyone upset her, he insisted on dealing with it. And if she reached out to him, he would come.

People in her lair thought that he gatecrashed their parties just for the fun of it. In truth, he came because *she'd* be there. It was his way of sharing special occasions with her without giving away their blood connection.

So, yeah, he was a dad of sorts. He and Alfie had both played a part in raising her alongside her mother. The three of them got along pretty well.

"Then I'll spread the word around our lair that if anyone sees him, they aren't to speak of what occurred here," said Jolene. "They'll just think I'm aiming to fuck with him again."

Well, her Prime *did* relish driving Lou crazy—they bickered often, neither much liking the other. "What exactly are you going to tell them happened?" asked Naomi.

"Not the full truth, obviously," Jolene assured her. "But it's always best to dance around the truth than tell an outright lie. I'll say that a silly group of fanatical clerics for some reason decided you were going to birth the Antichrist. People will only laugh."

Nodding her head in approval, Naomi plopped the empty cups on the tray she'd set on the coffee table. "In their shoes, I'd definitely laugh." She pyroported to the kitchen—a gift that was basically a variation of Lou's ability to teleport.

She couldn't pyroport far. Only several feet away. Lou, on the other hand, could teleport from realm to realm. Celestials generally lost that ability when they fell, but he'd retained it.

He wasn't a mere angel, though; he was a seraphim. He'd been God's favorite once. And due to that favoritism, he'd been awarded much power. *Too* much. A level that exceeded even that of archangels. Seraphim weren't psychically built to host such a level.

Naomi thought it might have contributed to why he'd reached a mental point where he'd become a problem for those in the upper realm. Power corrupted, didn't it? And the Uppers didn't kick celestials out without *very* good reason.

The fall had further warped his conscience and character. It had also twisted his gifts. That, in turn, had put a slight twist on *hers*. And having the biological and psychic makeup of both a siren and a very powerful fallen seraphim meant that she wasn't a normal demon by any stretch of the imagination.

But she was very, very good at hiding that.

Having placed the tray on the counter, intending to wash the mugs later, she returned to the living room.

"They shouldn't have been able to sneak into this house without being seen by imps in the neighborhood at some point," grumbled Alfie. "There aren't even any signs of forced entry."

"I doubt that was the first time those clerics had done a little breaking and entering while on holy quests," mused Naomi.

Tobe shot her a hard look. "If you'd activated your alarm system, they wouldn't have gotten inside."

"I was in a rush earlier. I forgot." She had a habit of being late. *And* forgetful, for that matter. "I won't forget again." Hopefully.

Tia heaved a sigh. "It seems like crime is forever on the rise. There's no end to it. The *nerve* of some people is shocking. They seem to think they're above the law."

"Complains the woman who swindles people every day of her life," quipped Alfie.

Tia glared at him. With her white headscarf, boho floral dress, large hooped earrings, and endless number of bangles, she looked the part she played to every human who entered her psychic shop. *Fake* part. She sniffed at her mate. "That's hardly relevant here and now."

"Honey, it's *always* relevant," Alfie contradicted, mirth twinkling in his brown eyes. "It's a shame you're not a real seer. You might have otherwise seen this coming."

"What do we do with the swords?" asked Beck.

Ciaran pursed his lips. "I suppose we could sell them."

"I don't care what you do with them so long as they're gone," Naomi told him.

He lifted one off the floor, and his expression morphed into a grimace. "What the hell is that smell?"

Jolene frowned. "Smell?"

"It's like a mix of decay and body odor," he elaborated.

Jolene sidled up to him and leaned in to give the sword a quick sniff. Her face scrunched up. "Dark magick."

Naomi blinked. "*Dark* magick?" Her mind drifted back to when one of the Elioluds had sliced her; to how she'd felt something far from holy trying to ease inside her.

Jolene's lips thinned. "Now just why would a bunch of devout clerics use a weapon embedded with dark magick?"

"They wouldn't," said Tia. "The strength of a cleric's power depends on their faith in God. To purposely utilize any sort of black craft would sever their connection to that holy power. They wouldn't have been able to toss magick at Naomi."

"Meaning they had no idea their swords were enchanted," Beck surmised.

Tia's head whipped round to face Naomi. "They didn't hurt you with those swords, did they?"

"Only once," replied Naomi. "I wasn't stabbed, just sliced. A sliver of what I now realize was dark magick tried infecting me, but my fire burned it away."

Alfie blew out a relieved breath. "The Elioluds must have gotten their hands on those swords via a person they didn't know was a dark practitioner. Though *why* a dark practitioner would sell them weapons, thus empowering them, makes no sense to me. They're not exactly allies."

Indeed. The two sides hated each other.

On the surface, it seemed that dark practitioners and clerics were polar opposites. Dark practitioners were self-serving and on a constant quest to obtain more power, often worshipping cruel deities. Clerics, on the other hand, considered themselves divine servants and sought to please God rather than themselves. But both magick-users would torture and kill in the name of whatever being they worshiped, so they weren't *terribly* different.

Khloë helped her brother gather up the blades. "I'll start digging into these clerics tomorrow." She spared Naomi a quick glance. "Hopefully I'll have something to tell you when you come to Urban Ink on Monday for your tattoo." Khloë worked as the receptionist at the studio.

"No rush," said Naomi. "As I said, they're all dead. There's no further harm they can do at this point." Unless there were in fact more of them. Fingers crossed that wasn't the case.

CHAPTER THREE

Standing in his front doorway the following afternoon, Luka watched one of his sentinels pull up in the courtyard. Beyond it were acres of manicured land, tall trees, and high brick walls.

His estate was expansive, just like the long, stately three-floored home in which he'd lived for many years. Beside it was an annex that housed his bodyguards. The demons who permanently guarded his home lived on the grounds in what was originally a guesthouse.

As the head of his syndicate, he naturally had many enemies. Luka had been born into this life. He knew nothing else. He'd been groomed from an early age to step in as Prime when the time came. He had held the position for years now, which he hadn't done by taking chances. So though it was rare for people to give him issues, let alone attempt to trespass on his personal territory, he ensured it was heavily guarded.

His sentinel, Raiden—who'd been sent to collect Iain—exited the car and then pulled open the rear door. Out slid a slender dark-blond male, his compact shoulders stiff, his scarred brow creased.

"He's looking worried," commented Mikhail. He and his brother—both of whom Luka had relayed the Naomi/Iain situation to—had planted themselves either side of the front door.

"So he should. I generally don't have people brought to my home unless they've displeased me," Luka pointed out. It wasn't as if he and Iain were friends. Having a virtual—and yes, mostly criminal—empire to run, Luka worked a lot and didn't make much time to socialize.

He waited until both demons had climbed the steps before he said, "Prompt as ever, Raiden. It doesn't go unappreciated." Luka was a busy man on a tight schedule. "Iain, we'll talk inside."

As they entered the house, Mikhail walked in front of Luka while Nikandr covered his back. They strode along the marble flooring of the circular foyer and then further into the building, passing many doors.

As well as basic rooms such as the den and the kitchen, there was everything from a well-equipped gym to an indoor atrium that featured a large fish tank built into a wall.

It would quickly become clear to any who entered his home that Luka liked the finer things. Everything was top-notch and stylish. Every surface shone or glimmered.

But yes, there was an austere feel to the place. He could admit that he'd forsaken comfort for opulence. Ella had been right in saying that it looked like a showroom, not a home. There were no personal touches anywhere that would indicate who lived here—not even a single picture or portrait.

Finally, they reached the living room, which Luka only used to receive guests. "Drink?" he offered Iain, waving him toward the sofa.

"I won't say no," the psi-demon replied, a nervous tremor to his voice, as he sat.

Luka's guards and sentinel took up positions around the room while he poured both himself and Iain a whiskey.

Taking a tumbler from him, Iain nodded his thanks.

"You don't look too good," observed Luka, sinking into the sofa across from him. It was no exaggeration—the demon appeared feverish, just as Luka would expect from someone caught in the spell of a siren song.

Iain's lips twitched. "Such flattery."

"What have you been doing with yourself lately?"

"Not much. Just spending time with my newborn nephew; helping my sister with taking care of him."

"Really? Because that's not what I heard." Luka sipped his drink. "In fact, it's your other sister who's been helping her. A lot of your time has been spent harassing a siren from Jolene Wallis's lair," he stated, disgust bleeding into his voice.

There were plenty of moral lines that Luka would cross—and had done many times—but none involved hurting women or children, either emotionally or physically. Even Belial, who enjoyed inflicting pain, would never cross *that* line.

Iain went rigid, color rising in his cheeks. "I wouldn't call it harassment," he said stiffly, managing to sound both offended and sheepish.

Annoyance creeping over his skin, Luka slowly lifted a brow. "Naomi Chamberlain asked that you cease contacting her, yes?"

The psi-demon pressed his lips tight together. "Yes." A reluctant whisper.

"Repeatedly?"

"Yes." Again, it was a mere murmur.

"But you've ignored her wishes and continued to reach out to her in numerous ways?"

Iain ground his teeth. "Yes," he quietly bit off.

"Even though you know she wants you to leave her alone, you keep contacting her, sending her gifts, and showing up at her home uninvited. Tell me how that doesn't constitute harassment."

Iain looked down at his glass and then took a gulp of whiskey. "You're under the thrall of her song, so I can—"

"No." Iain's head snapped up. "That's not the case at all. I've told Naomi that."

"You're insulting your own intelligence if you insist on believing that. Look at the facts in front of you. She's a siren. Her song preys on people and induces obsessions. And here you are, utterly obsessed with her. It's pretty fucking obvious that you're not in your right mind."

The psi-demon bristled, his chin flicking up. "I love her, Luka."

Abraxas rolled its eyes, finding him pitiful.

"No, you *think* you do," Luka contradicted. "If you really cared for her, you would respect her wishes and leave her alone. Her song has you all muddled up."

"It may seem that way—"

"Because it *is* that way. Denying it doesn't change the truth."

The corners of Iain's eyes tightened. "You're going to take my word over Jolene's? It can only be her who asked you to keep me away from Naomi."

"It wasn't only Jolene." Luka sipped at his drink again. "Naomi herself requested that I cut you from her life."

Iain sucked in a breath, pain flickering in the depth of his gaze. "She . . . she didn't mean that."

"Oh, I assure you she did. And you *will* stay away from her, Iain."

Anguish seeped into the psi-demon's blue eyes. "Don't ask that of me."

"I'm not asking you. I'm explicitly *stating* that you're to leave her alone. You *need* that distance from her, Iain, or her song will keep you under its spell. In a couple of weeks, it will have worn off and you'll see I'm right that this is obsession you feel."

Iain drained his glass and then placed it on the side table. His gaze snapped back to Luka, a hint of challenge there. "Have you ever been in love?"

"No."

"Then how can you be sure that's not what I'm feeling?"

Dagon snorted, wondering how someone could be so delusional—siren song or not.

"Have you taken a look in the mirror lately?" Luka asked. "You're pale. Sweaty. Flushed. Your eyes are cloudy."

Iain plucked uncomfortably at his collar, his gaze sliding to the side. "Okay, so maybe her song *is* affecting me. But my feelings for her are still real." A stubborn tension tightened his jaw. "If she could just see that, if she could just realize that I'm not delusional, she'd give me—*us*—another chance."

"You think that Naomi—someone who's dealt with many obsessed men—can't tell the difference between siren-induced emotions and genuine feelings?"

Belligerence danced in Iain's eyes as he leaned forward. "It's the truth, Luka. The absolute truth."

"It's fantasy," Luka countered. "Even if I was wrong on that, it wouldn't matter. Because no one has the right to force their wants on another person. You're going to leave her alone, Iain—not only because it's what's fair to her, but because I *fucking told you to*." Infuriated by the psi-demon's persistence, Belial shoved its way to the surface and glared at him. "If you dare disobey us on this, I will whip you until you are raw and bleeding—and then I will whip you some more."

Fear falling over his face, Iain eased back slightly in his seat.

Luka regained supremacy over Belial, rolling his shoulders. "Are we clear?"

The psi-demon swallowed hard, his expression souring. "Yes."

"Then say it."

"We're clear." The words were torn out of him.

Luka finished his drink. "Raiden, take Iain back home."

The sentinel pushed away from the wall. "Sure thing."

Iain rose from the sofa and followed Raiden to the door. Pausing, the psi-demon half-turned to look at Luka. "Maybe one day you'll fall hard for a woman. If you do, you'll understand how I feel right now, and you'll know what this will cost me."

"*Or* you'll discover with time and distance that you're wrong in what you presently believe, and you'll be thankful that I directed you to stay clear of Naomi." Luka flicked a hand. "Go."

Obediently, the psi-demon left with Raiden.

Mikhail took a few steps toward Luka. "Spelled by a siren song or not, the guy is definitely fixated on her."

"So it would seem." It wasn't something that Luka could relate to. He'd never even developed so much as a remote fondness for any of the women in his past. He'd never experienced obsession, adoration, or possessiveness toward them.

As a child, he had been wildly territorial of what was his. He hadn't merely refused to share his toys, he'd hidden his favorites from others. His father had handled it by taking any such favorites from him.

Andrey Belinsky hadn't done it to be cruel. He'd simply wanted to crush Luka's tendency to form attachments—for the head of a crime family like theirs, attachments could be weaknesses.

There were many lessons that Andrey had taught his son in his efforts to prepare him for a position that, placing him as it would at the top of the hierarchy, would set him slightly apart from the rest of his lair. Those lessons had paid off, but it meant that Luka didn't know how *not* to be alone. He instinctively shied away from emotional intimacy, as did his inner entities.

"Don't be surprised if he ignores your order," said Nikandr, moving to stand beside his brother. "Naomi's song has him all tied up in knots."

"And those knots are tight," added Mikhail. "He might feel in so much emotional pain that risking your wrath would be worth it if only he could convince her that he truly does love her."

Chewing on that, Luka twisted his mouth. "Have one of our demons keep an eye on him, just to be sure."

Mikhail gave a curt nod.

Luka pushed out of his chair. "I have a meeting to attend. Let's get moving."

Swiping an old tee from her dresser, Naomi shook her head. *Some people are their own worst enemy*, she telepathed Tobe. *It isn't as if Stefan wasn't warned what would happen if he didn't back off.*

He actually seemed shocked that I followed through on my threat, said Tobe. *He genuinely feels that he should be an exception to your 'I don't meet with clients' rule. I feel that he should fuck off.*

Samesies. Naomi closed the drawer. *Why he'd think that he'd be an exception, I have no clue.*

He seemed to believe you'd be flattered that he admires your work so much he's determined to meet you.

She huffed. *I guess all his success has gone to his head.*

Success he only has because of you.

Naomi hung her tee over her shoulder and then dragged open a lower drawer. *How did he take being told that I won't be producing art for him anymore?*

Badly. Real badly. He knows that without you his career will tank.

I'm not sure it'll tank. There are other ghost artists he could hire. Naomi nabbed a pair of sweatpants she regularly used when painting. She reserved her Sundays for letting her creativity stretch out, and she had a bare canvas waiting for her in the spare bedroom that she had made into a workroom.

But they'd have to be able to imitate the exact style you've used for his art—it's that style that's given him so much success. If they fail, it'll be game over for him.

Then he'd better hope they don't fail.

Just then, her doorbell rang.

It seems I have a visitor. I'll talk to you again later, okay? She frowned when there was no response from Tobe. *Hello?*

Sorry, got distracted.

What exactly are you doing?

Trying to dodge red laser beams so I don't set off an alarm system.

Naomi cursed, dumping her clothes on the bed. *You are unbelievable.* Intending to lecture him later, she pled, *Be careful.*

Always am, he assured her breezily.

And it was such a lie.

Barefoot, she skipped down the stairs and glanced through the front door's peephole. Her breath caught. *Luka.*

She backed up a step, raking her teeth over her lower lip. She'd thought he might return to the pizzeria at some point, but not show up *here*. There was no reason for him to know where she lived, and she wouldn't have expected that he'd go to the trouble of finding out. Her entity liked that he had; wanted to know why he was here.

She studied her reflection in the tall wall-mounted mirror, checking there were no stains on her lavender dress. Well, she wanted to look presentable around him—so sue her.

She opened the door ... and her belly dropped. Everything about him was just so *raw*. His magnetism, his sexuality, his power, his presence—all of it.

"Hi." The word came out all breathy.

He gave her a swift but bold eye-bang, need bleeding into his gaze and turning it dark as flint. "Naomi," he greeted simply. The gravel in his impossibly sexy voice scraped at her nerve endings in the most delicious way.

She looked past him to see one guard leaning against his car while the other remained in the driver's seat. She refocused on Luka. "How did you find out where I live?"

A fluid shrug. "It wasn't hard." He arched a daring brow. "Are you going to let me in?"

She stepped aside, giving him enough room that their bodies didn't brush as he entered. She could actually admire how boldly he stalked right through to the living area without waiting for an invitation. This wasn't a man who waited for anyone or anything.

The boldness continued as he nosily swept his gaze around, taking in everything. His audaciousness was knotted with a tangible confidence that skated the edge of arrogant.

He had a certain energy. It was unsettled. There was an undercurrent of restlessness ... which she supposed could be coming from his inner entities.

Naomi stopped a few feet away, needing a little space from the sheer *potency* of him. She subtly cast her tingling nipples a frown. *Do not get hard and embarrass me that way.*

"I talked to Iain," he said, turning to her.

She folded her arms. "And?"

"He acknowledged that your song has affected him, but he refuses to believe that his feelings for you aren't nonetheless real."

Naomi sighed. "I've heard that before," she mumbled.

"From him, or from others?"

"Others, so it doesn't surprise me that he'd make the same claim." She could understand why they would choose denial. Who wanted to believe that they weren't fully in control of their thoughts and feelings? "You told him to leave me be?"

"I made it clear that he is to stay out of your life—as did Belial, which gives him further incentive to do as ordered. Nobody likes fucking with Belial."

No, they didn't. Even her lair swerved getting on the entity's bad side, especially since ... "It has a habit of beheading imps."

"Only when they break my club rules. Though Belial actually got bored of decapitating them. It likes variety in its murderous diet."

What else could she say to that but, "Good to know." Her pulse started to skip as he walked toward her. And then he was *right there*, leaving mere inches between their bodies. He smelled good. She didn't know what cologne he wore, but it was smoky and rich.

"If Iain attempts to make contact with you again, I want you to telepath me straight away. I realize that, as a siren, you won't be at all weak and can likely handle yourself. But this isn't about whether you need protection or intervention. It's about managing the situation. The fact is that any interactions with you will please him, whether they be positive or negative. We don't want him to feel rewarded by reaching out to you."

Huh. Good point. And since she had zero interest in dealing with more of Iain's crap ... "All right."

"Good," he said, his gaze so damn intent, so unshakably focused in a way that was plain unnerving.

She'd heard some refer to Luka as a proverbial snake. But as he looked at her right then—his gaze searching, probing, studying her with a burning intensity—he made her think of a wolf circling its prey. Which loudly rang her hormones' bells, and now tension was snapping and popping in the air.

Naomi cleared her throat. "Thank you for dealing with Iain and taking the time to relay your conversation with him." She glanced at the front door. "Well, if that's all . . ."

"You don't want me here," he sensed, a hint of mirth in his gaze.

"It isn't something you should take personally. I don't like having most people here." Pure truth.

"There are some exceptions?"

"Yes. I don't know you well enough for you to be one of them."

"You will."

She double-blinked. "Excuse me?"

"You don't strike me as the type to miss much, so you'll know that you've captured my interest. I only recently exited an arrangement, and I don't jump from one bed to another. I intended to give it time before approaching you. I've decided that time is now up."

Naomi stilled, hit by mixed reactions. Her feminine parts all but swooned while her mind recoiled slightly in unease. Was it really a good idea to get involved with someone who was so damn perceptive he might well figure out what she strived so hard to hide?

If all he wanted was a one-night stand, it wouldn't be such a big deal. But she didn't get the sense that that was what he had in mind. And still she didn't find herself blurting out a hard no.

She should. She really should. It was a matter of self-preservation. And yet the words just didn't—

"Naomi?"

She mentally fumbled as his voice severed her line of thought. Blinking at him, she asked, "Hmm?"

His gaze bored into hers. "You back with me?"

"I never left."

After a long moment, he cocked his head. "Do you know why I stick to arrangements?"

"No, why?"

"Relationships are difficult for my kind. Each of my inner entities has its own personality, needs, wants, desires, likes, dislikes—it goes on and on. They're separate individuals, and it isn't always the case that they agree on things. Even when they do, it may be that I'm not in agreement with them. In other words, the four of us aren't always in sync.

"Belial, in particular, tends to have an opposing opinion. It is deliberately contrary, though mostly due to boredom. Few things snag its attention—people included. And it does not at all like for me to ignore its wants. So, for instance, I might like a particular piece of art. Belial, however, may not. Annoyed that I nonetheless purchased it, the entity might well destroy it out of spite if in a mood over something."

"Wow." She could see how a legion might become as arbitrarily stubborn and darkly dominant as Luka was rumored to be. From an early age, you'd have to learn how to hold your own against three inner entities all craving and angling for control. "It's got to be weird having three demons."

"It's all I've ever known. The point I'm making is that short, shallow arrangements are easier. Anything more would require myself and my entities to all feel very strongly for a woman—the same woman, more to the point. We never have, and it would be a lie to say we lament that. We are content as we are."

That he was clearly such a solitary person was kind of sad—for him, at least. Not so much for Naomi in this context, though. Because as potential bed partners went, he'd be safe. This was a person who didn't let people close. It meant that he would keep a distance between them. He wouldn't poke into her life and uncover secrets that needed to remain in few metaphorical hands.

"We don't even always want the same woman in our bed, but my entities won't fight me when it comes to you." His gaze slid over her face. "You hold an appeal for all four of us. They each intend to fuck you raw, which is *nothing* compared to what I'll do with you."

Her belly fluttered at that. The dude had a way with words.

His eyes darkened with warning. "Let it be known that there will be no other men for you while you're in my bed."

She raised a brow at his audacity.

"Before you ask, yes, that exclusivity goes both ways."

"You're barreling forward like you're certain I'll be along for this ride."

He raised a brow right back at her. "If you had any objections, you would have voiced them already."

True. As she wasn't into playing hard to get, she didn't bother with denials. "Do you really think this would be a wise idea? I'm trying to keep Iain out of my life. You're his Prime. If you and I started something, shallow fling or not, it would make matters worse."

A line dented Luka's brow. "How he would feel about it means nothing to me. Does it mean something to you?"

"No. I'd just prefer not to do anything that could exacerbate an already precarious situation."

"Iain won't put another foot into your life – I made that clear already."

She nibbled on the inside of her cheek, pensive. It was long moments before she spoke again. "So, to review, you want—"

"You. Often. Whenever and wherever. *However* I want." Luka's cock throbbed as her pupils dilated. He'd been hard since almost the moment he walked in here. Partly because of her song, but also because their chemistry was alive in the air, thick and oppressive. It seemed to stroke over his skin, tug at his will, and form an itch in his fingertips—an itch to touch, grab, haul her to him.

He pulled in a breath through his nose, dragging her scent into his lungs. Stupid, really. Because the more he filled his senses with her, the more it would feed the relentless, molten need coursing through his system. "The only stipulation I want to put into place is that we're exclusive."

"Women talk and, well, I heard through the grapevine that you don't insist on exclusivity."

"Generally, I don't. It depends on a few things."

"Such as?"

"Like I explained before, it's not always the case that my entities and I are all interested in taking a particular woman to our bed. Unlike the rest of us, Belial is territorial by nature. If it *is* invested in seducing the female in question, it will refuse to share her. It is *very* interested in you. Something I would imagine may unnerve you, given its reputation.

"You don't need to fear any of my demons. Dagon is moody and will lie to you because that's what it does to people. Abraxas will lay the charm on you and expect your complete adoration. Something of a sadist, Belial will bite and quite possibly spank you—it has a thing for your ass. But you're safe with them, just as you are with me."

Her nose wrinkled. "I'm not really into spanking."

Belial grinned, now wanting to do it to her all the more, which was rather typical.

Just then, Nikandr's psyche bumped Luka's. *A guy I recognize from a picture in Naomi's background check is heading up the path. Pretty sure it's her psi-mate. He noticed me and your car; doesn't seem too happy that you're here.*

The latter could be because the imp presumed that Iain must

have made another move . . . or because he didn't want someone with Luka's reputation near his anchor. "It would seem that your psi-mate is here," he told her.

Moments later, knuckles rapped on her front door.

Muttering something beneath her breath, she unfolded her arms and left the room. When she finally re-entered, it was with a glowering male imp at her back.

Naomi cleared her throat. "Tobe, I'm guessing you recognize Luka Belinsky. Luka, this is my anchor, Tobe Burke."

Luka inclined his head at the imp, who gave him a curt nod in return.

"What has Iain done now?" Tobe demanded.

"Nothing," Naomi replied. "Luka came to tell me that he's spoken with Iain as promised; that the asshole will now leave me be."

Tobe narrowed his eyes on Luka, suspicious. "And that necessitated you coming to her home? You couldn't have delivered the message via Jolene?"

Yeah, this imp *definitely* didn't like the thought of Luka near his anchor—his protectiveness came across loud and clear. While Luka didn't particularly give a fuck what anyone thought of him or his intentions toward Naomi, it would do him no favors to make an enemy of her psi-mate. So rather than convey that he owed the imp no explanations, he said, "One of my demons has been harassing Naomi. The least I can do is assure her in person that the matter has been handled."

Tobe grunted, not seeming particularly appeased. He also planted his feet, making it clear that he wouldn't be leaving. Disappointing. Luka had hoped to have more time alone with her. To be specific, he'd hoped to take her upstairs and explore every inch of her. Which Tobe had likely sensed for himself, hence his insistence on staying.

Luka would normally have taken a seat to indicate that he wouldn't be leaving either. But he didn't quite have a claim to Naomi yet. She hadn't rebuffed his advances or disagreed over exclusivity, but that was the most he had right now. He needed verbal consent from her.

Plus, her loyalty was to her anchor. If he and Tobe ended up arguing, it would be *Luka* she'd ask to leave. He didn't want that.

Refocusing on her, Luka said, "Remember to call out to me if Iain pulls anything." *I'll be back very soon*, he added telepathically, letting sexual intent color his tone.

Heat bled into her eyes, and she swallowed hard.

Satisfied that she wasn't telling him to stay away, Luka swanned out of the house.

CHAPTER FOUR

The next day, Naomi parked her car in the lot outside a very popular nightclub. A club that hid the entrance to the Underground. And what was the Underground? More or less a subterranean version of the Las Vegas strip that was mostly exclusive to demons.

There were places to eat, shop, dance, drink, gamble, compete, and ... well, pretty much anything. Demons naturally sought thrills and dopamine rushes, so this was a good place to not only enjoy downtime but open up a business of your own.

The Underground's founder, Knox Thorne, was both the mate and anchor of Jolene's granddaughter Harper. She happened to co-run Urban Ink and would be very soon giving Naomi her newest tattoo.

Naomi slid out of the car and let her eyes skim her surroundings. Several cars were parked nearby, but no people stood around. The club wasn't yet open for business, so there wasn't a queue of clubgoers waiting for entrance either.

Making a beeline for the building, she felt the spot between her shoulder blades begin to burn. Halting abruptly, she glanced over her shoulder. No one. There was no one. But ... she could *swear* she was being watched.

After giving her surroundings one last visual sweep, she again headed for the club. Maybe Iain was following her from a distance so as to avoid being noticed. Dammit, she'd hoped that Luka's warning would do the trick.

Luka.

Snippets of their conversation last night still ran riot around her brain. She couldn't lie: being pursued by such a scorching-hot motherfucker who embodied a massively amplified bad-boy vibe ... well, it was something of a turn-on. Call her weird, but she liked that he'd thrown out a declaration of intent. He hadn't put out feelers to check if she'd be receptive first; he'd quite explicitly and confidently told her that he wanted her.

Her demon liked his boldness; liked that he wouldn't be prepared to share her—the entity wasn't a fan of flings that didn't entail exclusivity. Not because it was possessive but because it felt that Naomi deserved to be the sole focus of whatever male sought her out.

While her demon wouldn't fight her on allowing Luka into her bed, Tobe sure would. After the legion had left her home last night, her anchor had whirled on her and said, "*He wants to nail you. You know that, right?*"

"*So aptly put,*" she'd quipped.

"*You don't want to get involved with him, Nome. You've heard the rumors. It ain't a secret that he's an ice-cold motherfucker. He won't be good for you.*"

But she didn't need Luka to be good for her—she wasn't looking for anything serious or permanent. Better still, neither was he. She'd met plenty of people who held themselves apart from others, but most did it subconsciously. With Luka, it was deliberate. They could enjoy a brief fling—and she had the feeling that she truly *would* enjoy it—and then each go their own way. It was a far too appealing thought.

Well, a girl had to eat.

Inside the club, Naomi headed to the basement. The demons manning the elevator let her pass, at which point she began a long-ass downward ride. The contraption slowed to a stop, and the doors opened.

Stepping out, she was hit by an abundance of street sounds. Voices talking. Distant music. Muffled laughter. Phones ringing. Heels clacking as people walked back and forth along the strip and filed in and out of the various premises.

There were bakeries, coffee houses, delis, bars, specialty stores. You name it; the Underground would have it.

She walked in the direction of the tattoo shop, shrugging past the many pedestrians. The Underground was as busy as always. Cart vendors were around. The occasional busker could be seen. Street sweepers did a good job of keeping the strip as litter-free as possible.

Finally arriving at her destination, Naomi stepped into the exceptionally neat reception area. The scents of ink, paint, coffee, and citrus disinfectant surrounded her.

Urban Ink was the epitome of cool. Sketches, metal art, and decals decorated the white walls, which were a contrast to the dark hardwood flooring. Muffled chatter mingled with the buzzing of tattoo guns and the rock music video playing on the wall-mounted TV in the reception area.

She spotted Harper straight off. The sphinx was wiping down the leather recliner at her station while talking into her cell phone. The other three tattooists—Raini, Devon, and Piper, who'd all been part of Naomi's lair until they mated—were at their own stations, their focus on their respective clients. At the rear of the studio were some doors, a sink, autoclave, and tracing table.

Crossing to the reception desk, Naomi waved at Khloë.

The imp's gray eyes lit up. "Hey, you're here. And late."

"This surprises you?"

"Not in the slightest."

And so it shouldn't. "Can you let Harper know I'm here?"

"Sure. Harper, your next client is here!"

Naomi sighed. "As always, you are pure class and grace."

Khloë grinned, gently patting her messy dark bun as if it were a perfectly styled updo. "Aren't I just?"

Her gaze on Naomi, Harper held up her index finger as she spoke into her phone.

Naomi gave her a nod.

"Hey, Naomi," a stunning blonde succubae greeted from her station.

Naomi felt her lips curve. "Hi, Raini. How're things?"

"All good," Raini assured her.

As she rested her tattoo gun on her shelf, Piper's pale-green eyes flitted to Naomi. "I bumped into your mom the other day. She said one of your exes was bothering you. Is that a thing of the past yet?"

"Whatever his Prime said seems to have gotten through to him," Naomi told the dark-haired nightmare, not wanting to get into specifics in front of a shop full of strangers. "The guy has stayed off my radar since then."

"Good," said Devon, skidding her wheeled chair a little closer to the recliner at her station. "Weirdos are *everywhere* these days. Including behind the reception desk near you."

Khloë frowned at the hellcat. "I might be quirky—".

"'Insane' would be a better descriptor," muttered Devon, using her arm to knock her ultraviolet ringlets over her shoulder.

"—but I'm not even half as weird as your homicidal spawn."

"Hey!"

"What? Anaïs is a death dealer. Which I love her *because* of, not *in spite* of."

Raini snickered. "Of course you do."

"Whatevs." Khloë turned back to Naomi. "We should just ignore them. It's so enjoyable. Let's talk about something else. Ooh, by the way," she went on, lowering her voice, "I haven't found out anything interesting about the clerics yet."

"Unsurprising," said Naomi. "They *weren't* interesting."

The imp planted a palm on her desk. "You know, we could show a picture of the emblem to one of the Black Saints," she suggested, referring to a local motorcycle club whose president was mated to Luka's anchor.

"Why would we do that?"

"They're fallen angels, Nome. They might know of a monkhood that wear clothes bearing that particular emblem."

Naomi pulled a face. "I don't think we need to go asking the Black Saints about it. They'll only wonder where you saw the emblem, and I'd rather outsiders weren't poking their noses into this. You'll find the answers without them."

Khloë inched up her chin proudly. "Of course I will. I'm awesome that way." Her gaze shifted to a guy who'd materialized beside Naomi. "Yo, what can I do for you?"

Stepping away, Naomi glanced over at Harper, to find that the sphinx was heading her way.

Casting her an apologetic look, Harper sank her fingers into her dark hair tipped with gold. "I'm really sorry, Naomi, but I need five more minutes."

"I don't mind waiting, it's fine." Considering that Naomi consistently lost track of time and had to often apologize for making others wait, she had no room to complain anyway.

Her smile one of both relief and gratitude, Harper said, "Thanks. I'll be as fast as I can." Then she was gone, putting her phone to her ear once more.

Naomi took a seat on the leather sofa and swiped a tattoo portfolio from the coffee table. Crossing one leg over the other, she hummed to the music playing on the TV as she idly flicked through the portfolio.

Someone sank onto the sofa beside her. "Cool place, right?"

Naomi looked up to see the guy who'd entered the studio only moments ago. Average height and wide-shouldered, he had a scruffy appearance, but it seemed deliberate. Gel kept his ash-blond hair in an unkempt clump. His short beard was wiry and uneven. Wrinkles graced his clothes, but they were designer and otherwise high-quality.

His smile was friendly, but it didn't fully reach his brown eyes. They were fixed on her, a little glazed over with a sleazy, objectifying lust.

Naomi handled the moment the same way she handled any guy who did that. She pasted a haughty, disinterested look on her face and gave a superior sniff designed to fracture his friendly act. And it worked—his smile faltered, and a hardness slid into his eyes.

"Right," she agreed before turning her attention back to the portfolio, essentially dismissing him.

He cleared his throat. "This your first time getting a tattoo?" he asked, all ease and pleasantness, except for the note of irritation in his voice.

Without looking up, she gave a slight shake of her head. "No."

"What should I expect?"

"Pain."

A snicker popped out of him. "At least you're honest. You know, I feel like I've seen you before, but I can't think where. It was recently." He made a speculative sound and then, moments later, clicked his fingers. "An imp. I saw you with an imp. Tobe something."

Her scalp prickled, and her inner demon tensed. Because there'd been something probing in his words.

So, what, he wanted information of some kind about Tobe?

Naomi telepathically reached out to Khloë. *Take a photo of this dude and text it to me. I want to know who he is.*

The imp's psyche brushed hers. *Give me two minutes and I'll have that info for you.*

"I only recognized Tobe because I bought a painting from him years ago," the guy added.

"Hmm."

"How is he doing?"

Naomi slowly turned a page. "Fine, as far as I know."

"He's an interesting fellow who lives an interesting life. But then, most imps do. Say . . . have you ever met any of the ghost artists he works with?"

Unease crawled its way up her spine. She kept her voice casual as she replied, "Nope."

"Ah. You two aren't close friends, then?" He drew out the word "friends" a little, and it seemed like a prompt—an attempt to have her correct him on her connection to Tobe.

He knew they were anchors, she thought. It made her wonder what else he knew but didn't want to reveal, intent on appearing to know little about Tobe. She met his gaze. "Look, if you have some interest in dating him, I suggest you—"

"Oh no," he interrupted, his eyes widening. "I'm a straight male with a mate and kids."

The "mate and kids" part was a clear lie, but she chose not to call him on it. "There are people who wouldn't let that hold them back."

"I suppose you're right. But no, I have no interest in him *that way*." His oh-so-friendly smile returned. "I was considering whether to contact him about acquiring more artwork, that's all. But then it struck me that I could go straight to the source instead—it often works out cheaper."

"Can't help you with that." She returned her attention to the portfolio.

"He's never mentioned any names?"

"Nope."

"That's a shame."

Just then, Khloë's mind touched hers. *My dad recognized the dude. His name is Daniel Phillips. He's a PI.*

Hmm, interesting. Send me that photo. I want to show it to Tobe.

Way ahead of you on that—I did it about five seconds ago.

Naomi shot the imp a look.

Khloë lifted her shoulders, all innocence. *What? I'm bored and nosy—it's a bad combination in an imp if you expect to keep them out of your business. You know this already.*

Naomi rolled her eyes. The sound of footfalls approaching made her look to the side.

Reaching the sofa, Harper smiled. "Sorry about the wait, Naomi. Come take a seat."

Gladly. Naomi returned the portfolio to the table and, not even sparing the PI a glance, stood upright.

Abruptly, Tobe's psyche crashed into hers, humming with anger. *A fucking PI approached you?*

Yes, though he didn't identify himself as one, Naomi replied as she started following Harper to her station.

What the hell did he say?

He acted like he'd recognized me from having once seen me with you, but I'm pretty sure he knew we were anchors. He said he met you years ago when buying a painting from you, and then he asked me if I'd met any of your ghost artists. He wanted names, claiming he'd rather buy a painting from 'the source'. Obviously, I pled ignorance.

There was a pause. *I'm thinking that he might have been hired by Stefan. If Phillips found out that you're my anchor, he might have thought I shared personal details with you about my connections. Do you think he suspected you of being one of the artists?*

Not at all. He would surely have otherwise hinted at it, or at least asked if she was into art.

Let's keep it that way.

Oh, he's leaving, she noticed. *I guess he's done with the questions.*

He might nose around for a little longer. Be on the lookout.

I will.

"Everything okay?" Harper asked, gesturing for Naomi to settle on the recliner.

"Yes," Naomi replied, taking a seat. "I was just having a little telepathic chat with Tobe."

"Ah, how's he doing? Still far too reckless for his own good?"

"Oh, totally."

The sphinx gave a soft snort, her reflective blue eyes swirling as they shifted to an oak brown—they changed colors frequently. "That's no shocker. Well, you ready for this?"

"More than."

Staring down at the sniveling male on his office floor, Luka ordered, "Get him out of here."

Two of his demons snatched the beaten hellbull up by his arms, making no effort to avoid his injuries. His answering whimper was music to Belial's ears—it had briefly participated in making the bastard bleed.

Once the hellbull had been dragged out of the room, Luka turned to a security guard who manned the entrance to the gambling den. "I highly doubt he'll come back to Infernal. If he does, be sure to express what an exceptionally bad idea it was."

"With pleasure," said Abe, no happier with the motherfucker who'd tried blackmailing one of their waitresses. "I'll spread the word that he's banned."

Luka cut his gaze to Valen, one of his sentinels. "Dig up whatever dirt on the hellbull you can find. Expose it to his nearest and dearest."

It was only fair, considering the bastard had threatened to do the same thing to the waitress if she didn't feed him information about Luka. A beating wasn't enough of a punishment.

Valen gave a curt nod. "It'll be done."

His jaw hard, Luka stalked out of his office and strode toward the private stairwell. The buzz that came with the release of violence rode his system, flooding his veins and sharpening his senses like adrenaline.

With his bodyguards at his heels, he descended the stairwell until he arrived at the second floor. The guard manning the door there opened it wide with a respectful nod.

Luka prowled into the den's luxury VIP area, aware of the brothers still following close behind him. Gentle lighting rained down from the glimmering chandeliers above him. Soft patterned carpeting ran throughout. Velvet sofas in shades of royal blue or soft lilac were dotted around, always accompanied by backlit tables. The chrome bar was a shorter version of the one situated beyond the roped-off set of steps that led to this section.

The classy feel continued in the main area, with its leather sofas, strobe lights, and purple and blue LED uplighting.

There was chattering, glasses tinkling, alarms pinging, machines blooping, dice tumbling, and dealers calling out. The air-conditioned air bore the scents of cologne, perfume, citrus freshener, alcohol, and hot machinery.

He swept his gaze over the den, not worried he'd find anything untoward occurring. For one thing, the guards monitoring the place via the domed cameras never missed a thing. For another, it was rare that any problems cropped up. People weren't exactly eager to piss off legions.

The exclusive den had many, many members. Some occupied themselves at roulette wheels, card tables, or the brightly lit slot machines. Others lounged around sipping drinks. Then there were those who preferred the basement, which featured fighting cages.

Luka immediately claimed the L-shaped sofa he routinely chose. The twins joined him, seating themselves on either end of the piece of furniture.

A smiling waitress appeared almost instantly. Though *not* the waitress who usually worked this corner of the VIP area. "Can I get you any drinks?" asked Draya.

Luka waved off the offer of a drink while the brothers politely declined too.

Still the banshee lingered. "I take it you dealt with the hell-bull?" she prompted softly, moving closer.

Luka inwardly sighed. A relatively new employee, the curvy blonde caught male attention easily. And yes, she'd initially snagged his. She'd also flashed him plenty of invitational smiles, making her interest in him clear.

Luka had gone no further than mild flirtation due to having only recently ended a brief fling. He had planned on making a move eventually, but then he'd laid eyes on Naomi, and his interest had shifted. Though Draya had sensed that shift, she persisted in flirting with him.

"I did." His response was curt. Invited no further conversation. Most people scurried away when he spoke in that tone. To her credit, she didn't let it chase her off, though a hint of nerves showed in her body language.

"And I'm confident that you made it hurt. Are you sure you don't want a drink?" she offered, a suggestive note to her voice that said it wasn't all she was offering.

"I'm good."

She licked her lips, seeming uncertain. "Call me bold, but you don't look it. Is there nothing at all I can get you?"

The head waitress materialized, her brow creased. "Draya, I don't know why you're over here—go serve the customers in *your* section. This one is mine, as you well know."

Irritation flared in Draya's gaze, but she quashed it fast. "Apologies, Bianca, I was—"

"Don't care," said Bianca, as no-nonsense as always—a trait her mate Valen adored. "Go." She waited until the other waitress was out of hearing range before turning to Luka. "She wants in your pants, in case you didn't know."

"I do know."

Bianca sniffed. "Anyone here want drinks?"

They all answered in the negative.

"Holler if you change your mind." With that, she walked off.

Nikandr spared Draya a subtle glance and then looked at Luka. "I thought you were planning to hit that at some point."

Luka draped an arm over the back of the sofa. "I'd considered it, but then I changed my mind."

"I'm guessing it was a certain siren who brought about that change," hedged Mikhail, his eyes smiling. "I get it. She's stunning, not to mention your type. Have you done anything about it yet?"

"I made my intentions clear to her last night. I only left as soon as I did because her psi-mate showed up."

"So she's on board?" Nikandr checked.

"I got the sense that she is, though she didn't verbally confirm it. I'll find out for sure later tonight when I go back to her place."

Luka scraped his teeth over his lower lip. "I had intended to hold out a little longer, but then Iain brought her fully onto my radar by fucking up so spectacularly." If he was honest, he didn't like knowing that the psi-demon had touched her. His entities loathed it.

"On that note ... by all reports, Iain is staying away from her as ordered. But I'm keeping a tail on him until I'm confident that his obsession has worn off."

"It shouldn't take too long," said Nikandr. "Right?"

"Another ten days or so. Two weeks at most," Luka estimated. "If he'd met and bonded with his anchor, it might have helped him recover quicker."

"Speaking of anchors, I doubt Naomi's psi-mate will be good with you edging your way into her life," said Mikhail. "He didn't seem happy that you were at her house. She might turn you down so as not to be at odds with him."

"She might," Luka allowed. "Especially when it can't be denied that he has reason to dislike my being around her. I didn't exactly support Ella's involvement with Viper, so I'd be a hypocrite to condemn Tobe for voicing his objections out of protectiveness. As for whether she'll turn me away to placate him ... I suppose I'll find out soon enough."

CHAPTER FIVE

Naomi had just finished washing the last dish in her sink when a knock came at the front door. Her belly did a little flip. Because it could only be Luka, couldn't it? He'd warned her that he'd be back, and he didn't strike her as someone who'd procrastinate.

She set the dish on the drainer and then wiped her hands on a small kitchen towel. *It might not be him*, she told herself as she walked through the house. *You live among most of your lair—any one of them could have decided to pay you a visit.*

But as she looked through the peephole, she saw that she'd been correct in her initial assumption. Luka stood outside, staring *right at* the peephole as if he somehow knew that she was peering through it.

She pulled back and adjusted the strap of her dress, a sizzling excitement crawling through her system. Given who Luka was and what he could do, she supposed she should at the very least be a little conflicted about reaching out to take what he'd offered.

Or, more specifically, declared that he wanted. But, well, that simply wasn't the case.

Mentally, she'd gone back and forth over it throughout the day. Really, she didn't see a true reason to turn him down. He'd only want something light. He wouldn't shove his nose into her business. And if the rumors were true, he had some serious game in the bedroom.

Where were the negatives?

Oh, there were likely some. But she knew that she'd nonetheless cave at some point, so what did it matter? It was really just a matter of when.

When might as well be now, mightn't it?

Her entity certainly thought so, having no reservations about him; still a big fan of the danger and power he embodied.

Bracing herself for the up-close impact of him, Naomi opened the door. And her breath did a little hitch. Because there was really no bracing yourself for Luka.

God, he was one magnificently masculine bastard. A bastard as imposing as the need he roused in her. She wasn't sure it would go away unless she actively slaked it. *Another* reason to hesitate turning him down.

His gaze traveled down her body in what was nothing short of a blatantly hot eye-fuck. Their gazes collided again, his own holding a predatory light that made her demon stir in delight.

He didn't ask if she was going to let him inside. He just arched a brow—a gesture that seemed both a dare and a challenge.

Moving aside to allow him entrance, she waved at the twins. Like last time, one leaned against the vehicle while the other waited in the driver's seat.

After closing the front door, Naomi did as she had the previous night and followed Luka into the living area, coming to a halt in the center of the space.

He turned to face her, his eyes pinning her with a penetrating, assessing stare. "I'd begin by asking how your day went, but I think we'd both rather I just get to the point."

He wasn't wrong on that score.

He planted his feet. "Last night, I told you exactly what I want from you. Unfortunately, your anchor arrived before we could reach the part of the conversation where you told me if we're on the same page."

"I didn't get the impression that you doubted we were." *Arrogant bastard.* He somehow made that arrogance work for him, though.

His lips hitched up. "A person doesn't always act on what they want. In this case, I fully intend to do so." Her heartbeat accelerated as he covered the small space between them in one smooth glide. "The question is . . . do you?"

She worried her lower lip. "A voice in my head keeps telling me that I'd be dumb to get involved with a demon who runs a criminal empire." A voice that sounded a lot like Tobe's.

Luka's eyes dipped down and boldly traced the shape of her mouth. "But?" he asked, his gaze sliding back to hers, hunger pooling there and acting as a punch to her gut.

"But . . . I find that I don't care."

Pure male satisfaction bloomed in his eyes. "That's a good thing, Naomi."

Her entity agreed. "That remains to be seen."

He dragged a fingertip down the side of her face. "I've told you, you're in no danger with me. I'm not a good person—that I'll admit. But no harm will come to you at my hands, or at those of my demons."

"Not even Belial?"

His eyes bled to black, the air cooling as one of his demons surfaced. The hint of cruelty in the depths of its otherwise flat gaze told her that it was likely Belial. "I will not hurt you," it said. "Unless I think you will like it."

She swallowed, admittedly a *tiny* bit intimidated by this entity. She wasn't afraid of it, just instinctively wary. So much malice lived in its gaze. Her own demon kind of liked that, though. "Pain doesn't do anything for me."

"Hmm, we shall see."

"No, we won't. You'll take my word for it."

"You do not fear me, do you?" the demon hummed. "This pleases me."

She felt her brow pinch. "I thought you liked terrifying people."

It lowered its head toward hers, its black gaze all too penetrating. "Not you." The entity retreated ... and Luka's eyes bored into hers. "Does that ease your concerns?" he asked.

She dipped her chin.

He fingered one of her curls, and her heart slammed against her ribcage. There was nothing sexual about his touch, but it didn't matter. Excitement still rushed through her blood. Anticipation still drummed over her skin. And now she was near to vibrating with the most basic of needs. She couldn't lie, it shook her.

He shook her.

Her demon was no less affected by him, because it wasn't just preternatural power he wielded. It was the sheer power that came from being so very and unabashedly *male*. The guy, unknowingly or not, brandished it like a weapon. And now her body was an absolute mess—heart pounding, hormones drunk, feminine parts tingling.

"So you're agreeing to be mine for at least the next few months?"

"Yes." Her voice broke, and something lit his eyes at the little crack in her composure. Something predatory and indecent.

He edged even closer, sucking up all her oxygen. "*Only* mine," he pushed in a thick whisper, the soft words fanning her face.

She licked her lower lip, and his eyes tracked the movement. "Yes."

"Even if your anchor objects?"

"Even if."

"Even if your family objects?"

"Even if. Quite frankly, it's not their business."

Satisfaction crawled through Luka, and his entities relaxed. "Good."

She lifted and dropped her shoulders. "So, what now?"

"Now" —Luka dipped his face to hers again, watching her pupils dilate—"I'm going to *take* you. Use you like the plaything I'll make you. And then I'll use you some more." He knotted a hand in her hair and tugged her head back slightly. "But not here. I want to fuck you in your bed."

Her tongue swiped out to lick at her bottom lip again. "Okay." She led him upstairs and into a very feminine bedroom that was all lavender paint and white-gloss wood.

He only distantly registered the details, his attention on her. An attention that dropped to her lips again. "I want at that mouth." So he took it, sweeping his tongue inside. Her taste—sweet and succulent—sprang into his system, planting a flag in his sensory memories.

Keeping a tight grip on her hair, he devoured her greedily. Her song had been pattering insistently at his skin and willpower since he arrived. Sexual chemistry had just kept brewing between them, rising with every breath they took. And now an all-consuming vicious need slashed at him, drew metaphorical blood, and tore at his composure—painful in its intensity yet bringing his cock to full attention.

Drawing back from the kiss, he dragged his gaze over her from head to toe, a sense of determination beginning to unfurl in his gut. A determination to have, take, dominate. He released her hair and took a step back. "Lose the clothes."

She swallowed. The tension between them intensified, thickening the atmosphere as the seconds ticked by.

He thought he might have to repeat his order, but then she slowly pulled down the side zipper of her dress. *Good girl.*

She tugged the straps over her shoulders and allowed the material to swish down her body, leaving her in white lacy underwear that stood out against her tanned—and sparsely inked—skin.

Carnal hunger tightened his belly, fierce and potent. She was seriously fucking beautiful. A sensual masterpiece.

Her movements unhurried, she shed her shoes and underwear. Every inch of her—soft, curvy, perfect—bare for his view, causing pure, molten lust to slam into him.

He strolled toward her, anticipation a drumbeat in his veins. He loosened his tie and pulled it off, keeping his movements slow, letting the tension simmer and stretch. He raked his gaze down her body, mapping it, as he blindly tossed the tie onto a plush chair. "That tattoo looks fresh," he commented, referring to the pretty and incredibly intricate rose on her thigh, which also featured a small butterfly.

Her gaze fell to his hands as he tackled the buttons of his shirt. "Harper Wallis did it for me earlier today. I'm a fast healer, so it's only a little tender now."

In other words, he didn't need to be careful with her. *Noted.* "Belial is jealous that someone else marked your skin." He slipped off his shirt and draped it over the back of the chair.

She stared at his chest, tracing over the tribal ink there. "Mother, may I?" she said to herself with a soft sigh.

Feeling his lips curve up, he crossed to her, looking his fill, drinking in the perfect sight she made. The scent of her need spiced the air between them; baited him, dared him to touch her. Again the drive to *take* gnawed at his control. His entities stirred restlessly within him, each wanting at her.

Naomi cleared her throat. "I'm naked, but you're not taking advantage. So lame."

He swept his thumb over the pulse beating fast in her neck. Her skin was soft, cool, and perfumed with the scent of vanilla. "I'll be taking every advantage in just a moment." It wasn't an exaggeration.

"Your pants are still on. Also lame."

"So impatient. Are we in a rush?"

"*I* am. You've gotten me all hot and bothered. I'm an instant-gratification girl."

"You're *my* girl for the time being, so you'll get gratification when I decide—not before."

Naomi broke out in a shiver as the coating of dominance in his voice wrapped around her like liquid steel. Waves of intensity all but rolled off him as he loomed over her, male greed swamping his gaze. Her demon hummed in interest, curious as to just how deep his dominant streak ran.

She would no doubt soon find out. And the quicker the better. Her body was bursting with anticipation. She needed him to touch her. She didn't even care where; just needed his hands on her.

"I should warn you," he said, his pitch dropping an octave.

"Warn me of what?" she asked, a slight croak in her voice.

"I won't be the only one who plays with you tonight. My demons ... they'll take turns with you. They'll each make you come. And then so will I."

That wicked promise trailed down her spine like teasing fingertips, and the atmosphere turned electric.

His hand crept up her nape, seized a bunch of her hair, and jerked her head back, wrenching a gasp from her. "We will use you however we please. All four of us. And you will take whatever we give you."

So he wanted to talk her into an orgasm. Fabulous. She parted her lips to speak—

And his mouth dropped down on hers.

The kiss was hungry and sensuous, interlaced with a hotly sexual promise. Chemicals rushed through her system, dizzying her thoughts.

His free hand gripped her hip and pulled her flush against him. She grabbed at his shoulders and arched into him. The press of his solid, powerful body against hers was just *yowzah*.

A growl drummed its way up his throat and poured into her mouth. He drew back, lifted her, and propped her butt on the edge of the bed—all in one smooth move. Invisible hands pushed her further up the mattress. Hmm, *someone* was telekinetic.

"Stay." He raised his palms, emitting gleaming gold and black threads of power. Two shot to her wrists; the other two went for her ankles. And then the buzzing threads yanked, spreading her into a starfish position and holding her wrists and ankles against the mattress.

What in the blazes of hell?

She pulled against the binds, but there was no give. She was caught. Pinned in position.

Her belly pitched as shards of excitement buried themselves there. She felt exposed and vulnerable, yet more than ready to roll.

She looked up at Luka, her words dying on her tongue as she saw he was now naked—a thoroughly magnificent sight. There was so much muscle and ink, and damn, she wanted that long, thick cock inside her.

Like, right now.

His eyes breezed over her with a burning intensity, admiring every line and curve. Her skin prickled at being in the spotlight of his absolute focus. She felt a little like a priceless piece of artwork at an exhibition.

"You're tying me to the bed?"

He kneeled on the mattress. "I have to be sure you don't fall off."

Yeah. Right. "At least let me have one hand free."

"No. I don't want you to touch or give. Not tonight. I want you to feel. Take. Shatter into tiny little fragments—defenses and all. That's when you'll *really* feel me. Everywhere." The temperature took a dip as his eyes bled to black, the whites disappearing. "Then we will possess every part of you," said whichever entity had surfaced, its voice a monotone.

Her pulse having a meltdown, she watched as the demon settled itself flat on the bed, its head level with her pussy. Tendrils of excitement twisted her stomach into a tight knot.

It ghosted the tip of its nose along one of her slick folds. "You smell a little too good." Hands curled around her thighs as a warm, velvety tongue licked at her slit. And that same tongue quickly swept her away.

Time, the room, *the world* seemed to disappear. All she knew was *that mouth*. Skilled licks, flicks, and stabs were interspersed with nips, bites, and nibbles. Sweet and sensual words of praise whispered over her wet flesh—some spoken in English, others in Russian.

Being unable to move was as frustrating as it was heady. She couldn't arch into its mouth, could only take. And take she did. Until, caught up in an endless loop of exquisite sensation, she came so hard that stars danced in her vision.

Jesus Christ. Little judders racking her body, she tried to get a hold on her breathing. No joy there.

The demon nuzzled her pussy and then slid up her body. "I like the taste of you. I am going to want more."

Demonic entities weren't much for compliments and praise, unlike *this* one. It was smooth and seductive, a note of sexual power in its otherwise toneless voice. "Abraxas," she guessed, recalling Luka's descriptions of his inner demons.

Its lips winged up. "What a clever girl you are." There was a ripple in those black eyes. Like a pebble landing in water. Then its expression changed from an amused satisfaction to something much more intense.

"And we have waited longer for this than we wished to," said the demon, the sexual hint of power now gone from its voice. It sounded put out. Sullen.

Another entity had surfaced, she realized. "You're Dagon."

"No," it denied.

Luka's previous words came back to her: *Dagon is moody and will lie to you because that's what it does to people.*

"Yes," she insisted.

Its eyes narrowed. "What makes you so sure?"

"I have a very good bullshit detector."

The entity hummed, not appearing too pleased about that. Then it jammed two fingers inside her.

She jolted, her eyes going wide. "Give a girl a warning, would you."

"Quiet now. I prefer that my toys do not talk." Its mouth descended on her breast just as it began pumping its fingers in and out of her, hitting her G spot just right.

She could only lie back and enjoy as the entity alternated from gentle to rough while it suckled, nipped, and scraped its teeth over each of her nipples.

She'd heard of breast worship. This wasn't worship. It was gluttony. The entity devoured her breasts, repeatedly scoring them with its teeth.

Meanwhile, it slowly upped the pace of its hand little by little ... until eventually it was slamming its fingers into her pussy hard and fast.

Her orgasm hit just as hard and just as fast, appearing out of nowhere. She fractured with a choked cry, her head flying back, her inner muscles rippling.

The fingers withdrew from her, and then lips breezed over her cheek. "I want to see you covered in my marks," said the entity, the merest note of cruelty in its tone. A note that hadn't been there before. "Bruises. Welts. Bites."

Belial, she thought. "Welts? Fuck that shit – I'm not into whips."

"Pity."

"Yeah, for you."

It slid its hand down her body. "This is going to hurt just a little."

She tensed. "What is?"

"Luka should have warned you really."

"Warned me what?"

"That we can do this." It planted a splayed hand on her stomach and ... God, it was like it *pushed* an orgasm into her body. A supernova explosion of pleasure/pain spiraled through her system. She screamed, shook, bucked, almost blacked out.

Teeth bit into the swell of her breast. "Again."

More pain-laden bliss struck, violently flooding her body and numbing her mind.

"One more."

Her body lit up like a goddamn firework yet again—there were snaps and crackles and bangs. At the same time, the skin beneath the demon's palm began to heat. She hissed at the sizzle of pain even as it turned into pleasure.

The entity was branding her, she realized.

The burn of it overlaid the other decadent sensations, added to the pleasure rocketing through her, and *shit*, she might cry with the intensity of it.

Finally, her release subsided. Her body went limp, officially running on empty. She didn't close her eyes; it was more like the lids collapsed.

Synapses. Officially. Fried.

That's when you'll really feel me. Everywhere.

She understood what he'd meant now. Her defenses were down, her body didn't feel like her own, all her layers peeled back, leaving her core-self exposed.

Shaking and drained and gasping for breath, she probably would have curled up in the fetal position and zonked out if she could have moved.

"Now it's my turn." The voice was pure sex—and it was *all* Luka. He lowered his full weight onto her.

Her nerve endings were so raw she flinched at the amount of skin-to-skin contact.

"Trapped under me, just how I want you."

"I sort of figured that out when you bound me to the bed."

"As I said before, I can't have you falling off."

"I'd snort if I had the energy."

Palming her delectable ass, Luka positioned her to take him and nudged the broad head of his dick inside her. Even through the condom he felt the scalding, addictive heat of her.

Her eyelids lifted, revealing two sex-drunk pools of gray-green. "I can't come again," she rasped, her throat seeming dry. "I can't."

"Of course you can. Because I *want* you to." He snapped his hips forward, slamming home. Her swollen muscles clamped down on him, a husky cry left her throat, and he groaned at the feeling of her tight wet heat coating his cock.

His control fractured, fell at his feet in a shower of shards. He rode her so hard it was brutal, forcing his dick deep, loving the sight of her bound beneath him. Loving that she was helpless to do anything but take whatever he gave her.

He let himself get lost in her. In her softness, her warmth, her moans, her submission, the ripples of her inner walls.

Walls that tightened and turned almost unbearably hot, telling him she was close to coming.

He snaked his hand between them so he could roll and flick her clit. His own release was almost on him. It began to build, coil, spasm. And then it exploded outward just as her pussy clamped down on him.

They came together. Hard. Long. Until the strength oozed out of them both.

He gave her his full weight, planting his face against her throat. She didn't move ... and it took him a few moments to remember that she *couldn't* move.

He released her wrists and ankles from the iron grip of his power. "How are your shoulders?" he asked, his voice lazy.

"I don't know," she all but slurred. "I can't feel anything from the neck down."

Raising his head, he met her slumberous gaze. "You all right?"

Her brow pinched. "Why wouldn't I be?"

"Being fucked by a legion and their three entities can no doubt be ... intense." He didn't get the impression that it had been too much for her, but he wanted the verbal confirmation—as did his inner demons.

Her dismissive expression waved away his concern. "I'm good."

Satisfied, Luka accepted that with a slight nod. His inner entities settled, though they weren't surprised by her response.

He withdrew his cock slowly, knowing it wouldn't be long before he was back inside her. He rolled to his side, placing his hand on her belly.

Her gaze seemed to sharpen with remembrance. "Was it Belial that branded me?"

"Yes."

"What does the mark look like?"

He peered down and blinked in surprise. Humor plucking at him, he invited, "See for yourself."

"I will in a minute. Not sure I can lift my head yet." She nibbled on her lower lip. "That *other* thing it did ... you know, where it made me come just by putting a hand on my stomach? All *four* of you can do that?"

"Yes."

"Gotta admit, that's a little unnerving. It makes me wonder what else you can all do. You won't ever do that to me in public, right?"

He frowned. "Me? No." He paused a beat. "Belial might, though."

"Really?"

"Really."

She pulled a face. "I think it would be best if you told it not to ever do that."

The entity snorted at that, finding her quite entertaining. "Belial does as it pleases a lot of the time," Luka said, sweeping a hand over the brand on her stomach.

"You look amused. Why? What did that damn demon do?" She lifted her head, and her face went slack. "What the hell is this?"

He shrugged one shoulder. "Belial wanted to leave bruises and welts on you, but you said no to being whipped. So it ... improvised." And it was rather smug about it. She now had what looked like welts criss-crossed over each other, overlaid by gray bruises.

She glared at him. "This isn't funny."

"I'm not laughing."

"You *want* to. Which is quite frankly confusing. It doesn't at all bother you that your demon so boldly branded me?"

"Why would it?" He slowly pushed his fingers inside her, humming as her slick pussy clenched them tight. "*This*" —he swirled his fingers—"is all the fuck mine for the next few months. Seeing my entities' brands on you won't bother me any."

"And if *my* demon decides to return the favor?"

Luka pursed his lips. "I suppose turnabout is fair play."

CHAPTER SIX

A light blaring sound filled the room a week later, slashing right through Naomi's concentration. She blinked, taking a mental step back from her work. *Cell phone alarm*, she realized.

Whenever she let her creative side free, she lost all sense of time. Loud-ass alarms were essential or she'd struggle to snap out of her zone. In this instance, it was a reminder that she needed to get ready for her shift at the pizzeria.

Grimacing in disappointment, she set down her paint palette and brush. The tarp spread out over the hardwood floor made a crackling sound beneath her feet as she walked over to where her phone rested on the windowsill. She tapped the screen, switching off the alarm.

Her arm a little tired, she rolled her stiff shoulder with a low groan. Though she'd much rather keep painting, it was likely best that she was forced to take a break.

She was never glad to leave this particular room. She *loved* her workspace. There was ample lighting—both natural and artificial—and a tip-top ventilation system. She'd brought things into the room that inspired her—carvings, vases, small sculptures, and also framed paintings of various artists, which she'd hung on the walls. The plentiful scents were both comforting and inspiring: oil paints, pine canvases, turpentine, and linseed oil.

Her corner storage area held a cabinet, drawers, and cubby shelves with baskets for all her supplies and tools. But plenty of those objects ended up in places they shouldn't, like vases or jars or old coffee tins, because organization wasn't really her jam.

No one could call the room tidy. It was chaos at its finest. Blobs and streaks of paint were just about everywhere. Empty mugs, discarded water bottles, old paint rags, and granola bar wrappers had managed to find homes in places they shouldn't. An overflowing trash can sat beneath the utility sink near her small coffee/tea station.

Her work spot was right in the center of the room, her large easel angled in a way that caught the natural light streaming through the window. Though the room was cluttered, she had enough space around her spot that she could inch back from the easel and view her work from every angle.

Other easels of different sizes were propped against a wall alongside her paintings – some finished, some unfinished—as well as bare canvases. Many other objects were also pushed against the walls, including a stepladder, buckets, crates, a small refrigerator, stool, drawing table, and workbench. There was also a bookcase, which held reference and art books.

After washing her brush in the utility sink and scrubbing her hands with mint soap, she nabbed a mango smoothie from her mini refrigerator and swiftly knocked it back. It wasn't until right then that she realized just how thirsty she'd been. When in her zone, there was no guarantee that hunger, thirst, or even the need to pee would penetrate.

Not wanting to interrupt her unnecessarily while she worked, her loved ones only ever reached out to her if they needed to make contact. Not Luka, though, as he had no idea about her main profession. Hence his earlier *I'll be at your place no later than nine* telepathic shoutout.

Not wanting to tread excess paint through the house, Naomi kicked off her sneakers before leaving her workspace. She then locked the door with the key that she typically kept on the top of the frame. She always kept it secured shut. If Luka wondered why, he hadn't asked.

Though he tossed some personal questions her way, they were never *too* personal, and his intention was usually only to change the path of the conversation. She pulled the same verbal stunt if he approached a topic that she didn't like to cover. And so they often went around in circles, only revealing snatches of this and that to each other.

Even if what they had wasn't simple and shallow, she wouldn't have easily told him about her *real* source of income. Luka wouldn't frown upon the illegal elements of her career path—he didn't exactly show much respect for the law—but she preferred to keep it private.

It occurred to her that if he were to uncover it, he mightn't be comfortable with the idea. Luka seemed to be protective by nature. While there was no danger in being a ghost artist, there were risks. Risks that she'd be caught painting replicas or creating fake lost paintings, or that she'd be hounded by clients like Stefan.

The mere thought of that idiot made her demon's mouth tighten. At least it seemed that Stefan had given up on trying to sniff out her identity. She hadn't seen or heard anything more from the PI, and Tobe hadn't been contacted by him either. A good sign.

Mentally setting the subject aside, Naomi made her way into her bedroom and through to the en suite bathroom, where she shucked her paint-streaked clothes. She hadn't yet informed Tobe or anyone else about her involvement with Luka. As she'd told him, it was none of their business. Why tell them only to have them attempt to talk her into exiting what was proving to be a very enjoyable arrangement?

Due to how busy he was, she hadn't seen Luka every night over the past week. When she did have him here, he was often called away at some point to deal with this or that. It was only to be expected, considering he was a Prime who also ran an actual demonic criminal empire. It didn't at all bother her that so much of his time was taken up, because it gave her the space and privacy she needed to paint.

In sum, things were going as well as she'd hoped.

After showering, styling her hair, and slapping on a little makeup, Naomi pulled on one of the black dresses she considered work attire. Finally ready to leave, she dropped her cell into her purse, activated her alarm system, and then exited the house.

The multi-lane traffic was calmer than it tended to be during daytime hours, as was the area itself. Not many pedestrians could be seen strolling along the sidewalk. But she spotted some of her neighbors pottering around. One was taking out the trash, another was unloading shopping bags from her car, and a third was walking his Labrador.

This particular street was home to several of her lair, as were many of the ones nearby. Demons didn't have territories, but they often grouped together. It gave them better protection.

As she crossed the road, an itch built between her shoulder blades, giving her that familiar feeling of being watched. Frustration tightened her jaw.

Without breaking stride, she peeked over her shoulder. There didn't appear to be anyone around, but she didn't think her imagination was simply going wild. Someone was definitely watching her—her demon felt equally certain of it.

Iain, maybe? Or that damn PI she'd just been thinking had left the picture?

Her lips thinning, she faced forward again and shook her head. Whoever it was, they'd better keep out of sight or they were going to end up with her foot up their ass.

Arriving at the pizzeria, she pushed open the door and breezed inside. "Hey, all. Sorry I'm late." The place wasn't yet open—wouldn't open for another five minutes—but she should have gotten here earlier.

Alfie looked up from behind the open kitchen. "Girl, I'll swear you are blind to the passing of time."

Well ... yeah. That fit.

Naomi hurried to her locker in the breakroom, locked her purse away, and then took up position at the hostess station.

Donna sidled up to her with a pretty smile. "So, are you going to show me your new tattoo or what?"

"Not right here—it's high up on my thigh. I'll show you later, when we're alone."

"I'm thinking of getting one myself, but something small. At least the first time."

"The girls at Urban Ink have a waiting list, so get on it as soon as you can." Hearing the door creak open, Naomi looked over ... and felt every muscle in her face freeze.

Iain gave her a tremulous smile as he entered. "Naomi," he whispered, so much reverence in his tone that nausea gripped her gut.

Fuck.

Ignoring the low curses coming from Alfie and Donna, Naomi watched the psi-demon carefully as he took slow, shuffling steps toward her—his eyes hazy, his skin clammy, his cheeks red and blotchy.

Her demon gritted its teeth, exasperated beyond belief with this guy. The entity wasn't familiar with empathy, so it gave not one measly shit that he was in the grasp of a siren song.

"I did it," he said with a proud smile.

Naomi felt her brow crease. "Did what?"

"Stayed away for a whole week. My feelings haven't changed, though. That means they're real," he insisted. "This is *proof* that they're real."

Conscious that people would begin piling inside at any moment, she suggested, "Why don't we talk in the breakroom?" There would otherwise be a public scene for sure.

Sending him away wouldn't work. Threatening him wouldn't work. *Nothing* ever worked.

He considered her suggestion for a moment. "Privacy would be best."

Heading for the breakroom, she exchanged a brief look with her stepfather as she telepathed him. *Don't worry, I'll handle this.*

No, sweetheart, Belinsky needs to be the one to handle it, said Alfie. *You can take care of yourself, I know, but Iain isn't going to listen to you—not while he's caught up in your song. Nothing you say will penetrate.*

He was right on that. Iain had disobeyed his Prime, yes, but he would leave if ordered to do so by Luka. She could toss as many orders and threats at him as she liked; could even set the guy on fire—none of it would make a difference. He was determined to prove that he loved her. Plus, she'd assured Luka that she'd call out to him if such a scenario occurred, hadn't she?

As she closed the breakroom door behind her and Iain, she telepathically reached out to Luka. *Sorry to interrupt whatever you're doing, but Iain's here at the pizzeria.*

"You look good." Iain swallowed hard. "Beautiful. Always do. God, I've missed you so much. It's been hard to stay away."

A male mind stroked over hers, vibrating with anger. *I'll be with you very soon*, Luka told her. He probably meant to have someone teleport him to the pizzeria, then.

You can teleport to the private dining room you used before. It's empty right now. We're in the breakroom – it's just a few doors down from there. Noticing Iain edging toward her, she slammed up a hand. "No."

His brow furrowed in confusion, but he halted.

"Iain, a week wasn't going to be enough for my song to wear off. You needed to stay away for at least two. Now you'll have to start all over again."

He shook his head. "What? No. No, I don't need longer."

God, she hated this. Hated seeing what her very nature did to people. Hated having to say things that hurt them in an effort to get through to them. It sucked every time. "You shouldn't have come here, you should have—"

"I *need* to be where you are."

"No, you need to listen to the people around you. You need to take their advice for your own sake."

His jaw clenched. "I am sick and tired of people telling me how I feel. I *know* how I feel. They can't possibly have any clue what's going on inside me."

"You're feverish, Iain. The kind of feverish that comes with being under the influence of a siren song."

"That doesn't mean my feelings are false!" he shouted, spittle flying from his mouth. "I would know if they were!"

Evidently not. She shot him a hard look, her entity baring its teeth in anger. "Do not yell at me."

He squeezed his eyes shut. "I'm sorry, I'm sorry. It's just maddening having people question your state of mind and insist that you're delusional. I know the difference between love and obsession."

"How could you love me when you barely know me? Seriously, *think* about it. Consider how crazy it is that you'd feel so deeply for someone you weren't around for very long."

"It's not crazy, it's—"

The door slammed open and hit the wall with a bang. Luka prowled inside, his bodyguards and an additional demon hot on his heels. He was an absolute vision of rage—eyes cold, jaw tight, neck corded, skin mottled, body stiff.

The flesh on the side of his face stretched and undulated, looking as if a snake writhed underneath it. The same happened to his throat and hand, and she knew it was his inner demons.

Her breath caught, unease gliding up her spine. Her entity tensed, though in fascination, not fear.

The three demons behind Luka, however, stilled nervously. Iain paled, snapped his mouth shut, and took two steps back.

Luka raked his icy gaze over Naomi, as if to be sure that she hadn't been harmed. He then cut it to Iain, his glare now gleaming with malice. "What in the unholy fuck made you think it would be a wise idea to come here?"

Luka couldn't quite believe that the bastard had dared do it. Iain was a lot of things, but he wasn't stupid. And he fucking *knew* that Luka didn't bluff. The guy had been well aware that a world of pain would await him if he went against Luka's order. And yet here he was.

Worse, he didn't look the slightest bit fucking remorseful.

Displeased at having been caught disobeying orders, yes. Terrified of what would now happen to him, yes. But not at all sorry. As if he had the *right* to be wherever Naomi was.

Fury heated Luka's blood, making him clench his teeth so

hard his jaw ached. Equally enraged, his entities kept pushing against his skin; he felt it ripple as they slithered beneath it. Not even the terror plastered over Iain's face mollified them.

Flexing his fingers, Luka stalked toward him. "You've developed a masochistic streak, have you? Is that it?"

Backing up so fast he staggered, Iain lifted a staying hand. "No. No, I just *had* to see her."

"And you did." Towering over the psi-demon, Luka cocked his head. "Was it worth what you know will happen to you next?"

Fear a dancing flame in his eyes, Iain hunched his shoulders. "I just wanted to—"

"I didn't ask what you wanted," Luka bit off. "Because what you want from Naomi means not one thing when it happens to be something that she *doesn't* want." Not even Abraxas, who basked in female attention and felt entitled to it, would push itself on a woman who wasn't interested.

"But that's the thing, she wouldn't ask me to stay away if she knew I truly did love her. I'm trying to make her see that she's mistaken. If she'd only listen—"

"The person who's not listening is *you*. You're choosing to cling to your delusions rather than face reality. The fact is that Naomi has not one wish to have you in her life—no matter what you feel for, about, or toward her."

"Luka—"

"We had a conversation at my home in which I made it perfectly clear that you were to stay away from her. Naomi has also made that clear. Jolene, too, has made it clear. Belial did as well, and it warned you what would happen if you disobeyed us on this."

"I didn't ignore your orders. I kept my distance from Naomi like you asked. But my feelings for her never dimmed."

Impatience fairly rattled Luka's bones. "You only kept your

distance for *seven days*. Of course they haven't dimmed. And you're not stupid enough to think they should have. You just decided to ignore the facts because it suited you to do so."

Iain looked away, his eyes seeking out Naomi. "I—"

"No," Luka snapped, drawing the psi-demon's attention back to him. "Don't talk to her. Don't even fucking look at her."

Iain opened his mouth to argue ... and Belial had officially had enough. The entity rose to the surface abruptly, taking control, relishing how Iain's face turned even whiter.

"Daniil is going to take you now," it told him. "I will join you shortly. We are going to have some fun, you and I. Well ... it will not be fun for you. But I will certainly enjoy every moment."

Regaining supremacy over the entity, Luka spared Daniil a look. "You know where to put him."

The tall blond demon crossed to a spluttering Iain, snatched his arm, and teleported him away.

Luka turned to Naomi, who stood very still, her expression unreadable. "Are you all right?" he asked.

"Yes," she replied simply.

Luka squinted, unsure he believed that. Dagon, to its supreme annoyance, couldn't tell if she'd lied or not. Its irritation would no doubt have tickled both Abraxas and Belial if it weren't for their black mood.

Luka looked at his guards. "Give us a minute."

The twins obligingly left the room.

He switched his attention back to Naomi, walking toward her. "Did the fucker touch you?"

"No, he just desperately tried convincing me that his feelings were genuine. He was beyond the point of being reasoned with." She grimaced. "It always creeps me out when someone fixates on me so intensely. It's like they lose who they are little by little," she added, guilt threaded through each word.

Luka frowned, inching closer to her. Her scent swirled around him; beckoned him, enticed him, urged him to reach out and touch her. An urge he didn't fight. "Don't feel guilty, Naomi," he said, palming her nape. "He isn't in that state because of you."

"My song—"

"Snared him, yes, but it hasn't taken his choices from him. As you yourself once pointed out to me, he's still responsible for his words and actions. If he'd done as you asked and left you alone, he would have recovered months ago. But he didn't do that. He hasn't respected your wishes at any point. He's all about himself. That isn't on you." He squeezed the back of her neck. "It's a reflection of his basic personality."

She licked her lips. A simple sight, and yet brutal lust bit at him. A lust that shot straight to his dick and fed the sexual tension that was always present when they were close. He should be used to it after a week in her bed. Should have developed some sort of immunity to her song. *No such luck.* It sang to his system even now.

The sex between them wasn't merely good, it was fucking phenomenal. Memories of it—of the softness of her skin, of her nails digging into his back, of how she arched into his every thrust—played through his mind constantly.

"I know," she said, her voice thick in a way that told him she wasn't immune to the tension. "I still don't like seeing him that way." She thrust a hand through her hair. "I didn't expect him to show up here. I thought he'd listen to you."

"So did I, but I was having him monitored just to be sure. He must have known, because he made every effort to give his watcher the slip." And the bastard had been successful—something Luka wouldn't have foreseen.

He'd underestimated just how determined Iain would be to have contact with her, and she'd essentially paid for that. Luka wouldn't make that mistake again. "On the day I release him, I will assign you a guard."

Surprise rippled over her face, and her brow knitted. "That's not necessary."

"Oh, but it is. He should never have gotten near you tonight. I will not allow it to happen again."

"He isn't a danger to me."

"At present, no. But you said yourself that things might get ugly. Men have threatened you in the past when in his state. They've even tried to harm you." Which made Luka want to fucking kill them.

"But—"

He reached up with his free hand and loosely cupped the side of her jaw. "No, Naomi, I'm not budging on this." He brushed his thumb over her lower lip. "I will not risk him harming you. As you already know, you're mine for the foreseeable future. That places you under my protection, which I take very seriously. It's as simple as that." His eyes dipped to her mouth of their own accord. "Now, I need to go deal with Iain. But I want a taste of you first."

He stole a kiss that was slow, teasing, and deep, feeling the tension gradually leach from her muscles. Pulling back, he hummed. "If I wasn't wound so tight with fury that I could trust I wouldn't be far too rough with you, I'd take you here and now. It will regretfully have to wait." Releasing her, he let his arms fall back to his sides. "I'm going to be . . . busy tonight." Busy dealing with Iain. "But I'll see you tomorrow."

She gave a curt nod. "Tomorrow."

CHAPTER SEVEN

Luka strode out of the breakroom, his blood still buzzing with rage. He looked at Daniil, who had evidently returned and now stood with the twins. "Take us to Iain."

Their surroundings blurred briefly as Daniil teleported them out of the pizzeria and straight to an underground vault. Located in an isolated spot of the Nevada desert, it was constructed of thick soundproof walls that were cracked and moist with damp.

It was windowless and dimly lit. The only light came from the weak, flickering bulbs placed sporadically around the vault. The air was ripe with the scents of fear, old blood, terror, rusted iron, and a defeated despair.

It was one of Belial's favorite places in the entire world.

"You may go," Luka told Daniil, who promptly disappeared.

Luka stalked along the narrow passageway that split the short rows of cramped detention cells. Only two were presently occupied. A badly hurt demon was curled up asleep in the corner of the first. Iain stood at the back of the other, his palms pressed against the walls as if he might disappear into them.

Luka halted in front of the cell. "I would imagine that being here has stirred up some extremely unpleasant memories for you. People who are brought to my vault generally don't do anything that would result in a second visit. There have been exceptions, of course. I hadn't thought that you would be one of them. We both learned that your threshold for pain is far from high."

Iain cast a fearful look to his right, knowing what lay beyond the cells. Knowing of the furnaces, pits of water, interrogation rooms, and—finally—torture chambers.

Each chamber was worse than the one before. All contained various instruments and machines—some medieval, some modern. The severity of the crime dictated how many chambers you were taken to and the length of the torture sessions you endured.

Many words had been used to describe the happenings here in the vault. Sadistic. Barbaric. Hellish. All were accurate.

And Iain knew that well.

He'd been here before. He'd experienced the kind of suffering that would deter anyone from breaking rules or ignoring orders again. But threats of pain or not, demons weren't easy to control—hence why Primes couldn't afford to be merciful.

Iain skirted the old bloodstains on the stone floor as he came to the front of the cell. "I understand why you are angry with me. But I did what I did out of love."

A snort popped out of Mikhail, and Nikandr dragged a disbelieving palm down his face.

"It's true," maintained Iain, curling his hands around the iron bars, his expression a plea for mercy.

"It wouldn't matter either way," said Luka, "because this isn't about what you do or don't feel for Naomi. It's that you discounted my order to stay away from her."

"No, I *did* stay away from her."

"Temporarily. That wasn't what I ordered you to do, was it? *Was it?*"

Iain squeezed his eyes shut. "No."

"No. What did I instruct you to do?"

Exhaling a low sigh, he met Luka's gaze. "Leave Naomi be."

"Leave her be. Make no attempt to contact her. Stay out of her life." Luka arched a brow. "Did you obey me?"

"No. But it's not as if I hurt her."

"So I should just overlook your behavior? I should excuse your actions?"

Iain mashed his lips together for a long moment. "You would understand if you'd ever felt for anyone what I feel for her," he burst out.

"Maybe. But you would still be punished. Because you disregarded not only my orders but Naomi's wishes." Luka should have made it public that he and Naomi were involved. Announcing his private business wasn't something he generally did. If he had, if his claim to her had been common knowledge, just maybe Iain would have done as ordered.

Or maybe it would have provoked the psi-demon to do exactly what he'd already done.

"I just want her to *listen* to me," Iain claimed. "Nobody is listening."

"It's you who's failing to hear people. I mentioned that already." And Luka was fucking tired of repeating himself. "It's going to take you a few days to recover both mentally and physically from what I'm about to do. I won't be releasing you right away, though. I think it might be best to keep you here until Naomi's song has worn off."

Iain's eyes went wide. "What? No." He let go of the cell bars and backed up.

"If you don't get better, the situation will escalate. You could harm her in your frustration at being unable to own her. I can't have that. I *won't* have that. Naomi's mine."

Iain's head jerked back. "What do you mean, yours?"

"Exactly what I said." It was time Luka made it clear. His entities were in firm agreement on that.

The psi-demon shook his head hard and fast in denial. "No. No, she's not—"

"In my metaphorical bed? Oh, she is."

Lines of jealousy creased Iain's face.

"And I will never allow any harm to come to what's mine," Luka added. "You . . . *you're* a threat to her."

"I would never hurt her."

"Says every stalker ever. That's what you've become, Iain. Part of why you went to see her today is that you can't cope with the idea that you might not be on her mind."

"That's not true."

Deep inside Luka, Dagon hissed at the lie. "You want to be center-stage in her thoughts, just as she is in yours—consequences be damned," accused Luka. "Well, those consequences are going to involve an agony that's beyond your imagining."

Belial grinned, eager to begin. It would relish the slap of a whip lashing skin, the crunches and cracks of bone, the whimpers and screams of fear and pain.

Neither Abraxas nor Dagon got any real kick out of such things, but it pleased them that this male would pay for refusing to leave Naomi alone.

Iain backed up even further, his breaths coming fast.

"There's nowhere to go. Nowhere you can hide. No way for you to escape. And you have no one to blame for what's coming but yourself."

*

Seated at one of the pizzeria's breakroom tables, Naomi narrowed her eyes on her anchor. "Stop it."

Leaning against the wall looking deceptively casual, Tobe widened his eyes. Eyes that gleamed with hot anger. "What?" he asked, all innocence. "I'm not doing anything."

"You're planning to fuck with Iain in some way—likely by setting his house on fire."

"It really is an effective way to get a message across," Lachlan cut in, standing a few feet away with Alfie. "I can personally attest to that."

Beside Naomi, her mother threw the imp a frustrated look. "Don't encourage him."

"I really don't think he needs encouragement," Lachlan told her. "His mind is all made up."

Naomi gave her psi-mate a beseeching look. "Tobe, let's not reward his behavior with attention; it does no good. And it'll only give him another reason to contact me or mine." That was what Iain would do, in his current frame of mind—use Tobe's retaliation as an excuse to reach out to her. Not that the idiot appeared to *need* excuses, but it seemed better for Tobe not to interfere anyway. Especially since Luka would be mad at him for getting involved and causing whatever damage Tobe had in mind. That was the last thing she wanted.

Her inner demon didn't care so much what "seemed better". It wanted Iain to suffer, so it would be behind any plan that ensured that.

Tobe pushed away from the wall. "I agreed to handle this in non-violent ways, Nome, but none have worked. He ain't listening. Someone needs to make him listen."

"Luka will," Tia interjected. "I have no doubt that Iain is going to be punished severely for ignoring his Prime's directives."

"Which he will have known in advance," said Tobe, his tone

clipped. "And yet the bastard came here anyway." He rolled his shoulders. "A statement needs to be made."

"A *firm* one," Lachlan added, to which her anchor nodded.

"I support this plan," Alfie piped up, his expression hard.

Tia glared at her mate. "I don't. Right now, we have Belinsky on our side. That will change if we go around destroying his demon's possessions or property."

Lachlan's brow pinched. "We can be subtle."

Naomi snorted at him. "You don't even know what that word means."

The imp managed to look offended. "Are you calling me stupid?"

"No, I'm saying you're willfully ignorant of anything you don't want to understand or accept." It could be maddening at times.

"I don't know what you mean," Lachlan claimed.

"And there you go proving my point," said Naomi with a slight wave of her hand.

"It's funny how men act differently when in the throes of an obsession," mused Tia. "Some turn stalkerish, professing undying love. Some turn aggressive, resenting the impact you have on them. Others avoid you desperately in an effort to snap out of it, knowing on some level that their feelings aren't real."

"You've dealt with this sort of thing in your time?" Naomi asked her.

"Often," Tia replied. "The thing with the Iains of the world is they seem foolish and weak with all their love bombing, so we can make the mistake of not being careful around them. That's something you can't do, Naomi. They're often the most dangerous, because their thought patterns are off and they're more obsessive than most."

Right then, the door creaked open and Jolene walked inside, her jaw tight and her face blank. Her eyes, though? They glittered with ire. She closed the door as her gaze found Naomi. "Tell me exactly what occurred here." It was nothing short of an order.

Naomi explained, starting from when Iain first arrived. The more she spoke, the darker her Prime's expression became. When she reached the part of the story where Luka had assured her that she had no need to feel guilty, Tia spoke. "He's right—Iain's behavior isn't on you."

"I know that intellectually, but seeing what my song can reduce a person to ... I can't help but feel bad about it," Naomi admitted.

"Is that why you don't want me to dish out some payback?" asked Tobe. "You hold yourself responsible? Because if so, that's some ridiculous bullshit right there."

"Not *totally* responsible," Naomi clarified. "I just feel as if I should have seen that there was a flimsy ego beneath all that self-assurance and bravado he displayed. I've always considered myself an observant person."

"And you are," Jolene asserted, taking a seat across from her. "You would see through an act. But with Iain, I don't think it was an act. I believe it was a case of someone fooling themselves so successfully that what they were hiding went unnoticed by others."

Tia laid her hand on Naomi's. "None of what's happening is your fault. The blame does not lie with you."

"It lies with that asshole who refuses to face the facts and plain ignores what you want," Tobe insisted. "He needs some ... convincing. A little help to make him see the light."

Naomi shot him a pleading look. "Give Luka a chance to do that."

"I already did," her psi-mate reminded her. "Whatever he said or did wasn't enough."

"Which is quite shocking," Jolene noted. "People generally don't test Luka."

And no one could blame them for that. "He put a tail on Iain just to be on the safe side, but Iain managed to give them the slip."

"Determined little bastard, isn't he," Jolene muttered.

"Well," began Tia, "I have a feeling Luka is gonna work harder to ensure that Iain finally keeps his distance from you."

Naomi dipped her chin in agreement. "Luka was furious just now. He swore that Iain wouldn't get near me again." She hesitated to add the next part, since it would clue people in to her fling with Luka, but it wasn't as if they wouldn't notice when he finally put a man on her. "He also declared that he's going to assign me a guard once Iain is released."

Tobe's brows snapped together. "A guard? The fuck? Why would he do that?"

Naomi scratched her cheek. "Well . . ."

Her anchor went rigid. "Tell me you didn't. Tell me you didn't let that merciless motherfucker into your life in any way.'

"Um . . ."

Tobe cursed a blue streak, his face flushing with anger. "Why the hell would you even give him the time of day? You can't honestly think you're safe with that guy. You know who he is. You know *what* he is. You know what he's capable of—everyone in this room has heard of the messed-up shit he's done. Why oh fucking why would you ignore all that? You're smarter than this, Nome."

She lifted a calming hand. "I get why you're worried, I do. And yes, I've heard the rumors. But never have I heard any claims that he harmed a woman. Have you?"

Tobe opened his mouth to respond, but then seemed to mentally falter. "That's not the point," he finally said.

"It very much is. I'm well aware that he's dangerous. But I've not once felt threatened by him." Intimidated, yes, but *as a woman* ... because he was lethally seductive. "Neither has my entity. It doesn't feel that I'm unsafe with him. It actually kind of likes him."

Tobe cast her a dismissive look. "Your demon likes danger, that's why. It's an absolute nut and enjoys violence. If it wasn't for the fact that you two have an understanding, it would be giving you all sorts of problems."

Well, yeah. But that didn't need to be relevant.

"Belinsky doesn't have relationships, Nome," Tobe went on. "He has flings. Keeps them short and sweet."

"It hasn't occurred to you that that's all I'm looking for right now?"

His mouth snapped shut. "Even if you are, it doesn't mean that you have to have one with him. It isn't as if you're not spoiled for choice. You could have your pick of guys." He looked around the room, taking in each person. "Someone back me up here and tell her that he's not what she needs."

"Your issue here isn't merely that Luka is dangerous, Tobe," Jolene claimed. "You don't like that he's going to assign her a guard because you feel he's trespassing; you feel that, as her anchor, it's your job to protect her."

"Well, it is," Tobe asserted.

Jolene raised a finger. "But it's Luka's job to keep Iain in line, not yours."

He frowned. "So you support this? You usually don't like other Primes poking their nose in or trying to handle shit for any of your demons."

"I'm the one who requested that he involve himself in the first place," Jolene reminded him. "I could ask that he drop his intention to put a guard on Naomi, but what would that achieve? He isn't going to step aside if he's involved with her—she'll be classed as having protected status. If he and I are at odds, it'll create a hole in her security. I won't have that. It's best I work with him. Besides, if he says she's under his protection, he should damn well back it up—especially when her current problem is one of *his* demons."

Tobe turned to Tia and Alfie, clearly intending to ignore Jolene's comments because they didn't suit him. "You two have to be opposed to this."

"Not really," said Tia. "Naomi being with Luka gives him more incentive to keep her safe. As she herself said, no rumors about him have ever implied that he's violent toward women. So I don't consider him a danger to her. And I appreciate that he's had her back—not all Primes would care how Iain's behavior impacts her; many would lie for him and take his side."

Alfie rubbed at his nape. "I'm not crazy about Naomi having Belinsky around. He can be cold and cruel and a whole bunch of other unpleasant things. *But* he clearly isn't someone who would overlook women being preyed on, which says he does have some scruples. That is more than can be said for Iain—a person you yourself thought would be good for her in the beginning, Tobe. None of us anticipated what would happen. One thing I think we can be certain of is that Belinsky won't ever fall victim to a siren song."

Apparently still unwilling to drop his concerns, Tobe looked at Lachlan. "You'll back me up, right?"

Blowing out a breath, Lachlan lifted his shoulders. "Naomi's a grown woman who has the right to make her own choices. Expecting her to defend or change them won't get you far. If there's one thing I've learned from raising a strong-willed daughter, it's that the more you object to what she's doing, the more determined she'll be to do it."

Tobe gritted his teeth, his nostrils flaring. "I just want you to be safe and be with someone who deserves you," he said to Naomi.

"And I adore you for that," she told him. "You'll just have to trust my judgment when I say that I don't feel I'm in danger with him. If that changes, I'll walk away. Now can we get back to the subject of Iain and how I'd really prefer it if you let Luka handle him?"

"We can, but it doesn't mean I'll agree to what you're asking," said Tobe. "You wouldn't overlook a woman behaving toward me the way Iain is toward you."

Naomi heaved a deep sigh. She really couldn't deny that.

"Which is all the more reason why Iain needs to be handled subtly," Lachlan chipped in.

Naomi rolled her eyes. "An example. Give me one example of how you might subtly handle him."

Lachlan looked off into the distance, twisting his mouth.

"*And* he's got nothing," said Naomi.

He frowned. "I was thinking. You didn't give me a chance to answer."

"You don't *have* an answer."

"I don't see the problem in making our statement in a very definitive way. In the name of the sanctity of retaliation—"

"Don't," interrupted Naomi, throwing up a hand. "Just don't. I honestly *can't* with you."

"You sound like my daughter," he complained.

"I'll take that as a compliment. Raini's awesome. Now I really should get back to work." Naomi rose to her feet. "Tobe . . ."

He exhaled heavily. "I'll do as you ask and not retaliate."

"That was a lie," she accused.

"Of course it was. We tried things your way. It didn't work. We let Belinsky try things his way. That didn't work either. Now it's time to step things up, and nothing you say will talk me out of it."

CHAPTER EIGHT

Once Tobe and the others had left, Naomi returned to her position at the hostess station. It was hard to be her usual gracious self when frustration simmered in her blood. Frustration at Iain, at Tobe, at her inability to convince her anchor to hang back. So her every smile was stiff, her every "Enjoy your meal" empty. As such, it was a relief when the end of her shift rolled around.

Hooking the strap of her purse over her shoulder, she said her goodbyes and left the restaurant. Her skin prickled as the cool evening breeze whispered over her. Damn, she should have brought a jacket.

No less annoyed than she had been earlier, her pace was faster than usual. Strident, even. But it faltered when she felt someone watching her. *Again.*

She couldn't help but frown. Unless Luka had released Iain, it couldn't be him. It didn't seem likely that the legion would have let him go so soon. As such, there'd be no reason why Luka would have put a tail on her already.

Whoever was following her had to be the person who'd followed her all the way to the pizzeria. She'd thought it was Iain. But now? Well, it could be the PI. She doubted it was clerics—if there were more, surely they would have attacked before now.

In her current mood, she wasn't feeling inclined to ignore that someone thought it acceptable to shadow her. She couldn't confront them here and now, though. A few humans lived around these parts, and there were plenty of things they shouldn't see.

What she needed to do was lure her follower to an isolated spot where there'd be no CCTV. And she knew just the place.

She headed for the nearby industrial space that her lair owned. Many of them used the place to store items that had "fallen out of a truck" or to privately engage in other illegal activities, but that was off-topic.

Reaching it, she walked to a spot where no human eyes would be able to see shit. Then she turned, ready to face her tail. "Come out, come out, whoever the hell you are," she sang.

Someone stepped out of the shadows ... but it wasn't the PI. Nor were any of the six other people who inched forward to gather near him. All were strangers, but the emblems on their black clothes told them *exactly* who she was facing.

Motherfucker.

Did they always travel in groups of seven? Maybe. If she recalled rightly, it was considered a holy number in the Bible. That could have something to do with it.

"Where are they?" the cleric in the center of the group demanded, his piercing eyes flinty, his square jaw hard. Like the others, he appeared freshly shaved, had not one hair on his head, and was armed with a sword that gleamed with magick.

Naomi went for confused. "Excuse me?"

"Our brethren," he elaborated, impatient. "Where are they? They came for you, and they have since disappeared."

"Brethren?" she echoed, scrunching her face up, feeling the molten force within her slinking upward in a predatory fashion.

He sneered. "Do not plead ignorance. You must have had something to do with their disappearance, though I fail to understand how." He looked her up and down in a superior manner.

Well wasn't he a precious little misogynist.

She shook her head, her skin heating with the power humming just underneath it. That same heat bled outward, upping the temperature. "I have no clue who or what you're talking about, and I want no part of whatever this is."

"That is too bad, because we cannot in good conscience allow you to walk away. Not when you will otherwise cause much destruction to this world. Or, more to the point, your future child will."

Naomi sighed. "Look, Brother John—"

"My name is Adrian."

"Adrian, whatever. I've had something of a shitty evening—"

"And it's about to get worse."

For *them*, yes. Because if they weren't going to walk away, she had no option but to kill them.

Her demon wanted to rise. Take over. Attack. Destroy.

You and I have a deal, she psychically reminded it.

It only huffed in response.

Naomi narrowed her eyes as she swept them over the other clerics. "Who are you?"

"Agents of God," the one on the far right claimed in a gruff voice. Somewhere in his fifties, he appeared to be the eldest of the bunch. "Our brotherhood has done his work for many, many centuries."

"Well, it's not really *his* work, is it? He didn't tell you to do this; you're acting of your own accord and you *claim* it's the will of God. That's a little different."

"Wrong, we are his servants; it is our duty to preserve the greater good," Gruff Voice piously upheld.

"Is that so?" She flicked a look at his blade. "Where did you all get your swords?"

He frowned. "Why?"

She shrugged. "Just curious. They gleam with a power I don't think is anything close to pure. Tell me, do they hold the smells of sweat and rot?"

The clerics all stiffened.

"Yeah, that means dark magick is embedded in the blades. I gotta wonder why God's servants would use anything like that."

"Nonsense," Gruff Voice spat. "What you smell is the pain and suffering threaded through the holy blood that blessed the steel."

Wait, what? *Holy* blood?

"Earth-bound angels may have been called back to their realm, but our savior did not abandon us," Gruff Voice bragged. "He sent one of his messengers to us; gifted us with weapons. Whoever wields those swords also wields the will of God."

Naomi blinked. "Hold up, you think—"

"Enough now. It is obvious that you are stalling. Perhaps you think you will be saved."

Adrian inched up his chin. "That will not happen. Your death is a must."

Knowing she'd get no more out of them, Naomi gently dropped her purse to the ground. "Shame you feel that way. Well, it's a shame for *you*. Because I'm not the one who'll die here tonight. I lied before. I met your brethren. They actually tried to kill me. They're all dead now."

"Who killed them?" Gruff Voice demanded, his voice a whip.

Naomi let her mouth curve. "I did."

Adrian hissed. "You lie."

"Nope. And all this is a waste of your time. You misunderstood the prophecy; didn't translate it correctly." She switched to the ancient tongue as she quoted, "'For she who bears the mark is the progeny of the devil.'"

"'And that child will lead an army of demons'," Adrian finished, sticking to English.

Naomi paused. "Could you maybe say that part in its *original* language? Then I can tell you what bits you mistranslated." They most certainly had not correctly translated it, because *she* was the child in question, and in no reality would she lead any show of force, let alone a demonic army. She was too damn lazy for that.

The stout cleric beside Adrian looked up at him. "That she is familiar with the prophecy means *he* got to her first. She could be carrying his spawn as we speak."

"If you're talking about Lucifer," she began, "*no way* would I ever have his child. You're wrong in believing that I'll birth the Antichrist, but I suppose you're not going to listen to me."

"You are right, we know better than to take the word of a demon." Adrian's jaw tightened. "Where are our brothers' bodies?"

"Tell me about your monkhood and I will tell you where they're buried," said Naomi.

Adrian slipped Gruff Voice a look. "You're right. She is stalling. Let us end this." He lifted his sword, his eyes focused on Naomi intently. "It is not your fault that you must die at our hands—you were chosen by Lucifer, not the other way around. As such, I will make this quick and as painless as possible."

Naomi felt her face harden. "*I won't.*" The blistering-hot power awaiting her direction began to boil like water in a pot ... and then she released it. A red-violet fire roared to life around her, licking at her flesh.

The clerics inched back, turning their heads slightly away from the overly bright flames, their eyes narrowing but not leaving her. Horror and shock danced over their faces, warring for supremacy.

"What are . . . ?" Adrian trailed off, gawking.

Naomi didn't answer him. Didn't wait for the Eliouds to make their move. She struck first, throwing up her hands and letting loose rivulets of red-violet liquid fire. They splashed over two clerics, drenching them, burning them, making their skin peel and blister and steam.

Her demon smirked at their screams of agony. The sounds blended with chanting and a battle cry that had her head snapping to the side—just in time for her to see twisting vines of pure-white magick sailing toward her.

Well, shit.

She tried to dodge them. Failed. They slammed into her, zapping every nerve ending like electric jolts.

"Fuck," she hissed, her flesh throbbing. It would have hurt a lot worse if it weren't for the flames covering her skin.

Gruff Voice laughed in triumph. "I don't know what you are, but I do know you are no match for us."

Her entity threw him a harsh glare, but Naomi smiled. "You really think that, huh?" She pyroported behind the asshole and took him out with a violent twist to his neck. He flopped to the ground, sword and all. "Seems you were wrong."

As magick came toward her from several angles, she pyroported to another spot . . . and another . . . and another . . . and another.

The clerics swore and spun and attacked blindly, missing their target every time. Chanting, crackling, yelling, and the snapping and popping of fire filled the air.

Throughout all the chaos, her inner demon smiled.

Well, it did love chaos.

Naomi landed behind a cleric, but another blindsided her before she could strike. *How rude.* She lashed out at the interfering bastard with a full-on blast of fire, setting him alight. His cries of pain were a blissful song to her entity.

Four down, three to go.

Another charged her, hurling magick her way too fast for her to dodge it. The blow was like boiling-hot darts sinking into her skin. *Fucker.*

Naomi retaliated with a stream of red-violet fire that swiftly became a snake. The serpent went right for the cleric's face, making him stagger back so fast he fell. The fiery snake landed on him and bit into his cheek. His back bowed, a loud cry of pain tearing out of his throat as the scorching-hot venom took instant effect.

Ha.

Her peripheral vision screamed a warning.

She looked to her left to see Stout Guy advancing on her. Wicked fast, she grabbed a fallen sword and slammed it up in time to parry his blow. More, she infused fire into the blade, let it crawl up the steel and then into his own. As it reached the hilt, he released the weapon with a cry. Both swords crumbled to nothing as they fell.

While he stared at his blistering palm, she released a stream of flames that set him alight. Which was right when she sensed that Adrian was going to make a run for it.

Naomi twirled *mega* fast and pyroported in front of him. "And then there was one," she said with a smirk.

His eyes wide in a terror that delighted her demon, Adrian took unsteady steps backward. "He has already claimed you as his bride, hasn't he? He has given you his powers."

She zapped his blade with fire, unsurprised that he dropped it before the flames could reach the hilt. "You mean Lucifer? I'm not his bride, but to some extent, he *did* give me power." He'd contributed to her DNA, after all. "Tell me, are there more of you?"

He clamped his mouth shut.

"*Now* you're going to be quiet? You were rather chatty before. Really, it's best that you don't fuck around," she warned. "I'd have no problem hurting you. It would genuinely mean nothing to me."

He turned to flee.

But she pre-empted him.

She pyroported in front of him again, smiling when he stumbled to a halt. "We're not done here." She blasted out a line of flames that quickly formed a circle around him.

His eyes went wide in alarm, his body braced to run through the flames.

"Try it," she dared, letting the fire engulfing her body ease up until it died down altogether. "The pain you'll feel will be like nothing you imagined could exist."

Seraphim fire purified, purging a soul of all guilt and wrongdoing. But Lou's ability to do so had become warped by the fall, meaning his fire not only contaminated the soul itself but proved noxious to a person's system—and Naomi's fire did exactly the same thing.

"You didn't answer my question," she prodded.

Adrian notched up his trembling chin. "Do what you will to me. I will never betray my brothers."

"Don't be so sure of that." She tossed a bunch of fiery serpents into the circle.

Fear washed over his face, chasing away the belligerence. He backed up, went to run ... and then stilled as he seemed to remember that there was nowhere to go.

He hopped from side to side, trying to avoid the snakes, but they were too fast. They slithered up his body, hissing, snapping their jaws, flashing their fangs, flicking out their tongues.

Adrian trembled, flinched, and cried out in pain as their scales scorched every bit of flesh they touched.

"Are there more of you?" she asked.

Lines of agony etched his face. "Yes," he spat out, resentment coloring his tone. "Many others. They will come. They will keep coming until you are dead."

"You see the problem, then, because they won't succeed in killing me. They're basically on a suicide mission."

"They will triumph. Good always triumphs over evil."

"Lord above, you are a bunch of nutcases." The fact was that "holy" didn't always equate to "good", just as "demonic" didn't automatically make a person evil. But she didn't suppose he'd be willing to listen to reason.

Naomi telepathically reached out to her Prime. *Hey, Jolene, hope you're not busy. I have a cleric here who you might want to meet.* She gave the woman her exact location.

Returning her attention to Adrian, she tilted her head. "Tell me more about the messenger who gave you these swords."

He squeezed his eyes shut, his cheeks turning mottled. "No. No, I can't."

"Oh, you can. And you really, really should."

Ciaran materialized a few feet away with Jolene.

The Prime swept her gaze around, taking in the burning corpses. "Good Christ. I suppose it was too much to hope that all the clerics on your ass were dead." She grinned at Adrian. "Hello there. You must be one of these idiots who think Naomi here will pop out the Antichrist at some point. Well, you should know that I'm even crazier than you are—and that's saying something. Taking that into consideration, it would be best for you to answer any questions we might have. And I have quite a few."

"As do I," said Naomi. "He was just about to tell me about the person from whom they received their swords. What is the messenger's name?" she pressed.

"I ... I ..." Adrian trailed off, his eyes rolling back into his head, his body trembling. All of a sudden, his legs gave out, he dropped to his knees and slumped forward, face-planting on the ground.

He didn't get up. Or moan in pain. Or move even an *inch*.

The fuck?

Naomi waved a hand, extinguishing the snakes and flames. "Is he all right?"

Ciaran squatted beside the cleric and checked his pulse. "No, he's dead," he said with some astonishment.

Naomi felt her lips part. "You're kidding. How can he be dead? I didn't have the snakes bite him, just scare him." Her demon's shoulders sagged at the anticlimactic feel to the moment.

"Not sure how it happened, but he's a goner." Ciaran rose to his feet. "It was like his body just ... gave out."

"Like he died from being asked a question," mused Jolene, her eyes squinty.

Naomi blinked. "How is that possible?"

"You've heard of preternaturals who can program a person's brain and body to self-destruct in the event of particular triggers such as phrases or questions, right?" asked Jolene.

Naomi felt her brows slide together. "You think that's the case here?"

"It's possible." Jolene took a suspicious look around. "I think we should get out of here and finish this conversation in private."

"I agree," Naomi told her. "Just let me clean up my mess."

All business, she used her fire to ensure that every trace of the clerics was gone, blades and all. Ciaran then teleported the three of them to her living area.

Slumping into her armchair, Naomi sank a hand into her hair. "What a fucking night."

Jolene shot her a look of disappointment. "You should have reached out when the clerics first showed up."

Naomi winced. "I was in a bad mood after that crap with Iain earlier. I wanted an outlet for my anger."

"Understandable, I suppose," Jolene grudgingly conceded. "I can still wish that you'd requested backup." She paused, taking a seat on the sofa. "I've telepathically contacted your mother, Alfie, and Beck. They will be here soon."

"Khloë's on a weekend break with Keenan," said Ciaran, standing near the fireplace, "so I'd rather just tell her about this tomorrow."

"That's fine." Naomi tried telepathing Tobe, but it was like hitting a psychic wall. She sighed. "Tobe seems to have shut a mental door, because my attempts to contact him aren't working."

Ciaran's gaze turned inward, and then he said, "Nor are mine."

Naomi looked from him to Jolene. "Am I the only one thinking that whoever put a trigger in the cleric's mind also gave him his sword?"

"No, that would be my guess as well," said Jolene. "Dark practitioners have been known to use such things."

"Get this: the cleric said that the person who brought the blades to the monkhood was one of God's messengers; that he came on behalf of God himself. And the more I ponder on that, the more I wonder if the messenger is a dark practitioner posing as an angel."

Ciaran blinked, his head jerking back. "An angel?"

"It was the tone of voice the cleric used as he spoke of him. There was awe and reverence there." It tweaked Naomi's radar.

Ciaran squinted. "Could a dark practitioner pull something like that off, Grams?"

"If he was powerful enough, yes," replied Jolene.

"I might have wondered if the 'he' they talked of is an actual angel, but no way would the Uppers make their current situation worse." After Uppers had targeted Ella and her baby for death merely due to a dislike of her breeding with a fallen celestial, they had earned themselves the wrath of every demon. They had called home all earth-bound angels for fear that demons would hurt them in lieu of those responsible for the attacks on Ella.

The celestials would want to lie low until tempers cooled so that they could come to earth once more. It would rankle with them that there was absolutely no angelic presence here at the moment. As such, the absolute last thing they would do was go after yet another demon.

"I agree with that much," said Ciaran. "But why would a dark practitioner get involved with a monkhood of clerics?"

Jolene tapped her fingers on the sofa's armrest. "While most dark practitioners like to feed off demonic power, others prefer holy power. They often capture angels for such purposes. There are presently no celestials on earth, but clerics can channel divine power as they're descendants of the Nephilim. It isn't a stretch to think that a dark practitioner might therefore use clerics, feeding off their faith and the holy magick they can wield."

Now *that* would make sense.

"While dark practitioners know much about demons, they aren't firmly entrenched in our world. They're not extremely knowledgeable about all preternatural species—about our natures, our abilities, our origins. Hell, some of them sacrifice virgins to Lucifer, having no clue what he's really like. They wouldn't know that he couldn't possibly conceive the Antichrist, so they wouldn't be able to enlighten the clerics."

"Do you think the dark practitioner in question even cares about the prophecy?" Ciaran asked.

Jolene pursed her lips. "He might. It depends on what exactly it states. If it doesn't in any way impact him, probably not. Unless he feels that preventing the birth of the Antichrist would please whatever deity he worships—a deity that may or may not be real. Some of the ones they revere are actually completely fictional."

"One of the clerics quoted more of the prophecy," Naomi told them, "but not in the ancient tongue, so I don't know what the exact translation of it is. But they believe I'll birth the child of the devil, who'll then lead an army of demons." She let out an aggrieved sigh. "I need to somehow get my hands on that prophecy so I can hear it in full. We have way too many unanswered questions."

Jolene made a sound of agreement. "I'll relay all of this to Khloë; it might help her narrow the search she's running on old-ass prophecies. We'll get answers soon—I believe that. Khloë's never let me down yet."

Opening a smoothie the next morning, Naomi glared at Tobe over the rim of the bottle. "It's your own fault that you didn't hear about it sooner. I tried telepathing you last night. Others did as well. But you'd closed a mental door—probably because you didn't want me bugging you to let Luka deal with Iain."

His arms folded, Tobe leaned back against her cherrywood kitchen counter. "You could have left me a text or something."

"It wasn't as if I'd been hospitalized or anything. My wounds were minor, and they healed fast." Naomi knocked back some of her drink. "Where were you anyway?"

"I went to a house party."

"A house party?"

"Yes. I needed to wind down. It did the trick. Now, tell me the full version of what went on last night. I only heard the 'appropriate for people who don't know Lou's your dad' version—it's circulating around the lair like wildfire."

Between swigs of her smoothie, Naomi relayed the entire event to him. "Though the cleric said he has many more brothers, a person's definition of 'many' is subjective. It could mean there are a dozen more clerics. It could mean double that number. Or it could be that there are many, many more."

Tobe dug his teeth into his lower lip. "At least we're now aware that they're directly working with a dark practitioner, however unknowingly. That's something."

Naomi stiffened as a mind brushed hers—familiar, masculine, edged with dominance—and then Luka's voice flowed into her head: *I recall you saying you won't be working tonight, so I'll come to you earlier than usual. Will six p.m. suit you?*

So formal, she thought. It almost made her smile. *Works for me.*

Good. A pause. *Just so you are aware, I will be keeping Iain under lock and key until I'm satisfied that his obsession with you has worn off.*

Taken aback, Naomi double-blinked. *Uh, okay. Wasn't expecting that.*

It's necessary. Even after the ordeal he endured at mine and Belial's hands, he swore point-blank that his feelings for you are real. I don't trust that he won't seek you out again if he's free to go about his business.

"Who're you talking to?" asked Tobe.

She held up a finger, urging him to wait.

He wouldn't be able to return home anyway, Luka went on, *since it somehow caught fire last night. You wouldn't happen to know anything about that, would you?*

Naomi felt her lips flatten. *No, not at all.* But she had a very good idea who would.

If you say so, he said, all skepticism. *Six p.m., Naomi.*

Six p.m., she echoed.

His psyche lightly bumped hers, and then he was gone.

She refocused on her anchor. "I thought you said you went to a house party."

His brows dipped. "I did."

"Really? Because Luka just told me that Iain's home went up in flames last night." There was no way he wasn't responsible.

"Yeah. House party."

She shook her head. "Unbelievable."

"Chill," said Tobe with an unconcerned flick of his hand. "Belinsky has no reason to connect it to our lair."

"*Common sense* ensured that he connected it to our lair."

"Well, he can't trace it back to anyone, so he can't *prove* whatever he suspects." Tobe's expression turned dark. "I still think you letting him into your life is a seriously bad call. *But* . . . I thought on what Lachlan said. He's right. You don't have to defend your choices to me or anyone else. So I won't go confronting Belinsky or anything. I reserve the right to be disapproving and moody about you sleeping with him, though."

Feeling her lips twitch, Naomi dumped her empty bottle in the trash can. "Very mature of you."

He grunted. "You've got enough problems in your life right now; you don't need me adding to them. And Jolene made a good point—opposing Luka will only create holes in your security. No way would I ever be down with that. Especially now, when you have not only Iain but those damn clerics targeting you."

"Speaking of Iain . . . Luka just informed me that he's keeping the guy locked up until my song no longer has him in its clutches."

Tobe's head twitched to the side. "Really?"

"Yup. Not even under the strain of whatever torture session Luka and Belial put him through did he drop the whole 'I love Naomi' thing."

Her anchor winced. "That's bad."

"I know. And it's why Luka doesn't trust that he will stay away from me. Hence his decision to keep him detained."

"It's the right decision. I approve," Tobe added grudgingly, clearly annoyed that he agreed with *any* decision that Luka made.

"It's just a shame it had to go this far," she said with a sigh.

"Now all we have to deal with is the clerics. I don't think it'll be too hard to remove them from the picture. Even with a dark practitioner's aid, what's the worst they can do?"

Famous last words.

CHAPTER NINE

"Okay, I change my vote—I'm pro Luka moving into our compound," Darko told Ella.

Ghost raised a hand. "Yeah, same here."

Luka frowned at the two fallen angels lounging on the sofa of his den. "Vote?" he repeated, confused.

"Blackjack suggested it first," Ghost explained. "Some were up for it, some were against it. I was on the fence. At this point, I'm *all* in."

No less confused, Luka exchanged a look with each of his bodyguards, who were standing at the back of the room. Their expressions were a mixture of baffled and amused.

Every member of the Black Saints MC club appeared tough as fuck, but they were also a little on the crazy side. How Ella happily lived among them, Luka had no clue. "I'm not even going to ask what this is about." He figured it was best not knowing.

Darko's brows slid together. "It's not obvious?" He spared a look at the infant in Luka's arms. "Whenever you hold her, she conks out. And she *stays* like that."

"So?"

Exhaustion fell over Ghost's face. "So Lilibeth is like that kid from *The Ring*. She doesn't sleep."

"She *does*," Ella cut in from the armchair opposite Luka's. "It's just that she sleeps in small bursts throughout the day. A few minutes here and there. Which we don't really understand, because it's not normal."

Was there a "normal" for a baby who was a product of a demon and a fallen archangel? The president of the Black Saints MC club hadn't confirmed the rumor that he'd once been one of the infamous seven archangels, but Luka deeply suspected it was true.

"All her health checks have come back just fine, so it doesn't negatively affect her," Ella added.

"But the rest of us?" Ghost let out a pained sigh. "We're fucking tired."

His eyes on Luka, Darko raised a placatory hand. "Don't take this the wrong way, but I can't work out why she's so relaxed around you."

Luka peered down at Lilibeth. With her mop of short dark hair, chubby cheeks, and eyes blue as diamonds, she was cute as fuck. "I'm a little surprised by it myself." He wasn't what anyone would call soothing.

Just ask Iain.

Six days he'd been in Luka's vault now. Six days during which he'd been . . . *pressured* to face reality. But the psi-demon's mental state still showed no signs of improvement. Something that didn't bother Belial in the least, because it meant that the entity got to play with him more. Abraxas and Dagon, however, were as frustrated as Luka with Iain's seeming determination to cling tight to his delusions.

Ghost looked at his brother. "We should rest while we can."

"Agreed," said Darko. "I'll take first watch."

Abraxas smirked, amused by how the two acted as though they were in the middle of a war zone.

Luka turned to Ella. "Does Lou still show up to visit Lily whenever he feels like it?"

She exhaled heavily. "Yes. Even though she telekinetically slaps him, he just keeps coming back for more. He finds it hilarious. Though I haven't seen him in about a month."

"I thought you were teaching her *not* to slap." Really, Ella had to teach the infant not to do many things. Extremely advanced for her age, Lily could make various displays of power. And she did it ruthlessly—something that he and his entities respected.

"Viper told her she can do it to Lou whenever she feels like it," said Ella. "So she does. Her new thing is telekinetically shoving people. She gave one of your waitresses from Infernal a little push the other day at my store."

Luka felt his brow crease. "Which waitress?"

"Draya," Ella elaborated, idly plucking at her red bangs. "She bent over the stroller, smiled at Lily, and proceeded to let out a stream of baby babble. You know how my girl finds that condescending."

Any child so advanced would. "I had no idea you knew Draya." Neither female had mentioned it.

"Oh, I didn't until recently. She started coming to my store a lot. She always chats so sweetly to me, like we're old pals. She even asked me to lunch last time."

Luka felt his brows snap together. "Lunch?"

"I blew her off, because I could tell that it wasn't a genuine overture of friendship. She hopes to buddy up to me as a way to get to you." Ella's lips set into a thin line. "She's not the first woman to have tried it. Probably won't be the last."

He clenched his jaw, infuriated that she would try to use Ella that way. "I'll have a word with her."

Ella flapped a hand. "Don't bother. It's fine. Really. She buys a whole heap of stuff. Only to suck up to me, sure, but sales are sales."

"When did she last seek you out?"

"Umm ... a few days ago."

Luka frowned, surprised. Draya hadn't once approached him since he'd made his involvement with Naomi common knowledge, so he'd thought the banshee had chosen to move on.

Ella sank back into the chair. "Be aware that she was asking a lot of questions."

"What kind of questions?"

"All revolved around you. Where in Russia you came from, why a quarter of your old lair migrated here, what the likes and dislikes of your demons are, why you avoid long-term relationships."

Dagon grumbled a sound of annoyance at the nerve of Draya, who had no right to such information. She wasn't even a member of their lair, for Christ's sake.

"It was as if she was trying to profile you so she could better get close to you," mused Ella. "From the stuff she was saying when she first tried befriending me, it seemed she thought that something might happen between you two. But then rumors recently began to circulate that you had Naomi Chamberlain in your bed. Draya seems quite put out by that."

"I never led Draya on. We briefly flirted. That's it. Not once did I verbally express an interest in taking it further." And now that it was apparent Draya wouldn't respect his well-known preference for privacy, he would never take it further. He was careful to choose bed partners who wouldn't push him to confide in them or share overly personal details. Then nobody would be disappointed.

"The flirting was clearly enough for her to feel hopeful that you'd take things up a notch," said Ella. "She seems hurt that you passed her up for Naomi. Draya had not-so-nice things to say about her."

His demons went rigid in an anger that also tightened Luka's jaw and made his nostrils flare. "Is that so?" he asked, his voice soft but vibrating with a menace even *he* could hear. "What exactly did she say?"

Ella's eyes widened and lit up. "Ooh, someone's protective. Intriguing. You generally place your bed buddies under your protection while they're in your life, but it was a formality in the past. You never appeared to *feel* protective until now."

He barely stopped himself from stiffening. "That isn't the case here."

"And now you're denying it. Again, intriguing."

The truth? Yes, his protective instincts were easily riled up when it came to Naomi. Hence why, despite still having Iain in his custody, he had assigned her a guard earlier than planned.

Though he'd told Konstantin to keep his distance, Naomi had still spotted him. She'd walked right up to the guard and asked who he was. Konstantin had told her, after which she'd telepathed Luka to snippily demand an explanation for why he'd put a man on her without informing her.

I was curious to see how long it would take you to notice him, Luka had replied. *It's reassuring that you did so this quickly.*

Why reassuring? she'd asked.

His response had been blunt and to the point. *Because your safety is far more important to me than I'd anticipated it would be.*

She hadn't said anything more about it, telepathically or verbally, since.

A soft snore popped out of Darko, and it was then that Luka realized both fallen angels were asleep. Some guards they were.

He supposed he should take it as a compliment that they so implicitly trusted Ella and Lily's safety with him.

"Admit it, I'm right," pushed Ella, leaning forward in her seat.

Luka squinted. "I really loathe it when you're bored. You turn into a meddling, nosy—"

"You're defensive," she noted, her lips curving. "That's telling."

"Not defensive, just uninterested in addressing your incorrect assumptions. You're free to believe what you want. Now, you didn't answer my question. What did Draya say?"

Ella lifted her shoulders in a mocking challenge. "Is it important, considering Naomi apparently doesn't matter to you?"

Luka pressed his lips tight together. Honestly, Belial wanted to shake her right now.

"I've never had cause to really talk to Naomi beyond saying hi and stuff, so I asked some of the demons in her lair about her."

He felt his brow pinch. "You normally don't express an interest in women I bed."

"You don't normally make frequent appearances at their place of work and stare at them like you want to devour them. With Naomi, you did that even before you made your play—I heard all about it. And it tells me two things. One, you liked to watch her a whole lot. Two, you were ensuring that other men noticed your interest in her to deter them from making a play of their own. It made me curious."

It really was frustrating how well Ella knew him.

"Harper and Khloë used a whole bunch of words to describe your siren. Spunky. Protective. Loyal. Sharp. Secretive. They also said that she's like you—has a small circle of people around her who she lets close; others she holds at a distance. Also, *again* like you, she apparently keeps her sexual associations short and shallow."

"Hmm."

Ella smiled. "You really don't want to discuss her with me, do you? Why not? You're evasive in general, but your bed buds aren't usually off limits when we natter."

Yes, well, he'd rather his anchor didn't sense something she'd blow out of proportion —that he liked Naomi more than he'd expected. She possessed the very qualities that Harper and Khloë had listed, all of which appealed to him. Plus, with Naomi, there was no artifice, no practiced moves, no scripted lines. She talked to him. Listened to him. Her smiles were easy, her warmth was genuine, and her laughs were open.

As a rule, Luka never found himself wanting to know his bed partners beyond surface level, but she intrigued him. Honestly, he felt uneasy at the curiosity she roused in him. A curiosity he'd tried and failed to douse so far. It would surely flit away with time.

"You have a pretty active life," he said to his anchor. "Why take time out of it to stick your nose into mine?"

"Same reason you're all up in my business. You want what's best for me in all areas of my life. Well, right back at you."

"I appreciate your concern."

"No you don't."

"No, I don't. It's fucking irritating."

Ella's shoulders shook with a silent laugh. "At least I'm not sitting here insisting that you drop Naomi the way you insisted I drop Viper. All I want is to hear you admit that you have more than a sexual interest in her. I mean, it's not as if it isn't clear as day for someone who knows you as well as I do."

Luka gave her a flat stare. "When are you going home?"

Another quiet laugh made her shoulders shake. "I'm on the right track here, I know it."

Darko snored so loudly he woke up both himself *and* Ghost.

Looking around, he double-blinked, sitting upright. "What was that noise?"

Luka shot him a frown. "It was you. Snoring."

Darko's gaze lowered to Lily. "And she stayed asleep. Seriously, man, you have to move to the compound."

"Not happening," Luka told him.

Ghost's brow furrowed. "Don't be selfish."

"Not selfish, just not going to be a live-in babysitter," said Luka. "I have too much shit to do anyway—I'd hardly ever be here."

"He's right on that," Ella chipped in.

Darko's shoulders sagged in defeat. "There's no hope, is there? We're gonna have to go without sleep for the rest of our lives."

Ella rolled her eyes. "Don't be dramatic. It's not like you have her with you twenty-four/seven. Honestly, I've never known a bunch of grown-ass men to whine so damn much."

"We're sleep-deprived," said Ghost, his voice rising slightly. "What do you expect?"

A snuffle came out of Lily as she stirred in Luka's arms. Her eyelids fluttered open, and startling blue eyes met his.

Darko groaned and elbowed his brother. "*Now* look what you did. Idiot."

"I am, I am a total idiot," Ghost admitted, sad and defeated.

Luka peered down at Lily. "Hey, there. How was your nap?"

A bright smile of contentment was her response. She aimed her gaze across the room, seeking out her mom.

Ella pushed out of the chair and crossed to him. "Come on, then."

"She wants you to pick her up?" Luka asked, knowing the little girl could telepathically communicate her wants and feelings with images and impressions.

"Yes," confirmed Ella, scooping her up. "She also wants her diaper changed."

Both fallen angels leaned back, shrinking away from her.

Ella thankfully dropped her earlier subject, and they chatted about general things for the next hour. She then stood, announcing, "Time for us to go. Lily, say bye to Uncle Luka."

An immature psyche lightly touched his.

Luka smiled at them both. "Later."

Ella patted his arm. "We'll revisit the subject of Naomi another time."

No, actually, they wouldn't.

Luka escorted his visitors to the front door, waved them off, and used the security app on his phone to open the electronic gates for them to exit the estate.

"I don't like that Draya was asking Ella so many questions about you," said Mikhail behind him.

Luka closed the door and then turned to face his two guards. "Neither do I. Draya has some front. It pisses me off more that she thought to use my anchor like that." He stalked back into the house, and the twins followed.

"I'll bet it also pisses you off that she apparently talked smack about Naomi," Nikandr hedged, a teasing note to his voice. "Let's face it, Ella was bang on the mark. You're protective of the siren. More, you actually like her."

Luka only cast him a cool look. His phone beeped, signaling that the outdoor gate sensors had detected the vehicle passing through. He pressed the button to close the gates and then pocketed his phone.

"You can at least admit it to us," Nikandr persisted.

Luka sighed. "You're as nosy as Ella."

"He can't help it," said Mikhail, sidling up to his brother. "He's always been determined to know everything."

"That's you," Nikandr told his twin.

"Actually, it's both of you," said Luka.

Konstantin's psyche knocked his. *Know you're busy with your anchor, but I thought you might want to know something.*

Luka stilled. *Is Naomi all right?*

She's fine, Konstantin quickly assured him. *I've been tailing her all day, and, well . . .*

Well what?

For the past twenty minutes, I haven't been the only one watching her.

Biting into her burger, Naomi stretched her legs beneath the small table. She'd stopped off at her local fast-food restaurant on the way home from her parents' place. Though she hadn't initially felt terribly hungry, that had changed when she walked inside and was hit by the scents of onions, sauces, and hot meat—whether fried, greasy, or grilled.

All kinds of activity surrounded her. Cashiers called out numbers at the stainless-steel counter. Lines of people griped at indecisive customers who were hemming and hawing at the self-ordering kiosks. Workers bustled around wiping dirty tables or mopping up spills. Parents went back and forth from the play area to check on the shrieking kids who were running riot there.

Naomi's little seating area was packed. Customers walked about carrying trays while searching for tables. A group of teenagers were laughing and snapping pictures at the corner booth. A couple who clearly had a case of puppy love were chatting and chuckling and making kissy faces at each other. A mother handling three overly loud youngsters looked close to planting her face on the table in exasperation.

Konstantin currently stood outside—he rarely followed her into any buildings unless they were so spacious he'd lose sight of her from the windows.

Because your safety is far more important to me than I'd anticipated it would be.

Those telepathic words from Luka clutched her chest tight whenever they drifted to the forefront of her brain, which was far too often in her opinion. When he'd first said them, shock had chased away her agitation and left her floundering. She hadn't known what to say, so she hadn't responded.

It was well known that Luka was exceedingly protective of his anchor and his honorary niece—any possible threat to them would be instantly marked for death. That was how he rolled. Naomi just hadn't expected that side of his nature to ever be directed at her.

Luka evidently hadn't expected it either.

Neither of them had spoken of it since that day, as if in silent mutual agreement that the matter was best left unaddressed so they could keep things uncomplicated.

Initially, she'd worried that perhaps Konstantin might stick *too* close to her, presenting a risk of him uncovering her secrets. But he kept a certain distance from her at all times, and he never entered her home.

Still, Tobe didn't much like the protective display from Luka. But really, Tobe didn't like anything the legion did—including breathing.

Jolene, on the other hand, was pleased about Konstantin's presence. She felt he would make any watchful clerics reluctant to launch another attack—they were careful to move about undetected, so they would notice him for sure. The harder Naomi made things for the clerics' preternatural helper, the more likely said helper would come out of the metaphorical shadows and involve themselves, thus also exposing their identity.

Metal scraped tile as a large family pushed some tables together. They were clearly celebrating one of the kids' birthdays, because the youngest was wearing a birthday badge and holding a balloon. *Too cute.*

Smiling, Naomi took another bite of her now half-eaten burger. Picking up movement at the nearby condiment station, she reflexively looked over ... and froze.

Well, if it wasn't the PI, Daniel Phillips.

Her demon squinted, irritation skittering through it. Because although he didn't appear to be paying Naomi any attention, busy gathering up sauces and napkins, it seemed too much a coincidence that he'd be here the same time as her.

Could he have followed her here? She had sensed that she was being watched, but she'd thought it was Konstantin—it hadn't occurred to her that she had more sets of eyes on her. She wouldn't make that mistake again.

Daniel turned, seemed to idly glance her way, and did quite a convincing double-take. But not convincing enough for either her or her entity to fail to see through his act.

He boldly approached her table, his lips curved. "Oh, hello again." He tipped his head to the side. "Remember me?"

"Nope," she lied.

His friendly smile faltered. "We met at the tattoo studio last week. Urban Ink?"

"Oh. Right. Of course." She lifted her cup, which was damp from condensation. "You're the dude who has a secret thing for Tobe."

"No. No, that genuinely isn't the case." He flicked a look at the chair opposite her own. "Mind if I join you?"

She slurped some of her soda through her straw. "Depends what you want."

"I'd just rather not eat alone." He sat down without holding out for an invitation. "You waiting for someone?"

She set down her drink. "Nope. So if you were hoping you might bump into Tobe ..."

"Really, I'm not looking to date your anchor," he stressed with a chuckle, peeling the crackly wrapper from his burger. "I'm honestly mated. *Happily* mated."

Such a little liar. She would have thought a PI would be better at it. "Then why are you sitting here with me?" And looking at her with sex in his eyes—something that earned him a sneer from her demon.

He shrugged one shoulder. "No reason in particular."

A loud thud was followed by a harsh curse. Naomi winced in sympathy as she noticed that a customer had dropped their tray, sending their order scattering over the tiled floor.

"My name's Ed," Daniel fibbed, pulling her attention back to him.

"Naomi." She took another bite out of her burger.

"You live around these parts?"

"Yes. You?"

Shaking his head, he picked up three of his fries and shoveled them into his mouth—classy. "I'm just heading home from work after meeting with a client."

"Client?"

"I'm a graphic designer."

"Huh."

He let out a self-deprecating chuckle. "Yeah, not exactly a job that involves living life on the edge. Pays the bills, though." He sank his teeth into his own burger. "And it means I get to exercise my creative streak." He spoke around a mouthful of food.

Her demon pulled a face at the unpleasant sight.

"I don't have what it takes to be a painter or sculptor or anything. But I can work art-magic with a laptop." He paused as the nearby family began singing "Happy Birthday" while clapping in time with the tune. "What about you? You strike me as the creative type."

Chewing the last of her burger, she barely refrained from narrowing her eyes in suspicion. "Why?"

"I don't know. I can usually spot a fellow artist. Call it a gift."

Unease tiptoed up her spine. "I like painting my nails. Does that count?"

Mirth gleamed in his eyes. "I don't see why not. A canvas is a canvas, whatever shape or form it takes."

She dipped a fry in her ketchup and bit into it, her instincts tingling. It bothered her that he'd asked if she was creative. Was he assuming that she was one of Tobe's ghost artists? There was no reason why he should. Then again, she'd been pretty defensive and tight-lipped at the tattoo studio. Perhaps it had made him suspicious.

It might be best, then, to give him a whole other reason why she'd been rude to him at Urban Ink; let him know that he wasn't fooling her and never had.

"Something wrong?" he asked. "You seem . . . tense. I'm a good listener, if you want to offload."

"I don't, but thanks."

"You sure?"

She ate another fry. "Positive. I mean, why would I talk to someone who likes feeding me a bunch of bullshit, Daniel?"

He paused mid chew, his amiable expression freezing.

"Yes, I know your real name. I knew it the day I met you, just as I also learned you're a PI."

His eyes flickering, the frozen friendly look on his face faded fast and turned hard. "How?"

"Imps can find out pretty much anything. The one at Urban Ink took your photo and sent it to a contact of hers—they telepathed her your identity in moments. She passed it on to me."

"Since when do receptionists check people's identities?" he bit off.

Her entity smiled, *loving* the aggravation in his tone. "They don't. But you're not as good a liar as you think you are—everything about your tone, body language, and word choices tweaked my instincts. I asked her to do me a solid and find out who you really were."

He tightened his grip on his burger, oblivious to the sauce oozing out of it.

Naomi tossed a fry into her mouth. "Now, going by how you like dragging the conversation round to Tobe, I'd say you have a client who wants info about him. You're wasting your time trying to get anything out of me, and you'll struggle just as much when it comes to anyone else in my lair."

His nostrils flared. "I'll pay you."

"Not interested." She shook her mostly empty cup, hearing the ice rattle, and then drank more soda through her straw. "Even if I knew the answers to your questions, I wouldn't tell you—not for anything."

"It's not like I'm asking for information that would do him harm."

"Doesn't matter. His business is his business to share or not to share. Go to him."

"I would if he'd tell me anything." He squinted, as if something had occurred to him. "Have you telepathed Tobe? Is he on his way?"

"No. I'm not going to drag him into your orbit. You want to talk to him, you need to approach him like a big boy." Done with her food, she used a napkin to wipe the salt and grease from her fingers. "You also need to stop watching and following me."

An ugly smirk graced his face. "When either you or Tobe tell me what I want to know, I'll back off. Until then, you'll just have to deal with me."

She eyed him intently. "I didn't peg you for stupid. Hmm. I

guess you never can tell." She dabbed her mouth with her napkin and then tossed it in her empty burger box.

"I should be worried about what a little siren can do to me?"

"Yes, actually. But it's mostly me you need to worry about."

Naomi went rigid. Because those words hadn't come from her.

CHAPTER TEN

Naomi looked up slowly. There beside her table was Luka, glaring down at Daniel through eyes that were pure frost. A slight chill went down her spine, sending a sweep of goosebumps up her arms. And not in a good way.

Shit.

She had hoped to keep him out of this situation, but she'd known there was a chance that Konstantin would spot Daniel following her if the PI was still around. She'd been prepared for this moment. She just wished that it hadn't arrived, because Luka would likely insist on involving himself in the situation.

Her demon wasn't quite so bothered by that. But that was mostly because it was curious as to what he would do. The entity wanted a peek at his merciless streak.

Freaking typical.

Naomi became aware that the volume in the restaurant had lowered slightly. Demons would recognize the legion in an instant. Humans wouldn't, but considering everything about him at that moment screamed "threat", she understood why some might sit up and take notice.

Luka's gaze slid to her . . . and their chemistry aimed and fired. The crackling force tautened the air as it hit. Every synapse in her system seemed to go electric. Her body never failed to come alive around him, even at moments like these.

Needing a reprieve from it, she returned her attention to Daniel. He was gaping up at Luka in shock, his face slack, his previous smirk nowhere to be found. That the PI seemed so surprised to see the legion would suggest he hadn't yet heard she was sleeping with him.

"Luka Belinsky," he breathed.

"You have me at a disadvantage," said Luka, his voice low and smooth even as danger looped through every word. "You clearly know who I am. I have no fucking idea who you are."

"D-Daniel Phillips."

"And you're bothering Naomi because?"

Daniel hesitated, clearly scrambling to come up with some bullshit excuse.

"You do not want to lie to me," Luka recommended.

"I wasn't harassing her or anything. I just had some questions for her. I'm a PI."

"Hired by whom and to do what?"

Daniel licked his lips. "I . . . I can't discuss my cases or my clients."

"You will with me."

"I really can't—I'm legally bound to share very little."

His patience a thing of the past, Luka edged closer to the table, raring to strangle the little shit. "You seem to think you have a choice here. You don't. Let me speak plainly. I don't give a fuck what assurances you granted your clients or what legalities are in place that prohibit you from revealing details. Naomi is under my protection. If you insist on making yourself a problem for her, then *I* become *your* problem. That's how this works."

The blood drained from Daniel's face—a sight that pleased Belial. "I didn't know that she had protected status. I swear I didn't know."

"Now you do. And you can either tell me what I want to know, or I take you somewhere we can get more ... comfortable. And you'll *still* tell me what I want to know."

Daniel swallowed so hard it looked like it hurt. "I-I have a client that's interested in meeting a ghost artist who works with Naomi's psi-mate. The artist wishes to remain anonymous, so Tobe won't reveal their identity. I was hired to find out who they are and obtain their contact details."

"What does that have to do with Naomi?"

"Anchors share secrets with each other. I thought maybe Tobe had mentioned names of his ghost artists to her."

"I've already told you I don't know any," she said to Daniel.

So they'd come into contact before now?

The PI lifted his shoulders. "I'm struggling to get answers for my client, so I thought I'd try again."

"Well, you did," said Luka. "And it was fruitless. It would be just as fruitless if you questioned her again. But you won't do that, will you?" It wasn't a question; it was a straight-up order that carried a promise of very dark consequences.

Fear flickering in his eyes, Daniel shook his head. "No. No, of course not."

Abraxas snorted at his cowardice, finding him pathetic. Luka's other two entities agreed with that assessment.

Luka cut his gaze back to Naomi and held out his palm to her.

She slowly placed her hand in his as she pushed out of her seat. It was only then that she seemed to notice that the twins and Daniil were a few feet behind him. "I just need to put my rubbish in the—" She cut off as Nikandr grabbed her tray and did it for her. "Right."

"Let's go." Luka splayed a hand on her back to guide her away from the table.

She threw him a quick look. "Konstantin telepathed you about Daniel," she guessed.

He dipped his chin. "He'd noticed that someone was watching you. When I arrived, he said the person was at your table. It was clear by your body language that he wasn't welcome."

Mikhail led the way as all five of them exited the restaurant and then, with Konstantin sliding in behind them, walked into the side alley. Once they were deep in the shadows and away from human eyes, Luka looked at his teleporter. "My house."

Surprise flickered across Daniil's face. Understandable. Luka didn't bring his bed buddies to his home. But right then, his protectiveness a feral thing, he wanted Naomi in the place she'd be safest.

Their surroundings momentarily blurred before altering completely, and suddenly they were all standing in his foyer.

Luka swept his gaze over his demons. "Leave us." After the four males had obligingly exited the house, he refocused on Naomi. She was glancing around with her lips parted, taking in the winding staircase, marble flooring, and sparkling chandelier.

"Wow," she breathed.

"You never mentioned that you'd been approached by a PI," said Luka, a bite to his voice.

She shrugged, visibly unfazed by his annoyance. "Why would I? It wasn't necessary for you to know. It had no bearing on anything." She didn't add that it wasn't his business, but the implication was there in her tone and expression.

Luka felt his face harden, and all three of his demons bristled. Because this *felt* like his business. "If there's a threat to you, I need to be aware of it."

"He's not a threat, just a pest."

Perhaps so, but ... "That isn't the point."

"Look, you don't tell me all of what goes on in your life. And why would you? I'm not entitled to know your business. We've made no commitment to each other."

"You're under my protection."

"Super. But it doesn't change the facts. Come on, Luka, you wouldn't have told me if *you'd* been approached by a PI. You can't have it both ways."

"Why not?"

Even as irritation scraped at Naomi's skin, she couldn't help but chuckle. "I can't even whine about how much of a handful you are. I knew what I was getting into. But don't think I'll stand for any bullshit," she softly warned. "That isn't who I am."

"Yes, I've noticed," he muttered. "If the PI bothers you again, I want to know about it."

"I doubt he will. You scared him."

"Even scared people do unadvisable things."

"True enough. Iain's an example of that." Thinking of him made her nose wrinkle. "Is he doing any better?"

Luka's lips thinned. "Not yet. He persists in maintaining that he's not under the thrall of a siren song."

Guilt nipped at Naomi's heels, which annoyed her entity. Yes, yes, it was *misplaced* guilt—she knew that well—but it didn't make how she felt any less real. The guy was willingly undergoing torture to prove that he truly loved her, for God's sake.

She sank her hand into her hair, momentarily stilling as Luka's gaze followed the movement before taking a slow glide down the length of her curls. It was nothing short of a visual caress that was as potent as any touch, causing her belly to flutter and her demon to preen.

"I didn't fail to notice that you gave me no guarantee you'd contact me if Phillips made a nuisance of himself again."

Tenacious bastard. Her demon rolled its eyes, though it respected his level of perseverance and liked that he was so protective of Naomi. "If I hear from him again, I'll tell you. Now, do I get a tour of this palace or what?"

Luka gave her a long look, as though he was debating whether he should run with the change of topic. Finally, he said, "I don't see why not."

Naomi followed him through the house, stealing little peeks at the various rooms—and there were many. The place was the height of luxury and amazingly clean, but it had no soul. Which was kind of sad. "You have a lot of guards," she noted.

"It's more of a deterrent than a precaution. Only two demons have ever managed to scale the walls of the estate undetected, but they didn't make it to the house. They were seen and detained before they had the chance. You're safe here, Naomi. Safer than you'll be anywhere else."

Well, the clerics would be unlikely to get past his security—that was reassuring. She doubted any would attempt to infiltrate the place, but she still felt better knowing that they had little chance of success if they tried.

"I'd get lost in a place like this in no time," she said as they walked toward the foyer's staircase. "How long have you lived here?"

Without breaking stride, Luka briefly glanced at her over his shoulder. "A while."

"Don't overload me with information," she mocked.

"I won't," he deadpanned.

Upstairs, he resumed his tour, pointing out rooms. Reaching a particular door, he pushed it open and ushered her inside. "This is the master bedroom."

Moving to stand in the center of the large space, Naomi took a slow look around. Now *this* room had a Luka vibe to it. It was neat and masculine and a little moody. Dark woods, oak flooring, luxury bedding, walls the color of desert sand. And it smelled like him; like power, amber, and sandalwood.

She zeroed in on the king-sized four-poster bed. "I'll bet this room has seen a lot of action," she teased.

He regarded her with a serious expression. "I don't bring women home."

Oh. "So why bring *me* here?"

"Because I wanted to."

"That's it?"

"That's it."

"Do you always do what you want to do?"

"Most of the time." Luka crossed to her, so much heat bleeding into his gaze that her breath caught.

As if on cue, her body started charging up—skin heating, muscles tightening, nerve endings prickling, insides buzzing with anticipation.

Gently but firmly taking her chin between his thumb and forefinger, he let his eyes cruise over her face, tracing and mapping every feature, as he often did. "A man could so easily develop an obsession with this face, and that has nothing to do with you being a siren." He lowered his head so there was only inches between his lips and hers. "Offer that mouth to me, Naomi."

No problem. She joined her lips to his, and their sexual connection clicked into place. Need rushed up, breezing through her as their kiss went straight to full-on carnal. The breath left her body as he pulled her flush against him, allowing her to feel his cock hardening.

She unashamedly arched into him, one hand curved around

his nape while her other grabbed at his shoulder—fingers squeezing, nails digging. She almost mewled in complaint when he drew back.

He used his fingertip to trace the shape of her mouth. "I want this stuffed full of my cock again."

Minutes later, they were naked on the bed—him sitting upright against the headboard; her positioned on her hands and knees between his spread thighs while she sucked him off.

Knowing what he liked, she kept the suction tight, pausing occasionally to lick at the head or the sensitive spot beneath the crown. All the while, Luka urged her on, scratched her scalp, played with her hair, whispered praise—mostly in Russian.

Occasionally she'd see shadows moving behind his eyes; little glimpses of his entities watching closely. So it didn't surprise her when Belial took over.

"Let's see how pretty you look when you're choking." Its hand tangled in her hair, the entity started thrusting up its hips, fucking her mouth deep enough that she struggled to breathe. She gagged, choked, coughed. And *still* it pumped its hips.

Well, what else could she expect from a sadist?

It was only when her vision blurred with tears that she felt the grip on her hair loosen. Flicking her gaze upward, she saw that Luka was back in charge.

"I have a question," he said.

Arching a probing brow, she slid her mouth all the way down his shaft and then sucked hard as she slowly drew her lips back up.

Pure male contentment moved over his face, and he lowered his eyelids slightly. "Are you on birth control?"

"Yes. Why?"

He swiped his thumb over the outer edge of her lower lip. "I want to come inside you tonight. I want to blow my load as deep as it will go."

Sincerely surprised by his request, she blinked and licked her lips. "Uh ... okay," she answered lamely.

Satisfaction bled into his gaze. "Get up here."

Naomi scooted forward, planting a knee either side of his hips. She set her hands on his upper chest, her fingers resting on his collarbone.

He curled an arm around her, smoothed a hand over her butt, and then dipped a finger inside her from behind. "You're soaked."

She felt her face flame. "Yeah, well." That was all she had. She was *brilliant* like that.

"You're going to ride me now. But first ..." He closed his mouth over hers and sank his tongue inside. They kissed hard and greedy as he skimmed his hands all over her—squeezing, palming, shaping—his touch bold and entitled in a way that her demon found thrilling.

Releasing her mouth, he dipped his head and latched onto a nipple, sucking so strongly it hurt.

She drew in a sharp breath. "Luka ..."

He gave the taut bud a quick nip and then splayed his palm on her lower belly. He swept it upward, stroking as much skin as possible, pressing the tips of his fingers down as if to stamp his prints on her. "Mine," he said, skimming his hand up her throat to grip her jaw. "Aren't you?"

Before she had the chance to even *think* to respond, her demon rushed to the surface and took over. "Yours to fuck," it told him. "That is all. Remember that."

His own eyes bled to black again, a surly glint appearing in their depths. *Dagon*. "Maybe we feel that our claim runs deeper." A pure taunt.

Her entity sniffed. "I do not care what you feel. Facts are facts."

"You're right. They are." Dagon splayed its hand tight around her throat, and a slight hissing sound filled the air as it burned a brand onto the skin there, conveying what it believed to be a fact.

Her entity narrowed its eyes. "Do not push me too hard."

"I could say the same to you."

Luka reclaimed supremacy before the situation could escalate, which visibly relieved Naomi. "Don't worry," he said, dragging her so close that her nipples stabbed his chest and the folds of her pussy cradled his cock. "They may bicker, but there won't be a physical altercation. My demons wouldn't take it that far."

"*Mine* might," she mumbled. "It doesn't care what would be considered 'too far'. While it wouldn't rejoice in whatever drama it caused—it's more a fan of mayhem and destruction—it also wouldn't give a rat's ass."

Luka clamped a hand on her hip, using his other to line his cock up with her entrance. "Now you're just trying to turn my demons on."

She shook her head. "Those three are so weird."

"They can live with that. Now, take me inside you."

She held onto his shoulders as she bore down, her breath hitching, her eyes falling shut. She kept going, taking inch after inch until finally he was balls-deep in her scorching-hot pussy.

He abruptly snagged her nape and took blatant ownership of her mouth. Kissed it. Nipped it. Ate at it. Plundered it. Until he had to pull back, his lungs burning for air. "Fuck yourself on me."

Still clinging tight to his shoulders, Naomi bounced up and down on his shaft with not one bit of restraint. Her breasts jiggled and slapped at her body so temptingly Luka reached out and filled his hands with them. He plumped and shaped and squeezed them tight, possession coursing through him.

She dug her nails into his skin, her eyes going hazy, a flush sweeping up her front to stain the fresh brand on her throat.

Just looking at it made his balls ache. He wouldn't have thought the sight of a mere mark could evoke such a response from him, but pure male satisfaction beat in his blood, entangled in both arousal and proprietorship.

He wasn't supposed to feel possessive of her. Or protective. Or so fucking greedy for her—for more and more and more of her—that it quite frankly rankled.

He started slamming her up and down on his cock, his hands gripping her ass with an insistent hold that said he had every right to move her how he wanted her. His belly tightened and twisted and pulsed as his release approached fast, making his shaft swell inside her.

Pitching up his hips to ram his cock deeper, Luka slipped a hand between them. Thumbing and rolling her clit, he ordered, "No closing your eyes when you come, Naomi. Look right at me while you shatter around my dick."

The next roll of her clit knocked her over the edge. A choked scream crawled up her throat as her orgasm hit, making her pussy ripple around him.

He dropped her hard on his dick over and over while also roughly rolling his hips. A deep groan traveled up his gut as he finally imploded, emptying his balls inside her.

"What the fuck is that?" demanded Tobe the next morning, his face like thunder. He'd been smiling right up until the brand on her throat caught his attention. It would catch *anyone*'s attention, because it was nothing close to subtle. A slender snake was looped around her neck, the head settled near the column of her throat, its lower body trailing down the valley between her breasts.

Stepping aside to allow him to enter her house, Naomi sighed. "It's really not obvious?" Brands looked like tattoos, but a demon would easily tell the difference.

Tobe stalked inside, setting his hands on his hips. "Which one of Belinsky's entities did it?"

"Dagon." Naomi closed the door, adding, "Luka and his demons were riled up about the PI making an appearance at the restaurant—which I presume you've come to discuss." She'd telepathed him about it only twenty minutes ago. After ranting about fuck-head PIs and mega-prick clients who wouldn't just back down, he'd informed her that he'd be at her house shortly. "Dagon left this brand so that it'd be clear I'm under the protection of a legion." Only Luka's breed of demon left snake brands.

Tobe pointed at it. "*That* isn't just a warning. That's a very clear statement of possession. Throat brands generally are." He shoved a hand through his hair. "I suppose I should just be relieved that it was Dagon and not Belial. We don't want that sadistic fucker feeling territorial of . . . What's with that look on your face?" His expression crumpled in a sort of dread. "Ah, shit, Belial branded you as well, didn't it?"

If Luka's prediction was correct, Abraxas would one day mark her much the same way. *My demons see your skin as their own personal canvas*, he'd told her this morning.

Wonderful.

"This isn't good, it's—" Tobe snapped his mouth shut, as if recalling how he'd previously reassured her that he wouldn't try convincing her to walk away from Luka. "How is your entity feeling about all this?"

"It likes that Luka and his demons are protective," she replied as she made her way into the living area. "It's undecided how it feels about the possessiveness, though. By virtue of being a siren, I've stirred up territorial feelings in lots of males—which sometimes made things go tits-up." They could become jealous. Overbearing. Far too intense.

Personally, she couldn't envision having such an issue with Luka. He was no slave to his emotions, her song appeared to have no real sway over him, and he didn't strike her as a naturally jealous person. Still, her demon would be leery for the moment.

"Has it branded him?" asked Tobe.

"No. My demon never brands anyone. You know that."

"So it's not possessive of him?"

Naomi hesitated. "Well ..."

Again Tobe's expression creased—this time with exasperation rather than dread. "Ah, shit."

"It's a *little* possessive. I don't even know exactly how or when that came to be." It had sort of crept up on the entity. "You don't need to get ... Are you sulking?" Because it *looked* like it.

"I liked being the only guy your demon felt territorial toward—go sue me."

Naomi inwardly sighed, and her entity let out a long breath. It would be easy to dub Tobe's feelings as immature and petty, but jealousy often came into play with psi-mates. It was part and parcel of it.

She crossed to him and hugged him tight. "No one could ever be to me who you are. No one." An anchor bond was a special, singular connection. "Not even a person I took as a mate." That would be a whole different but equally strong type of connection.

"And I'm your favorite person ever," he pressed, placing a palm on her back while his other hand caught her hip.

Crossing her eyes, she echoed, "And you're my favorite person ever."

"And you'll always love me most of all."

"Feeling needy, are we?"

"And you'll always love me most of all."

She drew back, exhaling heavily. "I can't possibly promise I'll love you more than I'll love my own mate. You know that. Stop being childish."

His lips hitched up. "But you're so cute when you get all irritated like this."

Squinting, Naomi flipped him off. "Are we going to talk about the PI now or what?"

"Sure." Tobe sank into her armchair. "Though I would have preferred to hear about it last night, not this morning. You should have telepathed me while you were at the restaurant."

"I had a strong suspicion that he hoped I would so that he'd have a chance to talk with you." Naomi took a seat on the sofa. "He's probably having a fuck of a time following and tracking you—you're a slippery little shit."

Tobe grinned. "Thanks."

Only an imp would be so proud of that. "I don't think I'll see or hear from him again. It seems he's terrified of Luka. I wouldn't be surprised if he drops this case altogether, since he's having no luck getting answers. I'm just not sure how easily Stefan will let this go and focus on getting himself a new ghost artist."

Tobe tipped his head to the side. "How much did you tell Belinsky about all this?"

"I didn't add anything to what Phillips told him, which was simply that he has a client who wants the identities of your ghost artists. He didn't specifically name Stefan as his client, but I can't imagine it being anyone else, all things considered."

Her psi-mate nodded his agreement. "I did contact Stefan and tell him to call off the PI. He denied hiring him, but it was obvious that he was lying. Anyway, back to what I meant to ask before. Have you told Belinsky what your main source of income happens to be?"

"Nope. He won't guess that I'm one of the artists. I've never shown him my workroom or even told him about my love for art. Not that I think he'd blab about it, I just prefer to keep it on the down-low. And considering he has no interest in getting to know me because he wants to keep things light, I don't see any way he'll find out."

Again Tobe dipped his chin. "You're good at keeping secrets. On another note, has Belinsky released Iain yet?"

"No. Iain persists in insisting he loves me, according to Luka." She blew out a tired breath. "My song *really* swept him under. He won't consider he's mistaken even under the pressure of actual torture. He's determined to prove us all wrong."

"Some guys in his situation can get seriously wrapped up in their delusions. It's the reason why sirens were known for singing people into throwing themselves off cliffs once upon a time. They didn't do it for fun, they did it because those men became too dangerous to themselves *and* to the siren they'd become obsessed with."

She nodded, having heard all the stories. "Being kept away from me should eventually snap him out of it, though, right? Even *this* caught up in my song, he's not a hopeless case."

"He'll snap out of it. I'm just not sure what mental state he'll be in when he does. He'll carry a lot of shame. Maybe even some resentment toward you."

"Yup." She sighed. "Hopefully he won't make himself an issue. I'm pretty sure Luka will see to it that he doesn't."

"He'd better."

She squinted at Tobe. "Promise me you won't threaten Luka."

Tobe's eyes went wide. "Why would I threaten him?"

"Because you're in full-on protective mode, and it makes you do inadvisable stuff. Now, *promise me*."

He huffed. "Fine. I promise you that I won't threaten him."

Knuckles rapped loudly and rhythmically on the front door. Tobe cocked his head. "I know that knock."

So did Naomi.

"I'll let her in." He was off the sofa before Naomi could move to leave the room.

She heard the front door open, and then... "Boy, do I have a story to tell," announced Khloë.

CHAPTER ELEVEN

Intrigued, Naomi sat up straighter. "I take it this is about the clerics," she said as the imp strode into the living area.

"Oh yeah." Khloë plopped her butt on the other armchair, looking mighty pleased with herself. "I found—*Whoa*, is that a brand?" She leaned forward to get a better look at Naomi's throat. "That's, like, the furthest thing from subtle ever. Luka's demons don't fuck around when it comes to making statements, do they?"

"No, they don't," grumbled Tobe. "Back to the topic of the clerics . . ."

"We gotta wait for the others to arrive," said the imp. "I gave Grams and Ciaran a heads-up that I have some juicy stuff to share. You should contact your mom and Alfie, Naomi; they'll want to hear this."

Naomi telepathed Tia. *You and Alfie might want to head to my place. Khloë has news.*

Her mother's response came fast. *We'll be five minutes.*

Refocusing on Khloë, she asked, "Did you and Keenan enjoy your weekend vacation?" The imp's mate was an incubus who belonged to Knox and Harper's lair.

"Totes. We were both supposed to have today off work so we could do stuff together, but Knox needs him for 'sentinel business'. Keenan felt bad that we had to cancel our plans, but I told him it's fine; I'll just spend the day relaxing and then have a quiet night at home."

Resettling on the sofa, Tobe snorted. "No way Keenan would ever think you're having a quiet night in. He's probably just choosing to believe it because it allows him to function better while away from you."

Khloë crossed one leg over the other. "Did you know that he *still* makes me promise not to blow shit up when he's gone? Like I can't be trusted to make good decisions if left unsupervised." She shook her head, incredulous.

"You really disagree with that assessment?" asked Naomi. *She* personally didn't.

The brunette sniffed. "When I'm in the mood to be affronted, yes."

Right then, Ciaran teleported Jolene and Beck into the living area. It wasn't long later that Tia and Alfie arrived. Of course, *everyone* felt the need to make *some* comment about Naomi's brand-spanking-new brand. No one said anything negative about it, though—only Tobe had a real issue with it so far.

Once everyone had taken a seat, Naomi looked at Khloë and prompted, "So, you have intel."

The imp grinned. "I sure do."

"Let's hear it," urged Jolene, sitting on the sofa between Khloë and Tia.

"It turns out that the clerics are part of an old-time order called the *Lemures*," Khloë revealed. "It's Latin for—"

"Ghosts. Specters. Phantoms," finished Naomi.

Nodding, Khloë planted her hands on the armrests. "It's alleged that—much like noncorporeal entities—these clerics move about unseen, undetected, and leave no traces of themselves behind."

"Hence the name of their order," Alfie mused, perched on a stool he'd taken from the breakfast bar.

"Uh-huh," Khloë agreed. "It was founded by the first generation of Eliouds. It has a strict no-women-allowed rule, though the members aren't celibate. They believe in continuing the Elioud lines; they just have no real use for females. Charming. They are devout followers of God and will do absolutely anything in his name, including kill. They'll target any supernatural creature they don't consider holy if they decide it's God's will."

Naomi hummed. "Rather bloodthirsty for men of the cloth, aren't they?"

"Indeed," said Khloë, her tone prim. "They don't see it as murder. In their view, they're on holy missions. Their beliefs hold sprinkles of various religions—mostly Catholic. They consider themselves first and foremost to be tools of God."

Jolene idly rubbed the pad of her thumb and forefinger together, her expression thoughtful. "So their beliefs are passed down from father to son."

"Yup. Though they're also suspected of abducting young boys and then fully indoctrinating them into the monkhood," Khloë explained, her face tightening. "Presumably those boys are oblivious Eliouds who the clerics have managed to track down."

Naomi bit out a curse. "And they dare consider themselves holy. There ain't anything good and just about snatching and conditioning kids, no matter your reason." It disgusted even her demon.

Khloë made a haughty *mmm-hmm* sound of agreement.

On the stool next to Alfie, Beck scratched at his sideburns. "Other than picking off whatever preternatural creature they deem fit, what else do they get up to?"

Khloë twirled her ankle. "There are whispers that over the years they've been responsible for the deaths of *many* people—like those who were attached to religious scandals, led Satanic cults, claimed to be Jesus reborn. Stuff like that."

"And they seem to believe in prophecies," added Tia, "so when you think how many ancient ones didn't come to pass, you have to wonder if the *Lemures*—or maybe similar orders—had something to do with it."

Naomi leaned forward in her seat, her gaze on Khloë. "What about the prophecy that they're currently so wound up over?"

"I found it in a dark corner of the web, but I've had no joy translating it." Khloë whipped out her phone, tapped the screen several times, and then handed it to Naomi. "This is a snapshot of it that someone somewhere took. It was written by a seriously ancient seer who predicted many events—some of which came to fruition."

Eager for answers, Naomi's demon pressed against her skin as she studied the image on the screen. It was a crinkly yellowy-cream page on which a short paragraph had been scrawled. Beneath it was a symbol. She felt her belly clench. "That's my birthmark."

Tobe cursed. "What does it say?" he pushed, leaning into her.

Naomi read it aloud in English. "*In the days when angels retreat from the earth a time of change for the Lemures shall come. For she who bears the mark is the progeny of the devil and will join with a demon they call a legion. As one, in the city of sin and lights, they will destroy the Lemures and he who would lead them to darkness.*'" Lowering the phone to her lap, she frowned. "That's . . . sort of accurate—at least to a point."

"Yeah," said Ciaran, sitting on the floor with his legs bent at the knees. "Angels have returned to their own realm, and the city of sin and lights is obviously Vegas. Those details right there warned the clerics of when you'd need to be found and just where you would be."

Naomi nodded, handing the phone back to Khloë. "I get now why they think that I – well, my Antichrist child—will lead a demonic army. They mistranslated the part that says 'a demon they call a legion.'"

"The prophecy isn't referring to an army, it's referring to a single person," said Ciaran, following her train of thought. "Probably Luka. Because it stands to reason that if he finds out about the monkhood coming at you, he *will* want it stamped out—and you'd definitely want a hand in that, so you'd work together."

Beck twisted his mouth. "There really is truth in the prophecy after all, then."

Tobe looked at Naomi, his expression none too happy. "Can't say I like that Belinsky might end up involved in all this, but I like this bullshit with the clerics a lot less. Their determination to end you will be as much—if not more—about the prediction that the kid they believe you'll birth will lead to the eradication of their precious order."

"Yes, they're seeking to protect themselves," said Tia. "As for 'he who would lead them to darkness', that's obviously the dark practitioner."

"He won't have liked the part of the prophecy that predicts his death," Jolene noted. "He'll know that the first descendants of Nephilim spouted genuine premonitions; he'll be sure to heed this one just to be on the safe side. I have no doubt that he fully supports the clerics in targeting Naomi."

"Them coming at me is, ironically, what put them on my

radar." Naomi raised her shoulders. "I wouldn't have even looked their way if they hadn't."

Jolene sighed. "Sometimes it seems like prophecies *cause* what they predict will happen. If the seer hadn't written that, no cleric would ever have thought to come after you."

Tia turned to Naomi. "Are you going to tell Luka about all this? I mean, the prophecy mentions him."

Naomi balked at the idea of dragging him into this crap. Besides . . . "We don't know for certain that *he's* the legion in question. Though, yes, I'll concede that he very probably is. He's the only one of his kind who considers me under his protection."

"It makes sense that he'd try to remove a threat to you," Alfie agreed. "Do you even know any other legions?"

"No." His kind were relatively rare. "I'd rather not involve him in this unless I have no choice. It isn't as if I can be one hundred percent honest with him about the situation. I'd have to withhold some details and fudge others. Luka is extremely astute; he'd sense that he didn't have the full story." And he wasn't likely to overlook that. As such, he and Naomi would likely end up arguing—and possibly even walking away from each other. She wasn't ready for the latter yet.

"Okay, I get why you'd hesitate to bring him into it," said Ciaran. "But if he *is* the legion in that prophecy—and even you agree that he most likely is—he's going to find out about it sooner or later."

Naomi lifted a finger. "Not necessarily. Like Jolene said, such predictions seem to *cause* what they state will happen. If I told him now, it would be because of what that ancient paragraph says, *not* because I want to tell him. I'd be fulfilling a part of the prophecy all by myself."

Ciaran inclined his head. "True."

Jolene smoothed a wrinkle out of her blouse. "We can hope

that we manage to obliterate the *Lemures* and their helper without Luka's aid. If there does come a point where he has to be told about it, well, we'll cross that bridge when we come to it. In the meantime, let's focus on locating the *Lemures* and identifying the dark practitioner who's pulling their strings."

"How do we do that?" asked Beck.

No one spoke for a long moment.

"Our only real chance might be to catch a live cleric and be *very* careful how we go about questioning him so we don't trigger his brain to shut down," said Naomi.

Considering that, Jolene dipped her chin. "Some will make a try for you soon enough. We need to have a plan of action for how to handle it when they do. Because you won't be handling them alone next time—sorry to break into your fun, but this situation calls for a little delicacy."

"Agreed," said Naomi, though her entity was disappointed. "Let's get started on that plan."

"We'll need coffee for that," declared Tia, rising from her seat. "Who wants drinks?" After orders were called out, she said, "Come on, Nome, you can give your old mom a hand."

Eye-roll. It was obvious that her mother just wanted to get her alone. Still, with an aggrieved sigh, Naomi left the sofa and followed Tia into the kitchen. "Clearly you have something to say about the brand on my neck," she said.

Her mother switched on the coffee machine. "Well, it's quite a brand. And it somewhat answers the question that was rattling around my head."

"Which is?"

"Just how invested Luka Belinsky is in my baby."

Naomi pulled mugs out of the cupboard and set them on the counter. "He's protective and possessive, but that's as far as it goes."

"That's not to say things will remain that way. He might decide he wants more with time." Tia paused. "You should bring him to dinner one night so me and Alfie can—"

"Present you with an opportunity to interrogate him? Nope."

"I don't interrogate people," Tia protested. "I ask questions because I'm interested."

"And nosy. Let's not forget nosy. You'll also listen to his private thoughts and then blab about them to your nearest and dearest." Which could be bad, given what Luka did for a living.

Tia gasped in offense. "I would never."

"Yes you would. Even if only to Alfie. I don't need to point out that Luka has secrets he needs to guard tightly."

"I just want to get a sense for how interested in you he truly is."

"Well, guess."

Tia huffed. "Such a horrid child. It's a good thing I love you."

"Is it? Is it really?"

Her mouth curving, Tia playfully swatted her arm. "We'll drop this subject for now, since we have plans to make. But don't think we won't be revisiting it at a later point."

"Can't wait," Naomi deadpanned.

Ending his phone call, Luka looked at the twins lounging on his office sofa. "Floyd's membership has been officially revoked." It wasn't something he did lightly to people ... purely because he didn't have to. Rarely did members at Infernal do anything to warrant such a thing.

The ex-member in question, however, had assaulted two security guards and the pit manager last night. Why? Because he hadn't wanted to part from a slot machine despite the fact that a minor case of power failure—one that had now been rectified—had necessitated an evacuation.

Floyd was a hardcore gambler who wore diapers so he wouldn't have to take bathroom breaks. When he sat down at a machine, he did not like to move—not for anything.

"Maybe it'll be good for him," said Mikhail. "He treats gambling like it's his goddamn job."

Nikandr rubbed at his nape. "I don't envision him stopping. He'll just go to another gambling venue."

Luka leaned forward in his chair and rested his phone on the desk. "Probably." Demons had addictive personalities, so they were more susceptible to becoming slaves to the thrills of gambling. He'd met his fair share of Floyds over the years. It generally took something major to make them change. "I doubt even the pain that Belial put him through will make a difference, though I'm sure it will stop him from coming back here."

A knock sounded at his office door.

"Come in," he called.

Draya took tentative steps inside, flashing him a shy smile. Dagon huffed, annoyed purely on the basis that this wasn't the she-demon it wanted to see. Belial merely looked away indifferently. Even Abraxas, lover of female attention though it was, felt no pleasure at the sexual appreciation in Draya's eyes. Its interest lay only with Naomi.

Draya waved at the twins. "Hi, guys." Fiddling with her fingers nervously, she refocused on Luka. "Uh, could we talk alone for a sec? It's, um, a private matter."

He studied her expression, noting her anxiety, wondering if something had happened between her and another employee. He'd made it crystal clear to all of them that they were to seek him out in such an event.

He reached out to the twins on their telepathic channel. *Wait outside.*

You sure you don't want to keep us here as a buffer? She might have come to throw an offer your way, Nikandr warned.

Or there's something wrong and she wishes to share it. I'm not so arrogant that I'd automatically assume this is about me.

Mikhail telepathically snorted. *Yes, you are, but we'll pretend differently.*

Ignoring that, Luka gestured for the brothers to leave and then waved Draya toward the chair opposite his. "Have a seat."

She did so, a bright but tremulous smile curving her mouth. "Last night was crazy, huh? I've never seen any of the members here lose it like that before. Floyd was out of control."

"It's been handled," Luka assured her.

"Oh, I don't doubt it. You're nobody's fool. You woulda thought he'd consider that before he attacked your employees." She shook her head in amused mystification.

Luka sank back into his chair, waiting for her to explain why she'd come. She didn't. "You said there was a private matter you wanted to discuss?" he prompted.

She blew out a breath and shifted in her seat. "Okay, so call me forward, but I'm not one for playing coy. I kind of got the vibe from you that you were into me."

He held back a sigh.

"You're not one of those guys who flirts with every breath he takes. It's a deliberate thing with you, and . . ." She trailed off with an awkward grimace. "It wasn't my imagination, right?"

"No," he admitted.

Her brow furrowed. "So then, what changed? You met the siren and just lost interest in me?"

The siren. There was something depersonalizing in the way she spoke those words. It rubbed him up the wrong way. "Meeting *Naomi* changed things, yes."

Draya's expression cooled. "And you couldn't have told me that? Couldn't have sat me down and explained that despite all the flirting that previously went on, nothing was going to happen between us?"

Luka bristled, as did his demons. She spoke as though he owed her something. Not once when a woman had flirted with him had he felt that she was then obligated to follow through on it in some way. That line of thinking was pure bullshit.

"You showed some interest in one of my bartenders when you first started working here," he reminded her. "Then you withdrew it. Did he get on your case over that?"

She pressed her lips tight together. "No." An almost indiscernible mumble.

"Would you have thought it fair or acceptable if he had?"

She looked away. "No."

"No, because flirting doesn't always mean someone has intentions to take it further, or that they have to," he pointed out.

"It seemed like you meant to."

Luka arched a brow. "Why? Did I say something in particular that made you think that?" He *knew* he hadn't.

She opened and closed her mouth a few times before finally answering. "You didn't, no."

"Did I put out a warning to others that you weren't to be touched?"

"No."

"Did I do anything to give you a solid indication that my intention was to make a move on you?"

She heaved an annoyed sigh. "No, it was just a feeling I got." And she seemed to believe that that "feeling" was all that counted.

"We can both agree that I didn't lead you on with false promises, then?"

"Yes," she replied, her voice tart. "But when we talked, there was something there. A connection."

Those words had him doing an internal double-take. "A connection?"

"You felt it," she insisted. "We both did."

His inner demons stared at her, nonplussed. "Draya, I can honestly tell you that I felt no such thing," Luka bluntly stated. "I can also tell you that, Naomi or no Naomi, I would have made no move on you. I don't want a woman in my life who'd not only try to get an in with me through my anchor but wouldn't respect my need for privacy."

Her eyes went diamond-hard. "You're pretty big-headed to think that my being friendly with Ella has anything to do with you."

His patience wearing thin, Luka leaned forward in his seat, bracing his lower arms on the table. "Don't insult my intelligence. You plied her with personal questions about me, so your purpose for seeking her out was more than fucking obvious."

Draya snapped her mouth shut. "I see no point in continuing this conversation. It's not making our situation any better."

"*We* don't have a situation. There's no *we* at all. I'm your employer, nothing more. Unless, of course, you'd like to quit your job. Is that where this is going?"

She paused. "Miss out on the tips I get here? No. No, I'm not quitting."

"Then keep things professional from here on out and stay away from Ella. If you don't, you won't merely be fired, Draya. I don't tolerate anyone fucking with my anchor."

The she-demon swallowed hard, her eyes flickering, and then haughtily squared her shoulders. "Understood." She rose from her chair, her back ramrod straight. "I'd like to get back to work now."

Luka flicked a hand toward the door. "Then go."

She turned stiffly toward it and calmly left the room.

The twins returned, closing the door behind them.

"She's not a happy bunny right now," Nikandr noted. "Neither are you," he added, studying Luka's expression. "What did she say that put that look on your face?"

Luka relaxed in his chair. "Several things I didn't like." He brought the brothers up to speed, giving them a short summary of the conversation.

Nikandr scowled. "I get that her ego will have taken a hit when you chose to pursue Naomi rather than her; that's understandable. But believing that anyone—male or female—is obligated to take flirting further is a messed-up mindset."

Mikhail nodded hard. "Fuck, I flirt all the time. It means shit."

"To be fair, bro, I don't think women always realize it's supposed to be flirting—you're not that good at it," teased Nikandr, his lips tipping up when Mikhail cursed him in Russian.

Raiden's mind abruptly bumped into Luka's, a sense of urgency buzzing along his consciousness. *I know you didn't want to be interrupted, but we have a major situation here.*

Luka felt his brow crease. *What sort?*

Iain seems to be on the verge of going rogue, replied the sentinel.

Fuck.

CHAPTER TWELVE

Mere minutes later, Daniil teleported Luka and the twins to the underground vault. Luka took the lead as they strode down the passageway, making a beeline for Iain's cell, allowing the relative darkness to envelop them.

If Iain was on the verge of turning rogue, it could mean two things. Either his psyche was splintering, or he was prepared to willingly surrender control to his entity as a means of escape. It wouldn't be the first time someone had left their demon to deal with the consequences of their actions.

Whatever the case, this wasn't good.

The only thing stopping a person's inner entity from giving in to their unfeeling nature was the balance they received from sharing their soul with someone. When a demon took over, they had no balance.

To turn rogue wasn't to lose your sanity. It simply meant that a demon would lose any and all interest in reason or rationality.

They would kill because they could, no motive required. And they would not stop until somebody killed *them*.

Nearing Iain's cell, Luka saw the prisoner leaning against the bars, each hand loosely clasping one. Raiden watched him uneasily from a short distance away.

A flickering bulb cast light over Iain's face, giving Luka flashes of pure black eyes. It was then he realized that Iain wasn't in charge at that moment.

Luka stopped a mere foot from the cell, meeting the entity's probing gaze head-on. His own inner demons stirred, watching it very carefully.

It glanced around. "If it were not for the bars keeping me prisoner, I would like it here," it said, its voice cold and flat. "So much pain and blood and fear—the emotional echoes are strong."

Luka tipped his head to the side. "You're going to take advantage of Iain's fractured mental state?" Entities were protective of their human half, but that wasn't to say they wouldn't commandeer full control if they could.

"He thinks he is fighting by sticking to his claims. It is not fighting. It is refusing to allow himself to see reality. That is *weakness*," it sneered.

"So you yourself know that he isn't—"

"Deeply, madly in love with the siren? Yes, I know that. So does he on some level. He just will not face it." Its lips momentarily curved. "It infuriates him that you now bed her."

"I don't much care. What I want to know is if you are going to retreat."

The demon straightened, pushing away from the bars. "He needs to see the bigger picture."

Luka narrowed his eyes. "You mean to scare him into realizing what will happen if he doesn't pull his head out of his ass."

"Nicely put."

So Iain *wasn't* on the verge of turning rogue; wasn't having a psychic breakdown due to the strain of fighting his demon's insistence for dominance. It was simply that his entity wanted him to wake the fuck up and accept reality. "Will it work?"

"Perhaps. The thought of being lost forever terrifies him. That terror is fueling him to rise. He needs to find his strength. If he does, I will subside. If he does not, I will reign."

Luka twisted his mouth, trying to think of how he might aid the entity. "Would seeing his sisters help him?" he asked, knowing the siblings were tight; that there was a chance Iain would listen to them.

The demon pursed its lips, considering. "Their encouragement may make a difference, yes."

"Then I will have them brought here."

"It would be best that you do not stay," the entity recommended. "Your presence enrages him far too much. It will make him less reasonable and receptive."

Luka had already concluded that much for himself. "If you choose to reign, you will die," he warned. "I cannot, will not allow you to live."

The entity's bored expression didn't change in the slightest. "Which is why I would prefer that he feel spurred to fight me. No one wins if he does not."

Having tossed back the last of her smoothie, Naomi set the empty bottle on her coffee table. "I can't imagine what Iain's going through right now," she said to Luka, who sat beside her on the sofa. "To have your own entity keep you suppressed like that . . ." She would for sure feel betrayed in his position.

Angled in his seat to face her, Luka gave her a severe look. "Do *not* feel guilty. None of this is on you. And if Iain doesn't choose to fight his demon, that won't be on you either. He's a big boy; siren song or no, he can make his own decisions."

"I know that. I just can't quite believe things have gone this far." She crossed one leg over the other and slipped her joined hands between her thighs. "What do you think the outcome will be?"

"Iain held out against me and Belial, but that was more to stubbornly get across that he believed himself to be right in all he claimed. His entity may have more success with him. He doesn't want to die; he will if his demon takes over. I can't allow a rogue to live unless I keep them permanently in my vault."

"Which is no life."

"Exactly. The demon wouldn't wish for such an existence anyway."

She sighed. "It must *really* be pissed at Iain to pull this move." A person's inner entity wouldn't easily do something that would upset them.

"Oh, it is. It's very sure he's fooling himself, and it doesn't like that vein of weakness in him." Luka draped an arm over the back of the sofa. "Has no other man taken so long to snap out of their obsession with you?"

She shook her head. "My song affected Iain on a level that it didn't others. I keep wondering if maybe I should have reported the problem to Jolene sooner; if he would have shaken it off by now if you'd intervened at an earlier point."

"Either way, you still hold no blame here."

"It sucks that sirens have no way to unravel the metaphorical spells we unintentionally weave over people. It doesn't seem fair that we don't have that inborn power."

"Ella did attempt to find a literal spell that would release Iain from your song's thrall. Unfortunately, none exists."

Kind of curious about his relationship with his anchor, she asked, "How did you first meet Ella?"

"I needed new wards for Infernal—the others were suffering from wear and tear. I heard she was the best at constructing them. I wanted the best. While she was outside the club building wards, I telepathed her from inside to ask how long she'd be. As soon as our psyches touched, I knew she was my anchor." He paused. "What about you and Tobe?"

"I've known him since we were kids, but we never had cause to touch minds until one day eight years ago. He'd telepathically reached out to tell me to be careful; that I was being followed."

Luka tensed, squinted slightly. "Followed?"

"It was an ex. I dealt with it. Haven't seen him since." Naomi paused. "Has Tobe contacted you at all?"

"No. Why?"

She gave a stiff shrug. "No reason."

"Let me guess ... he isn't pleased that you're in my bed, and you're worried that he'll eventually come to me about it?"

"It's not a jealousy thing, if that's what you're wondering. He's just hyper-protective, and you're a man with a whole lot of enemies."

"He thinks you'd be safer away from me and that you can do better?"

"Yes, pretty much. Why are you half smiling?"

"I said similar things to Ella regarding Viper." Luka thought it ironic that he'd now be hearing the same said of him. "I didn't want Viper in the picture. He and I had some unpleasant conversations in the beginning." As such, Luka really wouldn't be able to judge Tobe if he did choose to make his reservations clear in person. "Ella's mother and aunt weren't crazy about her involvement with him either. Are your family on the same page as Tobe regarding me?"

"My mom isn't bothered by it. My stepfather has his reservations but only spoke of them once."

Luka twined a strand of her hair around his finger. "He runs the pizzeria where you work, right?"

"Right."

"You live an unusually quiet life for an imp." Even *he* had heard the note of suspicion in his voice, so it was no surprise that she stiffened. "Why do you only work part-time?"

Her casual shrug seemed a little forced. "Alfie doesn't need me full-time."

"Hmm," Luka responded. "Is that the only reason?"

"Why? What's with all the questions?"

He blinked at her defensive tone. "I want to know you." He almost smiled at how she eyed him, wary and uncertain. That was Naomi, he'd come to learn. Always cautious of people's motivations.

"Why?"

"Because," he replied simply.

He couldn't pinpoint why curiosity clawed at him often around this she-demon. He'd known many women. Bedded many women. Until her, none had intrigued him beyond a surface level. He found himself wanting to pierce the guardedness she wore like a layer of perfume.

It was really no wonder that his defenses had steadily grown to read her as a threat. She was . . . not quite under his skin, but scratching at it, demanding entry. An uncomfortable feeling. "I didn't anticipate that you would matter to me, but you do."

She swallowed. "Maybe you're just caught up in the siren spell."

"You know that isn't true. You'd be able to tell if I was." It would be a lie to say that her song hadn't impacted him. The pull she gave off was pure sexual magnetism, so it had of course contributed to his attraction to her. But she was so beautiful, sensual, and compellingly self-assured that she would have snatched his attention with or without it.

"There were sirens in my past," he added. "I felt their call, just as I feel yours. But the effect of their song wore off fast, and none of them kept my interest." He gently tapped her nose. "You're a different matter."

"And you're not sure how you feel about that, are you?"

"No, as it happens, I'm not. I generally don't like to find myself in unfamiliar territory."

"So why aren't you ending our arrangement?"

"I really can't say, because I don't have an answer."

Finding herself at a loss here, Naomi stared at him in silence for long moments.

I didn't anticipate that you would matter to me, but you do.

The words kept swirling around her brain. This dude had a talent for knocking her mentally off balance with just a few words, and she wasn't too good at rolling with it. "You say that I matter to you, but you haven't been in my life long. There are things about me that you don't know."

"Oh, I'm well aware that you're hiding parts of yourself from me. There's no point, Naomi. I'll find them."

Alarm bells started blaring in her head. It was a struggle to keep her breathing even. Because this ... She really hadn't expected to ever find herself in this position.

Luka could be nosy and something of a meddler, true, but he'd resolutely kept a distance between them. Yes, they talked sometimes; tentatively shared this and that. But neither had ever pushed when a no-no topic was broached. As such, he'd given her *not one clue* that he would make this little declaration.

What should she do now?

Easy.

Pull away. End their arrangement. Ask him to leave. Self-preservation demanded it. Because who knew what he'd do if he discovered that Lou was her father?

She'd like to think that he would keep it to himself. If he didn't, though, a whole heap of problems would ensue. More, given the "quirk" that Lou had passed on to her, Luka would be sure to look at her differently if he knew the full truth. That bothered her far more than it should.

So, yes, she should usher him out.

But she didn't.

Well, it wasn't that simple. He *pulled* at her somehow. Not in the mere sense of her feeling drawn to him—that would be a freaking understatement at this point. It was more than that. She just couldn't put it into words. Or maybe she didn't want to examine the matter too closely. Whichever.

The protective moat she'd built around herself . . . she had the distinct feeling that he could cross it if she wasn't careful. Which was all the more reason for her to tell him to leave, wasn't it? And yet, she *still* didn't.

Her demon didn't weigh in on the matter, equally torn. It *liked* Luka. Liked him for Naomi. And it felt that if anyone would accept her secrets and keep them safe, it would be him. But the entity didn't *trust* in that, so it didn't wish to push her in either direction.

"Naomi?"

The sound of her name sent her thoughts scattering. "Hmm?"

He looked close to sighing. "You stopped listening, didn't you?"

"Only with one ear."

He snagged her nape with his palm, holding her gaze. "You don't have to be wary of what's happening here."

"What *is* happening?" she asked, her heartbeat kicking up.

"I don't know. Maybe something. Maybe nothing." He tipped his head to the side. "Is it really so bad that I want to know you?"

"No."

"But?"

"But it's best that you don't go looking for the parts of me I keep hidden. You wouldn't like what you uncovered."

"It wouldn't change that you matter. Not for me, not for my demons."

"You can't know that."

"Yes, I can," Luka assured her, unable to imagine that anything about her could be so terrible. He released her nape and splayed his hand around her throat to palm Dagon's brand. "We want you in a way we've never wanted another woman."

"That's just physical," she croaked.

"If that were true, we wouldn't be having this conversation." He leaned toward her slightly. "Keep your secrets, Naomi. I won't nag you to part with them."

"Really?"

"Really. I have plenty of my own." He flicked a look at the ceiling. "I don't need to know what's behind that locked door upstairs, or if—like many in your lair—you have an illegal mode of income. I just want to know you better. That's all."

Naomi nibbled on her lower lip, still the picture of uncertainty. She pulled in a long preparatory breath and then exhaled heavily. The unease bled out of her expression little by little, and her shoulders lost their stiffness. "Okay." A low whisper.

Satisfied, Luka felt the corner of his mouth hitch up.

The temperature abruptly lowered as her eyes turned pure black. "You will keep to your word and not push her," the demon told him. *Told* him. With all the authority of a queen.

Luka's brows lifted in surprise. "I will respect it when there's something she doesn't want to share," he promised, but the demon's hard expression didn't soften.

"If you discover what she fears you might, you will keep it to yourself." Malice churned in its eyes. "If you reveal her secrets and cause her harm, there will be a reckoning. I will bathe in your blood once I am done with you."

His entities had mixed reactions to that proclamation. Abraxas huffed, affronted that it didn't have the demon's utter devotion. Belial smirked, liking its vengeful streak. Dagon was offended that the entity would even *think* Luka was lying ... even though lying was all Dagon really did. Luka, well, he wondered why Naomi's demon would feel so confident that it could take him down.

"It won't come to that," he assured it. "I'm not in the habit of revealing people's personal business."

The entity's only response was a steady glare of warning. Then it retreated, and Naomi's eyes were back to their usual gray-green.

"So," Luka said, "your demon doesn't trust me."

"No. But don't take it personally," she advised. "It's mistrustful by nature."

"Then we have that in common."

His mind flicked back to the entity's comment. *If you discover what she fears you might* . . .

It was the word "fears" that stuck out most, because what could Naomi possibly fear him discovering? What could be so monumental that it would drive her demon to threaten him that way? Not many entities would dare. In fact, he couldn't recall any having done so in the past.

"Your demon wasn't bluffing just now." Letting his hand slip away from her throat, he threaded his fingers through her hair. "It meant what it said. It would truly seek to make me pay if I brought you harm."

"It's very protective of me."

"Good. So am I. In which case your demon doesn't need to worry that I'd ever commit an act that would negatively impact you. I don't expect it to take my word for that. I have the feeling that it won't anyway. But I'm making the statement nonetheless."

She studied him closely, and her lips twitched. "It bothers you that my demon isn't being friendly toward you," she correctly sensed. "It doesn't dislike you, Luka. The opposite, actually. But for my entity, 'like' and 'trust' aren't mutually compatible."

"Hmm, I can relate."

"But it still bothers you."

"A little," he conceded. "My demons aren't too pleased about it either. But I'm sure your entity will relax around us eventually. We can be patient."

"Can you?"

"No."

Her smile went up a notch. "You're spoiled."

He gave a small, unapologetic shrug. "I'm used to having my own way. Comes with having been a Prime for so long, I suppose."

"Well, since there's nothing I can say that will improve your mood regarding this particular subject, maybe we could switch topics. Or . . ."

"Or?"

"Or go upstairs, get naked, and fuck each other stupid. Personally, I'm leaning more toward the latter. You?"

Like that, his mindset shifted and his body began to stir. "I think we've done enough talking for one night."

"I couldn't agree more. Glad you see things my way."

CHAPTER THIRTEEN

Yawning, Naomi slid a reference book back on the bookcase in her workspace. Having finished her most recent project, she'd already cleaned her hands in the sink and was now tidying a few things away. The rest of the clutter would have to stay where it was, because she had somewhere she needed to be.

At this hour on any other Monday, she would have been pulling a shift at the pizzeria. But the other hostess had wanted the extra hours so she could save cash for her upcoming trip. This made it easier for Naomi to go ahead with plans to meet with Luka this evening.

A week. It had been a week of Luka following through on his intent to get to know her better. He plied her with questions, edging as close to her secrets as he could all while sticking to his promise not to push her. That had made her demon relax a little more around him.

She didn't get the sense that he was making an active attempt to build something with her. More that he'd simply decided not to fight his wish to learn more about her.

To an extent, it made her uncomfortable. She was used to being ogled. Objectified. Leered at. Hit on. Treated as arm candy. She wasn't used to having someone around who wanted to *know* her.

Since turnabout was fair play, she'd tossed some questions his way. To her surprise, he'd been fairly open with her, though he avoided any mention of his family and he *never* spoke of his illegal business dealings. The latter was no surprise.

Although they'd shared a bed for two weeks at this point, they so far remained trapped in an endless loop of indecently carnal hunger. She felt all but enslaved by it at times.

Turning away from the bookcase, she grabbed her cell phone from the drawing table and made her way out of the room. After locking the door behind her, she padded through her bedroom, into the en suite, switched on the light—

A creak on the stairs.

She went completely still, her nape prickling. Well, it would seem that she had company. Rather than uneasy, she felt a tingle of anticipation.

She closed the bathroom door and flicked the lock as she telepathed Jolene. *It seems the clerics have taken the bait.* Her demon all but clapped its hands with glee.

Her Prime's psyche stroked hers. *I was confident that Martina would come through for us.* Jolene had assigned her daughter to flirt outrageously with Konstantin and distract him enough that any watchful clerics would take advantage and slip into Naomi's place.

It was something they'd had Martina do on several occasions since the clerics last attacked, never knowing if they were lingering; always hoping they were and that they'd snap up the opportunity to get to Naomi.

Stick to the plan and keep them occupied, Jolene went on. *The rest of us will be at your house shortly.*

Okay. You'll find us in my bedroom, Naomi told her.

She waited a good twenty seconds and then flushed the toilet, giving her intruders the impression that she was simply doing her business. She washed her hands for real—well, she'd just pressed the flush button, which wasn't exactly hygienic—and then dried them.

A spike of adrenaline quickened her pulse as she exited the room. Sure enough, several Eliouds were gathered around. There were more this time. Fourteen in total. All were bald and clothed in their cleric gear, magick-infused swords in hand.

Her demon smirked, pleased that there were plenty for Naomi and the others to kill. It would for sure enjoy the show. How typical.

"I'm starting to think that you and your brethren don't like me." She scanned the large group. "So many of you. How curious. I suppose I should be flattered that you felt it necessary to have so much backup. Though I had thought that maybe you guys only worked in groups of seven."

A cleric with brown bushy brows shot her a glare. "Apparently you can too easily handle one unit, since our other brethren have disappeared."

"So two groups came along this time." As always in response to a threat, the twisted seraphim power that she harbored stirred. Seeped upward. Pooled beneath her skin. Began to heat the room. "At this point, though, I would have thought you people would stop coming at me. I mean, are you not tired of losing brothers?"

"So it is as we suspected: they are dead," mused a young, baby-faced Elioud.

"Where did you bury them?" Bushy Brows demanded.

Naomi gave him a smile of mock pity. "There wasn't anything left to bury. I figured they'd prefer that, though. You *Lemures* don't like to leave evidence of yourselves behind."

There was an almost collective intake of breath. Bodies tensed, and unnerved looks were exchanged.

"Yes, I know about your order," she continued. "If you wanted to keep its existence quiet, you should have scrapped the emblem on your clothes—it's like wearing ID." They really should have thought of that.

"It doesn't matter that you know who we are," Baby Face decided, tugging at his collar, his cheeks flushing from the heat.

"It does matter that you're being manipulated by a dark practitioner who's posing as an angel. He gave you those swords, right? They aren't blessed, they're enchanted. But hey, I don't suppose you'll take my word for that."

The bland expressions aimed her way confirmed that no, they didn't believe her.

"Also, you misread the prophecy," she added. Not that the *actual* translation would make them leave—they wanted her dead so that her child wouldn't rid the world of their order. Still . . . "I'm not going to birth the Antichrist. I won't have a child who'll lead an army of demons."

Bushy Brows sneered, using the back of his hand to swipe at the sheen of sweat on his forehead. "You expect us to believe anything the whore of the devil would say?"

Whore? *Fuck you, asshole.* "You act so very pious for a bunch of people who believe in kidnapping little boys and dragging them into your monkhood to be brainwashed."

Baby Face flushed. "We are not brainwashed, we are enlightened."

Ah, so *this* guy had been one of the abducted. "If that were the case, you'd know the truth. You don't. You've come here on the basis of a prophecy that, in reality, you don't fully understand."

"And it was a tremendously unadvisable thing to do," Jolene chipped in.

The clerics whirled to face the demons who now stood at the other side of the room—Jolene, Tobe, Ciaran, Khloë, Beck, Tia, and Alfie. Curses flew out of their mouths, and they shifted uneasily.

"So very, very unadvisable," Naomi agreed, her lips curving.

The expressions on the intruders' faces darkened. They angled their bodies in a way that enabled them to keep an eye on both her and the newcomers, aiming to appear unfazed. But she could see that their confidence had taken a blow.

Of course it had.

All the demons held a ball of shimmering hellfire in their hand, making it clear that they were up for a battle.

Bushy Brows looked at her. "So this is how you defeated our brethren. You had others aid you. If you think such backup will make *us* leave, you are wrong. This time, you are outnumbered." He raised his sword, his jaw firming. "We will kill them, just as we will kill *you*."

Naomi smiled while her demon snorted. "What a wishful thinker. It's kind of cute." She called on the power bubbling within her, feeling her smile fade as predatory determination poured through her system. "You shouldn't have come here, but I'm rather glad you did." Her power rushed out in a torrent of fire that lit her up from head to toe.

Shock gracing the clerics' faces. Some eased back while others threw up their hands to shield their eyes from the radiance of the flames.

Bushy Brows gaped at her. "Merciful God," he breathed.

"Yeah, I don't think he'll be coming to save you." She paused. "Catch." She hurled a fiery serpent right at him.

Cursing, he raised his sword high and sliced at the snake, but the blade passed harmlessly through it. And then the serpent was on him, sinking its fangs in with a hiss.

Her entity let out a little cackle.

The demons across the room acted fast, pitching orbs of hellfire at the Eliouds.

Some clerics ducked. Some darted to the side, crashing into their brothers or the wall. The others jerked as the orbs hit home, burning their clothes and scorching the skin beneath.

To their credit, all but Bushy Brows recovered quickly. Chanting sounded as magick came rushing out of the clerics—some glowing streams heading for Naomi, some aiming for the other demons.

Naomi struck with a thin blade of red-violet fire, slicing through one, two, three streams.

But she missed the fourth.

It rammed into her hard enough to knock her back a step, electrifying her nerve endings. *Motherfucking ow.*

Her fellow demons took their own lumps but retaliated fast. Ciaran slammed three clerics with telekinetic power, sending them flying backwards. Khloë let out a spray of electric-blue fire bullets, making two clerics drop to the floor. Tobe lashed out with psychic hits that flattened another two. Jolene, Beck, Tia, and Alfie lobbed a series of crackling orbs at the others—all the clerics staggered backwards, crying out in pain.

Adrenaline pumping in her blood, Naomi joined Ciaran in porting behind people to snap their necks. Boring, yes, but they wanted the fight over with quickly so they could focus on what was important: getting answers from the last Elioud standing. Even as her demon understood, it was supremely disappointed that it wasn't a bloodier scene.

Just as she dropped a dead body, another cleric settled his

glower on her, held his sword high above his head, and yelled some sort of war cry. "Kill the whore!" he ordered.

His brothers echoed his cry, raising their weapons, and then they all charged at her.

Laughing, Naomi 'ported to another spot and watched them skid to a halt, snapping their heads around as they searched for her. The other demons in the room took advantage, striking at the clerics, forcing them to divide their attention yet again.

It was a messy battle. Flaming orbs and electric-fire bullets whooshed across the room. Streams of pure-white magick and red-violet flames flew back and forth. Telekinetic waves rippled through the air, hitting their targets like a train. The faint zaps of psychic hits could be heard among the cries, curses, and roars.

The Eliouds were pitiless in their attack. When they weren't launching magick, they were aiming to slash and stab people with their swords. None scored hits on Naomi this time, but she didn't know if she could say the same for those in her lair.

As for the damage? Portraits hit the floor. Glass smashed. Splinters came off the wooden furniture. Stray hellfire collided with the walls, leaving scorch marks.

Wonderful.

Clerics flinched. Screamed. Fell. Dropped swords. Eyed their injuries in horror. *Literally* burned alive as her acidic fire ate at them.

Sensing movement, Naomi turned.

But not fast enough.

A sword slashed her arm, causing a blazing fiery pain—*fucking ouch*—to race down it. More, she had the same sensation as last time: a sliver of something malevolent creeping inside her.

"Fucker," she spat, even as her inner fire rose up to incinerate the sliver and heal her wound.

Baby Face's brow creased in confusion as her flesh reknitted.

Confusion that was swiftly chased away by a fanatical hatred. "Die!"

"Nope." She scorched his blade with power, forcing him to drop it, and—

"Don't kill him, he's all that's left!" shouted Jolene.

Bummer. Naomi had wanted to make him pay for that slice. Instead, she pyroported behind him, wrapped her arm tight around his neck, and then squeezed hard.

He choked on a breath and struggled against her hold. As a demon, she was stronger than him, and he couldn't get himself free. He desperately clawed at her arm and tried stomping on her feet. She thought he'd start lobbing magick at her, but it was as if he wasn't thinking, too caught up in sheer animal panic.

She didn't release him. Didn't loosen her hold. Just kept on choking him out.

His struggles weakened until finally he lost consciousness.

Naomi let him drop to the floor and then looked around. The rest of his brethren had been slain. Her lair members were all on their feet, but a few looked a little the worse for wear. "Anyone need healing?"

Ciaran waved away the offer. "I've only got minor burns, they're healing already." The others echoed his sentiment, except for her mother and her anchor.

Tobe stared down at the slice on his chest. "It's only shallow, so I'd say it ain't a big deal, but I felt dark magick enter my bloodstream."

Naomi pressed her hand over his wound, calling her inner fire to the surface, letting it heal him as it would her. She then gave the same treatment to the slashes on her mother's neck and arm.

All seraphim could heal. Her power might not be pure like theirs, but it could still perform that ability. It had come in handy often over the years.

"Nobody else has an injury they want rid of?" she double-checked.

"We're all peachy," said Alfie, and the others nodded in agreement.

Smoothing back the hairs around her face that had escaped her stylish updo, Jolene said, "I believe we're ready for step two in our plan. Let's move the cleric over to the bed."

Beck scooped him up and unceremoniously tossed him over his shoulder while Jolene snatched up a fallen sword.

Naomi used red-violet fire to incinerate every trace of his brethren's existence, including the other blades. Meanwhile, Beck positioned Baby Face on her bed while Jolene propped the sword up against the dresser. Tobe then quickly injected him with a drug that was a slightly stronger version of truth serum.

Khloë rubbed her palms together. "Fingers crossed this all goes well and we get the answers we need."

"Your fingers aren't crossed," Ciaran seemed to feel compelled to point out.

"You're so literal sometimes," his sister griped.

"Right, all of you step away from the bed and stand behind Tobe," Jolene ordered. "The human should wake any minute."

They did as instructed, at which point Tobe threw up a shield that would hide their presence. Jolene then knocked back a vial of something she'd bought from Ella—it was basically liquidized glamor magick. Her facial features seemed to blur, swim, ripple, then re-form into a completely different face. Her features hadn't *truly* changed; the magick simply made them *appear* different to whoever looked at her.

Jolene turned to them, hand on hip, and patted her hair. "Well, how do I look?"

"A lot like my grandmother," Beck said honestly.

The Prime smiled. "Excellent. She has a sweet face that screams 'You can trust me.' That will help."

Hopefully, yes, it would. They needed the cleric to feel comfortable with Jolene. To see her as no threat and lower his guard, if only a little.

They wouldn't be able to squeeze information out of him via even the most gentle interrogation. Questions relating to the monkhood and the dark practitioner would no doubt trigger his brain and body to conk out. That meant they would have to make him share *willingly*.

People did that during conversations if they felt relaxed and safe. The truth serum would make him more inclined to be open; it would remove his hesitation to keep secrets. So as long as Jolene stuck to clever prompts, she should be able to make him blurt out helpful information.

"This had better work," muttered Tobe, rolling his shoulders.

"Fingers crossed it does," said Khloë.

Ciaran sighed. "*Again*, you're not actually crossing them."

"*Again*, I'm doing it mentally."

"Why not just do it physically?"

"I'm tired."

Jolene raised a hand, gesturing for silence. "Quiet. He's starting to stir." She perched herself on the edge of the bed, plastered a gentle look on her face, and focused on him.

Soon, his eyelids began to flutter and he mumbled nonintelligible words beneath his breath. He looked up at Jolene, his eyes a little glazed over. "Who are you?"

"Someone who means you no harm," Jolene replied, her voice soft and lulling. "I found you outside in my yard. You're hurt. It seems something happened to you."

His brow furrowing, he lifted his head to take stock of himself, noticing the burns on his chest and arms. Confusion deepened his frown. "The last thing I remember is leaving the monastery with my brothers."

"I didn't see anyone else outside."

"Her protectors must have slaughtered them," he concluded, though he seemed to be speaking to himself. "Any who try to kill her don't come back."

Jolene lightly patted his hand in comfort. "Others may not have survived, but you did. You're a strong one. And you'll be back on your feet soon enough. Then you can return to your monastery."

He swallowed, distressed. "The brothers there won't be pleased that we failed. And *he* will be angry."

He being the dark practitioner, Naomi guessed.

"No one will be angry with you," Jolene assured him.

"Yes, yes, they will," he insisted. "I was supposed to kill her."

"Maybe you did."

A line dented his brow at that. "You're right. I don't recall killing her, but I might have." Hope lit his eyes. "It could be why I survived."

"Exactly. You'll return a hero, not a failure."

He nodded. "I'll be rewarded, just as promised."

"I do love rewards. Especially if they involve chocolate."

"This one isn't chocolate. It is so much more." His gaze went out of focus. "He's so pure and whole. He shines so bright it's sometimes hard to look at him. But how can we not look at him? Even without wings he is magnificent. And now I will ascend like he promised."

Naomi sent out a telepathic comment that would reach every demonic mind in the room. *Sounds like the dark practitioner has definitely somehow convinced the clerics that he's an angel.*

We need to find out where the monkhood is, Tobe asserted, his fingers flexing. *If we don't take them out, they'll keep coming.*

Relax, we'll have the information we need soon. Jolene refocused on the cleric. "If you need a ride home, just say so. I'll drive you wherever you need to go."

"Are you sure?" he asked. "The monastery isn't local."

She flapped a hand. "That's fine."

"It's over an hour's drive away."

"Not a problem. I'd feel better dropping you off. That way I'll know you got home safely."

A grateful smile graced his face. "Thank you. You're so nice."

Naomi barely held back an amused snort. By the looks on her companions' faces, they were in the same boat.

Jolene raised a hand, as if she'd just remembered something. "Oh, I think I might have found something of yours outside. It was lying beside you. A very impressive sword."

He gripped her hand, a sense of urgency in his expression. "Do you have it?"

"Yes, I brought it inside. It's right over there." She pointed at where it rested against the dresser.

Relief made him release her hand with a long breath. "Thank you. I'll need to take it back to the monastery with me. It was given to me by someone very special."

The supposed angel, I'm guessing, said Khloë, to which Naomi nodded.

Jolene bit her lip in contemplation, most likely wondering how she could push him into revealing more. "I'm glad you have someone special in your life," she said at last. "My children, ah, they're my world."

"He's a whole other kind of special," Baby Face told her, his expression one of awe and wonder. "If you met him, you would understand. Just looking at him makes me feel closer to God."

Gag, said Khloë, dramatically hunching forward as if she'd puke.

"How lovely," said Jolene. "You're lucky to have met him, then."

"So lucky," he agreed, his eyes fairly sheening with happiness. "God sent him to us; gave us these blades. His holiness is channeled through the steel. You don't even need to deliver a killing blow—you just need to be able to sink it into someone. God's power will do the rest."

Naomi rolled her eyes. *Magick will do the rest*, she corrected. *He's so pitifully delusional I feel kind of sorry for him. Especially when I'm pretty sure he was someone the monkhood abducted as a kid.*

We can't allow him to live, Nome, said Tia. *He would keep coming for you. The clerics won't stop. The dark practitioner wouldn't permit it if they tried.*

She knew that, but it still sucked.

Jolene patted the cleric's hand again. "Let me know when you feel ready to leave. Now, be warned, I don't have what you would call a pigeon's instincts, so I'll need you to give me very clear directions or we're apt to get lost."

His lips hitched up. "I can do that. The monastery is tricky to find unless you know where to look, but it's not all that far from what is in my opinion the best ghost town in all of Nevada."

Jolene went still, and then her mouth curved. "I do love ghost towns. The one closest to the Grand Canyon is probably my favorite."

"My favorite is—"

"Why in the underworld is there a priest in my daughter's bed?"

CHAPTER FOURTEEN

Naomi felt her eyes drift shut. *Unbelievable.* She looked up to see her father standing at the foot of the bed in a ratty tee and stained jeans, a bag of chips in hand. His curious gaze studied the cleric like he was an insect. That gaze then narrowed on her Prime, as if he sensed the use of glamor and was striving to see through it.

Lou smirked. "That you, Jolene? I'm getting your usual *mess with me and die* vibes and—Ooh, shiny," he added, his attention snatched by the sword.

"*Don't* touch it," Jolene snapped as he walked toward it, making the cleric jerk in shock at her abrupt change in manner.

Lou glared at her. "I wasn't going to steal it, just look at it."

"You look with your eyes, not your hands," Jolene reprimanded.

His lips curved. "Harper's always saying that to Asher."

"And I really shouldn't have to say it to a man your age, but here we are."

He gave her an incredulous look. "Who are you kidding,

acting all aggravated? You *love* having an excuse to give me shit. It's a balm to the boredom that plagues your dark, ghoulish soul." He moved closer to the bed and said to the cleric, "Really, don't let her fool you—she's the kind of person hell itself would reject."

Her demon closed its eyes in the same exasperation Naomi felt.

Her lips thin, Jolene sighed at him. "You just can't help but fuck things up, can you?"

Baffled, Lou blinked and rocked back slightly on his heels. "What exactly am I fucking up? Speaking of fucked up, why does the room look like a tornado hit it? And why is there a priest in Naomi's bed? And where *is* Naomi?"

"Naomi," the cleric mumbled, his eyes going increasingly wide with terror and realization. "Wait, this is her home? This is ... You tricked me," he accused Jolene.

"No, I did not."

"Of *course* she did," Lou told him with a snort. "I don't know exactly what happened, but I am quite sure she messed with your head somehow. It's what she does."

Jolene edged off the bed and threw up her arms.

Naomi tapped Tobe's shoulder and indicated for him to drop the shield. As he did, the cleric let out a loud *gah* of horror.

She stared at Lou. "Dad, honestly, you have the *worst* timing."

His gaze snapped to her, and his lips bowed up. "There you are. And what, pray tell, is wrong with my timing? Or anything else about me? I am perfection itself."

He was *something*.

"The priest. Your bed. Far too weird. What's going on?" Lou pressed.

Baby Face sat up, shrinking away from Jolene. "I want to leave. *Now*."

The Prime exhaled heavily. "All right. My grandson here will take you someplace else. Mostly because it'd be strange for

Naomi if we killed you in her bed." Jolene looked at Ciaran and tipped her chin toward the cleric.

The guy's eyes bulged. "No, wait!"

Ciaran didn't. He crossed to the cleric, snatched his arm, and teleported away.

"Will someone please tell me what's happening here?" asked Lou, dipping his hand in his bag of chips. "The suspense is killing me."

Naomi rolled her shoulders. "Fine. But don't freak out."

His brow pinched. "Why would I freak out? I'm an extremely calm and composed being. Very little bothers me on a deep level." He tossed a chip in his mouth.

"So here goes." Naomi thrust a hand into her hair. "A bunch of clerics have been trying to kill me because they think I'll birth the Antichrist and eliminate their order. Oh, and a dark practitioner is helping them."

Lou paused mid chew, going rigid, his eyes turning cold as frost. Moments later he resumed chewing—the process slow, stiff, angry. The bag of chips went up in a small burst of ultraviolet flames. He spat a very ugly curse and then began pacing back and forth.

Naomi and the others remained silent, giving him a chance to walk off his rage. Ciaran had just teleported back to the room when Lou marched over to the sword and—*snap*.

Yeah. He split it right down the middle.

More ultraviolet flames appeared beneath his palms, sinking into both halves of the broken weapon and eating them whole so they were quickly reduced to tiny particles. Particles that he promptly dumped on the floor.

"Calm and composed," mumbled Tobe beside Naomi. "Right."

Lou whirled on her. "I need specifics."

So she told him everything, watching as his expression turned darker and darker.

"I shouldn't only be learning of all this now! Why did you keep it from me?" It was a whiny demand.

"Why do you think?" She would have thought the answer was obvious.

"I have no idea. I'm such an approachable, understanding person—ask anyone."

If she did, they'd laugh their tits off at the mere idea that any such descriptors could be applied to him.

"Not to mention that I'm your *father*," he reminded her, stabbing his finger into his palm. "I have a right to know these things."

Tia went to his side, her hands raised in a placatory gesture. "It wasn't a matter of excluding you. We just wanted to be careful how we approached the situation, and we didn't have enough information to go on anyway. You would have wanted details that we simply didn't yet have."

"You knew that a dark practitioner was involved, though." He sniffed. "That problem, at least, is easily solved."

Khloë frowned. "It is? How?"

"I'll just kill all the dark practitioners in Vegas," replied Lou, as if the solution were obvious. "Then we can be sure he's dead."

Naomi barely held back an aggravated sigh. "That's a bit of an overreaction, don't you think?"

"Nope. And why would you care if they all die? They're terrible, terrible people. The things they get up to" —he shuddered in disgust— "are pure evil. They should be eradicated for the greater good."

Beck frowned. "What do you care about the greater good?"

"Not one thing," said Lou. "But I want my daughter to be safe. A dark practitioner is a threat to her. Slaughtering them would remove that threat. Ergo . . ."

Naomi stepped toward him. "While I appreciate that you want to protect me, I'd rather you didn't go on a killing spree."

"Wouldn't be the first time," he pointed out.

"Who did you kill before?" asked Khloë.

"A bunch of angels." Lou folded his arms, inching up his chin in superiority. "They deserved it."

Khloë's nose wrinkled. "Why?"

"Because they did."

Alfie tipped his head to the side. "And that conclusion has roots in pragmatism or is just something you claim to excuse your actions?"

Lou's face scrunched up. "Why would I want to excuse what I did? That kind of thing is for people who feel . . . you know . . . remorse. I would genuinely pity those who experience that emotion if I had it in me to give a rat's ass."

"And yet you judge others so much," said Beck. "You don't think that you're perhaps equally cruel?"

Lou pointed at his face. "Perfection itself, remember?"

Jolene rolled her eyes. "Your 'solution' won't help us. Unless the first dark practitioner you kill is our boy, you'll only scare him into lying low by massacring his kind. He might even go underground, making it harder for us to find him and dragging out this whole thing. More, he could decide to come at Naomi another way. A *harder* way. Like with preternaturals instead of clerics. Humans who have a trace of Nephilim blood and thereby possess an aptitude for holy magick are far less of a threat."

Lou leaned back, eyeing the Prime curiously. "Wait, you think you can talk me into ignoring that this is happening? Is that what you're trying to do?"

"What I think is that if you want to get involved, you need to go about it more stealthily for Naomi's sake," said Jolene. "No dramatic displays of power or vengeance."

"Says an imp—the very personification of dramatic displays of, well, everything."

"Be a parent, Lou, and *think of her*."

"I think of her all the time. She is always in my thoughts." He thumped a fist over the right side of his chest. "I hold her here."

"In the large cavity in your chest where a heart should be?"

"Now *that* was uncalled for." Lou crossed to Naomi and curled an arm around her shoulders. "Fear not, my dear girl. I will make this problem go away completely. You'll see." With that, he disappeared.

Ciaran rubbed at the back of his head. "I could be wrong, but I don't think he intends to listen to us."

Naomi puffed out a breath. "No. No, neither do I."

"Thanks to Lou," Jolene began stiffly, "we're unlikely to get the address of the monastery from the cleric. I'll question him regardless, but it isn't likely to get me anywhere. Even under threats of torture, he'll protect this person he's convinced is an angel."

"He did give us a few clues to go on," Beck reminded her. "He said that the monastery was over an hour's drive away. That means it's approximately sixty miles from here, though I'm not sure in what direction. He also said it was near a ghost town. There are several in Nevada, but I think there are only two that are roughly in a sixty-mile radius from here. I'd have to check."

Jolene folded her arms. "We might be able to locate it using these clues, though we're only likely to get an approximate idea of where it might be. Damn Lou for showing up. Things were going so well. We could right now be in possession of all the answers if he hadn't appeared and messed everything up."

Naomi pulled a face. "I feel like I should apologize for him."

"You certainly don't have to make apologies on his behalf," Jolene stated.

"Do you think he really will aim to kill every last dark practitioner he can find here in Vegas?" asked Ciaran.

Jolene drew in a breath through her nose. "Yes, I do. And I'm feeling quite certain that he won't be in the least bit subtle about it."

What with how the start of her evening had played out, Naomi had briefly considered canceling her hookup with Luka. She wouldn't exactly make the best company—too tired, too distracted, too annoyed that Lou had foiled their plan.

Her entity had pushed her not to cancel, feeling there was a very good chance that Luka could fuck the emotions badgering her *right* out of her system. Which was something of a valid point. And really, Naomi didn't feel like staying at home after what had happened. She wanted to get out of there and *breathe*.

Hence why she was pulling up outside the huge black iron gates of his estate with Konstantin behind her in his own vehicle.

Her nerves doing a little dance, she telepathed Luka. *I'm outside.*

Moments later, the gates swung open slowly. She drove forward, following a driveway that was so thickly bordered by trees she couldn't see anything beyond it. Only when she reached the courtyard did the tree tunnel end.

Naomi parked her car and slid out, as did Konstantin. The expansive and perfectly maintained grounds were as impressive as Luka's home. While Naomi wasn't particularly wowed by luxury, she could certainly appreciate the timeless elegance of the building before her. *And* the man who right then opened the front door.

Countless times she'd had him in her bed, and yet there were still occasions when the sheer impact of him struck her hard. He was just so tall and solid and entirely too fuckable. Right then, he pinned her with a dark, scorching-hot gaze that made a cord of excitement wind its way through her. Yeah, she'd been right to come here.

She stalked up the path. "Hey."

"Naomi," he greeted, the word somehow sounding like pure sex.

The twins came up behind him and piled out of the house, giving her a brief nod, then walked off to join Konstantin.

As she stood before Luka, his scent wrapped around her and their ever-present chemistry ballooned.

He opened the door wider, silently indicating for her to enter.

She'd only taken a single step inside the house when he caught her mouth with his. He didn't ravish it as she would have liked. He indulged in a few teasing little sips before pulling back, sheer want darkening his eyes, sparking a wickedly carnal need to flicker to life in her lower stomach.

"Drink?" he offered.

After the evening she'd so far had ... "Sure, why not?"

She followed him into the den and over to the bar, which was all shiny black marble. Leaning against the low counter behind it, she watched as he poured them both a whiskey, admiring the bunching and rippling of muscle beneath his shirt. The sight almost made her release a happy sigh.

She gratefully took a tumbler from him. "Thanks." Sexual tension simmered in the air as they each drank from their glass, their gazes connected the entire time. Her demon stretched, basking in the staticky tension.

"I wouldn't have originally pegged you for a whiskey drinker."

She recalled how he'd been surprised the first time he'd offered her a drink and she'd chosen whiskey. "I get it from my stepfather." She took another sip from her glass, and Luka's eyes dipped down to her throat, watching as she swallowed. Those same eyes then lifted to settle on her mouth, staring at it so hungrily her belly clenched.

"What did you do with yourself today?" she asked.

His gaze returned to hers. "Same as usual. Met with my sentinels. Dealt with lair issues. Tended to ... other matters."

Illegal matters, she thought.

He took another swig of his whiskey. "And you?"

Naomi hesitated. She couldn't tell him that she'd spent most of the day painting. He might wonder if she was one of the ghost artists who worked with Tobe. It wouldn't be much of a stretch, would it? Especially considering the PI had badgered her.

"It wasn't a trick question, Naomi," he said, his lips quirking.

"I allowed myself a day of relaxation." Not untrue. Painting *did* relax her. Really, things had been going great until the freaking clerics made an appearance.

His eyes sharpening, Luka tilted his head slightly. "What's wrong?"

She meant to wave away the question, but he cast her a pointed look.

"You could say *nothing*, but it would be a lie," he softly accused. "We both know it."

Inwardly, Naomi sighed. While she didn't regret that she'd let this far-too-astute male into her life, she still couldn't help but find his level of perceptiveness irritating at times. "Things just weren't as relaxing as I'd intended them to be." *Understatement.*

He stepped closer, blocking out the rest of the room, as if he might shield her from the world. "Why not? What happened?"

She exhaled heavily. "Something that ... It wasn't necessarily *bad*." The clerics had taken the bait, several more were now dead, and Baby Face had confirmed their suspicions. But she hadn't learned enough from him to put a fast end to this bullshit, and now *Lou* was involved. "It just didn't go as I'd hoped."

"You can't give me more details than that?"

"Not in a way that would satisfy you." Because she'd have to leave out too much, which meant ... "It'd only lead you to have more questions."

"Questions you can't answer?"

"Yes." Taking another sip of her drink, she lifted a finger. "And before you think to complain, just remember that I didn't whine when you failed to cough up deets on the 'other matters' you mentioned earlier."

He lowered his head. "I respect your need to guard your secrets, Naomi, but I'm not fine with anything that puts that look on your face," he added, softly tapping her cheek.

If he wasn't careful, she'd start to wonder if he cared. Something she almost said aloud as a joke, but then he was talking again.

"If you tell me what's wrong, I'll fix it."

Ugh, did he have to be so protective and supportive? It felt way too nice, and made it harder for Naomi to blow him off. Something that amused her entity. "The offer is appreciated. I'll bear it in mind."

"Be sure that you do."

"Now can we move on from this? I came here hoping you'd distract me and improve my mood. So far, that isn't happening."

Luka stayed silent for a long moment, watching her carefully. "All right, we'll move on. Just know that I'm here if you need me, even if only as a sounding board."

"A sounding board? Pfft."

"Why *pfft*?"

"I'm not dumb, Luka. You'd never be content with simply *knowing* the issue."

"I wouldn't?"

"No. You only offered to be a sounding board in the hope that I'd tell you what you want to know. Then you would have gone meddling in whatever ways you felt necessary."

Luka felt his lips bow up slightly. "Maybe." In truth, there were no maybes about it. The idea that something—or someone—might be bothering her grated on him and his demons. "But only because I want you safe and well." He paused. "Do you have another obsessed admirer on your hands? Is that what's wrong?" Konstantin hadn't reported that any males were giving her issues or tailing her, but ...

"No, nothing like that. While we're on the subject of admirers, though, are you still planning to release Iain tomorrow?"

"Yes." Though with some reluctance. "I could have done it days ago, really. The effects of your song have fully worn off, and he readily admits that he was under its thrall. But I wanted to give it a little extra time." It wasn't so easy to free a prisoner who might wish harm to a person who mattered to you. Iain had assured him that he bore Naomi no ill will, but Luka suspected there might be some resentment there.

"He's definitely back to his normal self?"

"He is." Luka drained his glass and then set it on the counter. "His demon wouldn't have retreated if that were not the case."

"True," she conceded with a slight tilt of her head.

"He wanted to apologize to you in person, but I made it clear that he's not to go anywhere near you. He swore to me that he'd stay away. Still, as I've already told you, Konstantin will remain your guard until we're all satisfied that Iain will no longer be an issue for you."

"I don't foresee him making waves again, but I'm not going to put up a protest."

Taking her empty tumbler from her, Luka placed it beside his own. "Good. It would have made no difference. I'm protective of what's mine. And you" —he snaked a hand around her throat, watching her pupils dilate— "are very much mine."

Luka sipped at her mouth once, twice. Her lips parted beneath his, and he swept his tongue inside. He snagged her nape as he feasted on her, slow and thorough, licking at every crevice of her mouth.

For him, kissing was usually a means to an end. The beginning of a dance. Not something he found himself moved by on any level. But the taste of Naomi made a wave of visceral lust wash over him and torch his insides.

Growling, he snatched her by her hips and propped her on the counter. He stepped between her legs, saying, "Let's see if you did as I asked." He skimmed his hand along her inner thigh, pushing up her dress as he went ... and his fingertips brushed over her bare pussy. "No underwear. Good girl."

"I'm always good."

"Only when you want to be. Which you usually do, because you're all about instant gratification and don't like to be made to wait for what you need. Other times, you test my patience for the fuck of it. Belial happens to enjoy those occasions."

"Because it then has reasons to spank me?"

"It really doesn't feel it needs a reason to do that, but yes. Your ass turns such a pretty shade of red."

"So will your face if Belial ever takes shit too far." Naomi shivered at the low chuckle that breezed out of Luka. The wicked sound made static sparks skip along her skin, raising the little hairs there.

"Noted." He started stroking her pussy, his finger sliding between her folds, rubbing her clit, circling her opening, squeezing her folds together so they in turn squeezed her clit.

Oh God. His touch was soft yet ruthlessly demanding,

insisting on her submission. It also held a taunting edge, keeping her in a state of suspense. "Is this you punishing me for not being totally forthcoming with you?" she asked, her breathing a little choppy.

He looked surprised by the question. "This isn't a punishment."

"Then why are you dragging it out?"

"Because I can," he whispered, lathering some of her slickness over her clit. "You're mine to do with as I wish. And right now, I wish to tease the fuck out of you."

Wonderful.

He traced the snake on her throat with his tongue. "I do like this brand."

Just this morning, she'd found herself admiring the sight of it in the mirror ... and her inner smile had died when she thought of how she'd eventually have to watch it fade. It was the downside of such possessive marks. You got to literally *see* the entity's interest in you dim little by little, until eventually it was gone.

"What is it?" he asked, his eyes narrowing slightly.

"I don't want to tell you." She groaned as his finger sank inside her.

"Why not?"

"It'll give you too much power."

His eyes gleamed. "I like power."

Yeah, she knew that.

"Tell me," he coaxed, lazily thrusting his finger in and out of her.

"Don't wanna."

"*Naomi.*"

She shook her head, bucking as a second finger slipped inside her.

"Tell me." He curved his fingers and pressed them on just the right spot, but he didn't rub, didn't thrust, didn't do anything.

He just kept them right there like that, both a promise and a threat. "What were you thinking about?"

A low whimper slipped out of her. "That I'll have to watch the brand fade at some point. We both know it'll happen sooner or later. Probably sooner. You once told me that your demons tire of things and people easily. And, well, I'm not gonna like it much." Neither would her entity, in truth, but it didn't want him or his demons to know that yet.

Long seconds ticked by as he stared at her, his gaze unreadable. Then his fingers began to move, rubbing over that hypersensitive spot inside her. "None of them are anything close to bored with you. Nor am I."

She moaned as he took her mouth again with blatant possession. Their tongues tangled as he kept pumping his fingers into her, driving her closer and closer to an orgasm.

Then it hit.

She arched. Moaned. Bucked. Scratched at him.

The release subsided, and she sagged against him—panting and shaking, her inner muscles still fluttering around his fingers.

Warm lips settled at her ear. "If I wore your demon's brand, I wouldn't like knowing I'd have to watch it grow fainter; that it would one day vanish as if it had never been."

Drawing back to meet his eyes, she studied them closely; found only sincerity there. "So we're even."

"We're even."

CHAPTER FIFTEEN

Parked outside her mother's psychic shop the following Saturday, Naomi downed the last of her smoothie. Located not far from a small theme park, the shop wasn't close to Tia's home. The woman didn't drive—her license had been revoked again—so Alfie generally took her to and from work. Today, however, he had car trouble. As Naomi was due to meet Tobe at a jewelry store near the shop, she'd offered to pick her mother up.

She screwed the cap on her empty bottle and stuffed it into a cupholder. Tobe wanted help selecting a birthday gift for his grandmother, who collected brooches like it was her purpose in life.

Really, when it came to demons, you couldn't go wrong with any kind of jewelry so long as it was shiny. Even if, like Naomi, you weren't a person who wore bling a lot, your inner entity would still go gaga for the stuff.

She nabbed her keys and slipped out of the car. A breeze

whispered over her, cool and refreshing. Though it was early evening, plenty of pedestrians dotted the sidewalk—strolling, window-shopping, or stopping to chat with others.

Using her key fob, Naomi locked her vehicle. She waved at Konstantin, who'd parked a few car spaces behind her. She'd been keeping a close lookout for signs of any other tails, but she hadn't spotted any. There'd been no more peeps from the *Lemures*, but a few notable things had occurred . . .

Several well-known hangouts for dark practitioners had exploded—*thanks, Dad. Subtle is thy middle name*.

Jolene had approached a former dark practitioner who—anxious to compensate for the misdeeds he'd committed in his younger years—acted as a consultant for all things dark magick. He'd examined the cleric's sword and explained that it was bespelled to psychically weaken its victims, making them easier to defeat. *Lovely*.

Luka had released Iain, who had so far completely avoided Naomi. Still, Tobe had taken it upon himself to confront the psi-demon and issue some warnings of his own. Iain had admitted that his obsession with Naomi had been a result of her song and had claimed he was deeply embarrassed. He'd also assured Tobe that he had no intention of making contact with her.

Here's to hoping.

Naomi crossed the street and strode toward Tia's shop. A black awning shaded the storefront. Two red neon signs hung in the window—one saying *Psychic Readings*, while the slightly smaller one below it said *Open*.

Oblivious humans and demons popped into the store all the time, either for consultations, out of curiosity, or to buy merchandise.

Tia was always available to do readings. The angel cards, crystals, and supposed palm readings were all for show, though.

Really, she used a mix of her exceptional intuition and her demonic ability to pick up surface thoughts. Some people had natural shields that kept their thoughts protected—Naomi was one of them —but her mother was still damn good at reading her.

Naomi had spent a lot of time here as a kid, since her mother had liked to do the whole "And this is my daughter—she inherited the family gift" thing. Tia would telepathically tell Naomi something about the human, such as what they were thinking at that moment. Naomi would then repeat it aloud and watch the client's face go slack in wonder.

Maybe she should have felt bad about fooling all those people, but Tia had made it seem like a game, so she'd initially found it fun. Later, though, it hadn't felt right. Her mother had said, "We're part of an imp-dominated lair, sweetie—we never do what feels right."

As a kid, watching her mother work, Naomi had admired how well Tia could read people. Even as an adult, she still found it impressive. Tia took in every micro-expression; noticed anything about a person's voice or body language that gave away details. But it had been somewhat annoying for Naomi when she was a teenager who wanted to sneak off and do unadvisable things, because it was hard to get a lie past Tia.

Naomi pushed open the shop door, causing the chimes there to jingle. The smells of herbs, scented candles, and incense tickled her nose.

The color scheme was all blues, purples, and pinks. Framed ethereal pictures hung on the walls. Soft mystical music played low in the background. A seating area was set directly across from the cluttered cashier's desk. The lighting was gentle—a combination of flickering candles and old lamps that featured purple shades.

Various merchandise was scattered around—some in glass cases, some on shelves, some near or on the cashier's desk. There were also candles, crystals, angel statues, books, herb packets, pendulums, charm bracelets, essential oils—on and on it went.

Naomi blinked in surprise at the sight of Tobe leaning over the desk, smiling at the blonde imp behind it, who wore a gypsy-style dress. "I thought we were meeting up at the jewelry store," she said to her anchor.

He gave a dry look. "Oh hi, Nome. Yes, I *am* fine, thanks."

Naomi rolled her eyes. "I know you're fine. I spoke to you, like, two hours ago when we agreed to meet up."

"Yeah, and I knew you'd be late—which you are, in case you haven't noticed—so I figured I'd wait for you here. It gives me an excuse to chat up Yuliya."

The receptionist grinned at him. "You never need an excuse to do that, honey." She looked at Naomi. "Don't let him give you crap for being late. He walked in here no more than thirty seconds before you."

He gaped at her. "I can't believe you threw me under the bus like that."

The blonde gave an unapologetic shrug. "Sisters before misters."

A snort popped out of Naomi. "Is my mom around?"

"She's in the back room getting ready to close up," replied Yuliya. She switched off the music. "You can go in there if you want; her last client of the day just left."

"Great."

"I'll wait here," said Tobe, his eyes fixed on Yuliya like she'd disappear if he looked away.

Smiling to herself, Naomi made a beeline for the back room. Pushing aside the privacy curtain, she slipped inside. Dressed in her usual bohemian getup, her mother was in the process of blowing out the candles that were set around the room. "Are you ready, Madam Tia?"

Her mother cast her a smile. "Almost. Thanks for picking me up, sweetheart."

"Not a problem. You wiped my ass for, what, two whole years? The least I can do is give you a ride home when you need it."

Tia chuckled. "Well, when you put it like that..." She crossed to the circular cloth-covered table that had center-stage. "I haven't spoken to you much this week, so I didn't get a chance to ask... How are things going with you and Luka?"

Naomi gave a blasé shrug. "Fine."

"Just fine?" Tia prodded as she began pushing the chairs closer to the table.

"Just fine."

"Huh. Must be something else that has you looking so content. The resting bitch face has gone. You're a woman who is quite clearly satisfied with her life—I can tell. That man is doing *something* right. Maybe you should let this one stick around."

Naomi felt her brows slide together. "What do you mean 'let'?"

"I mean that you have a habit of cutting men loose as soon as things get serious." Tia reached across the table to snatch up the pile of angel cards sitting near the crystal ball. "You avoid emotional intimacy. Yes, you have secrets to guard. But that isn't the only reason you do it."

Feeling a little defensive, Naomi folded her arms. "Oh, it's not?" she asked, snippy.

"No. Throughout your life, no matter your age, you've been bombarded with male attention. All sirens have that problem. There are enough sickos in this world that grown men are attracted to us when we're *children*. We have to deal with them trying to stroke our hair, lure us closer, or watch us play in the park. It makes our skin crawl. Makes us feel preyed on. Makes us feel dirty and objectified."

Naomi ground her teeth, recalling those occasions. Recalling the greedy gleam in the eyes of those men. "It must have been harder for you. You must have picked up some of what they were thinking, even seen flashes of what they were imagining."

Tia swallowed, slipping the angel cards into a velvet pouch. "I did, but it doesn't make my experiences worse than yours. Things get no better for sirens as we grow. It affects all our interpersonal relationships. Your friends distanced themselves from you when you were teenagers. One did it because it creeped her out that her dad would stare at you. Another did it because her boyfriend was so affected by your song. A third did it to please the jealous little bitches who bullied you simply because they didn't like that you took away the male attention they sought."

Naomi shoved back the memories that tried surfacing. Memories of how her friends had turned on or away from her. Memories of those previous friends laughing at what the bullies said or did.

"All of that impacts a person's growth," Tia went on. "Even when you were a kid, it made you try to fade into the background. You didn't want to be seen. Which hasn't changed. You won't even claim credit for your work because you don't want the publicity."

"Yeah, well."

"Hey, I'm not giving you grief here, honey. I get it." Tia placed the pouch of cards in her storage chest. "We reach a point where we loathe attention so much that we feel uncomfortable whenever we have it. Especially since it's mostly sexual. So when a guy comes along who, unlike those who came before him, has a genuine interest in us as a *person* . . . we don't know what to do with it.

"I had not one clue how to deal with Alfie seeing past me being a siren. I'd come to expect betrayal, resentment, and abandonment. I expected it from him as well, and I almost pushed him away because of it."

Naomi frowned. "I didn't know that."

"Thankfully he's a patient and perseverant man who doesn't give up on those he cares for. The point is that I was like you once upon a time—I walked into every relationship expecting it to go south. Expect *more*, Naomi. You deserve more. Reach for it."

"You act like Luka's offered me more and I threw the offer back in his face. He hasn't."

"But he might. I've been assured by multiple people that you have his focus in a way no other woman has."

Naomi's pulse spiked. "What people?"

"I don't name my sources." Tia's gaze briefly lowered to Naomi's throat. "You've worn that brand for weeks now. It hasn't faded the tiniest bit. And my guess is that it's not the only one on your body. Ah, I'm right."

"I didn't say that."

"You didn't have to—your expression answered for you. If there comes a point where he suggests taking things up a notch, don't reflexively back away."

Her mother talked as if it would be a natural thing for him to make such an offer. Talked like Luka would easily grow to want something permanent, but could he really give so much of himself to another person? Naomi wasn't sure. She didn't know if someone like him could ever really belong to anyone.

Her demon had the same doubts. Luka was just so solitary, so self-contained. And his mental walls were pure steel. There'd be no sneaking past them, chipping at them, or poking holes in them. He'd have to willingly lower them for her, and she wasn't certain he ever deliberately would.

"Your secrets are by no means small, but that doesn't mean he won't accept them," Tia added.

Naomi swallowed hard. "What if he can't, though? What if he found out and then couldn't look at me the same way?"

"Then we set him on fire. What else?"

A snicker popped out of her. "Yeah, what else. Now, if you're finished, I have shopping to do with Tobe. Get your shit so we can go."

"Only if you promise to think on all I've said."

"I'll think on all you've said." It would be hard not to.

Once her mom had grabbed her purse, Naomi switched off the lamp and then moved the curtain aside so they could both exit the room.

"Will it help if I say it in a different language?" she heard Tobe ask, his tone clipped.

Looking at the cashier desk, she noted he was having some sort of confrontation with a thin guy with a ponytail who wore rather flamboyant clothing.

"Will that make the words *finally* penetrate?" Tobe went on.

"You're being unreasonable," the stranger replied. "I'm only asking for a fucking name!"

"And I've told you too many times to count that you're never going to get it," Tobe pretty much growled. "If you'd just respected their wishes, they wouldn't have gotten annoyed by your persistence and then dropped you. This situation is of your own making."

Her scalp prickling in suspicion, Naomi telepathed her psimate. *Oh my God, is that Stefan?*

Tobe's mind bumped hers. *Yes.*

Naomi stilled. "Unreal," she hissed low.

Tia frowned. "What is it?" Her voice was equally quiet.

Naomi leaned into her and whispered, "See that guy Tobe is talking to? That's Stefan Brandt, the demon who hired a PI to ID me."

Tia's eyes widened a little. "Do you think he followed Tobe here?"

"Maybe. Either that or he spotted him when passing by and decided to take the opportunity to come talk to him." She and Tia headed down the hall toward the desk.

"I passed on my apologies through you," Stefan was saying.

"Only after threatening me didn't work," Tobe reminded him. "Then you had a damn PI bug my anchor. Do you really think I'm inclined to do anything for you at this point?"

"I called Phillips off," Stefan claimed.

"Bull*shit*. He quit after Luka Belinsky threatened him."

Stefan's eyes flickered. Yeah, the PI had quit all right.

The pair stopped arguing as Tia and Naomi neared them. Stefan's exasperation-filled gaze shifted to them but just as quickly returned to Tobe. He opened his mouth to speak . . . but didn't get the chance.

Tia got right up into his space. "Well, hello there, I'm Madam Tia. You're here for a reading, I'm guessing."

Stefan's brow furrowed. "Uh . . ."

"Unfortunately, the shop is about to close. But I suppose I can give you a free mini reading." She took his hand and turned it over. Running her finger along a line on his palm, she hummed. "You've had many relationships. Nothing lasting or serious. That will change, though. I can't see *when* she comes into your life, I just know that she will."

He tried stifling a smile that revealed he was a pure skeptic—something that Tia wouldn't fail to notice.

She tapped his palm. "See the way this line is curved and sloped? That tells me you are creative." Her eyes fogged over. "I see brushes in your hand. Paintbrushes. A studio with a window that has beautiful stained glass."

He double-blinked, his lips parting.

Naomi almost grinned. Tia was good at making people mentally reveal things. All she'd do was throw out a comment that would make them conjure up memories or scenes or images in their mind. Like now, when she'd told Stefan she saw him holding paintbrushes. He had unconsciously pictured his studio. According to Tobe, the guy *did* paint, he just wasn't all that great at it.

Tia hummed again thoughtfully. "You can be stubborn. Perhaps a little materialistic, though you can certainly afford to indulge that side of yourself." Her brow creased in concern. "I see a change there, though. You've lost ... something. I don't know what, but it's impacting your career. The money well may dry up if you're not careful."

His jaw tightened, and Naomi fought the urge to laugh. A quick look at Tobe confirmed he was experiencing that same urge.

"And here we have your life line. I—" Tia gasped abruptly, her expression turning horrified.

He glanced down at where she held his hand. "Uh, ow."

She loosened her grip. "I'm sorry, it's ... You need to get off the path you're on."

He went rigid. "Excuse me?"

"You're seeking something. An answer. A person, maybe?" She grabbed his upper arm, a sense of urgency plastered over her face. "You must stop. If you do not, *death will find you.*"

Honest to God, she sounded so convincing that even Naomi got the chills. Her inner demon thought the whole thing was hilarious.

Stefan pulled his arm free, eyeing her uncertainly. "I have to go." He spared Tobe one last *very* unhappy look and then scampered.

Naomi looked at her mother, who was dusting her palms together. "You enjoyed that, didn't you?"

"Loved it," said Tia.

"*I* loved it." Tobe bowed to the woman. "That was quite a performance. Brav-the-fuck-o."

"Whose name does he want?" Yuliya asked. "He was so careful with his word choices that I couldn't understand exactly who or what he was talking about."

Well of course Stefan had been careful. He wouldn't want the world to know that he used a ghost artist.

"Just one of my contacts," Tobe answered vaguely.

Naomi turned to him. "How long was he here?"

"He walked in shortly after you." *He's getting desperate, Nome*, Tobe telepathically added. *I'd admire his tenacity if it wasn't aimed my way.*

Do you think he followed you here?

Not sure. "Can we go do some jewelry shopping now? My grandmother has so many brooches it'll be hard to find her one that she doesn't already own. It ain't gonna be a quick process."

"We can go," Naomi told him. "Just as soon as you put back whatever merchandise you pocketed."

He put a hand to his chest. "You think I'd steal from my anchor's mom?"

"I think you'd steal from *your* mom, so why not mine? Besides, you do it without even noticing a lot of the time."

Tia sighed. "It's like a compulsion with imps. I think many of them are kleptomaniacs, because they don't even need half the shit they take. Tobe, either hand back what you swiped or lube yourself up to prepare for a thorough body search."

With a curse, he patted himself down, producing a spell candle, a mini figurine of a saint, a dreamcatcher keyring, and a tarot deck—all of which he seemed to conjure out of thin air.

Yuliya's jaw dropped. "But you were right in front of me

the whole time you were here. How did I not notice you take *anything?*"

"He's just that good," Naomi told her.

Tobe smirked. "Yeah, I'm that good."

CHAPTER SIXTEEN

Breezing through the doors of Infernal later that evening, Naomi glanced around. *Wow.*

She'd heard plenty about the gambling den, but she'd never actually been inside before. The rumors were evidently true—it was stylish and striking and inviting.

It also wasn't lacking in patrons. But then neither were any other gambling venues available for demons. Her kind became addicted to the rushes.

She knew where to find Luka—he'd given her clear directions to the VIP area when they'd telepathically chatted earlier today. Heading that way, she slowly wound through the various machines and tables.

Originally, they'd planned for her to go to his place. But, as it sometimes went, he'd gotten called away. Rather than them reschedule, he'd asked her to instead come to him. She'd agreed.

He'd make it worth her while for sure.

As Naomi approached the manned set of steps that led to the

VIP area, she gave the demon there her name and informed him that Luka was waiting for her. He confirmed it with someone through his earpiece and then unclipped the rope, allowing her to pass.

She'd no sooner reached the top step than she came face to face with Ella.

The redhead cast her a bright smile. "Oh, hi. Luka said you were coming. How're things with you?"

"Great. You?"

"Never better." Her brows slid together as her gaze dipped down to Naomi's neck. "What happened?"

"Hmm?"

"Some of your concealer is smudged, and I can make out a small bruise. Did someone hurt you?" Outrage flared in the incantor's eyes. "Luka's gonna *freak*."

Unlikely. "Luka has already seen it. Belial put it there, along with several other fingerprint brands that look like bruises."

Amusement chased away the ire in Ella's gaze. "Oh, I see. Belial's kind of a law unto itself."

"Yeah, I got that." It branded Naomi often, and the marks were never pretty. Welts, bites, stuff like that.

Ella edged forward. "If I wasn't in a rush, I'd ask you to give me the gossip on you and Luka."

Naomi felt her brow crease in surprise. "He's your anchor. Surely he talks to you."

"He's tight-lipped when it comes to a lot of things—you included, as it turns out. He won't even confirm any guesses I make."

"Sounds like he's just dicking with you."

"Hmm, maybe. Well, I have to go, or I'll be late for the movie; the girls will be waiting for me. I'd invite you to come along, but Luka would kill me if I managed to drag you away. Hey, you should come to our girls' night next Saturday at the Xpress bar. Originally it was only supposed to be me and Piper. Somehow, it became all her co-workers plus one of Knox's sentinels, Larkin."

Naomi pursed her lips. "Should be an interesting evening. I'm up for it."

Ella beamed at her. "Great! I'll get Khloë to pass on specifics once we have them."

Sensing the weight of someone's attention, Naomi looked to the side and saw a glowering waitress standing at the bar. "Is she glaring at you or me?"

Ella sighed. "Both, I expect. She tried to befriend me, but only because she wants to get in Luka's pants. He turned her down and told her to stay away from me. Also, he's now in *your* pants. Draya doesn't like any of that." The redhead flipped a hand. "Just ignore her. She isn't important."

"Here you are," said a gravelly, panty-dropping voice.

Naomi looked to see Luka almost on her. That easily, slivers of excitement rushed through her blood. Her system had quite simply come to associate him with mind-blowing pleasure. God, he had such sexual power over her body that it almost hurt.

Reaching her, he skimmed his fingertips up her bare arm and planted a soft kiss on her mouth. "You're late."

"Habit."

"I've noticed," he said, his hand clamping on her hip, heavy and blatantly possessive.

Guys had often touched her with possession—being a siren brought that trait out in them. But with Luka, it was more intense. Yet not creepy. Her demon had come to like it.

"Aw, you guys are cute," said Ella.

He frowned at his anchor. "I thought you'd left."

"I wanted to talk to Naomi a little first. I was just telling her how tight-lipped you are regarding her." She pouted. "It's not fair."

He shot her a look of mild exasperation. "Go home to your daughter and what's-his-name."

The redhead sighed. "I really wish you'd stop pretending you don't like Viper."

"It's no pretense, I assure you."

"Right," Ella drawled, all skepticism. "See ya later, Naomi. You both have a good night." She jogged down the steps and headed for the exit.

Naomi turned her attention back to Luka, almost sucking in a breath as he pinned her with a look so scorching it gave her goosebumps.

He leaned in and inhaled deeply. "You smell good."

"I try."

"You look good, too."

"Good enough to eat, if you catch my meaning?"

A slow, predatory smile curved his lips. "That'll come later, when we're alone in my office. For now, I need to be visible. There's a big fight happening in the basement. Issues are far less likely to crop up if members know I'm around."

"Issues like men so riled up from watching and betting on fights that they turn mean when they lose?"

"Something like that." Luka placed a hand on her back and guided her to an L-shaped sofa. A waitress appeared and took their orders before melting away just as fast. "How did your day go?"

"Fine."

"You have a tendency to overwhelm me with details," he deadpanned.

"There's nothing interesting to say, really. I woke. Ate breakfast." Painted a while. "Did some grocery shopping. Had lunch. Chilled out some. Ate dinner. Picked my mom up from work. Shopped a little with Tobe. Went home. Showered. Dressed. Dragged my ass here."

"Konstantin mentioned that your anchor got into an argument at your mom's store."

Freaking Chatty Cathy. "That was the guy who hired the PI. Your conversation with Daniel Phillips definitely did the trick, because he quit, so the client came straight to Tobe. It was no big scene, and he left pretty quickly. By the way, *your* anchor just invited me to go on a girls' night out with her and a bunch of females that includes Khloë and Harper Wallis."

"When and where?"

Naomi loved how he asked that with only curiosity. Her previous bed buddies and boyfriends hadn't liked her going out with friends; had wanted to keep an eye on her every moment, filled with a jealousy-induced paranoia that she'd betray them if left unwatched. They'd complained and made silly passive-aggressive comments. Luka didn't do any of that, and he was never upset if she had plans.

"The Xpress bar in the Underground next Saturday," she replied.

"I'll pick you up afterwards."

"Will you?"

"It makes sense, don't you think? You won't have the other girls to catch a ride with. Their mates collect them for the same reason I want to collect you: you'll be plastered, and I want to be sure you get home safely."

"To my home or your home?"

"Either works for me." Luka didn't care so long as he got to ensure she was safe. "Be warned that Ella may do her best to adopt you; make you her new best friend. You might find it an overwhelming experience." His psi-mate was a very strong personality. But then so was Naomi, though she possessed a quiet strength.

"So I won't have to worry about anchor-based jealousy?"

"No, Ella is very happy with Viper." Almost sickeningly happy, really.

"Was it hard for you when she took a mate?"

"In a sense. My issue was never that she committed to somebody—I wanted that for her. My issue was that she committed to Viper."

"You have something against fallen angels?"

Luka paused. The question had sounded idle, but he felt like his answer was somehow important. "No. I had something against my anchor being involved with someone who's rumored to be a very dangerous fallen archangel. And relationships between demons and fallen celestials aren't always known to end well. Things became slightly strained between us, but I came to realize that—in his way—he is good for her."

Her lips kicked up. "You say that so grudgingly."

Luka only grunted.

"It's pretty normal for demons to react weirdly to their anchors taking mates."

"It is, yes. In my case, it wasn't jealousy. That isn't an emotion I'm prone to feeling." Though, admittedly, Luka didn't like that another male had a deep, strong connection to Naomi. "You said that Tobe isn't jealous of your involvement with me. You two never slept together?" he asked, since it wasn't uncommon with anchors.

Naomi hesitated. "Did you and Ella ever cross platonic lines?"

Luka felt himself squint at her evasiveness. "You didn't answer my question."

"I will if you'll answer mine."

"We did it only once. It was a long time ago. Your turn."

Naomi's hand flexed slightly around her glass. "Tobe and I slept together a couple of times, but that was years ago."

As something very dark swirled low in Luka's belly, Dagon

rushed to the surface and complained, "The imp should not have touched you."

Her eyes widened. "Why not?"

"Because I do not like it."

"Luka slept with *his* psi-mate."

"Irrelevant."

Naomi felt a tired sigh ease out of her. Entities could sometimes operate on a whole other kind of logic. One that was often childlike in its entitlement.

"Did your demon touch him?" Dagon asked.

"No."

It studied her closely for a few moments. "You are telling the truth. Good. Never lie to me. I will always know."

She smirked. "No you won't. And that bothers you."

It grunted and then subsided, its black gaze quickly returning to Luka's own dark eyes.

"Dagon is a pure grump, huh," she muttered, amused.

Luka drank from his glass. "It feels chronically inconvenienced by life itself, so it's often in an unpleasant mood."

"Right now, it isn't the only one," she said as her peripheral vision was snagged by something. "That woman over there is giving you the stink eye. Like you betrayed her." It was making Naomi's demon want to throw something at her.

Luka's brow furrowed. "What woman?"

"The waitress at the bar. Ella said her name's Draya."

He looked close to sighing. "There was no betrayal. But in her view, some light flirtation was a firm promise that I'd be making a play at some point. She considers herself an injured party even though she admits that I did nothing to lead her on."

Naomi felt annoyance skitter through her. "It pisses me off when people do that. So many act like they're entitled to more from you just because you let them buy you a drink or joked around with them or whatever."

"You've had to deal with that?" he asked, a stiffness to his voice.

"Yup. Then I was often called a bitch or cock-tease for turning down what they offered. Everyone has the basic right to say no. I don't know why some people struggle to grasp that."

Anger glittered in his gaze. "Tell me who did that to you. Give me names. I'll deal with them."

"Kill them, you mean?"

"Same thing."

"No, it isn't. And it's a reminder that I should be careful when agreeing for you to 'deal' with things." She cast Draya a quick glance, finding the waitress now focused on the bartender. *Good.* "I would've thought she'd quit her job if she's so deeply unhappy with you."

"The tips here are good, especially in the VIP area," he said distractedly, his eyes tracking the movement of his fingers weaving into Naomi's hair. "Just ignore her."

"That's what Ella said."

"You should listen to her." Luka leaned into her. "Draya is my employee—nothing more. I don't want her. Why would I want other women when I have my pretty little plaything?"

"Why indeed." Naomi hummed into the light kiss he planted on her mouth. "Is she part of your lair? I only ask so I know what Prime might get upset with me if I end up scalping the bitch."

Luka's lips twitched. Oh, he thought she was joking? Yeah, no.

"She belongs to Maddox Quentin's lair," he clarified, referring to Raini's mate. "Have you always been part of Jolene's?"

"Yup. For which I'm glad. Imps aren't the most ethical of beings, but they're funny as fuck. My childhood was a happy one."

He angled his head slightly. "How long have your mother and stepfather been a couple?"

"Since I was a toddler."

"And your biological father?"

Don't tense, don't tense. "He pops in and out of the picture every few months," she said with a blasé shrug.

"I suspected he was around."

She stiffened a little at that. Forcing her muscles to relax, she asked, "Why?"

"A lot of people whose stepfather played a huge part in their lives would call him Dad, especially if they loved him. I can tell by your tone of voice when you speak of Alfie that you care for him deeply and consider him a father figure. But you refer to him by his name."

Naomi narrowed her eyes. "Have I mentioned before that I don't like how observant you are?"

Luka's lips curved. "No, but I picked up on that as well." He nuzzled the hollow beneath her ear. "I take it you'd rather not talk about your biological father."

"Maybe one day. Not today, though."

"All right." His gaze cruised intently over her face, sweeping over her cheekbones, tracing the outline of her mouth, delving deep into her eyes as if he might see all she hid from him.

She arched a brow. "Do you really have to stare all the time?" He truly did it a lot.

"No."

"Then you'll stop?"

"No."

Figures. "Is there a reason for that?"

"Yes." But he didn't elaborate.

Naomi exhaled a heavy breath. "I give up."

He stifled a smile and sipped at his drink. His eyes abruptly went out of focus, telling her he was having a telepathic chat.

She took a few swigs from her glass as she waited for him to finish.

Finally, his gaze sharpened on her. "I have to head down to the basement." He tossed back what remained of his drink and stood. "Wait for me here; I'll be no longer than a few minutes."

"No rush, I'll be fine." She admired his very fine ass as he walked away. Her demon made plans to grip it tight when they did the dirty later.

Not a bad idea.

To pass the time, Naomi did some people-watching in between taking more swigs of her drink. A drink she'd just finished when someone materialized in front of her. Instantly, her demon's mouth tightened. Because this particular someone was Draya.

The waitress smiled kindly and reached for Luka's empty glass. "Let me take this away for you." She carefully rested it on her tray. "You're from Jolene Wallis' lair. Noma, right?"

Oh Lord. Pretending that you didn't know someone's name was such an old and boring game. Deciding to toy with the bitch a little, Naomi grinned and said, "That's right."

Draya's pleasant smile trembled, irritation bleeding into her expression. She couldn't call Naomi on the lie without admitting that she *knew* her name wasn't Noma.

"Guess I shouldn't be surprised that you caught Luka's attention," she said, the slightest bite to her voice, as if it was taking everything she had not to snarl. "Every man's a sucker for a siren, huh?"

Naomi was no doubt supposed to feel upset at the implication that Luka wouldn't otherwise want her. *Snort.* "It makes it super easy to reel in guys."

Draya sucked in her cheeks slightly. "Well, heads-up—he doesn't keep women around for long, so enjoy it while it lasts."

"Oh, I am enjoying it. Very, *very* much, as it happens." Naomi handed the woman her empty glass. "I'm curious, though ... If you're so confident that I'll be out of the picture soon, why be bothered that I'm in it at all?"

Draya set the glass on the tray a little harder than necessary. "I didn't say it bothered me that you're around."

"You didn't have to. It's written all over you. Makes sense, really, since you have your eye on Luka. Yeah, I heard about it. As you stupidly see it, I'm in your way. Right?"

A condescending smirk curved Draya's lips. "If I wanted to lure him away from you, I could."

Naomi almost barked a laugh at the ridiculous claim. "That so?"

"It is." The waitress's grin died as Luka reappeared.

Naomi looked up at him, smiling. "She's funny. You didn't tell me that."

His expression dark, he bounced his gaze from her to Draya. "What's going on here?"

"Nothing," the waitress replied quickly. "I was just collecting empty glasses." With that, she hurried off.

"What did she say to you?" Luka clipped, staring down at Naomi.

"Nothing upsetting." It hadn't even been all that annoying. "It was more entertaining than anything else."

Seemingly unconvinced, he retook his seat and seized her gaze with his. "Tell me what she said."

Persistent bastard. "She merely advised me to make the most of my sexual time with you because you switch partners often ... and she claimed she could lure you away from me if she chose to do so."

Those inky-black eyes narrowed. "Did she now?" he asked, the words a little rough.

"As I said, it wasn't upsetting. I already knew that you kept your arrangements short and sweet. As for her latter claim, well, I don't believe that for a second. You told me that you didn't want her."

"And I don't," he verified. "What I do want is to inform her that she's to stay away from you in future."

"Can you put a pin in that? She probably approached me hoping that you'd pull her on it so that she'd then have your attention." Naomi leaned into him. "Don't give it to her, give it to me." She nipped his lower lip.

His pupils dilated. "Oh, I'll be giving you more than simply my attention."

"The question is when. Help a girl get herself some, would you?"

Mirth lit his expression. "Always in such a rush to get my dick in you. I suppose I should be flattered."

"Be flattered in your office. I'm good to go. So hold off on the warn-Draya-to-behave talk, yeah?"

With a long, put-out sigh, he stood and held out his hand. "Fine, I'll have one of my sentinels speak with her instead so I can go fuck you. But I have to say I'm feeling very used right now."

Naomi felt a smile tug at her lips. "Oh, you made a funny. I didn't think you could. Go, you."

CHAPTER SEVENTEEN

"Why do you always talk about nursery rhymes when you're smashed?" Devon griped, plopping a thin napkin over a condensation ring on the table.

Khloë's spine snapped straight, but then it promptly wilted as she swayed. Setting down her colorful cocktail, she glared at the hellcat beside her and lifted a finger. "A, I ain't smashed. Two, I don't always mention them. And before you try to argue that, *don't* try to argue that. Last of all" —her brows flitting together, she looked across the table at Larkin— "what was I talking 'bout before?"

Dipping her hand into a bowl of pretzels she'd swiped from the bar, Larkin weakly shrugged one shoulder. "Something about a dude called Humphrey sitting on a wall. I wasn't really listening, to be honest."

Khloë gasped, slapping a hand to her chest. "Why wouldn't you listen to me? I have such intriguing, thought-provoking, fascinating things to say."

"When?" Devon challenged.

The imp cast her yet another glare. "Every damn second."

Resting her head on the hellcat's shoulder, Harper snorted at her cousin. "Five minutes ago, you claimed we're all stuck in a reality TV show watched by aliens from Mars."

"Venus," corrected Raini, who had her feet up on Harper's lap.

The sphinx raised her head and looked at Raini. "What?"

"She said they're on Venus," the blonde elaborated. "I know 'cause I remember mentally chewing over whether Venus was a Greek goddess or a Roman goddess."

"Roman," Naomi told her.

Raini pointed a plastic drink stirrer at her. "Gracias."

"What does *any* of that have to do with little ole Humpty?" demanded Khloë.

Nabbing a pretzel from Larkin's bowl, Piper frowned at the imp. "Don't you mean Humphrey?"

"*No*." Groaning, Khloë turned to Naomi. "They don't listen to me, Nome," she whined. "It's almost like they're not interested in anything I say."

Naomi patted her shoulder. "It's not that they aren't interested—"

"It is," objected Devon, straight-faced. "It absolutely is."

Khloë flipped her the finger. "Fuck off home to your evil spawn."

Sitting up straight, Devon let out a dramatic horrified gasp. "You take that back. Anaïs is not evil."

Khloë pursed her lips. "We could go with 'callous'. 'Homicidal'. 'Princess of darkness'."

Ella almost choked on her drink, shooting Naomi a look of gratitude as she lightly pounded a fist on the redhead's back.

Devon leaned toward the imp. "Anaïs is *not* evil."

"It doesn't have to be a bad thing," Khloë told her.

The hellcat's brows drew together. "How could it *not* be a bad thing?"

Khloë shook her head. "You're so closed-minded."

Snorting to herself, Naomi idly glanced around. The Xpress bar was something of an upscale hot spot here in the Underground. She wasn't terribly fond of the neon strobe lights, but she otherwise liked the place. The DJ was class, the vibe was upbeat, and the drinks were good, albeit potent.

Occasional laughs or shouts rang out, piercing the blasting music. Smells were plentiful—perfume, cologne, beer, spirits, citrus. Every table and booth was crowded, as was the dance floor. Many people sat on the stools lining the long bar, including Konstantin. She'd invited him to join them at the table, but he'd politely declined.

Admittedly tipsy, she currently had a nice buzz going on. Felt all warm and floaty and tingly.

She took a swig from her highball glass, frowning as she realized . . . "It's empty. Crap."

Khloë slid a small glass toward her. "Have another shot."

Larkin grimaced at Naomi. "I wouldn't recommend 'em unless you like the taste of paint stripper."

"You've tasted paint stripper?" Khloë jerked back. "Ew. Ain't gonna lie, that's just weird—and I have a super high tolerance for weird."

Larkin tossed another pretzel into her mouth, her hand so unsteady she almost missed. "That's easy to sense. I mean, you don't think of yourself or Teague as odd. Which is like *whoa*."

"How can you call him that? He's your mate."

"*Still* an odd motherfucker."

Devon cocked her head at Larkin as she cut in, "I would never have pictured you with someone like Teague, but you two suit so well."

Larkin's face softened. "Aw. Samesies with you and Tanner. A hellcat and a hellhound? I wouldn'ta seen that coming."

Ella nudged Naomi gently. "I remember the times I'd go out for drinks with the girls before I met Viper. Being the only unmated female at the table made me feel a little excluded."

Hearing the question there, Naomi assured her, "It doesn't affect me one way or the other."

"Probably 'cause you're not exactly single," mused Ella. "I know you and Luka ain't in a full-on relationship, but I hope that changes. He's different with you. And so stingy with details when I ask him about you! As if he's, like, possessive of them or something."

"He's pretty elusive in general." But then so was Naomi herself.

"Yeah, he doesn't connect with people easily. It's like there's this wall between him and the rest of the world. I think his father put it there with all his 'let's prepare you for being a crime boss/Prime of a lair' lessons."

Luka hadn't spoken to Naomi of his upbringing. She'd only touched on the subject once, backing off on sensing it was a topic that he preferred to avoid. She didn't get the feeling that there might be some trauma there, just that he was especially private when it came to his family.

Ella bit into a cherry. "He was groomed to be hard. To make tough decisions. To be as ruthless as any demonic crime boss and Prime needs to be. Nobody taught him how to be part of something meaningful. So he hops from shallow arrangement to shallow arrangement, never seeing what he's missing. It makes me super sad."

Naomi raked her teeth over her lower lip. "I don't like to think of him having been mostly alone all these years, but it's his comfort zone."

"Oh, for sure. They don't come more solitary than Luka. But

he made room for me in his life, and then for Lily. Seems to me that he's making room for you, too."

Naomi pulled a face.

"You don't get that feeling?"

"It's hard to tell with Luka. I feel like he and I have somehow stumbled into a situationship. It's not an arrangement, it's not a fling, it's not a relationship. It's something, but nothing I can really define."

Ella gave a slow nod. "I think I get what you're trying to say. Are you hoping that the two of you will build on that?"

"Call me a coward, but I'm not examining *any* of what I feel too closely." If she did, if she learned that she'd officially grown to want more from Luka, Naomi might well shit her pants. Because what man could realistically accept all that she hid?

"No, I get that. It sometimes feels easier to just let things flow and see where it takes you; to not worry about the destination and just enjoy the journey. I did that with Viper. It—" Ella cut off as a fist slammed on the table.

Devon hissed at Khloë. "*Dammit, woman, my child is not evil!*"

The imp gave her a look of pity. "Saying it won't make it true, kitty."

Devon tried lunging at her, tipping over two glasses, sending the contents spilling across the table.

Naomi jumped to her feet—and promptly staggered—but not fast enough to avoid the spill. She gasped at the shock of cold liquid soaking through her red dress. "Crap."

Harper cursed, nudging Devon. "*Now* look what you did."

The hellcat flushed, righting the glasses. "I'm sorry, Naomi. Super, super sorry."

Naomi groaned as she peered down at the dubious dark stain right over her crotch area. "I look like I peed myself."

"Here." Ella handed her some napkins.

"Thanks." Naomi dabbed at the stains, but the napkins were too thin to help. Sighing, she balled them up and plonked them onto the table. "I'm gonna go clean up in the restroom."

"I'm really, really sorry," Devon repeated.

"Did you see how she made a grab for my throat? It's where Anaïs gets it from," Khloë mumbled. She and the hellcat then went back to bickering.

Naomi shrugged her way through clusters of people. Along the way, she glanced at Konstantin, who looked close to laughing at the state of her.

"Bastard," she mouthed.

He did laugh, then.

He also slid off his stool to follow her.

With a sniff, she ignored him as she disappeared down the hallway that led to the restrooms. She almost pouted when she discovered there was a long queue—something she should have anticipated really. It was a good ten minutes before she even made it inside. By that point, the stain was unsalvageable.

Ugh.

She dried the crotch area of her dress as best she could with the hand dryer so she at least wouldn't look like she'd had an accident. Once she'd washed away the sticky feeling from her hands, she exited the restroom and found Konstantin leaning against a wall further down the hallway.

The bastard *still* looked on the verge of laughing.

She threw him a dirty look as they headed back into the main area. He made his way over to a stool at the counter while she shouldered her way through the crowd.

A curse burst out of her as someone on her left stood on her foot. He quickly apologized and edged back. She gave him an "it's fine" smile and turned away ... only to realize that the person now directly in front of her was Iain.

Ah, hell.

He halted, his eyes going almost comically wide. "Naomi," he breathed. "Shit."

On high alert, her demon pushed close to the surface of her skin, ready to take over and attack if Iain gave the *slightest* indication that he meant Naomi harm.

Panicked, he scrubbed a hand down his face and then threw up both palms. "I know how this must look, I do, but I didn't follow you here." He licked his lips nervously. "My cousin asked me to meet up with him; I swear, I had no clue you were here."

Hearing the honesty in his voice, she said, "It's fine, Iain."

He didn't seem to hear her. "I *swear it*, Naomi, I'm not lying."

"I believe you," she assured him.

He paused. "You do?"

"Yes."

Air seemed to gush out of his lungs in relief. "Good." He scratched at his nape, awkward. "Listen, I ... I'm sorry. For everything I said and did over the past several months."

Naomi didn't respond. Both she and her entity were watching him intently, not liking the hint of desire in his gaze that he couldn't suppress, or the note of resentment mingled in with it.

"When I look back on how I acted, it feels surreal. Like it was a dream. Because those things I insisted on believing despite all evidence to the contrary ... I just don't see how I couldn't have seen the truth." He swallowed hard. "I wasn't myself."

"I know." She shrugged. "Apology accepted."

He gave her a tremulous smile. "Thank you. I appreciate it."

Konstantin materialized, fixing a hard glare on Iain.

His throat bobbing, the psi-demon backed away from her. "I'll, uh, I'll see you both around." He melted into the crowd.

Konstantin looked down at her. "What did he say?"

"He swore that he hadn't followed me here, and he apologized for how he acted when caught up in my song," she replied. "That's it."

The guard gave her a quick head-to-toe inspection. "You all right?"

"My dear Kon, it isn't the first time I've come face to face with a previously obsessed suitor, and it likely won't be the last."

"It's *Konstantin*."

Naomi smiled. "I know." She made her way back to her table, finding that the mess had been cleared up – *and* that Piper had fallen asleep. Aw.

Staring into her glass like she was trying to read tea leaves, Ella said, "There's something in my drink. I think it's alive."

Naomi peered into the glass. "Looks like a cherry stem."

"Could be a bug, though," Khloë chimed in. "Ooh, Ella, it could have had babies in your glass, and you could have *drunk* them."

"Hit her," Ella told Devon, who promptly obliged. The redhead grinned. "Thanks."

Devon's lips curved. "Any time. *Really*."

Naomi nabbed a stray shot from the tray and knocked it back. Yup, tasted like ass. It worked a treat, though. The alcohol went right to her head and brought back the buzz she'd lost at seeing Iain.

Ella eyed her curiously. "Something's wrong."

"I guess I'm a little irritated," Naomi admitted.

"How come?" asked the redhead.

"Iain's here." Naomi relayed her little conversation with him.

Ella's eyes narrowed. "Do you buy that it's a coincidence he's here?"

"Yes. But I don't know if I buy that he's sorry about what he did." Her demon certainly didn't. Could they really blame him for that, though, when it was only natural he wouldn't feel that the fault lay squarely with him? It wasn't like he *willingly* got ensnared by her song. But it wasn't *her* fault either—she couldn't help what she was.

"Well, coincidence or not, I don't believe I'm wrong in thinking that Luka will show up *any* moment."

Naomi frowned. "Why?"

"Konstantin will have told him what happened."

"Yeah, but Iain hasn't done anything."

"I don't mean Luka will come here for him. I mean he'll come here to check on you; make sure you're okay."

"He might telepathically reach out to—"

"Nope, he'll show up. And he'll probably take the opportunity to cozy up to you right where Iain can see. He'll want to get the message fully across that you're in *his* bed now, just in case Iain gets any dumb ideas."

Naomi snatched the last shot from the tray and downed it—again, the alcohol went straight to her head. She double-blinked as her head swam. "There'd be no point in doing something like that. This place is packed. Iain likely wouldn't even notice Luka's here."

"He would definitely notice, because he's looking right at you."

Naomi stilled. "What?"

"Yup. Don't look now. Don't give him the satisfaction of knowing you're talking about him. He's not close, but he's in a prime position that gives him a clear view of our table. It's hard to read his expression because of the dim lighting, so I can't say if he looks feverish and your song might have him in its thrall again."

"I'd need to be around him for at least an hour for that to happen. I don't intend for it to *ever* happen."

Khloë leaned in, her eyes bright. "What are we talking about? Seems interesting. Share, share, share."

Instead, Naomi asked, "Khlo, are you ever going to take that coaster off your head?"

The imp's brow creased in confusion. "Coaster?" Moments later, her eyes went wide with remembrance. "Oh, coaster!" She snatched it off her head and returned it to the table.

"You forgot it was there?" asked Larkin.

"Kinda." Khloë rubbed at her scalp, again looking the height of confused. "Why did I put it on my head again?"

"Something about a dare," said Larkin. "Again, I wasn't really listening."

Khloë shook her head. "You're a super tough audience tonight, Lark."

Sensing a presence at her side, Naomi twisted her head and slowly looked up. Her heartbeat kicked up, because there was Luka. As her feminine parts snapped to attention, she felt a lazy smile curve her mouth. "Ella said you'd show up."

"Did she?" An idle question. He took Naomi's hand and gently pulled her to her feet. Just like that, a bubble of sexual tension seemed to form around them, bringing them into their own little cocoon.

His eyes delved into hers, concerned. "Are you okay?"

Arching into him, she locked her arms around his neck. "Uh-huh. I'm riding a nice buzz right now. Don't ruin it."

He slid a proprietary hand down her back. "Iain didn't say anything more than what you told Konstantin?"

She pouted. "I said don't ruin it. Talk of Iain will ruin in." She nuzzled his neck. "You smell really, really good. Makes me wanna take a bite."

He let out a throaty hum she felt against her lips. "Come home with me, and you can do whatever you want," he said, pure sex coating every word.

A burst of anticipation hit her bloodstream. "Mmm, okay."

She didn't feel like staying now that she knew Iain was here anyway.

Satisfaction moved over Luka's face. "Good. First, though..." He kissed her. Slow. Hard. Deep. Greedily. The kiss went on and on and on—a loop of drugging, sensual delight. At last he pulled back, need darkening his gaze. "That should do it. Let's go."

"Wait, you're leaving?" Khloë turned to Luka. "No, no, you can't take her. She's the only person who listens to me. The others zone out. I mean, *look* at them."

Naomi glanced at the rest of the girls. Ella was singing out of tune, her eyes closed. Devon was doing some kind of weird arm-dance. Raini was using a cocktail stick as if it were a flute. Larkin was balancing pretzels on the head of a still sleeping Piper. And Harper was trying to fish a dollar out of her glass.

"See?" Khloë asked him.

"I do see," Luka told her. "But I'm still taking Naomi with me."

The imp sighed. "You both have sex in your eyes, so I can see you're not gonna be reasonable here."

Feeling her lips curl, Naomi waved at the girls. "Later, people!"

Kisses were blown, goodbyes were called out, take-cares were said.

It was only when Luka turned her that she saw Daniil and the twins were nearby, who had been joined by Konstantin.

The teleporter dropped her and Luka off at the den in his home before disappearing with the others. She and Luka were finally alone, one measly foot separating them as they locked gazes.

He stood still and watchful. A jungle predator rearing to pounce. His dark eyes were twin pools of lust, so many demands gleaming there. Excitement gripped her insides and twisted.

The sexual tension of earlier tautened, heightened, stretched like an elastic band.

With quick, deft movements, he tugged off his tie and threw it on the chair. "I haven't fucked you while you're smashed before."

She licked her lower lip, her belly fluttering. "I do hope you intend to rectify that here and now."

He grabbed her hips and hauled her to him so abruptly she crashed into his chest with a gasp. "Oh, I do." He dropped his mouth down on hers.

CHAPTER EIGHTEEN

Naomi moaned into the kiss he all but slayed her with—it was hot and bold and wild. She grabbed at his shirt as she kissed him just as hard. A growl drummed its way up his throat and poured into her mouth. The guttural sound, the vibrations of it, made goosebumps sweep over her skin.

His hands roamed over her, squeezing and shaping and teasing with such entitlement. Inside her body, all kinds of bells rang, whistles were blown, and fireworks went off. It left her damp and needy and so *ready*.

Herding her backwards, he divested her of her dress and bra in record time—and yeah, there was some tearing and snapping of cloth. So she felt in no way sorry when some of his shirt buttons went flying as she roughly tackled them.

What was good for the goose . . .

Her breath hitched as her back abruptly met the wall. Ribbons of power caught her wrists tight and pinned them high above her head. She couldn't lie, several parts of her clenched. Her demon gave a little shudder of delight.

She tugged against the buzzing threads, trying to free herself. She couldn't. There was no give. And a rush of agonizing suspense rolled over her.

Luka slipped off his shirt and threw it aside, revealing so much solid muscle and sleek tanned skin that her hormones didn't know what to do with themselves.

He moved closer, pressing his hard dick against her lower stomach, and put his lips to her ear. "I want to bury my cock inside you. Lock it deep. Leave it there. So you'll always feel me."

Her belly fluttered. "We can certainly make the first part happen."

He trailed a finger down the side of her face. "Don't get wet yet."

Naomi felt her jaw go slack. "Are you joking?"

"Not in the slightest."

Then the sensual torture began. Her neck was kissed, licked, and bitten. Her breasts were clutched, kneaded, and stroked. Her nipples were sucked, pinched, and twisted.

He didn't only use his mouth and palms and teeth; he used his telekinetic power. It was like having a second set of hands on her. The sensations . . . there were so many she couldn't fully process them; could only drown in them. And yet every cell in her body greedily screamed for more, more, more.

Control. Where was her control?

Nowhere to be seen.

She was moaning. Panting. Shaking. *Aching* to come. But each time she came close, he eased up; let the tension inside her dim. Then he'd push her high all over again only to stop once more before she imploded.

A tortured whimper slipped out of her just before he tore

off her panties. It was as much relief as it was pleasure when he finally, *finally* cupped her pussy.

He slipped a finger through her folds—*oh God, yes*—and then tutted. "I told you not to get wet yet."

"You set me up for failure is what you did. That isn't anything to smile about." But he was wearing one of his half-grins, the bastard.

A bastard who abruptly dropped to his knees.

He parted her folds with his thumbs and took a long lick. *Fuck*, that felt good. His hum of male appreciation went right to her core.

Then he ate her out. No teasing, no gentleness, no building her up to an orgasm slowly. He went to town down there, using that blessed tongue to lick and flick and swirl and stab. At the same time, he telekinetically squeezed her breasts and plucked at her nipples.

Her body couldn't take the overload of sensation much longer. The responses he wrenched out of it were melting her brain.

Her composure? Totaled. Absolutely totaled. She was a sexual wreck—mindless, breathless, speechless—and frantic to find the release she'd been chasing that he'd so far denied her.

She didn't get it then, either.

Before she could fracture, he was back on his feet, towering over her, his face a mask of greed, his raw sexuality sucking the oxygen right out of the air. "Know what you taste like?"

"What?" she rasped.

"Mine." The buzz of power surrounding her wrists disappeared. "Bend over the arm of the sofa."

Anticipation flowing in her veins, she somehow made her way to the couch on wobbly legs and did as he asked.

His belt jingled. A zipper lowered. Something hot, heavy, and hard smacked her butt.

A waft of cold whispered up her back, and she knew one of his demons had risen.

"Such a perfect little toy," it purred. *Abraxas*. "I would like to lock you away somewhere no one else can find you, so I can have you all to myself." It grabbed her wrists and wrenched both arms behind her back. "You wouldn't mind, would you?"

"Actually, yeah, I would."

It slid its palms to her upper arms. "Pity."

She hissed through her teeth as the flesh beneath its hands started to burn. The hurt fast became pleasurable, telling her that she was being branded. *Again*. "I—" She cut off as it slammed its cock home, sending a hot nick of pain arrowing up her inner walls.

Her breath hitched so abruptly she almost choked on it. After all the foreplay, she was wet but swollen and supersensitive, so the demon's rough possession was both pleasure and pain.

"You take my cock like it was made for you." The words came from Luka, so he'd evidently taken back the wheel. He hooked one hand over her shoulder and clamped the other around her wrists, keeping them behind her back. "Hold on."

He rode her impossibly hard. His hips snapped furiously forward again and again, plunging his cock deep, making her eyes fall shut in pure bliss. His belt buckle jingled with each smack of his flesh against hers.

"That's it," he grunted as she pushed back to meet his thrusts. "Deeper."

"If I go deeper, it's going to hurt."

"I don't care."

Taking her at her word, he released her shoulder and angled her hips slightly, allowing his dick to slide further in. *Fuck*. Then he was punching it in and out of her, his pace wild.

Possessiveness burned through him and jolted his system like a drug. No woman had ever affected him this way. None. He'd never coveted anyone the way he did Naomi. Had never been so greedy for every detail of their life. Watching her face, searching for little slivers she hid from him, had become an obsession.

She had become an obsession.

He couldn't even blame it on her being a siren. The attraction between them might have initially sprung to life due to the pull of her song, but that song didn't power it.

He curled over her, planting one hand on the sofa cushion, his other hand still holding her wrists. "I know you want to come. So come." He used telekinesis to flick her clit, and her inner muscles strangled him as she exploded, squeezing so fucking tight it nearly hurt.

Stifling a scream, Naomi turned her head and latched onto his arm with her teeth, biting just shy of drawing blood.

Pausing mid thrust, he spoke into her ear once her release subsided. "You bit me."

"So?"

"So, I bite back." He sank his teeth into the crook of her neck and fucked her even more furiously than before. Orgasm struck him abruptly, white-hot and wicked fast. His eyes went blind as euphoric currents surged through his system.

Panting, he dropped his face to her nape. "Are you going to bitch at me for restraining you again?" She did it sometimes, though only ever playfully. They both knew she loved it.

"Not tonight," she slurred. "Tonight I'm gonna openly admit that it revs my engines. But we won't speak of my confession in the morning, or ever again after that. 'Kay?"

He felt his lips bow up. "Okay."

"We agreed that we wouldn't speak of it."

"I forgot."

"No you didn't." Naomi lowered her spoon to her bowl and lifted her cup of tea. "You're just being an ass."

Sitting across from her at the kitchen table, Luka made a poor attempt to stifle a smile. "Harsh."

"Fact."

"Notice that I didn't take advantage of your being tipsy last night to try to make you part with your secrets."

"Which is why you woke to me sucking you off." Sipping her tea, she playfully glared at him over the rim of her cup. "But if I'd known that you were going to tease me regardless of your assurances, I wouldn't have bothered."

His smile widened a little. "Just so you're aware, you make Belial want to spank you when you get all prim with me like that."

"When does it *not* want to spank me?"

"Rarely," he admitted.

Naomi set her cup back down. "My entity is probably going to bitch-slap Belial one day. You know that, right?"

"I do." If his expression was anything to go by, he found the idea amusing.

"So long as you're aware." Lifting her spoon again, she scooped up more cereal and shoveled it into her mouth.

Just then, his cell phone beeped. Something that happened a lot in the mornings—a time when he was contacted by his sentinels and members of his Force–a band of demons who helped police the lair. They sent in reports, complaints, and all that jazz.

She knew that he'd also receive emails from his business associates, of whom he had plenty. Hence why, in between taking sips of his coffee and bites of his bagel, he'd replied to whatever messages awaited him. He'd told her that he liked to get a head-start on tackling any issues that lay ahead of him each day.

Chewing on her food, she watched his face darken as he stared down at the screen of his phone. "Everything okay?"

He inhaled deeply and then set his cell on the table. "Yes. Some demons simply need reminding that there are rules they must follow, so then long talks are necessary. Annoying, because I have a busy schedule today."

"Is confronting Iain anywhere on that schedule? Because I'm thinking it isn't necessary for you to do that."

"Why?"

"I genuinely believe it was a coincidence that we were both at the Xpress bar last night. It's not as if I go there often, so he had no reason to think he'd bump into me there. He wasn't rude to me. He even apologized for his past behavior."

"And maybe he meant it. Maybe he won't be any threat to you in future. But Konstantin will remain as your guard. He is of the same opinion as you, by the way; he believes it was a coincidence that Iain happened to be at the bar the same time as you. I trust both your judgments. So no, I won't be confronting Iain over it. But if he shows up where you are again, it'll be a different story."

"You trust my judgment?"

The surprise in her tone made Luka's brow pinch. "Yes, I do."

She cleared her throat, shifting awkwardly in her seat. "Oh. Good."

And there it was. That hint of vulnerability she tried to hide. One born of rarely having others look beyond her beautiful surface to see the shrewd, intelligent mind beneath.

When it came to sirens, people seemed to assume that they were one-dimensional femme fatales. In his experience, that wasn't the case. It certainly wasn't the case with Naomi.

His siren was no pretty, empty-headed ornament. She had more layers than an onion. She was sweet, quirky, caring, cunning, merciless, grounded, independent—on and on it went.

She was a whole juxtaposition of traits, really. Didn't fit in any one box.

She'd very quickly reeled him in, making his possessiveness grow and grow. His entities were in much the same boat, as evidenced by the many brands on her skin.

She currently wore a long-sleeved tee, so Abraxas' marks—the matching bands it had left on each of her upper arms last night—weren't visible. Something that annoyed the demon. It wanted everyone to see them.

Normally, Luka wouldn't welcome being branded, but it admittedly bugged him that he wore none from her entity. According to Naomi, it hadn't ever branded anyone; it simply wasn't bothered about even temporarily claiming people as part of its circle, no matter how territorial it felt toward them.

Luka's demons felt sure that her entity was possessive of him. Abraxas' theory was that the demon was waiting for something. It couldn't sense what, though. It only knew that a certain thing needed to happen—or maybe that Luka himself needed to do this certain thing—before the entity would lay any claim to him.

He couldn't imagine what this "thing" could be. He had too many unanswered questions about the creature before him. "Abraxas believes that your demon is waiting for something from me."

Naomi paused in the process of setting down her cup.

"It thinks that your entity won't act on any possessiveness it feels toward me until I give it what it needs. The look on your face confirms that that's true. So my question is . . . what exactly does it need from me?"

She carefully placed the mug back on the table. "I can't explain that right now."

"Why not?"

She hesitated. "My answer wouldn't make much sense to you, so you'd only find yourself with more questions."

"That doesn't mean you can't at least tell me what it wants from me. I won't pressure you to elaborate beyond that."

Her eyes narrowed. "All right." She exhaled heavily. "Acceptance. It needs you to accept . . . something."

"Something about you, or something about your entity?"

"Both, really. That's the most I can say on that, though. At least for now."

At least for now. Those words should have appeased him to some degree, but they didn't. She had been right in her prediction that he'd only want to hear more.

With the women in his past, *he* had always been the one with the secrets. It had eventually gotten to a point where said women had wanted him to open up. He'd never understood why it bothered them so much that he hadn't shared every little detail of his life with them. Now, he got it. Because now, he was invested in something; in some*one*.

"I can see that you're tempted to pressure me to tell you more, but you swore that you wouldn't," she reminded him. "You also once promised my demon that you wouldn't push if you hit on something I couldn't or didn't want to share."

Yes, and he was regretting it.

"But hey, if you really want us to start sharing more personal stuff with each other, I guess we could. I am ever so curious about the inner workings of the criminal empire you so successfully run." She lifted a daring brow, knowing full well that he wouldn't elaborate. It made Belial want to bite her.

"You know how to shut down a line of questioning, don't you?" Imps were experts at it, and his siren had evidently picked up their tricks.

She only smiled.

His attention shifting to those full and oh so bitable lips, he said, "Come here."

Her brow pinched. "Why?"

"Because I want that mouth."

"Then come get it."

"Are you sure you want me to do that, Naomi?"

"Why wouldn't I?"

"It might end with you getting bent over this table while Belial fucks you from behind, and then you *will* get a hot ass."

Naomi's lady bits predictably perked all the way up. "I'll take my chances."

That turned out to be a mistake on her part. Because she *did* get hammered by the entity, and it *did* spank the hell out of her. Although ... she supposed she couldn't really call it a 'mistake' since she'd admittedly enjoyed it despite herself.

More, Belial left another brand on her. A brand of its handprint, right on her butt. And when she ranted at it, it only gave her a sadistic smile.

She felt her lips thin. "Sometimes, I could swear you're trying to provoke my demon into branding you right back."

The entity shrugged. "Only one way to find out."

CHAPTER NINETEEN

Naomi dropped her gaze from the framed painting to the cards beneath it. Under *Please don't touch* was the name of the artist and also the price of the artwork. At the latter, she almost whistled. *Hefty.*

But then most of the pieces here at this particular gallery were.

Located in the Underground, it was quite an impressive place, all high ceilings and shiny flooring. The plain white walls and clever lighting helped emphasize the works displayed all around.

Still feeling bloated from her lunch with Tobe, she put a hand to her belly and blew out a breath. She usually spent her Sundays in her workroom, but he'd asked that they meet up at one of the ethnic restaurants here in the Underground, whining that they didn't see as much of each other now that Luka was in the picture.

Not *strictly* true. It was more that Tobe was finding it hard to adjust to her having another man in her life. Which wasn't unusual for anchors, so she made a point of making time for him.

He had requested that they stop off at the gallery on their way out so that he could speak to one of his contacts here. Yes, even upscale galleries with very elite clientele were willing to do business with imps if it meant better profits. Some even obtained work via Tobe on behalf of their clients.

Naomi didn't mind waiting. She'd always liked wandering around such places, and the ambience here was pretty relaxing.

People talked low as they meandered around or chatted with curators, so the echoes were mostly inaudible. The smells of sage, plaster, paint, and wood polish circulated through the air—some stronger in some sections than others.

There were plenty of pieces to admire – paintings, carvings, blown glasswork, and mass-media sculptures. The various sections appeared to be organized according to themes. Depending on the nature of the piece, some hung on walls while others were propped on tables.

A couple of paintings were actually hers. Of course, none were under her name—her clients had taken the credit. But it still gave her a burst of pride to see them displayed here.

Her mother constantly pestered her to stop hiding her light, to take the plunge and work to become an established artist. But truly, Naomi preferred it this way. It wasn't about hiding; it was just that the limelight wasn't for her.

Tia struggled to understand that, because she herself was a total extrovert who would embrace any attention that came with success. She failed to see how Naomi could possibly be happy in the shadows. Some people just were, though.

Hearing footfalls, she turned to see Tobe heading her way. "All good?"

"All good," he confirmed.

"Then let's head out." They skirted the room divider, walked through the open doorway into the sparse reception area, and then breezed out of the gallery. Spotting her guard, Naomi smiled. "Hey, Kon. I'd invite you to walk with us, but I know you won't."

"And so he shouldn't," said Tobe, his hand on her elbow guiding her forward. "His job isn't to keep you company, it's to watch your back. You'll just distract him."

She huffed. *I guess*.

As they joined the pedestrians walking in the direction of the Underground's exit, Tobe cast her a quick look. "I suppose you're meeting Belinsky later." A petulant grumble.

Naomi sighed inwardly. "Don't start grumbling about him again."

"It was an innocent comment. I was merely making conversation."

"Your idea of good conversation doesn't feature Luka."

"Did you make clear to him that I'm your favorite person?"

Dear Lord. "Why would I need to? It's highly unlikely he'd care one way or the other."

"Don't be so sure," Tobe mumbled. "He's far too possessive of you for my liking."

"You said you weren't jealous."

"And I'm not. Just like I wouldn't be jealous if you took a mate. Though I *would* be annoyed. It would ruin our plan to grow old alone together."

Naomi felt her brows knit. "When was that ever our plan?" she asked, mirth bleeding into her voice.

"Always."

She shook her head. "It ain't *my* future goal—let's be clear on that."

"Well, just make sure that Belinsky doesn't help you meet that 'future goal'. And before you go defending him, bear in mind that I have plenty of legitimate reasons for having reservations. He's a criminal."

Aware of the ears all around them, she telepathically shot back, *So are you. So am I.*

But we don't associate with mobsters.

You commissioned a painting for one literally last month, and I was the one who painted it.

Well, we don't torture people in a secret underground location.

Something about his tone made her narrow her eyes. *You broke into Luka's vault, didn't you?* She'd heard whispers about the place.

It is hell on earth, I'm telling you.

Exasperated by his lack of self-preservation, she barely managed to bite back a growl. *All Primes have a place they take people to be punished.*

Jolene doesn't.

Yes she does. You helped her build it!

Tobe spluttered. "Stop picking holes in my argument."

"I don't need to. The gaping holes are already there—I'm just pointing them out."

Finally they reached the elevator. He jabbed the button on the wall panel hard. *Have you told Lou about him?*

No, she replied. *I've only seen Lou once since he showed up in my bedroom when we had the cleric in our custody. He bragged about how, given the many deaths he'd caused, he had for sure killed the dark practitioner, and then he left. He's still mad at me for not contacting him about the monkhood initially.*

Right then, the elevator's metal doors slid open with a *ding*.

They stepped inside. Konstantin smoothly joined them and jabbed the "up" button.

Have you heard anything more from Stefan? Naomi asked Tobe as they began to ascend.

Leaning back against the wall, he folded his arms. *Nope. Haven't seen him loitering around either. I'm hoping that he's decided to let it go, but he's stubborn. Kind of like Iain.*

I don't think I have to worry that Iain will start being stalkerish again.

Considering he spent time in Belinsky's underground chamber of horrors, I'm not surprised he's happy to leave you be, Tobe jibed.

Naomi rolled her eyes. "He has a first name, you know."

"I do know."

"It wouldn't kill you to use it."

"I know that, too."

"Or to be nice—that costs literally nothing."

Impatience moved across Tobe's face. "Hey, have I broken into his house? No. Have I set him on fire? No. Have I hotwired his car and taken it for a joy ride? No."

"Those things really aren't a reason for me to pat you on the back. Fact is that you naturally *shouldn't* do those things."

"Whatever."

She exchanged an amused look with Konstantin.

Finally the elevator came to a halt. The three of them piled out of it, exited the club, and headed for the parking lot.

As Tobe walked her to her car, she said, "Thank you for lunch."

"We should do it more often." He gave her a pointed look.

Naomi poked his shoulder. "We had lunch on Wednesday. Stop being a diva." Ignoring his unintelligible mumble, she pressed a quick kiss to his cheek. "Take care."

"You too." He gave her a brief hug and then headed for his motorcycle.

Spotting Konstantin approaching his own car, Naomi gave him a little wave before sliding into her vehicle. She placed her purse on the passenger seat and then clicked on her belt, grimacing as the damn thing put pressure on her still-bloated stomach.

Hearing her phone beep, she plucked it out of her purse. It was a text from Ella: *You free on Thursday? Me and my sister go to a pool hall every Friday, but we're going Thursday this week. I want to introduce you to her and I figured it might be fun if you come with us.*

Feeling her lips curve, Naomi replied, *I'm up for it. Just let me know exactly where and what time.*

Ella's response came fast: *Awesome. We usually meet there around 6.30.* She added the address of the pool hall and then *See you there.*

Placing her cell back in her purse, Naomi heard Tobe's bike disappear with a loud rumble. She inserted her key into the car ignition and switched on the engine. Or tried. It only sputtered.

She tried again. Another sputter.

Frowning, she cocked her head. And heard a low, ominous rhythmic beeping. Her stomach took a nosedive. *Fuck.*

From the dark pockets of shadow beyond the parking lot, Jonah pressed his thumb down on his cell phone screen, and two cars exploded. He smiled, satisfied.

The devil's whore and her protector were now dead. Lucifer's plan had been foiled. The child would never be born.

And the monkhood would not perish.

"It is done," he said to his brothers, lifting his chin.

"So it is," agreed Henry flatly, staring at the flaming vehicles in the lot.

Jonah frowned. "You should be happy."

"I still do not like that we used bombs. That is not our way."

"Kushiel was clear that it was the *only* way," Oslo cut in, ever the peacemaker.

Henry's brow inched up. "If it was the only way, why didn't he suggest it at the beginning? And since when would God wish for us to use terrorist methods?"

Duncan's lips thinned. "It is not our place to question an

angel. He is a messenger of God. Yet you persist in doing so. It is no better than blasphemy."

"I didn't initially question him," Henry defended. "But he has ... changed." His gaze swept over each of the other brethren. "Is there not one of you here who agrees that Kushiel is not always so angel-like anymore?"

Some responded with only a stubborn look. Idris and Van, however, shifted uneasily while Griff and Magnus exchanged a brief glance.

Jonah himself was uncomfortable. Because the truth was that, yes, Kushiel was indeed somewhat different from when he'd first come to them many months ago.

The angel was still intense. Still wore an ethereal glow. Still carried an aura of power. But he no longer emitted peace and serenity. No longer exuded a calm presence that put the brothers at ease and made them feel close to God.

"The way he speaks to us now," Henry began, "as if we are servants to be ordered about and beneath his contempt—"

"But we *are* servants," Maynard interjected. "God's servants. Kushiel is his voice; issues his commands."

"Does he really?" Henry drawled, a hint of challenge in his voice. "Or are those commands his own?"

Alban lifted his shoulders. "Does it matter? Both Kushiel and our Lord want the same thing. They want what *we* want."

"But I will bet that God would not have raged at the rest of us each time our other brothers failed in their attempt to kill *her*," Henry hedged.

"Well, Kushiel will not rage this time," Jonah pointed out. "She is dead. The work of our Holy Father has been completed."

"Has it, though?" Henry asked.

Jonah felt his brow pinch. "Excuse me?"

Henry shrugged. "The translation of the prophecy still seems off to me."

Idris's back straightened. "I know the old tongues; my translation was exact."

"Maybe. But maybe not. I still maintain—"

"A large crowd has gathered in the lot," Magnus cut in. "We should leave. It is no good for us to hang about." He flicked his gaze around . . . and frowned. "Where is Oslo?"

Jonah looked at where their brother had last stood. The spot was empty. "Oslo! Oslo!" He spun around, calling his name repeatedly, the others doing the same.

No response.

Jonah turned back around. "I don't see . . ." He trailed off on noticing another absence. "Duncan?"

Magnus gripped Jonah's arm painfully tight, his eyes flickering. "We must leave. Now. Something is not right."

Jonah's stomach churned with apprehension. "I agree. But Oslo and Duncan—"

"We have to go," Magnus insisted . . . just as an unfamiliar male abruptly appeared behind him.

Feeling his eyes widen, Jonah yelled, "Move!" But it was too late. The newcomer fisted Magnus' tunic, and then they both disappeared into thin air.

Curses and gasps flew out of the seven remaining brethren.

His pulse quickening, Jonah conjured an orb of pure white magick, but there was no one to aim it at. He glanced around, his every breath now short and choppy. "Where are they?" *Who were they?*

He did a double-take as movement snatched his attention. "Duck!" he shouted as the unfamiliar male returned, materializing at Griff's back. Again his warning came too late. Both men vanished before he could toss the orb of magick. "Dammit!"

"Maynard and Idris have disappeared as well," Van informed him, his voice shaky. "*And* Alban."

Visibly panicking, Henry began dragging Jonah toward their vehicles. "We must leave now, we—"

An invisible wall slammed into them, knocking both to the ground.

The orb in his hand winking out, Jonah grunted at the pain that raced up his spine. *Telekinesis*, he thought. "Stop hiding and face us!" he demanded ... but nobody did. It was as he and Henry struggled to their feet that he noticed Van had also disappeared.

"They come at people from behind, we need to ensure that they can't!" stated Henry. He and Jonah went back to back, scanning the shadows. "I see nothing."

Nor did Jonah, but ... "They're there," he murmured, his nostrils flaring, anger and dread panging in his blood. "Whoever *they* are."

An invisible impact rammed into their sides, making them topple over like skittles.

Jonah felt Henry's body heat disappear; knew that he was now alone.

The click-clack of heels preceded a familiar woman stalking out of the shadows. *The whore*.

Squatting near Jonah, she glared at him. "You know, I'm sick and fucking *tired* of you idiots coming at me—not to mention furious that you almost killed my bodyguard. *He* has nothing to do with your prophecy, but you didn't care about that. So I'm *really* not gonna care that this will hurt." She fisted his hair, wrenched back his head, and bit into his neck.

Oh God, it *burned*. Burned like acid as she drank his blood. Drank and drank and drank. He cried out as that burn coursed through his body, weakening him on every level. Like her bite had injected something into him.

She finally unlatched her teeth from his skin and dumped him on the ground with a sneer. Then her gaze snapped upward, turning wary.

Even as pain racked his insides, Jonah tracked her gaze. A tall man in an elegant suit appeared, his expression cold, his dark eyes twin orbs of fury, snakes wriggling beneath his skin.

Jonah felt the blood drain from his face. "Lucifer," he breathed in horror.

The man tore his gaze away from the whore and slammed it on Jonah. "Oh no," he said, his voice flat and pure frost. "I'm something much, much worse."

Jonah was about to ask who could possibly be worse than Lucifer, but then the man threw a ball of flames at his head, and an all-consuming pain stole every thought from his mind.

CHAPTER TWENTY

As the dying cleric writhed in agony on the ground, Naomi swiped the back of her hand over her mouth and stared up at Luka. Her heart was pounding like crazy. He wasn't supposed to be here; he wasn't supposed to know, to have *seen* ...

Fuck.

Luka didn't say a word. He merely stared at her, flickers of menace moving in the depths of his cool gaze.

Her entity watched him warily, searching for any sign of abhorrence or rejection, but it couldn't get a read on him. Neither could she. He was too self-contained, too good at concealing his true thoughts and feelings.

Since he had no reason to be here, she could only assume that Konstantin had called on him. Before her car had exploded, she'd telepathed the bodyguard to insist that he get out of his own vehicle just in case her suspicions were correct.

Luckily, he'd listened.

She'd pyroported to him, found him unconscious—likely

having been thrown by the force of the explosion—but otherwise fine, and propped him up against a nearby lamp post.

Then she'd gone hunting.

The moment she had spotted the clerics, she'd called out to Tobe, who'd swiftly appeared with Ciaran. The two had helped her dispatch them. They'd needed to do it quickly and cleanly so as not to attract attention. She'd thought she could have the whole thing over and done with before Konstantin woke.

She'd been wrong.

And now Luka knew her biggest secret. Whatever he was thinking right now, well, it couldn't be anything good.

Materializing at her side with Ciaran, Tobe cursed at the sight of the now-dead cleric. "I thought we were gonna take him alive," he said to Naomi.

They *had* telepathically agreed that they would let this one Elioud live so they could question him, but ... "Luka wasn't aware of that."

Tobe glanced from her to the legion, his gaze turning both hard and wary. He stepped closer to her, evidently feeling protective. "If you're standing there judging her for something she has no control over, you can fuck right off."

Ignoring that outburst, Luka looked down at the dead male, his eyes narrowing on the emblem. His gaze locked with hers once more. "A cleric, I'm guessing. Why would he come for you?" he asked, his voice ice-cold.

Not a good sign.

Naomi's stomach plummeted. He was going to walk now, wasn't he? He couldn't look at her the same way anymore, just as she'd feared. "Does it matter?" she threw out, disheartened.

His eyes flared. "Yeah, it fucking matters."

Could've fooled me.

"This isn't the time or place to talk about this," Tobe stated.

Luka pressed his lips together. "You're right. It isn't."

Daniil materialized; he'd presumably been telepathically summoned.

"I need to go to my place," said Naomi, flicking a hand at her ruined clothing. "We can talk there."

"Alone," Luka specified.

Tobe stiffened. "Nome . . ."

"I'll be okay," she assured her anchor. "This conversation needs to be had in private." If Luka said even *one* thing remotely hurtful to her, Tobe would flip and launch himself at him. The legion wouldn't exactly stand there and take it, so the end result would be bad.

"Me and Tobe will get rid of the bodies," Ciaran told her.

Luka stiffened. "Bodies plural? The cleric wasn't alone?"

"I'll explain everything when we get out of here," Naomi said.

A muscle in Tobe's cheek ticked. "If you need me, Nome, reach out."

"I will." Moments later, her surroundings briefly blurred, and then she, Luka, and Daniil were standing in her living area. After a quick look at his Prime, the teleporter disappeared.

Luka raked his unreadable gaze over her. "Are you all right?" A stiffly spoken question.

Surprised he'd bothered to ask, she cleared her throat. "Fine. No wounds. Konstantin telepathed you?"

"Yes, he did," Luka verified. "The question is: why didn't *you*?"

She blinked. Her car had been blown up. A bunch of clerics had come for her. He'd witnessed her feed from one of them. And . . . "*That's* your question?"

"Oh, I have others." The words were low. Clipped. Curt. "Many others."

I'll bet.

"Tell me about the clerics."

Why should she, considering it was extremely probable that he had every intention of breezing out of her house never to come back? Then again, Konstantin could have died tonight. She hadn't thought she was putting him in danger by leaving him ignorant of the monkhood's existence; hadn't thought they would target him. That miscalculation could have resulted in the bodyguard losing his life. At the very least, she could explain the situation.

"The clerics are part of an order known as the *Lemures*," she explained.

"They were responsible for the car bombs?"

She nodded. "I heard them speak of it while Tobe, Ciaran, and I picked them off."

"Why did they target you?"

She hesitated, licking her lips. "They came upon an old-ass prophecy that was probably written by one of the Nephilim's first descendants. They translated it; believe it says that a specific woman will birth the Antichrist, who—with some demonic help—will destroy the order and the person pulling their strings."

Luka's brow furrowed. "What does that have to do with you?"

Naomi scratched the back of her head, grimacing. "They believe I'm the woman in the prophecy. We're quite sure that their puppeteer is a dark practitioner. He obviously puts stock in the foretelling, because he seems to think it necessary for his survival that I die."

"*We're* quite sure," he echoed. "Who's we?"

"Me, Tobe, my mom, Alfie, Jolene, her anchor, Khloë, and Ciaran." And Lou, but she wouldn't mention that *just* yet.

Luka's eyes went slitted. "Tonight wasn't the first time you'd encountered the clerics, then?"

Her nape prickled at the silken menace in his tone. "No."

His nostrils flared. "So you knew that danger dogged your heels . . . and you said nothing of it to me or Konstantin?"

Naomi inwardly winced. "Yeah."

There was a flash of something very dark in his eyes, but he killed the emotion fast, as if striving to maintain his cool. "How long have they been coming for you?"

"About a month now."

He clenched his jaw, his teeth grinding. "Are there more of them?"

"Probably. We tried to find the location of the monastery, but we've so far had no luck. We believe the dark practitioner is posing as an angel to manipulate them. He's calling himself Kushiel, from what I overheard. I'm pretty sure that's the name of the Angel of Punishment, so it would explain why he chose it."

"Why would the clerics believe that the prophecy refers to you?"

"It features a symbol that matches a birthmark I have."

Luka's brow creased. "I've explored every inch of you multiple times, and I've not seen a single birthmark."

"I started covering it with concealer after I came to suspect that it was what had led the clerics to me."

"When did they first come at you?"

"The evening you met Jolene at the pizzeria. A little over a week later, they surrounded me when I was on my way home from work. It was roughly two weeks after that that they broke into my home again. Then nothing until now."

"So essentially you've been in the direct path of danger since the day I came into your life, and I knew nothing of it," he summed up, his voice a low rumble of fury.

Naomi internally cringed. "Essentially."

A gleam of something hard and dark came and went in his eyes. Snakes seemed to slither beneath the skin of his face and throat, telling her that his demons were *pissed*.

Her stomach seized as she braced herself for him to blurt out *Fuck this shit* and go. Her entity, too, expected it—and planned to rip him a new asshole as he made his way out.

"I knew you were keeping things from me," said Luka, his voice eerily flat. "You were open with me about that much. But I didn't ask myself if there was a threat aside from Iain hanging over your head, because you never seemed in any way nervous or afraid."

She *hadn't* been scared, not believing the monkhood presented a real risk to her life. They could use magick, yes, but she was more powerful. She hadn't thought they would ever use explosives. "I wasn't—" She cut off as Luka stalked angrily toward her.

"Why didn't you tell me any of this?" He dipped his face to hers, pinning her gaze with his own. "*Don't* say that it isn't my business, Naomi. I declared you mine—I was very fucking clear about it. Any possible danger to you is absolutely my business."

She let out a heavy breath. "I said nothing for two reasons. One, I didn't want to drag you into this mess unless I absolutely had to. Two, I couldn't have told you the full truth; I would have had to lie to you."

"About what?"

She thought about blowing off the question. After all, he wasn't going to stay. He hadn't even addressed what he'd witnessed her do, shocking though it must have been, as if to block it out. Which meant he couldn't accept it.

Her demon urged her to keep quiet, feeling it owed him no answers. It wasn't merely angry with him, it was angry with itself. Because it had begun to believe that just maybe he would be able to look past Naomi's need to drink blood. The fact that she apparently didn't matter enough to him for that to be the case made her entity want to claw his face off.

And it *hurt*.

You don't know that he can't accept it, a voice in her head whispered. *You're making assumptions because you're bracing yourself for the worst.*

True. Was she doing him a disservice by deciding that he wouldn't overlook it? Maybe. The reality was that she couldn't truly know what his reaction would be unless she told him everything and helped him understand. If she didn't do that here and now, if he walked out as a result of that, she'd never know for certain.

And she found that she wanted to know.

"About what?" he repeated.

She dragged in a preparatory breath. "The prophecy isn't actually inaccurate, the clerics just didn't properly translate it. It doesn't state that I'll birth the child of the devil. It says that I *am* the child of the devil. Which is true."

He went completely still. "You're Lucifer's daughter?"

"Yes." A whisper.

"*The* Lucifer's daughter?"

"Yes," she repeated, her voice a little stronger this time.

"I thought that all his offspring lived in hell."

"I'm the exception." She worried her bottom lip again. "And as you saw for yourself, I inherited his curse."

Luka frowned. "Curse?"

"I don't know if this applies to all fallen angels or just him, but he was cursed when he fell. Cursed to need blood as much as he needs food and water to survive. And when passing his DNA onto me, he also passed on that."

"So you drink from people?" he asked, an edge to his voice that was jagged with possessiveness.

"Normally, no. My bite is venomous. It doesn't kill, but it

causes a *lot* of pain. Tobe has vampiric connections who make bottled drinks that contain blood and vitamins and stuff. They sell him batches of them every so often, and he gives them to me."

Realization visibly dawned on Luka. "Your smoothies."

"My smoothies," she confirmed.

A pensive glint entered his eyes. "You bit me the other night."

"I didn't draw blood, but it was a close call." A little *too* close. "I think you can understand why I've kept all this quiet from most people."

"Who does know about it?"

"Only the people who are also fully aware of the cleric situation—which includes Lou. He thought he'd killed Kushiel during his recent spree of murdering dark practitioners, but that clearly isn't the case." He was gonna be furious when he learned that.

Luka was silent for long moments, his expression still unreadable. "Acceptance. You said that your demon needed me to accept something. This is what you meant."

"Yes. You can't tell anyone about it, Luka."

An affronted anger rippled across his face. "Do you honestly think I'd do that?"

"I don't know, because I can't tell what's going through your head right now. It's not as if this stuff is light or cheery. Look, you have a right to be upset that I kept the information about the clerics from you. If there were Eliouds on some dumbass holy mission to end your life and you'd kept it from me, I would've been pissed as all hell at you. I just . . . I didn't want to lie to you. Keeping things from you is one thing. Lying is another. I couldn't have told you everything, so I decided to say nothing."

"Wrong, Naomi, you *could* have told me everything."

Exasperated, she challenged, "Would you have, in my position? Would you have spilled to me that Lucifer was your dad and that you needed to drink blood to survive? Would you have risked that I'd look upon you with sheer disgust?"

His brow pinched. "You thought I'd be disgusted?"

"Aren't you?"

"No. It isn't as if drinking blood is a fetish for you. You have no choice. What I am is angry on your behalf. This was Lou's curse. It should never have been yours." His gaze arrowed into hers, stripping her of her cool facade, seeing everything. "You expected me to walk away if I knew the full truth."

She gave a weak shrug and lowered her gaze to his chest. "I won't blame you if you do." Her demon would, though.

A long moment of silence passed. "You warned me that I wouldn't like what I heard if your secrets came to light. I was clear that you'd still matter to me regardless. And you do." He cupped her chin and tipped her head upwards, his dark eyes boring into hers, not letting her look away, giving her no room to hide. "I'm not going anywhere. And I've got news for you, Naomi—neither are you."

It took a few seconds for his words to penetrate. "Uh ... sorry?"

"I didn't anticipate that you'd become this important to me. I never saw it coming. Feels like it crept up on me somehow. We might not have admitted it to ourselves or to each other, but what we now have is as far from shallow as it can get. I have zero intention of changing that, or of letting you go."

"Since when?"

"Since a few minutes ago, when you looked up at me wearing a defeated, wary expression. I knew you expected me to leave you, and I realized that it isn't something I ever plan to do." He shook his head in mystification. "I have no idea how you did it, how you circumvented every defense I have, but you did. So here we are. It's done. All that's left for me to do is officially claim you as my mate, and I will. There's no going back now. Not for me, and not for you."

Luka had meant for his words to come out reassuring, but they sounded more like a threat. He had no gentleness in him right now. Hot rage coursed through his blood, fueling that of his demons. Their need for vengeance tore at all four of them, demanding satiation. Killing that cleric hadn't been enough. Not even close.

The clerics and their angel had marked Naomi for death. They'd targeted her multiple times. They'd attempted to take her from this world—from *him*—on four separate fucking occasions ... and he'd known nothing of it until tonight.

Only one need overrode the urge to hunt the fuckers. The need to tuck Naomi away somewhere safe. His protective instincts were on fucking fire, and the flames weren't going to die down any time soon.

He felt his skin stretch; knew his demons were again pushing at it as they writhed in fury. Could he blame Naomi for keeping them in the dark, though? Intellectually, no. Not when he understood exactly how important it was that she preserve her secrets.

On hearing that Lou was her father, shock had reverberated through his very bones. Many times he had contemplated what she could be keeping from him. He'd internally chewed on many theories. But not once, for even a single fleeting moment, had he considered *this*.

It explained a lot, though. Such as why she hesitated to get close to people, why she spoke so little of her biological father, and why said father wasn't around much. It was safer for her that way.

As for her need to drink blood ... yeah, that had been another shock. And again, it was only natural that she wouldn't easily share that with others. Still, a part of him was pissed at her for keeping it from him. Because this woman had some-the-fuck-how come to mean everything to him.

He'd been well aware when they first started their fling that burning off the sexual chemistry would be no quick or easy feat. But he hadn't even suspected that he might come to care for her, or just how fucking *encompassing* the feeling would be.

He'd known he was in trouble when he felt driven to come inside her. He'd willfully ignored it, not wanting to examine all he felt for her too closely; not wanting to see that other emotions were interwoven in the carnal need and primal possessiveness that gripped him tightly.

Bonding didn't come naturally to Luka. He wasn't good at letting people close. And the slight disconnect between him and his deeper emotions—which was no doubt a by-product of his upbringing—made it even more difficult.

He had always known that there was a high chance he'd spend his life alone. He'd just never imagined he would claim a woman, and he'd been unable to envision a scenario in which all three of his entities would be on board with it. So he'd prepared himself for a life of relative solitude. He hadn't prepared himself to be someone's partner. Hadn't thought there'd be a woman who'd put up with the ways in which his father's lessons had shaped him.

What he felt sure of was that he wouldn't make an easy mate. He knew how proprietary he could be of anything he formed an attachment to—his father had never been able to quash that tendency, despite his best efforts. When Luka became that firmly attached to something, he would hog and obsess over it . . . much as he did with Naomi.

"You're serious," she marveled, cutting right through his thoughts.

"Utterly," he confirmed.

She continued to stare at him in disbelief. "Luka, I just tossed some heavy shit at you. I fed from someone *in front of you*."

"You did. And I can't lie, it all came as a fuck of a shock. But none of it changes what I want or feel."

She spluttered. "Maybe not right now. But what about later? What about when the full impact of it hits you?"

"It already hit me. Even if it hadn't, my response would be the same when it did. I've never once struggled to walk away from a woman. Maybe that makes me an asshole, but it's how it is. Leave you, though? It isn't going to happen, Naomi, it's just not. Would you walk away from me if it was the other way around and I'd landed all that stuff on you?"

Her brow creased. "No."

"Then why do you find it so hard to believe that it doesn't change anything for me?"

She clenched and unclenched her hands, her breathing speeding up. "I thought maybe you *could* accept it, but I would never have expected that at the same time you'd declare that you wanted to claim me as your mate. I wasn't sure you'd *ever* do the latter. I figured the best I could hope for would be that you'd be prepared to try a relationship."

"Well, you were wrong. And it's a relief to hear that you were hoping I'd want a relationship, because it means we're on the same page. I know you generally avoid them, though I didn't know why exactly until now."

She swallowed. "It isn't just that I have secrets to guard. My relationships *always* went south. Guys inevitably reached a point where they couldn't deal with how my song snatches male attention. It isn't something I can control, but they came to resent me for it sooner or later. They were asses to me whenever other guys ogled or came on to me—as if I *like* that shit—and they'd even get paranoid that I was snapping up those offers and cheating on them."

Luka felt his mouth tighten. "The men in your past were weak pricks who made you pay for their own insecurities and jealousies. That isn't something I'd ever do, Naomi. If other men tried trespassing, I'd definitely have a problem with it. But it would be *them* who earned my anger, not you. And I'd never accuse you of cheating—you're far too loyal to betray someone that way."

She blinked hard. "You sound very sure of that."

"I am. I know you. You might have held back certain facts about yourself until now, but I still know you. And I know that we both want the same thing here—not merely for us to try a relationship on for size, but for us to make it permanent. You would have said otherwise by now if you didn't."

She clamped her lips shut. It settled something in him that she didn't deny it.

He slid his hands into her hair. "I've never before felt an urge to irrevocably claim someone as mine. But you I refuse to part with. And I'm pretty sure you don't want me to anyway. So accept that you're all-the-way mine now. You have to, Naomi. Neither myself nor my entities will give you any other choice."

"Your demons are on board?" she asked, surprised.

"When it comes to you, all four of us are completely in sync. We have been from the beginning."

He went to kiss her, but then Abraxas lunged for the surface and said, "I decided weeks ago that I would keep you."

She double-blinked. "You never said anything. And I can't say I appreciate that you didn't think to *ask* if I was good with that."

The entity shrugged. "It was a given that you would say yes to being mine."

She slid up an imperious brow. "Such arrogance."

Dagon pushed Abraxas aside, stealing supremacy. "Not arrogance. Fact." It gripped her shoulders tight. "We own you. We will always own you. There is no escape."

Belial took over then, saying, "It is best not to argue with this. To do so would make no difference. What's done is done." It then retreated, as if to stick around for a response was to suggest that she had a choice.

Naomi snorted at Luka. "Your entities are bold bastards."

"They are," he conceded. "And they meant every word of what they said. As did I."

"Even though I share Lou's DNA?"

"Even though."

"Even though I need to drink blood?"

"Even though." He framed her face with his hands. "Baby, I don't give a fuck that you need to consume blood to survive, so long *as* you survive."

Naomi swallowed again, her chest throbbing with emotion. Fuck, the guy knew how to hit her right in the feels. Her insides had melted more and more with each reassuring word he'd given her. She was close to getting all choked up. "You're sure?"

"Surer than sure." He softly dragged his fingertip down one side of her face. "Would you judge or reject me for having a dietary quirk like that?"

She snickered, her lips hitching up. "It's a little more than a dietary quirk, but no."

"Then there you go." He whispered his lips over hers. Gentle. So gentle. But his eyes were steely as they drilled into hers. "We're locking this down now. You're mine. I'm yours. Permanently."

Like she was going to argue. Not one part of her had any interest in doing so. And now, rather than wanting to make him bleed, her entity only wanted to keep him. Because he'd given it exactly what it needed—acceptance.

"No more secrets," he pressed. "If something happens in future, *you tell me.*"

She shifted uncomfortably. "There's one more thing I've kept from you."

"What's that?"

"It's better that I just show you." She pyroported them both straight into her workroom.

He frowned as the red-violet flames died down. "You don't conjure simple hellfire?"

"I can, but I'm only able to shape it into orbs. I can't use it to pyroport—that gift comes from the part of me that came from Lou. His fire is ultraviolet. But being both demon and fallen angel, it seems that my own fire is slightly different. Anyway" —she gestured at the room— "you wanted to know what was behind the locked door."

He swept his gaze around, taking in everything. "This is an art studio." His attention darted back to her. "You're one of the ghost artists Tobe's clientele uses." It was more of a statement than conjecture.

"Yes," she confirmed. "You don't look surprised."

He shrugged. "I'd already guessed."

"You'd *guessed*?"

"You sometimes smell of paint. Faintly, but still. And it was obvious by how few hours you work at the pizzeria that you had a second mode of income. It wasn't hard to put the pieces together."

Well, shit.

"Does your entire lair know?"

"No. I prefer it that way. I don't like—"

"The limelight."

"Right."

He cocked his head. "Are you the ghost artist the PI was looking for?"

"Yes, but he doesn't know that."

Luka squinted. "You're sure?"

"Positive. His client doesn't suspect it either. He barely even looked at me the time he showed up at my mom's store to talk to Tobe. It's only the clerics and their puppeteer who are a real issue."

His face hardened. "They won't be an issue for much longer. Fact is, they're already dead. No one gets to fuck with what's mine and live, especially when it comes to you."

Her demon shivered at that, and then rushed to the surface to take the wheel. "You will be good to her," it ordered. *Literally* ordered.

"Of course I will," Luka told it. "I want her to be safe, happy, and well, just as you do."

The entity sniffed. "I still plan to kill you if you hurt her."

"You seem very sure that you could."

"Because I am. And so should you be."

At a knock on the front door, Naomi's demon retreated. "That'll probably be Tobe and the others coming to check on me," she hedged. "He will have filled them all in." She pyroported both her and Luka to the hallway, and opened the front door.

Jolene entered first. "Everything all right here?" she asked, her gaze darting from Naomi to Luka.

"Everything is fine," Naomi assured her.

Tia, Alfie, and Tobe filed in behind their Prime. Naomi found herself on the receiving end of hugs, how-are-yous, and I'm-so-glad-you're-okays.

As they all poured into the living area, Tia slid Luka a quick look before refocusing on Naomi. "I'm guessing he's now fully informed where you're concerned?"

"I told him everything," she confirmed.

"Her secrets are safe with me, just as Naomi is," Luka swore. "I'd never betray my mate."

"Mate?" Jolene echoed, her voice overriding Tobe's muffled curse. "I had the feeling that things were heading in this direction. It's always nice to be right."

"I too suspected it." Tia eyed him closely. "After all, you'd be a fool not to have claimed my baby. And you don't strike me as a fool."

"I trust that you'll take care of her," Alfie said to him. "She'd allow nothing less anyway."

"Am I the only one who has reservations here?" Tobe pinned a hard look on Luka. "You may not mean to ever hurt her, but let's face it, you have a lot of enemies."

"No harm will come to her," Luka vowed, his expression solemn.

"Just because you say so?" Tobe snorted. "That isn't how it works. And I *swear* to you on all that's unholy that if anything happens to her—"

"You *promised* that you wouldn't threaten him," Naomi reminded Tobe, jabbing her elbow into his ribs.

Tobe's shoulders lifted and fell. "I'm an imp—my promises mean shit."

Lord above. "Let this be an exception."

"It's better if he and I come to an understanding from the start," Tobe insisted, all reasonable.

She flapped her arms. "What understanding?"

"That if you're harmed, I kill him. Simple."

"Kill a legion? Really?" Her demon snorted at the idea. He'd have more chance of baptizing a cat.

Luka slid closer to her. "Naomi, it's fine. I threatened Ella's mate many times. Most demons make such threats when it comes to their anchors. I wouldn't expect any different."

Tobe arched a brow at him. "So we have an understanding?"

"No," Luka replied. "Warnings are one thing. Come at

me, and you will suffer for it. Being Naomi's anchor won't save you."

Tobe stared at him for an agonizingly long moment. "Good."

She frowned, at a loss. "Why is that good?"

"Ruthlessness in a mate is a positive thing," said Tobe. "It means there's a better chance he'll do whatever's necessary to keep you safe. That works for me."

Her entity rolled its eyes. "Well, so long as you're happy," Naomi deadpanned.

Her mother smiled, amused, and then turned back to Luka. "I didn't formally introduce myself, did I? I'm Tia, Naomi's mom. This is Alfie, my mate."

Luka's gaze danced from Tia to Alfie as he inclined his head.

"You have exceptionally strong mental shields," Tia commented.

In other words, she couldn't read his thoughts. That was a relief.

"I take it you all want the full story of what happened with the clerics tonight."

"We do," said Jolene, sinking into the armchair. "Tell us."

So Naomi did. Naturally, her account was met with lots of cursing, angry outbursts, and promises that the clerics and Kushiel would meet a very painful death.

"That they would use bombs is far from holy," Alfie commented. "They're apparently prepared to step away from 'the righteous path' if it means protecting their monkhood."

"It won't matter what methods they use, they won't be successful," Luka swore. "And they *will* die for harming Naomi."

"Thus fulfilling the prophecy that the child of the devil, with the help of a legion, will take down the order and its puppeteer," mused Tia. "But had they just ignored the foretelling, it would likely never have come about. Ironic."

"I'd say we need to step up our attempts to find their location," began Jolene, "but we've poured everything we have into uncovering it. Even with the small clues we possess, our searches have been fruitless. It shouldn't be so damn hard to locate a monastery."

Luka turned to her. "Tell me about these clues. I'll add my resources to yours. Between us, we should be able to find these clerics. Just note that *I* will be the one to wipe them out."

A slow grin surfaced on Jolene's face. "It isn't me you'll need to beat to the punch. Knowing Naomi, she'll get there first."

Too freaking right she would.

After her mom, Alfie, Jolene, and Tobe left, Luka psychically summoned Daniil. The teleporter took them straight to Luka's den before then disappearing again. Naomi was about to suggest that they head upstairs and get started on making their mating official in a more physical way, but then Luka was on her.

His hands dived into her hair, his mouth latched onto hers, his kiss swept her away.

He stripped her just enough to have access to her best parts and then took her to the floor. He probed her pussy with his fingers, growled in satisfaction—presumably at how wet she was—and then plunged his cock inside her. He fucked her hard, staring into her eyes the entire time, and when her orgasm approached, her entity took charge.

The demon slid its hands up Luka's shirt and slapped them on his back; branded him right there and then, sending him over the edge and dragging Naomi with him. They lay there for long moments, striving to catch their breath.

"What does it look like?" he asked.

Knowing he was referring to the brand, she lifted her head to peer over his shoulder. "Uh, well, you now have a line of musical notes all the way down your spine."

"Musical notes? Representing the siren song, I'm guessing?"

"Yup." Sirens typically left such brands on their mates. "The top one is right there," she added, tapping his nape. "And since your hair is short, people are gonna see it easily enough." Her demon wanted everyone to know that this legion was taken.

A deep self-satisfaction bled into his eyes. "Good."

Her entity smiled, pleased by his response. "Yeah, it really is," Naomi agreed.

CHAPTER TWENTY-ONE

Wincing at the high-pitched noise that came down the line, Luka moved his cell away from his ear. He gave a quick nod of gratitude to Daniil, who'd moments ago returned him to his living area. Once the teleporter disappeared, Luka spoke into his phone again. "Was the girly squeal really necessary?"

"I'm excited for you—go sue me," said Ella. "While I'd thought that you *might* build something with Naomi, I wasn't sure you'd ever take her or anyone else as your mate."

"I still don't see how it necessitated squealing."

She huffed. "Forgive me for not wanting you to grow old alone."

"I'm a legion. I've never been anything close to alone."

"Having three inner entities isn't the same as sharing your life with someone. Now, tell me all about how you came to stake your official claim last night. I want to know how, when, what, why."

"That's a shame," he said, walking through the house as he

made his way to the foyer, intending to track down his siren, "because I have absolutely no intention of going into specifics."

Ella let out a prim sniff. "Fine. I'll just ask Naomi when we meet up at the pool hall on Thursday."

"She won't tell you either." There was too much they needed to hold back.

"I know," Ella grumbled. "She's as evasive as you are. You guys suck. And I mean that in the nicest possible way."

"There's no real way that telling someone they suck can be nice."

"Don't be so literal."

Reaching the foyer, he heard music playing low upstairs. Naomi had been running a bath when he was called away to deal with a lair matter. He'd hoped to be back in time to join her but, given she didn't play music while bathing, he was thinking he'd missed that boat.

Disappointing.

But there'd be other opportunities. Many others. Because she was his now—fully and forever. The knowledge fed something in him that he hadn't known was there.

As did the brand on his nape.

"I take it your demons are on board with your decision," Ella went on.

"On every level," Luka confirmed, climbing the winding staircase. They were also exceptionally pleased that Naomi's entity had finally branded Luka and staked its own claim.

"You feel certain none of them will later get bored and withdraw?"

"Positive. Naomi will never be free of them now that they consider her their mate." Luka's entities were hoarders; they did *not* let go of what belonged to them. "How's Lilibeth?"

"Perfectly fine. Don't try to change the subject. You have to give me more deets."

He sighed. "I don't recall questioning you so much about you taking what's-his-name as your mate."

"You *totally* questioned me over it. You said you couldn't understand why I'd want anything to do with Viper. You even contemplated killing him just to get him out of my life."

True. "I have to go," he said, arriving on the top stair.

"No you don't, you just *want* to go."

He shrugged, heading for his bedroom. "Same thing."

"Wait, before you ring off, we need to arrange a couples' evening. You, Naomi, me, and Viper—it'll be *awesome*."

Luka frowned. "No it wouldn't. So no, it isn't happening."

"Don't act like you hate spending time with Viper."

"It really isn't an act. And the couples' evening really won't happen."

"God, you're such a bore."

"I can live with that." He ended the call just as he entered the master bedroom. He paused in the doorway, finding Naomi standing near the futon, rummaging through the duffle she'd set on top of it and mouthing the lyrics of the song playing on her cell phone.

She was wearing a toweling robe, and her smooth, lightly tanned skin gleamed with a fine sheen of damp. Little droplets lingered here and there, inviting him to lap them up.

Glossy tendrils trickled down from where she'd gathered her hair into a high, messy bun. He wanted to sink his hands into it, to free her hair and wrap it around his fists.

Or his cock.

As if she felt his attention settle over her, she lifted her head and whipped it round to face the doorway. Their gazes clashed. Locked. Held.

Her pupils dilated as a hint of a smile pulled at her mouth. "You're back." She tapped the screen of her cell, and the music cut off. "All good now?"

"All good." Luka crossed to her. "I just spoke to Ella. I wanted her to hear our news from me. The demonic grapevine works at top speed."

"How did she take it?"

"Very, very well. Though she's not pleased that I won't give her all the finer details." He clasped her hips and tugged her closer. "She'll no doubt quiz you during your evening at the pool hall. She'll also probably push you to convince me to agree to a couples' evening involving us, Ella, and her mate, but trying to persuade me would be fruitless, so don't bother."

Naomi's brow pinched slightly. "Why would you be so against it?"

"Viper will never be my choice of company."

Her lips hitched up. "I don't think you dislike him as much as you claim. And if you want my opinion, it'd be better for you to just agree to her request. She'll only pester you until you do. And I'd like to meet her daughter."

Luka cocked his head as something occurred to him. "Given that Viper's a fallen celestial like Lou, it strikes me that you and Lilibeth may be similar in some ways. What kind of angel is Lou?"

"A seraphim. But with upgrades, shall we say. He was given far too much power as rewards for this or that, being God's favorite. I think it eventually corrupted him to the point that it twisted him. Or something. I don't really know, so I can only guess."

The seraphim were high-ranking, though they were a peg down from archangels. As such, Lilibeth would naturally be more powerful than Naomi. Still similar, though. Especially if Lou's curse applied to *all* the fallen. Luka couldn't ask Ella without giving some bullshit reason why he'd ever have such a question.

He trusted his anchor, but Naomi's secrets weren't his to share.

And, honestly, he felt better knowing that not many were aware of them. It was less risky that way.

Breeds of blood-drinking demons had once existed. Feeding on the essence of life had made them so incredibly strong that they were the most powerful of all. Not liking that, other breeds had slowly and steadily wiped them out.

If people were to learn that Naomi fed on blood, they would come for her. And that wasn't the only danger—many angels downright loathed even the thought of demons possessing holy blood. They, too, could come for her—especially if they learned that Lou was her father.

Luka slid a hand up her back. "You know that one of Viper's brothers is Lou's biological half-brother, right?"

"The one they call Jester, you mean? Yes, I know. Lou talks about him sometimes."

"Does Jester know that you're his niece?"

"Nope." Naomi planted her hands on Luka's chest. "Lou is super secretive about our familial connection, paranoid over my safety."

"I like that he's so protective of you." It also surprised Luka, because he hadn't heard many positives things about Lou. "You're not curious about Jester? I mean, he's your uncle."

"And he may therefore know about Lou's curse," she pointed out. "If he learns who I am, he might guess that I share in that curse."

"All the fallen might share in it."

"True. But they also might not."

"Haven't you asked Lou?"

"Yes. He said he didn't know, but that might have been a lie to keep me from wanting to hang with any of the fallen. He wouldn't risk any figuring out he's my dad for fear that they used the info to earn their way back to heaven or something. As I said before, he's paranoid over my safety."

"And with good reason." Luka stroked his fingers down her neck, tracing over the brand there. "How often do you need to feed?"

"Weekly, but I don't need much of it each time. Lou was worried that I'd go through short periods where I'd be in the grip of a kind of bloodlust, but that's never happened. Now that I have an anchor, it's all but guaranteed that it never will."

Which was yet another reason to be glad that she'd found her psi-mate, even if a part of Luka didn't like that she was so closely bonded to another man. "Tobe was right in claiming that you being mine could endanger you. Those who are entrenched in the criminal underworld will consider you off limits—anchors and mates always are. But demons outside of this life won't necessarily respect that, so precautions will be necessary. I take your safety very seriously. Something that can't have escaped your attention."

She squinted. "What you're saying is that Konstantin will be my guard on a permanent basis."

"Yes, and he won't be following behind you anymore; he'll be at your side. I have bodyguards as well," Luka reminded her. "It's par for the course when you're a Prime, just as it is for those who are deeply involved with one."

"But the clerics might try to hurt him again."

"He'll know to look out for them now. Though it's sweet that you'd worry for him, it's his risk to take—and he will willingly take it. He's *your* bodyguard, not the other way around."

Naomi let out a *humph*. "While I can't deny that it's better to take such precautions, I do worry that Konstantin will notice things he shouldn't if he's constantly around."

"He'll only be with you when you're out and about. You'll have privacy indoors, so he won't pick up on things you'd prefer he didn't." On *that* subject . . . Luka offered her his hand. "Come with me. I want to show you something."

Curiosity glimmering in her eyes, she placed her palm in his. "Ooh, what exactly?"

He didn't respond. He led her out of the room, down the hall, and into a spare bedroom that he'd recently emptied. It was spacious, with big windows that provided plenty of natural light. As she glanced around, he said, "I thought it would make a good art studio."

Her gaze shot back to his, surprised. "I . . . An art studio?"

"You had to know that I'd want you to move in here."

"I didn't think you'd want me to do it right away."

"You consented to being mine. I won't live apart from my mate." He tucked a stray lock of hair behind her ear. "I realize that you're used to living close to your family, but they're not exactly hours away from here. They're welcome to visit you any time."

Her brow flicked up. "Imps are welcome here? Really?"

"If they mean something to you, yes. Just make them vow not to steal anything. I'd prefer not to have to separate them from their fingers and toes."

Leaning back, she stared at him. "I can't quite tell if you're being serious about the latter."

Luka pulled her flush against him. "I know this is a big step, and you may feel that things are moving very fast. But I'm asking you to do it anyway. I want you here with me, where you belong." He swept a hand down her spine. "As a bonus, you'll be safer here than at your own house."

"First you want me to consent to having a permanent bodyguard, and now you want me to agree to move into your home." She sniffed, haughty. "Anything else you want from me?"

"Not at the moment. But give it time."

She snorted, her lips curling, and then nipped the tip of his ear—and not at all gently.

He rubbed at the small hurt, cursing in Russian.

"That's what you get," Naomi said with a prim little sniff. She cocked her head. "I've noticed that you speak Russian sometimes, though mostly only to curse or to whisper stuff when we're doing the dirty. Are you fluent in it because your parents spoke the language around you or because you once lived in Russia?"

Many times he'd been asked that question. Few times had he answered it, and never with women who shared his bed—his defenses had risen up in reflex and slammed up a mental wall. That didn't happen with Naomi; she wasn't just anyone to him.

"I was born there," he replied. "I spent some of my childhood there."

She idly dragged her fingertips along his nape. "Why did your parents relocate?"

"Ugly intra-lair problems eventually resulted in it dividing three ways. That wasn't enough to bring an end to those issues. The three lairs would cross each other in various ways, resulting in multiple deaths. My uncle had moved here years before; he invited my parents and some others to join the lair he'd integrated into. They accepted the invitation but soon after started their own lair, with my father as Prime—and crime boss."

She tilted her head. "How old are you?"

His lips quirking, he flicked her nose with his. "Much, much older than you."

"So I have a sugar daddy," she teased. "Never had one of those before. It's working out okay so far."

"Glad to hear you feel that way."

"Where are your parents now?"

"Somewhere," he prevaricated. "A crime boss doesn't get to leave this life unless he's prepared to go where he'll never be found. It's commonly done. They wanted out; said their time was over. They took my younger sister with them so that no one could use her to flush my father out."

Naomi frowned. "But not you?" she asked, a note of protective outrage in her voice that melted something in him.

"I was his heir. Which wasn't enough to guarantee that his role would become mine, of course. I was groomed from an early age to take over."

"No one tried using you to lure your father out of hiding?"

"It was attempted only once. The consequences convinced others to let it be. Most demonic crime bosses don't really want to drag retirees out into the open, because they plan to retire in the same fashion one day."

"Do you like being a crime boss?"

"Yes. It gives me and my entities what we need. All demons crave power, control, respect, and authority. The cravings are much worse for legions. Those things don't merely satisfy us, they play a part in stabilizing us." He trailed a fingertip down her throat. "Your own demon doesn't seem to yearn for those things, if your lifestyle is anything to go by."

"Being a siren comes with personal power," she pointed out. "Both me and my demon can control a person's actions with words alone; make them do whatever we want; render them at our mercy that easily."

"Knowing you have that ability over everyone you meet, should you care to use it, is enough to give your entity a sense of power and control?"

"Yes."

"But you don't get the same satisfaction from it as your demon," he stated.

Her eyes narrowed slightly. "What makes you think that?"

"You're not a person who seeks to control others. It may

comfort you to know that you can use such a gift in your own defense, but you wouldn't get pleasure from it."

"You say that with certainty."

"If I was wrong, you'd be stealing people's wills all the time to get whatever you want out of life. You don't do that. Nor do you battle for control in or out of bed. It just isn't something that feeds any part of you."

Naomi stared at him, thinking he knew her too well; realizing that she no longer felt uncomfortable with it. Nothing inside her tensed or bristled, and she felt no reflexive urge to pull inward. They were past that now. He'd accepted all she'd hid from him, and that meant everything to not only her but her entity. "Whereas you very much like to control those around you."

"I do." An easy, unapologetic agreement.

"You like to see them bend to your will."

He kissed his way down her throat. "Bend. Crumble. Break." He nipped her pulse. "I like it when you shatter for me."

"I like it when you make me shatter. You're rather good at it, as I'm sure you're well aware. All the ladies in your past no doubt made it clear." *Hoes.*

Okay, so that was harsh—they were probably lovely. It was just hard to think of them in a positive light when they'd touched her mate. Her entity would happily set them on fire.

"You said that your demons made relationships difficult, so flings are just easier," she recalled. "Have you ever been in a real relationship?"

Another nip to her pulse. "No."

"So you never came close to taking a mate?"

He met her gaze again. "There was a time when my father wanted me to take another crime boss's daughter as my mate. Since I couldn't imagine ever really committing to someone in a meaningful way, I contemplated it and agreed to meet with her. Things never went further than that, though."

"Why not?"

"I didn't like her. Neither did Abraxas. Dagon found her incredibly boring. Belial had no interest in her, and was very put off by sensing she had a masochistic streak."

Naomi felt her brows draw together. "But . . . Belial is sadistic."

"Too sadistic to find satisfaction in doling out pain to those who'd enjoy it."

"Oh," she breathed. It was only then that she realized . . . "It leaves all these injury-themed brands on me because it knows that I find it annoying."

His lips twitched. "Any kind of suffering feeds it—even emotional suffering. But it doesn't want to see you hurt or angry. It'll settle for irritation."

"I should really just kick it or something."

Luka's smile hitched up a notch. "Now you're just amusing it."

Hmm, no doubt.

"You didn't agree to my request before," he noted, his gaze snaring hers. "Move in with me," he urged in a whisper that was somehow both coaxing and forceful. "We could live in your house if it's what you really want, but as I said before, you'll be safer here. I'd prefer that we make this our home. Or we could find somewhere else; choose a place that is equally secure—whatever you want. The important thing to me is that we don't live apart."

She wasn't particularly attached to her house, only her workroom. But *this* room . . . yes, she could see herself setting up a workspace here. Could see herself living in this house, where she knew *he'd* be safest.

As Tobe liked to point out, Luka had many enemies. Her home was nowhere near as secure as this place. The harder it was for anyone to get to him, the better. Her safety was his priority, and that went both ways.

So she let her lips curve as she murmured, "Okay, I'll move in here."

Satisfaction lit his eyes, and his own mouth winged up. "Just what I wanted to hear."

CHAPTER TWENTY-TWO

"I'm just so fucking thrilled that you and Luka took the plunge," said Ella the following Friday as she slid clothes hangers back and forth on a metal rail, filling the air with clicks and clacks. "I originally found it hard to envision him committing to anyone, but when I saw him with you ... I don't know, I just got a vibe that there was potential there."

Looking away from where Konstantin stood near the door—his manner awkward as two moms flirted with him while their kids tried climbing out of their strollers—Naomi said, "I see now that I was ignoring that potential so I wouldn't be disappointed if nothing came of it." She paused, skipping a narrow aisle that was packed with people. "I hadn't let myself really acknowledge how much I wanted more from him."

"Well, now you have the *ultimate* more."

She did indeed, and she couldn't be happier about it.

As arranged, Naomi had met up with Ella and her sister at the pool hall last night. It was sweet how close the incantors were, being as much besties as they were siblings. But since Mia had needed to cancel her trip to the mall with Ella today, the girls had suggested that Naomi go in her place.

Ella's lips hitched up. "It's a big deal that he asked you to move in with him, you know. Luka's not great at sharing his space, no matter how huge said space is."

Naomi had spent the past several days transferring her possessions to his house little by little. There wasn't much left to move at this point. "I sensed as much, so I worried he'd find it weird. That turned out to be a senseless worry. He seems rather self-satisfied about the whole thing."

"Of course he is. Talking of self-satisfied . . . It's cute how smug he is that your entity branded him. I mean, he isn't obvious about it—you have to know him well to detect just how much it affects him."

Smug was a mild word for it, in truth. But her demon loved that sign that its mate was so *all* in; that its brand meant that much to him.

Word of Naomi and Luka's mating had traveled fast. News always did in the world of demons. That the demonic population understood he was off limits . . . well, Naomi could admit she liked it a whole lot.

"Don't be surprised if he puts a black diamond on your finger sometime soon," Ella threw out.

Naomi did a double-take. "Huh?"

"I know demons don't give them to their mates unless they are super certain about them, but there's zero chance that Luka doesn't feel that way about you. He would never claim someone lightly."

Very true. Naomi just hadn't considered it before.

"Will you freak out if he produces a ring?"

Naomi inhaled deeply, searching within herself. "No. Because just as he wouldn't claim a person lightly, neither would I. I'm super sure about him as well." As was her demon. And since it liked shiny things, it would gladly wear his ring.

Ella nodded, satisfied. "Excellent. Because I'm pretty sure you'd find it literally impossible to ever leave him. He wouldn't allow it. Not for anything," she added, adjusting the position of the running pants she'd tossed over her shoulder.

A few T-shirts were draped over Naomi's arm, her other arm supporting the weight of the plastic bags she held. They'd been at the mall a couple of hours now, so she was carrying several bags, though not as many as Ella—the redhead had splurged quite a bit when buying cute things for her daughter.

The mall here at the Underground was like most. The indoor building featured skylights, tiled flooring, lounge areas, retail stores, specialty kiosks, water fountains, coffee houses, smoothie bars, and a large food court.

You could buy practically anything—clothes, toys, electronics, houseware, skincare products, jewelry. You name it, some store within the mall sold it.

This particular store mostly sold casual wear and sporty gear, though there was a small racy lingerie section that seemed a little out of place. The inky scent of new clothing laced the air, along with those of perfumes and metal.

It was packed with lone shoppers, couples, clusters of giggling teen girls, and women pushing strollers. The echoes of voices, ringing of phones, whir of the air conditioning, and scraping of metal against metal mingled with the pop music playing over the store's speakers.

The strong lighting and white walls were a contrast to the dark faux-wood flooring. Large posters of women in various clothing stood out against the bright paint. Tall mirrors were scattered around. Red *SALE* signs hung on some racks.

"How did your anchor take the news about you and Luka?" asked Ella.

"He isn't thrilled about it." In a telepathic conversation days ago, during which it had become clear that Tobe felt slightly threatened by her having such a deep bond with another male, she'd said, *We've been over this; no mate could take your place in my life*, to which he had petulantly replied, *I know, but I don't have to like that Luka's made his own place in it, and you can't make me.* But at the end of said conversation ... "He told me that he sort of gives his blessing, though."

Amusement bled into the incantor's eyes. "Sort of?"

Naomi shrugged. "Tobe's a diva at times."

"And his nose feels a little pushed out, I'm guessing."

"A little."

"That's only to be expected, really. Demons often react that way to their anchors taking a mate." Ella nabbed a tester perfume from a rack and sprayed the air. Inhaling through her nose, she hummed. "Nice." She spritzed her neck and then grabbed an unopened bottle while returning the tester. "How has your family taken the news?"

"My mother's pleased—she was rooting for us. My stepfather said he's happy so long as I'm happy."

"I guess, what with the activities your lair gets up to, your family's not all that fazed by Luka's ... position, shall we say."

"No, they're not. Nor is the rest of the lair, so all is good on that front."

Ella skimmed her fingers over the sleeve of a jacket. "I suppose they also like knowing that if those weird clerics strike again, he'll be able to help." She checked the price tag, frowned, and moved on. "Not that you'll need much help against a bunch of humans ordinarily. But those who can channel divine power and are prepared to work with explosives? That's a whole other matter."

Yeah, due to the public nature of the attack, there had been no way to keep it quiet. All Naomi could do was control the narrative. She'd been unable to leave out the detail of the monkhood, since two of them had been caught on CCTV hovering near her and Konstantin's vehicles outside the entrance to the Underground.

She'd played it off as an idiotic bunch of religious fanatics insisting that she would birth the Antichrist by quoting some "apparent human prophecy that may or may not exist". Everyone thought it dumb and pitiful, since Satan lived deep in the bowels of hell, so there was no chance of the Antichrist being born here on earth.

Of course, if anyone got curious enough about the prophecy to go searching for it and translated it correctly, they'd realize that there was no use of the word "Antichrist"; that it had instead stated "the progeny of the devil". Such people might find it a little too coincidental that the prophecy also mentioned a legion, so they might wonder if Lou was in fact her father.

As such, she could only hope that no one tried digging it up. Given how hard it had been for Khloë to find it, though, Naomi didn't suppose she needed to be *too* concerned.

Dodging an oddly angled hanger, she refocused on the conversation at hand. "Konstantin checks both our cars for explosives every time we intend to drive anywhere now."

"The clerics probably won't make such a move again," Ella hedged. "It would be too predictable. But it's better to be safe than sorry."

Naomi inwardly grimaced, feeling a little shitty about misleading her mate's anchor. She couldn't tell her the truth, though. She had initially worried that it would upset Luka to have to lie to Ella, but he'd insisted that no exceptions could be made; that Naomi's safety took priority.

While it didn't surprise her that he'd be resolute about keeping her secrets, it did surprise her that he would so easily lie for her—even by omission—to his own psi-mate. What surprised her even more was that he hadn't again brought up her "dietary quirk". As if it just wasn't anything important.

He'd asked about the whole ghost-artistry situation, though. While he had admitted that the risks it presented to her bothered him, he hadn't tried telling her to give up her job. And when she'd showed him one of her paintings, he'd said, "Exquisite. Like you."

He *so* got lucky later on.

Wincing at the loud screech of a metal hanger grinding along a rack, Naomi looked over at Ella. "So, since you clearly feel I pass muster, when do I get to meet Lilibeth?"

The redhead grinned. "Any time you want. But beware, she's very advanced mentally and psychically. So no cooing or baby babble—she finds it condescending and tends to then dish out telekinetic slaps. Which I think is why Lou does it to her so much. He finds it amusing." Pausing, Ella moved aside so that a salesperson sporting a headset could squeeze past her. "Have you ever met him, Naomi? The devil, I mean?"

Naomi hid a smile. "Yes, I have. He gatecrashes a lot of our lair's parties. Much as he complains about imps, he likes that they're as shrewd and conniving as he is."

Ella chuckled. "I can imagine. He finds Lily fascinating."

Naomi knew that, because her father liked to talk about both Lilibeth and Asher—Harper and Knox's son. They amused him something fierce. He insisted on viewing himself as their honorary uncle.

Ella let out a small *oof* as her bulkiest plastic bag was knocked by a passing shopper and banged into her knee.

Naomi winced in sympathy. "Need help carrying anything?"

Ella's shopping bag crinkled as she readjusted its position. "I'm good, but thanks. Well, aside from these pants"—she touched the pair still hanging over her shoulder—"I can't find anything I like." She twisted her mouth. "I'm gonna check out the discount area. What about you?"

Naomi flicked a look at the tees draped over her arm. "I'm fine with just these. I'll need to try them on, though."

"Go ahead; I'll keep hunting."

While Ella headed to the discount area, Naomi strode into the unmanned changing rooms. She slowed her pace as she searched for an unoccupied cubicle. Hooks scraped a rail up ahead as a curtain was shoved aside, and then out walked Draya.

Oh, how awesome.

The blonde went still, tension creeping into her muscles and turning her jaw into a hard line. An ugly gleam in her eyes, she clung tight to a hanger she held and presented Naomi with a fake smile. "I heard about you and Luka," she said, an edge to her voice. "Congrats."

"Thanks," said Naomi, her demon liking the banshee's obvious annoyance.

"You know, I never would have predicted that he would fall victim to a siren's song. I thought he'd be tougher than that. Stronger than people like Iain. Life continues to surprise me."

Naomi almost rolled her eyes. "If you need to tell yourself that's what happened..."

"It's the only thing that *could* have happened," Draya snapped. "Nothing else would explain Luka claiming you. He has never once spoken of taking a mate. When his lair members at the casino sensed that I was interested in him, they all warned me that he didn't do permanence."

"Lots of people don't. Until they do. Until they meet someone they want to keep in their lives."

Draya gave her head a small shake. "Your song has him under its spell," she insisted, several emotions swirling in her eyes—irritation, bitterness, resentment, and ... embarrassment?

Naomi frowned. She'd expected jealousy; classic woman-scorned glares. Draya, though ... "You have the look of a person who feels they've been outwitted."

Draya's head jerked. "What does that even mean?"

"I think you know exactly what it means," said Naomi, the pieces falling into place. "He was just a mark to you, wasn't he?"

"A mark?" Draya tittered, dismissive, but more tension filled her frame.

"I knew someone like you once. She would choose a guy who she decided would make a good provider of luxury and diamonds and all those things. Once she'd used him up, she would move on to another mark."

Draya's eyes flickered.

"You meant to bag Luka, intended to get whatever you could out of him. You got the job at Infernal so that you could get close to him and learn his patterns, likes, dislikes; so you could question the staff there about him to learn even more. You also tried milking Ella for information about him, the kind that would allow you to profile him to some extent. Then you would have fashioned yourself into whatever you thought would make him keep you around." It all made sense now.

The blonde forced an exaggerated huff, but her discomfort was clear. "That's quite a theory."

"And utterly accurate, I'd say. You set out to swindle him, basically. Except it didn't work. He didn't want you."

Draya slammed a burning stare on Naomi. "Oh, he did. He likely still does. But he got distracted by your song. Well, *he* may have been snagged by it, but it won't have worked on his entities. They're not so easy to kid. They'll press him to end the relationship."

Naomi pointed at the brand on her throat. "Does it really look like they want to fight Luka on this?"

Draya's eyes narrowed. "How did you manipulate the entity into marking you?"

"I didn't. Dagon acted of its own accord. As did Belial and Abraxas when they branded me." But of course the woman would think Naomi had conned them somehow. "You see, I'm not like you. I don't seek to play men. Fact is, I don't have to."

An indignant flush crept up Draya's neck and into her face, while her ears reddened.

"Your plan would never have been successful, by the way. Luka's too smart for that. He would have picked up on all the red flags. He would have sensed your game, and he would have put a fast end to it. In short, you chose the wrong target."

Draya's lips flattened. "You could be right. But then you also could be wrong. So if he dumps you at some point in the future, I'll slide back into the picture. And I *will* have him. I'll show you how securing a mark is truly done."

"Not my style."

"Oh, *come on*. You're a siren. It's what they do. Choose, seduce, trap, exploit."

"No, it's what *you'd* do if you were a siren. I'm no user."

Draya let out a fake laugh. "Of course you are. Willingly or not, you're as much a manipulator of men as I am. I'm just honest about it." She looked Naomi up and down. "You're too much of an uppity, cowardly little bitch to admit it."

A feminine sigh drifted through the air. "Really, Draya, you hate your job so much that you want to get fired?" asked Ella. "Because that's what will happen after this."

Both Naomi and Draya looked at the redhead.

"Not an issue." Draya jerkily tugged at the hem of her floral blouse. "I was planning to quit anyway." With that, she marched out of the changing rooms.

Rolling her eyes, Ella crossed to Naomi. "I take it she's upset that Luka claimed you?"

"Not for the reasons I would imagine you're thinking," said Naomi. "She was never really interested in him as a person. He was her mark. She'd intended to hook him, use him, and then eventually drop him."

"Ah. So that's what she meant by the whole 'you're as much a manipulator of men as I am'."

"Yup."

Ella sighed. "He isn't going to be happy that she got all up in your face like that. You are planning to tell him, right? Because if you don't, I will. He's your mate. It's the kind of thing he should be made aware of."

"I know." It would totally feel like tattling about the mean girl at school to her parents, but she'd sworn to him that there would be no more secrets. "When I see him later, I'll tell him. He'll probably just do what you did and roll his eyes."

CHAPTER TWENTY-THREE

Watching from her living room sofa later that day as Luka paced like a caged jungle cat, Naomi inwardly sighed. "I really just thought that you'd roll your eyes."

He slid her a surprised look. "Excuse me?"

When he'd appeared to help her transfer the rest of her stuff to his place, she'd lapped up his little displays of possessive affection before casually tossing out that she'd had a brief chat with Draya. As was typical of Luka, he'd demanded every last detail. With each one she'd revealed, his expression had gone darker. And then a stream of Russian curses had all but burst out of him as he began to pace back and forth.

Well, who would like hearing that they'd been someone's mark? That they hadn't sensed such a thing? That they'd almost gone ahead and slept with a person who had set out to manipulate and use them?

Maybe Naomi should have kept the confrontation to herself after all. At least for a short while. He was already on edge due to the cleric situation. But then Ella would have informed him of it anyway, so keeping it quiet hadn't really been an option.

She rose from the sofa. "I can understand why you'd be mad that Draya thought she had a prayer of playing you, but—"

"That's not why I'm pissed," he said, coming to a halt.

She felt her brows slide together. "It's not?"

"No. I'm pissed that she dared go near you."

Aw, he was too sweet. "She didn't really have much of a choice, to be fair. The changing rooms weren't at all spacious, so there was no real way she could have physically avoided me."

Luka prowled toward her. "She could have stepped aside, let you pass, and walked right on out of there. She could have kept her mouth shut and her opinions to herself. But no. She decided to give you grief instead."

"She didn't touch me, though," Naomi reminded him. "She just—"

"Tried filling your head with shit and called you a cowardly little bitch," he finished, his tone clipped.

Naomi shrugged. "I've been called worse."

His eyes blazed, a murderous glint in their depths. "By who?"

"Uh, never mind. Doesn't matter. Forget I said anything." She fisted the front of his shirt. "Look, I'm not upset. What she thinks or feels means nothing to me."

"What she did is still unacceptable. Whether it bothered you isn't the point. She should *never* have dared pull that shit."

In total agreement, her inner entity nodded firmly. Unsurprising. Since it was evident by the lethal edge in Luka's voice that repercussions would be due, she asked, "What are you going to do?"

"Something she won't like," he answered vaguely.

Naomi exhaled heavily, knowing that she couldn't talk him

out of retaliating. This was who he was. A person who'd never let a slight to his mate go unaddressed. And she wouldn't want him any other way. Nor would her demon, who very much approved of his plan. *Typical.*

"Fine. Can we not talk about her any more, though?" She leaned into him, sliding her palms up his chest. "I'd rather we just finished moving this stuff to your place and then enjoyed our evening."

His arms came around her, his hands settling on her lower back. "You're sure you're all right?"

"Positive. Honestly," she assured him, but it didn't soften his expression any.

He cast her a look of reprimand. "You should have telepathed me the moment Draya opened her mouth."

"To what purpose? Luka, I'm not going to request you intervene to fight my every battle—especially the teensy ones. I don't need you to do that for me. And I wouldn't feel good about myself, about us, if I forced myself to lean on you for everything when it goes against who I am."

He clenched his jaw. "Why did you have to word it like that?"

She stifled a smile. "Oh, I'm sorry, does it cut into your argument?"

"Yes."

Her demon snickered, amused. "If you want a mate who'll turn to you for every little thing . . ."

"I want you. Only you." He nuzzled her face, his hand gliding down to rest on her ass. "I accept that this is who you are, but I reserve the right to complain when I don't get my way in everything."

"That sounds reasonable."

"Does it?"

"Uh, no, but whatever."

"And just *why* does that legion have his hands all over you?" demanded a new voice.

Naomi froze. *Ah, hell.* She very slowly turned her head. Lou stood a few feet away in a scruffy tee and faded jeans, a joint between his fingers, his angry gaze bouncing from her to Luka.

Turning to face him fully, she forced a smile. "Hello, Dad."

He stiffened. "What . . ."

"Luka knows you're my father. I had to tell him."

Lou's face scrunched up. "Why?"

"We claimed each other."

His eyes fairly bugged out of his head. "*Claimed?* You *claimed* each other?"

"Yes."

"When?" he demanded, a near-hysterical note to his voice that tickled her entity.

"Like . . . six days ago."

His expression firmed. "So the same day clerics blew up your car—something you failed to mention. I had to find out from someone else, which is what I came here to whine at you about. Something I would have enjoyed. But this" —he flicked a finger from her to Luka — "I'm not so jolly about." He peered down at his joint. "I'm hallucinating. That's what it is. Maybe Jester dosed the weed with LSD. Sounds like something he'd do."

Pausing, Lou inhaled deeply and then closed his eyes. "This isn't real. My baby girl is not mated. She's not. It's an illusion within an illusion. When I open my eyes, the legion will be gone. Like magick." He opened his eyes, his shoulders slumped, and he looked back at the joint. "The LSD is strong in this one."

Oh Lord. "You're not hallucinating. This situation is very much real. I claimed Luka. He claimed me. We're mates."

Lou's joint abruptly disappeared in a ball of ultraviolet flames.

His brows squishing together, he dropped his hand to his side. "How can you be mated? I didn't even know you were dating anyone."

"You didn't ask."

"And if I had?"

"I . . . I would have told you."

He shot her an indignant look. "You think you're going to get a lie past *me*, the ultimate connoisseur of deception? Really? And why would you date *him*, of all people?"

Naomi felt her brows snap together in affront. "What's wrong with him?"

"Uh, *everything*," Lou drawled. "His reputation is widely known. He's cold-blooded. Vindictive. Lethal. Volatile. He has *three inner entities*—even for me that's fucking weird."

She folded her arms. "And if he had only one entity and was none of those things you listed, you'd be fine with this?"

"No."

"So, basically, you wouldn't like him no matter what?"

"Basically."

Her demon rolled its eyes. Honestly, Lou was a total man child. "Well, that's just too bad. Luka's my choice. You'll have to accept that."

"Why?" It was a genuine question.

"As my father, you're supposed to be supportive."

"You continue to expect reasonable reactions from me. I have *no* idea why that is. We long ago established that I would always do outrageous things."

Absolutely true. However . . . "What other option do you have *but* to accept this?"

Lou twisted his mouth, pensive. "I could drag him down to hell."

Naomi stiffened. "You *promised* you wouldn't do that to

someone I care about ever again. I'm still traumatized by how you tossed poor Donatello into an abyss down there."

Lou's jaw tightened at the memory. "The little bastard bit me."

She scoffed. "No he didn't."

"Yes he did!"

"He was a turtle. They don't have teeth."

Luka shifted slightly, drawing Lou's attention. "Normally I wouldn't care what anyone thought of Naomi and me claiming each other. But as you're her father, I'll give you the assurance you need. Still, I'm going to say this to you only once; whether you believe it or not is up to you. I'm not a good person. I've never tried to be. I've done nothing to deserve having something as good as Naomi in my life. Nonetheless, I'm keeping her. There's not a single thing more important to me than she is."

Lou pulled a face, flapping a hand. "Blah, blah, blah, words are cheap, blah."

"*Dad*," Naomi groaned.

"I'm not wrong," he maintained, folding his arms. "I don't believe him. And I don't like him. And you can't make me be nice to him. So there."

"Your level of maturity is overwhelming."

Lou squinted. "I detected a hint of sarcasm there."

"Oh, it was no hint. It was *full-on* sarcasm." Naomi put her hands on her hips. "Why would you find it so hard to believe that he cares about me? Are you saying I'm unlovable?"

Lou wagged his finger at her. "Don't. Don't start trying to talk me in circles. I'm too stoned for that shit, it'll make me dizzy." He crossed to her and rested his hands on her upper arms. "Listen to me, men are the worst. Pigs. Liars. Adulterers. We have no practical relevance other than to help ensure the propagation of our respective species. That's it. That's all we have to offer."

"So what you're saying is you'd prefer I was into women?"

"Celibacy," he asserted. "Celibacy is the only avenue that leads to happiness."

"Are *you* celibate?"

"No. But I wouldn't know happiness if it took a steaming shit on my head, so we don't need to worry about me. Only you. Just. You."

Beyond exasperated at this point, Naomi said, "Maybe I should telepath Jolene and ask her to come over. She can help bring the tension down a few notches." Or, more accurately, the Prime would annoy the crap out of him—they'd been frenemies for years.

Lou stilled, his mouth dropping open. "Oh, you're diabolical."

Naomi grinned. "Thank you."

Releasing her arms, he dropped his own to his sides and let out a dramatic huff. "Is it so wrong that I want you to have a decent man in your life?"

"I thought you said all men are pigs."

"There are some exceptions. You could find one easy. They'd flock to you because they'd sense you're special."

She snorted. "If I had a decent man anywhere in my general vicinity, you'd hate him *because* he was decent. You'd say he was weak and boring and you'd throw things at him for fun. Tell me I'm wrong—and mean it."

Lou gave her a sulky look. "It's occasionally discomforting that you know me as well as you do."

"Just occasionally? I'd better put a little more effort into it."

His lips curled. "That's my girl." His smile faded as he glanced from her to Luka. "So it's a done deal? You insist on giving him a home?"

Naomi felt her brow crease. "He's a person, not a pet."

"He's a man. Men are pigs. Pigs can be pets. Ergo . . ."

"Oh my God, you are unbelievably ridiculous."

He frowned. "Why do you always say that?"

"Because it's so very true."

"What's ridiculous is you taking a legion as your mate. Come on, you're smarter than this!"

Luka stepped closer to her, his attention on Lou. "You're free to disapprove of me, but don't raise your voice at Naomi. I don't like it."

She winced. *Uh-oh*. Her dad was going to flip his lid for sure.

Except . . . he didn't. He didn't bristle. Didn't get mad. Didn't give Luka a load of shit. Hell, he didn't even look her mate's way. As if refusing to acknowledge not only Luka's words but his very presence.

She heaved a sigh. "You're going to pretend Luka's not here, aren't you?"

Lou shrugged. "It's that or beat him bloody. He's defiling my once-virginal daughter."

Naomi scratched her cheek. "Uh, sorry to burst your bubble, Dad, but I lost my virginity years a—"

"La, la, la, la, deaf ears."

Fuck this shit. "That's it, I'm calling Jolene."

Lou scowled. "Don't bother, I'm leaving. I'm gonna smoke another joint, eat some munchies, and pray to the lunar gods that this was all a funky-ass dream."

She tipped her head to the side. "Are there such things as lunar gods?"

"We'll soon fucking find out." He clicked his heels and disappeared.

Blowing out a long breath, she shoved a hand into her hair as she slowly turned to face Luka. He wore the look of someone who'd just been poleaxed. *Sigh*. Plenty of people wore that look after meeting Lucifer.

She cleared her throat. "So. That's my dad. Quite a gem, isn't he?"

"Hmm." After a long moment of silence, Luka raised a finger. "I have a question. Why would he banish a turtle to hell?"

"Jolene gave Donatello to me as a birthday gift. Lou didn't like that I was so delighted with it. He felt outdone and jealous. She made it worse by smirking at him smugly. And, as I'm sure you noticed, his thought processes aren't normal. So in his head, it was a perfectly reasonable reaction to throw the turtle into an abyss, never to be seen again."

Luka twisted his mouth. "Hmm," he repeated.

She expected him to ply her with more questions, but he said nothing, just stared into the distance, his expression blank. "You're still stuck processing him, aren't you? Yeah, it takes most people's brains a fair few moments to do that. You'll snap out of it soon. Want a beer while we wait?"

"Hmm."

She gave a nod. "Beer it is."

CHAPTER TWENTY-FOUR

Heading home from the pizzeria the next evening, Naomi slid Konstantin a quick look. The bodyguard was walking beside her rather than behind her—a new practice that Luka had warned her would be typical from here on out.

Due to his powerful build, there was zero chance he'd go unnoticed. Nobody's eyes would gloss over almost seven feet of roped, bulging muscles. He looked like a damn wrestler. That she so obviously had personal protection would hopefully act as a deterrent to anyone who would dare think to mess with her.

The current dark expression he wore only added to his don't-come-close air. She could guess what had put that look on his face.

She nibbled on her lower lip. "You're still mad at me, huh?"

He looked at her askance. "Why would I be mad? You only neglected to tell me—your personal bodyguard—that you had clerics on your ass, which interfered with my ability to properly protect you. Why would that bother me?" Sarcasm at its finest.

Naomi sighed. "I didn't think they'd strike while you or anyone else were near. They seemed set on getting me alone. I really am sorry that I kept you in the dark. If I'd known that they would even so much as *think* to use bombs... It just hadn't occurred to me that they would go that far."

"Which I can understand, because clerics usually rely on magick, and explosives aren't at all their style. But that isn't the point, is it?"

"No. And I'm sorry that they almost killed you."

He cast her a frown. "Told you before, that wasn't your fault. The apology doesn't need to come from you. My problem is that you hid from me that you had danger dogging your heels. That's something I needed to be made aware of."

"I wasn't trying to make your job more difficult than it is. I just wasn't ready to tell Luka everything, which meant I also couldn't tell *you*."

His frown deepened. "Don't know why you thought it necessary to hide that you're part celestial. Luka's the last person who'd care about something like that."

Wanting to be able to pyroport around the mansion at her leisure, she'd permitted Luka to inform his most trusted demons—namely his bodyguards and Konstantin—that her father was a fallen angel to account for why her fire wasn't normal. But he hadn't told them that her dad was Lucifer—they intended to keep that a secret from all.

None of the three had batted an eyelid on hearing that she had celestial blood. She supposed it was no biggie to them, given that they were around Lilibeth and the Black Saints often. They were used to hybrids like herself.

Luka would have liked to also tell Ella about Naomi being part angel, but he didn't feel comfortable doing so. Truly, neither did Naomi. If every fallen angel *did* share in Lou's curse, Ella—being mated to a fallen celestial—would be aware of that. As such, she would therefore also guess that Naomi had to drink blood. And while it wasn't likely that she would leak the information, neither Luka nor Naomi wanted anyone else to be aware of it.

The fewer people who knew of a secret, the easier it was to protect it. Simple.

Of course, Lou's curse might *not* be something that applied to all fallen angels, in which case Ella couldn't possibly guess about Naomi's "dietary quirk". However, it was worth noting that Ella was leery of all celestials due to some having tried to kill her when she was pregnant with Lilibeth. She would therefore naturally wish to know who Naomi's father was in order to establish if he should be considered a threat—something she would consult Viper about, since he would know of many fallen angels.

Sure, Naomi could lie and claim that she had no idea who her father was, but then they'd just go ask Tia. And yes, Tia could lie to them as well. But it made more sense to just tell the couple nothing at all rather than feed them falsities.

Snapping back to the conversation, she said, "It wasn't that I thought it would put him off. It wasn't about Luka at all. My mom never wanted people to know that I wasn't full demon because half-breeds aren't always welcome if they're part celestial. As such, very few people know. Even most of my lair are in the dark. I didn't intend on sharing it with Luka unless things got serious."

"You could have told him about the clerics without mentioning that you had celestial DNA."

"He would have asked if I was keeping anything else from him. I would have had to lie. I didn't want to do that. Whatever you might think, I didn't feel good about keeping things from him. Or from you."

Konstantin's expression softened. "I don't for a second think that you felt good about it. But I do think there's another reason you kept the stuff about the clerics to yourself."

"What's that?"

"You didn't want Luka to feel that he had to keep rescuing you."

Naomi blinked. Huh, now that she thought about it, there was *some* truth to that. "You could say that I was reluctant to drag him into anything else. First he had to step in to deal with Iain. Then the PI."

"And you didn't want him feeling that you're more trouble than you're worth," he surmised.

Again there was some truth to his assumption. "Kind of. Haven't you ever kept things from someone because you worried you'd otherwise lose them?"

Konstantin let out a long sigh. "Yeah. There was a lot that I didn't tell my mate about myself in the beginning. I wanted to hook her first and *then* lay it all on her. No woman in her right mind would have taken me on otherwise."

Curious, Naomi tilted her head. "Why is that?"

He glanced across at her. "I'll tell you my secrets if you'll tell me yours."

Yeah, not possible. "Some things are better left mysteries."

"Agreed." He paused. "You know, on reading your background check, I thought, 'Hmm, this girl has not one thing in common with my Prime.' But then I realized you're as evasive and secretive as he is."

"Yep, we're quite the pair."

"You're good for him. I didn't think he'd ever take a mate—legions struggle with relationships, and they don't always stake such claims. Plus, Luka is ... well, Luka."

"A very solitary being," she elaborated.

"Exactly. And he seemed fine with that. I figured he'd find it impossible to properly trust another woman so deeply anyway. I'm glad to be wrong."

"I shared your beliefs at one time, so—"

"Naomi Chamberlain?" a voice called out.

She tracked it, her head whipping to the side. A man was casually approaching them, nothing aggressive in his body language. Nonetheless, her insides seized. Because she recognized him straight away.

Stefan.

Konstantin slipped in front of her—for a tank, he could move fast. "Who are you?"

"Just a friend of her anchor," Stefan told him. His head peeked around her bodyguard, and his eyes locked with hers again. "We met briefly at the psychic store, remember?"

Her demon studied him closely, not sensing that he meant Naomi any harm but still not wanting him near her. "I remember."

"Can we talk?" He lifted his hands in a gesture of peace. "I just have some questions."

"I'm not interested in answering them. There's nothing I can tell you that Daniel Phillips won't have put in his report, so . . ."

Konstantin shot her a look over his shoulder. "*He* hired the PI?"

"Yes," she replied.

The bodyguard shifted, blocking Stefan's view of her. "It's time you left." A firm statement.

"I don't intend to hurt her or anything," Stefan assured him. "I just want to talk to her."

"She doesn't want to talk to you—she's made that clear. So I don't give a damn what you want."

"But—"

"You have five seconds—no more, no less—to get in your car and get the fuck out of here," Konstantin warned.

Stefan let out a loud sigh. "Oh, come on."

"One ... two ... three—"

Pitch-black darkness fell. *Pitch*-black. It seemed thick and endless, like she was standing in a void.

The fuck?

Her demon shot to full alertness as her heart began to race and—

Pain slammed into Naomi's head—sharp, heavy, hard. She sucked in a breath, stars bursting behind her eyelids, her stomach heaving.

She swayed, her legs trembling as pulsing waves of agony reverberated through her skull. The world seemed to be spinning around her. A world still so *dark*.

She fell to her knees, balancing on the mere edge of consciousness. Noise. There was so much noise.

Alarmed shouts. Pained cries. Crackles of magick. Hisses of hellfire.

She only distantly registered it, the agony racking her head all-consuming. It stole her breath, her focus, her strength. And it just kept battering at her.

A warm hand landed on her arm. "Naomi, come on, get up."

She knew that voice. *Iain.*

"I don't know who the fuck these people are, but we have to get out of here," he stressed.

Luka's mind all but crashed into hers, and then his voice poured inside—hard, demanding, filled with dread: *Naomi? Naomi, tell me you're all right.*

She tried to respond, she really did, but her head hurt too much.

Fuck, baby, hold on.

Iain grabbed her arm tighter. "*Now*, Naomi, get up."

"Sorry to say," came a deep voice from the darkness, "you won't be going anywhere."

Magick crackled again. A loud cry tore out of Iain. There was the thud of a body hitting the ground. All of which Naomi barely registered, the pain in her head becoming so great that she couldn't think of anything else. She sagged forward, her eyes falling shut as unconsciousness dragged her under.

As the office door closed behind Luka's now ex-employee, Nikandr whistled low from the sofa. "Two people quitting in one week—unusual." He paused before adding, "Though I suppose it's not surprising that Draya quit. She'd want to avoid you after what she did."

Yes, but whereas Sela had resigned in person, Draya had done it remotely—and with immediate effect.

"It isn't so surprising that Sela quit either, when you think about it," said Mikhail, beside his brother. "It was getting on top of her watching newcomers join all happy and excited but then, after years of being regulars, eventually turn miserable and hopeless because they can't stop."

"Yeah," muttered Nikandr. "Then she had to watch her friend's partner repeatedly come here and gamble away his wages when he had a family to support." He refocused on Luka. "You cut him off, but it didn't stop him from blowing his paycheck—he just did it elsewhere."

"I heard he threw a tantrum at a different venue, swearing that his car had been stolen from the lot," Mikhail threw in. "Turns out it got repossessed while he was busy playing blackjack."

That was the frustrating thing. Luka could ban someone from his club to prevent them from losing their funds, home, or other possessions, but they'd only submerge themselves in debt at another casino.

"Are you going to attempt to track down Draya?" Nikandr asked him.

Leaning back in his chair, Luka arched a brow. "She confronted and insulted Naomi. You think I'd let that slide?"

"Draya must think you will, or she would never have done it."

Mikhail pursed his lips. "She probably figures Maddox will protect her from you."

"He can try," said Luka. It wouldn't work. Neither he nor his demons were willing to ignore this.

Too many fucking people seemed to be under the mistaken impression that it was acceptable to upset his mate. He needed to make it abundantly clear that—

Konstantin's psyche crashed into his. *East corner of Shaler Road! Clerics!*

Luka's stomach dropped, a chill racing down his spine. He shot to his feet. *Daniil, my office*, he ordered.

"What's wrong?" asked Mikhail as he and his brother stood.

"Clerics." An acute sense of urgency clawing at him, Luka quickly reached out to his mate. *Naomi? Naomi, tell me you're all right.*

Her psyche slid weakly against his, and he sensed that she was barely conscious.

Dread clutched his gut. *Fuck, baby, hold on.*

Right then, Daniil materialized.

"Take us to the east corner of Shaler Road," Luka ordered.

Their surroundings blurred ... and then darkened. All he could see was blackness. No, wait, there were brief flashes of hellfire and magick. And a loud cacophony of sounds.

Sounds of battle.

Sheer panic shuddering through him, he conjured a ball of hellfire to break up the darkness, but it didn't help much. It did, however, gain him the attention of someone, because ribbons of magick sailed right at him.

He dodged them fast and then tossed the flaming orb. A loud yell of pain sounded, moments before the darkness abruptly lifted, like someone had snapped open blackout curtains.

Luka swept his gaze over his surroundings, searching for Naomi. Bodies littered the floor, some of them clerics. Several people stood around, including Jolene, Tobe, and Ciaran. Since the trio made no attempt to attack the others, he was assuming they were also imps.

He dismissed them, his only concern Naomi ... but she was nowhere to be seen. He touched her mind again, immediately sensing that she'd passed out. *Fuck.* "They took her." The words were torn out of him.

Blood rushed to his ears as rage, panic, and dread flooded his system, blindingly intense. There was another emotion. It had been so long since he'd felt fear that he almost didn't recognize it. Cold and near-overpowering, it seemed bottomless; he could so easily drown in it.

"She's alive?" asked Nikandr, his face creased in concern.

He nodded hard. "Unconscious, but alive."

Crouched beside a fallen Konstantin, Mikhail grimaced. "He's gone."

Another pulse of anger coursed through Luka.

"Where's Naomi?" Tobe demanded as he, Jolene, and Ciaran hurried over to them.

"The clerics seem to have snatched her right off the street," Luka gritted out, feeling his skin stretch as his demons writhed beneath it, furious beyond measure, their minds leaping to the worst-case scenario, ready to burn the fucking world.

Tobe growled at him. "I thought you had a man on her." The tension in his jaw made the words come out clipped.

"I did. The clerics killed him to get to her." Luka could hear his heartbeat thrashing in his ears, fast and hard. It hurt to breathe; it felt as if his chest was being squeezed so tight he couldn't get enough air. "The monastery is the likeliest place they've taken her."

"It has to be somewhere we haven't already looked," said Jolene, her eyes blazing with ire, her voice as stiff as her posture.

Having pooled their resources, she and Luka had managed to narrow it down to three locations. But when they'd investigated them, no building had been uncovered. There hadn't even been signs of life—each area had been barren and uninhabited by anything other than wild animals.

Nikandr shoved a hand through his hair. "I don't get it. Why would they take Naomi rather than just kill her here and now? They want her dead."

"I have not one clue," Luka bit out resentfully, his chest still weighted, his breathing harsh and uneven. *Wake up, baby*, he urged psychically. *I need you to tell me where you are.*

But she didn't.

A craving for vengeance heaved through him and pounded at his insides, threatening to cloud his thoughts. He breathed through it, held himself in check by sheer force of will—Naomi needed that from him right now. Later? Later, when he had the bastards who'd taken her in his custody, he could let that rage fly.

Hurting them wouldn't be enough. Making them bleed wouldn't be enough. He wanted to torture them. Dismember them. Castrate them. Whip them. Skin them alive . . . only to have a healer tend to their injuries so that he could do it all over again.

Daniil cursed, standing at a spot a few feet away. "What the hell is Iain doing here?" He squatted, examining the psi-demon. "Dead." He tipped his chin at a nearby unfamiliar male. "So is he, whoever he is. A member of your lair?" he asked the imps, standing upright.

Briefly glancing away from his cell—and what the fuck was he doing on his phone, as if Naomi wasn't the priority?—Tobe stiffly shook his head and said, "That's Stefan. He hired the PI."

Mikhail looked at Luka. "You think Iain was working with the clerics?"

"I don't know. It could be that he was following Naomi again and attempted to help her." *Naomi, talk to me, baby*, he pled.

Her psyche stirred. *I'm . . . Don't . . .*

Luka's pulse jumped, relief lancing through him. *Where are you? Tell me.*

Going by . . . symbols . . . monastery . . . temple . . .

He frowned. "She's awake, but she's psychically weak. And there's something off about the connection. As though it's being muddied—likely by magick."

"I can barely understand her," said Tobe, his gaze inward. "She's saying something about . . . a temple?"

I'll find you, Naomi. Some-the-fuck-how, Luka would find her. "I'm going to search the places where we thought the monastery might be again, starting with the first one."

"Whoa," began Tobe, "wait a second. The prophecy might state that you and Naomi take down the *Lemures*, but we want our pound of flesh too." He waved a hand, gesturing at himself, the other imps, and Tia.

"Fine," Luka bit out, "you can come along."

Tobe pursed his lips. "Or . . ."

"Or what?" Luka pushed impatiently.

"Or we use the GPS tags that I put on her shoes without her knowledge. Yeah, I know she's gonna rip me a new one, but I regret nothing. I already have the phone app trying to lock onto the tags as we speak. It won't give us her *exact* location, but it'll give us a general idea of where she is."

It was better than nothing. Later, Luka would be pissed at the imp for putting trackers on his mate. Right now, his priority was getting to her. *Just hold on for us, baby, we're coming.*

Jolene sidled up to him. "Don't worry, Luka. Naomi will be fine. Truth is, it's the clerics and their angel who are in the most danger."

Luka felt his brow crease. "What does that mean?"

She spared his bodyguards and Daniil a quick look. *Do they know about Naomi's parentage?* she asked Luka telepathically.

Daniil knows nothing. I told the twins only that her biological father is a fallen angel and then swore them to secrecy, he replied.

The Prime pressed her lips together, hesitating to continue.

Luka turned to his demons. "Give us privacy for a moment." Once the three were out of hearing range, he refocused on Jolene. "Speak freely."

"You have an honorary niece who's half celestial," began Jolene, "so you'll know that demons like Naomi are ... different."

"Yes, I'm aware," said Luka.

"It also often means that their inner entities are different. Sometimes even unstable to some degree."

"What are you getting at?"

"Presumably you've met Naomi's demon?" Tobe probed, though it wasn't really a question.

"Of course," Luka confirmed.

"I'll bet it's made brief appearances here and there to warn you to behave but hasn't really involved itself in anything happening around it," Tobe hedged.

"Sounds about right."

"It doesn't give a shit about anything except its own survival and that of the person with whom it shares its soul. Naomi's demon will protect her to the death, but it won't do that cleanly or carefully. It won't be subtle, won't show an ounce of mercy, won't be leery of attracting human attention. Because, in truth, there's nothing low-key about that demon."

Luka narrowed his eyes, his own entities locked on the male imp, sensing there was more.

"She and her demon have a deal," Tobe added. "Unless she's in the gravest danger, unless her life is *truly* at risk, it won't interfere; it will let her handle it. But if the threat is too big, if she's outnumbered, the entity gets to take charge and eliminate the danger. Naomi has to take a back seat."

Luka felt his brow furrow. She'd told him nothing of this. "And if the demon gets to take the wheel?"

"We'd better hope she's somewhere isolated. Somewhere no humans will stumble upon anything they shouldn't. Somewhere no random demons might witness what she can do and just how much power she carries. Because if they do—human, demon, child, adult, innocent, guilty—the entity will kill them all. It allows no witnesses to live."

CHAPTER TWENTY-FIVE

Just hold . . . baby . . . coming, said Luka, his psyche bumping hers. Naomi gently cricked her neck, trying to ease the ache there—an ache that had been caused by her head being slumped forward while she was out cold. Waking to find that she was bound to a chair by ropes of magick hadn't pleased her in the slightest.

Her little nap had been enough to make the dizziness pass, though. More, the pain in her head was subsiding now, enabling her to think. But she was still a little *off*, her psychic strength having taken a hard hit—hence why her demon hadn't yet struck at their enemies.

Whispers came from the clerics surrounding her. She ignored them as she scanned the temple yet again on the off chance that she'd missed a clue as to her precise location.

Among the religious symbols on the walls was the *Lemures'* emblem, so she had to be at the monastery. That was all she knew.

She mentally crossed her fingers that Konstantin was all right.

She tried thinking back to what had happened. She remembered the rush attack, remembered blasts of hellfire, remembered sensing more such blasts, as if other demons had arrived—likely alerted by how the unnatural darkness had fallen. She'd heard cries of sheer agony, and she hoped like hell that none had come from Konstantin.

She was pissed that she'd passed out. More, she was pissed that these bastards had managed to take her off guard—as was her entity. That anger seemed to feed the warped fiery power within her. It was already heating and rising in response to the danger.

The crowd stirred, and then the clerics directly in front of her started shuffling aside, making way for a tall figure. He had a real Jesus vibe going on with his beard, shoulder-length hair, and full-body aura of light.

The clerics bowed, but he paid them no attention. He took purposeful, elegant strides toward Naomi, his pale-blue eyes fixed on her intently.

Reaching her chair, he loomed over her in a clear attempt to intimidate her—his chin high, his back straight, his chest puffed out. There was an air of serenity to him. It was fake as fuck, of course, but very good.

"You must be the one who calls himself Kushiel," she said. Her demon was very still, watching him carefully; observing its target, biding its time as the heat of her inner fire built and built.

He gave her a placid smile. "I *am* Kushiel," he lied, so convincingly that it was almost impressive.

"Now that's not exactly true, is it?" she challenged with a chastising smirk.

He flapped a hand. "I do not expect you to recognize me. My kind do not consort with yours, after all. Feel free to telepathically call out to whoever you want, by the way," he added. "They won't understand much of what you say."

Yeah, she'd figured *that* much, considering she'd struggled to understand both Luka and Tobe when they'd telepathed her. It wouldn't have mattered if she did have a clear mind-to-mind connection to them—there was absolutely nothing around her that would clue her in as to where they could find her. Not that she needed saving, but still.

"It was quite arrogant of you to have only *one* bodyguard when you knew a divine force would come for you," he reprimanded condescendingly. "His soul will be in hell now, along with those of the other two demons."

She stiffened. He'd killed Konstantin? *This motherfucker.*

Anger and vengefulness swirled in her bloodstream. But not defeat. Not hopelessness. Not fear. Because these people had no real fucking clue what they were dealing with.

"Why am I here?" she bit out. Why hadn't he just killed her already? He *should* have. Which he'd learn soon enough.

"Three times my clerics made an attempt on your life. None ever came back to us." Kushiel tilted his head. "I got curious. Curious as to how a siren could be so easily defeating them time and time again."

"I would have thought that an angel would be grieving their deaths, not merely feel curious as to how they came about."

He ignored that. "You must be far more powerful than you seem. Divine power is quite lethal for demons." He crouched in front of her. "But not for you, apparently."

She forced herself not to flinch as he touched her cheek—another attempt to intimidate her, no doubt. Her entity hissed at him, preparing itself to pounce early if necessary. Naomi's psychic strength was returning, but it was a slow process.

He studied her closely, inhaling through his nose. "As I suspected, there is holy blood in you. You have a celestial somewhere in your family line."

Murmurs traveled through the crowd, coated in alarm and agitation. Oh, "the holy" did loathe it when demons possessed angelic DNA.

"Is that why Lucifer chose you to be the mother of his child? I would expect so."

Funny, he truly did seem to believe that she would birth Lou's kid. Maybe he put stock in the prophecy as a whole, not merely the part predicting his demise.

"You know what's interesting?" Naomi asked as the red-hot power within her pushed upward and started pooling beneath her skin, awaiting release.

"What?"

"That holy blood you mentioned? It hums when I'm around another who possesses it —angels and such. Not sure why, but it always has. It isn't humming right now. Which tells me that you're no celestial. But then I already suspected that. The clerics' swords all scented of dark magick. Swords that *you* gave them."

He didn't look fazed by her words. "If you are seeking to turn these clerics against me, it will not work," he claimed, the image of confidence.

"Don't be so sure of that. I overheard the last group of 'brothers' talking. One—think his name was Henry—claimed that you aren't quite as angelic as you first appeared."

His jaw tightened at that.

"Others agreed that your requests and responses weren't so divine in nature anymore. They were suspicious. I'll be surprised if there aren't others among this monkhood who harbor the same suspicions." She briefly scanned the large crowd, noting a few avert their gazes or shift uneasily.

"Such lies and manipulations," scoffed Kushiel, standing upright. He sniffed, haughty. "I would expect nothing less from the consort of Satan."

"Satan and Lucifer are two separate people. Any celestial would know that. The fact that you don't only supports my claim that you're no angel."

His eyes went hard.

"But hey, I'm sure you could easily prove me wrong. Calling on heavenly light, for instance, would do the trick. Fill the room with it here and now," she dared.

He forced a dismissive smile. "I do not have to prove anything to a *demon*."

"But it would put these clerics' minds at rest. As servants of God—a being you supposedly revere and love—they must indeed matter dearly to you."

"The only thing making these clerics uneasy is your existence. Of course, as of tonight, that will no longer be an issue." Kushiel clicked his fingers. Almost instantly, a bunch of clerics rushed forward to place buckets near her chair.

Naomi regarded him through slitted eyes as he conjured a ceremonial dagger. "Let me guess ... you plan to bleed me out. It's what a dark practitioner who feeds off anything holy would do. They'd drink my blood; use it in their rituals." A typical practice. "Of course, if you're *truly* a celestial, you'll have no such plan. You'll just kill me outright, because my blood would have no value to you."

He didn't react other than to glare down at her in annoyance, a light flush creeping into his face at the rise in air temperature.

She smiled. "I'm right," she accused. "You intend to bleed me out. How are you going to justify that to these people here?"

"A demon does not deserve to harbor holy blood. Being drained of it is an appropriate way for you to die."

She snickered. "That so?" He had an answer for everything, didn't he? "Look, these clerics might buy your brand of crap. But I don't. If you were truly an angel, truly favored by God, *you would not be here.* No celestials are permitted to walk the earth until demonic tempers have cooled. The last thing the people upstairs would do is make matters worse by targeting yet *another* demon."

"They made an exception for you, since it is essential to prevent the birth of the Antichrist."

"That would imply that you knew about the prophecy *before* you came here. You didn't learn of it from the clerics?"

He pressed his lips shut, his eyes flickering.

A grin tugged at her mouth. "Ah, you weren't aware of it until you came to them." Something he couldn't lie about, because the clerics would know. "If you had no knowledge of it, well, God had no reason to send you to these people, did he?"

"He did not go into the specifics of my mission, true," he clipped. "But he was clear that the Antichrist might soon walk this earth if I did not aid the clerics."

"Oh, I see. Explain one thing to me, then." She paused. "How is it that a supposed angel, who'd know and speak the old languages, wasn't able to tell that they'd mistranslated the prophecy?"

His brows flicked together, a mix of confusion, doubt, and interest rippling across his face. He wanted to hear what the prophecy *might* say, but he wasn't sure if he should believe her.

Right then, Luka's mind touched hers. *Naomi, we're ... Need ... finding ... flames.*

Uh, yeah, she wasn't too sure what he was saying. Not knowing how much of this would make sense to him, she replied, *Don't worry about me, Luka, I'm just dandy. I got this, trust me on that.* She paused. *I'll be home soon.*

Kushiel inched up his chin, sweat now dotting his forehead. "Just like Lucifer himself, you are a great pretender. Full of lies. No wonder he chose you."

"What-the-fuck-ever, dude. You and me both know that you're

no angel. You're not here on some divine mission. You've been manipulating these clerics since the moment you showed up on their doorstep. *I* know what the prophecy really states. *I* know what the Elioud predicted all those years ago. And if *you* knew, you would never have come for me."

"Cease trying to plant seeds of doubt in our minds—it will do you no good. I wouldn't bother begging, bargaining, or attempting to flee either. You could scream, but no one aside for us would hear you," he taunted.

"Why would I scream? You're no real threat to me. You never were."

"You think if you keep us all chatting it will give someone time to save you?"

Nope, she'd just wanted to keep him occupied while she psychically healed ... and she'd been successful.

He chuckled, as though she were pathetic. "Nobody is coming for you. Even if they did come to this very area, they would never find the monastery. So you see, you are going nowhere. I have you now. Your death is guaranteed."

It was almost cute that he truly believed that. "You should have killed me when you had the chance," she said as the molten force inside her bubbled and snapped. "It was a mistake on your part to let me live, just as it was a mistake to assume that I'd need rescuing. Bringing me here achieved one thing only—it allowed *me* to get to *you*."

She let her inner power rush out of her system. Red-violet flames roared to life around her body, incinerating the magick ropes. As Kushiel stumbled back, shying away from the brightness of the fire, her demon rose to the surface.

Luka ground his teeth, flexing his fingers. "I see nothing." The GPS signal had led them here, to a desert on the outskirts of

Vegas—an endless sandy landscape with rocks, cacti, shrubs, thick grass, and stunted trees.

It was an area that he'd searched once before, having identified it as a possible spot for the monastery. Back then, he'd found nothing.

Of course, he'd taken into account that the building could be somehow concealed, but there would be *some* signs of human life out here. Footprints. Vehicles. Tire tracks. Litter.

None of those things could be seen. Not during his previous search, and not now.

There were no sounds of human life either. A thick silence had fallen, broken only by the occasional rattle of a bush or flutter of wings.

He scanned his surroundings again—left, right, down, even up. The sun was beginning to set in the wide-open sky, turning a deep gold ringed with red. The clouds had taken on a pink/orange hue that held faint dashes of purple. Shadows were beginning to creep over the landscape, bringing with them a slight chill.

At least they wouldn't all be baking in the daytime heat while they searched.

"She's *somewhere* around here," maintained Tobe, his phone in hand. "She has to be."

"Unless the clerics removed her shoes and tossed them here," said Nikandr. "Though I see no reason why they'd feel it necessary to do that."

Luka had brought along the twins, but not Daniil—he'd had the teleporter focus on moving Konstantin and Iain's bodies. Only Nikandr and Mikhail knew of Naomi's angelic blood, and Luka wanted it to stay that way. If Tobe's prediction was correct, her entity would do nothing to hide its true nature when dealing with the monkhood.

The only others here were Tobe, Jolene, Ciaran, Tia, Alfie, and Beck—people already aware of Naomi's secrets. They hadn't called on Khloë, because her mate would have insisted on going into battle with her. No, that wasn't happening.

Urgency still pounding at Luka—an urgency to find, protect, avenge—he cricked his neck. His demons continued to writhe beneath his flesh, all edgy, hypervigilant, restless, and sending him psychic snapshots of the many revenge scenarios flickering through their minds.

Luka turned, the hard-packed sandy ground crunching beneath his feet, and stalked over to Tobe. He glanced down at the imp's cell phone. On the screen was an overhead map of the area, a thick red dot pulsing in its center. It only gave them a general sense of where Naomi might be. She could be up to half a mile away in either direction. "The signal can't get any more specific than that?"

"No," Tobe muttered, visibly frustrated by it.

Jolene set her hands on her hips. "The monkhood has to be using glamor magick to hide their monastery."

Luka had considered that. Since the clerics were able to channel divine power, the glamor would be strong. Still ... "There should be some evidence of people coming and going, though, shouldn't there? It isn't as if they can teleport." Almost itchy with exasperation, he called out to his mate again. *Naomi, we're close. Need a little help finding you. Can you call on your flames?*

Her psyche brushed against his. *Don't ... Luka ... dandy ... trust me on ... home ...*

He sighed. "If I understood her telepathic comment correctly, I should trust that she's 'dandy' right now." As if he'd be so easily reassured. "I had hoped that the mind-to-mind frequency would be clearer with close proximity, but that doesn't appear to be the case."

"Which means we can't rely on her to guide us," said Mikhail. "We'll have to set off on foot and search for her."

Nikandr nodded. "It would be best to split into groups and head in varying directions."

"Not necessary," Tia told them with a flap of her hand. "All we need to do is wait."

Luka looked at the imps, all of whom were far too calm for his liking. "Wait for what?"

"For her demon to make its move," replied Tia. "Trust me, it'll make enough of a fuss for us to know *exactly* where we need to head."

Mikhail squinted. "You really think her demon can take on a dark practitioner and a bunch of clerics? If that were the case, it would have done so before now."

It was Tobe who responded. "Naomi didn't give it the chance, because she knows that it can't be trusted to hold back." Pausing, he pocketed his cell. "Think of it as a rabid dog on a leash. You're not going to unclip that leash unless you have no other choice, because you know that the dog will attack without sense or control."

"As I said earlier," Jolene began, "the inner entities of demons with angelic blood can sometimes be unstable."

Which was one of the reasons why Luka hadn't particularly wanted Ella to mate Viper. A child carrying both angelic and demonic blood ... you never quite knew exactly what you were going to get. And then Luka had gone off and mated such a hybrid himself. Fate had to be laughing its ass off at him.

A light breeze brushed over him, carrying the scents of dry air and baked earth. "It might be better if we just ..." He stopped talking as a rumble built, snagging his attention. It vibrated along the ground, drumming at the soles of his feet through his shoes, making sand and pebbles dance and shift.

Alfie stumbled backwards, cursing as a thorny brush caught at his pants. "Well, I'd say that's courtesy of our girl. We just need—"

A *boom* reverberated through the air as rocks, earth, and sand seemed to explode upward a short distance away. Echoes of alarm and fear quickly followed, and then ... well, it looked like people were climbing out of a fracture in the desert.

"They were underground," Luka realized.

As one, he and the other demons raced toward the scene. Despite the distance, he could hear panicked cries, fire sizzling, and magick crackling. More ground near the fissure gave way, widening the gap, causing all those who'd clambered out of it to fall back down.

There were two more booms as the land on all sides of the fissure collapsed. Trapping the clerics and Kushiel, maybe? Ensuring that they had only one exit?

It occurred to Luka that maybe they'd been using a tunnel system to travel to and from the area, and that Naomi's demon had purposely blocked the passageways, but he didn't bother ruminating on it. His priority was getting to her.

More people climbed out of the fracture in the ground, led by a bearded male with shoulder-length hair and a white aura that quickly winked out.

Kushiel, no doubt.

Then a figure surrounded by red-violet flames levitated out of the gap in the landscape, and the tightness in Luka's chest left him. *Naomi*.

No, he realized, it wasn't Naomi. It was her demon. And it was backlit by massive rays of red, black, and orange light that almost hurt to look at.

Tobe slowed his pace. "This is why I said we needed to hope that she's somewhere isolated—her demon gives no fucks about being discreet." He gripped Luka's arm as he staggered to a stop. The other imps and the twins followed suit. "We should hang back."

Luka pulled his arm free. "Are you fucking kidding me?"

"I get that you want to help her, but *look* at her demon—it doesn't need us right now."

An oily black gust of power blasted out of the bearded male's palm, heading right for the entity. Red-violet flames clashed with the gust, ate it whole, and then incinerated the bastard just like that.

Luka's brows flew up.

A roar split the air as omnidirectional flames burst from the entity's body, reaching out to the clerics like devilish fingers. Fingers that were tipped with snake-heads. They latched onto ankles and dragged their captives backwards, tossing them into the strange light behind the demon.

Tobe flicked up a brow. "See what I mean?"

Yes, Luka did. Because he saw now what he hadn't sensed before. Saw the primeval dark divinity that his mate possessed. Her inborn connection to the sacred, defiled and twisted into something malevolent, was the source of her inner raw power. And her demon harnessed it like a master. Something his own entities found a complete turn-on.

"The demon is also clearly in a fury," Tia chipped in, "so there's a good chance it might accidentally kill us. The best thing for us to do is to keep a slight distance from it and deal with the stragglers." Her gaze sharpened on the men rushing their way. "Here they come."

CHAPTER TWENTY-SIX

Deciding the imps were right, Luka focused on the clerics ahead of him. He threw a hellfire grenade right at the swarm. Sand flew upward, fire roared, voices cried out, bodies hit the ground.

While several clerics took cover—hiding behind trees, shrubs, or wind-worn rock formations—others launched attacks.

Chanting filled the air moments before glowing white vines of magick soared toward Luka. They barreled into him, zapping his every nerve ending with burning-hot jolts of electricity.

Gritting his teeth at the fast-blistering burns, he snapped a telekinetic hand around his attacker's throat, cutting off his air supply until finally the cleric went limp.

More glowing white streams came his way as he dumped the body on the ground. He slammed up a telekinetic barrier, shielding himself from the blows, then shoved that barrier forward *hard*. It crashed into several clerics, knocking them clean off their feet.

His entities smirked—wanting their prey's fear, craving their blood, relishing their pain. And very much wishing that they could be at Naomi's side as her demon quite literally burned shit down.

Nikandr flinched with a hiss as a pure-white orb blindsided him. "Christ, they hurt like a bitch."

He wasn't wrong.

A bald head popped up from behind a boulder, and the cleric sent twirling ribbons of pure-white magick at Luka. They slammed into his leg so hard it almost gave out. *Fuck.*

Ignoring the cramping throb, he lashed out with a telekinetic blast that made the boulder explode and collapse on top of his attacker.

A large number of clerics bolted, heading left. A wall of red-violet fire shot up in front of them, blocking their path. Other Eliouds headed for the right, only to skid to a halt as they too found themselves facing a flaming wall.

Curses rang out from the *Lemures*. They were stuck, weren't going anywhere, and they knew it.

It made Luka's entities smirk.

Helpless rage clear in their expressions, the Eliouds attacked as a whole—some targeting Naomi's entity, the rest aiming at Luka and the demons near him. Hellfire. Chaos. Destruction. Magick. It all reigned supreme over the landscape right then. Thanks to stray blows, trees were split in half, shrubs caught fire, and rocks imploded.

Both sides fought hard. Nikandr and Mikhail remained either side of Luka, launching bolts and beams of hellfire, watching his back as he watched theirs. Tobe alternated between releasing blasts of hellfire and psychic blows. Ciaran frequently teleported from spot to spot, dodging magick hits, snapping necks, and reaching clerics who'd taken cover.

Meanwhile, Jolene had thrown up a shield that protected

herself, Beck, Tia, and Alfie from incoming magickal attacks as they aimed to take down as many clerics as possible with hellfire.

Having taken out yet another cleric, Luka spared a look at Naomi. Her demon was still firmly in charge, pursuing the Eliouds at a slow, purposeful, confident walk, still looking the pure embodiment of defiled divinity.

The heat radiating from it was blistering—waves of it danced in the air. Needing a reprieve, he shed his suit jacket and tossed it on the ground.

More flames burst out of the entity—some slicing clean through bodies to cleave them in half, others snatching them off their feet and throwing them into the rays of near-blinding light still at its back.

No, not rays of light, he realized, his lips parting. *Flames.*

The flames of hell.

"Fuck," he breathed.

"What?" asked Nikandr, swiping his palm over his face to wipe away the layers of dust there.

"A portal," said Luka. "Her entity has opened a fucking portal to hell."

"It *what?*"

Some clerics twisted to attack the demon, but the red-violet flames surrounding it seemed to take the edge off the impact of their blows, because it showed no signs of pain. On the contrary, it—

A heavy gust of magick punched Luka right in the solar plexus, sending the breath gushing out of his lungs. A second gust headed his way, pissing him off. He telekinetically deflected the magickal strike, retaliating with a telekinetic punch that made the cleric's head snap back so violently it broke his neck.

As the dead body slumped to the ground, Luka hurled an orb of hellfire at an approaching cleric. But the Elioud tripped over a clump of aloe spears, causing the orb to miss him. It collided with the branch of an acacia tree instead, setting it alight.

Once the cleric stood, Luka struck out again, using a harsh blast of telekinesis. The Elioud almost folded in half with the impact as he zoomed backward into a large rock formation, smacking his skull hard.

"Her demon's just toying with them really, isn't it?" It was a realization from Nikandr, not a question. "If it had wanted to, it could have wiped them out fast. It wants to feed on their terror and pain, not merely watch them die."

Luka sighed, using the heel of his palm to rub away grit from the corner of his eye. "Something like that."

Twisting vines of magick rushed at him from another angle, the pain like the stabbing of scalding-hot razor-sharp blades. Hissing, he telekinetically plucked his attacker off the ground and threw him at a tight cluster of his brothers, knocking two down. He then launched a hellfire grenade at the small group, taking them all out at once.

Again he stole a moment to check on Naomi. *There.* Her entity was closer now, and he could better see the portal behind it. A hellish background of shimmering fire, crimson skies, and scorched land. The relentless heat made sweat dot his skin.

His attention was snagged by a new presence not far from the entity—a figure engulfed in ultraviolet flames. It wasn't attacking Naomi's demon; no, it was aiding it, lashing out with whips of ultraviolet fire that wrenched agonizing screams out of its victims. Any time said whips missed their target and smacked the ground, they sent a brief tremor through it.

Mikhail frowned. "Is that . . . is that Lucifer?"

It would appear so. "He lives in hell, so he wasn't likely to miss a portal opening." Or to sit out a battle that involved his daughter.

"I guess he wanted in on the fun," said Mikhail with a loose shrug.

Luka's demons desperately wanted to surface and have their own fun, but he couldn't trust that they wouldn't attempt to get to Naomi, arrogantly sure that their mate would never harm them even in such a fury. He also didn't trust that they wouldn't wander into the portal out of morbid curiosity—they were easily distracted by shiny things.

Noticing a hoop of magick heading right for him, Luka jerked aside before it could hook around his neck. He was about to take his attacker out, but Nikandr did the job for him, lancing a beam of hellfire through the cleric's body.

Luka gave his bodyguard a curt nod of thanks. It was only a moment later that another cleric conjured an orb of magick and pitched it at him. He dodged it and retaliated with a telekinetic wave that sent his attacker crashing into a withered tree. There was a loud *crack* as splits spiderwebbed through the trunk. The Elioud hit the uneven ground hard, making a cloud of dust fly up.

There weren't many clerics left, he quickly realized. A barrage of hellfire, holy magick, psychic hits, and telekinetic power still flew back and forth, but most blows were demonic in nature at this point.

"We need to back up some," announced Tobe loudly. "We don't want to be too close to the last of these clerics when Naomi's demon and Lou target them. We could get caught in the crossfire."

"He's right," said Jolene. "Start retreating."

They all did exactly that, watching as father and daughter—both looking like walking flaming torches—stalked after the remaining clerics. Some Eliouds hid, some tried fleeing, and the rest fought back.

None managed to escape the creatures of fire.

They were whipped. Chopped in half. Set alight. Thrown through the portal.

Voices screamed. Begged. Chanted. Swore. Yelled out in anger.

One by one, the number of clerics went down ... and down ... and down. Until, finally, none were left.

Naomi's entity then turned its attention to Luka and the other demons, no hint of recognition in its expression.

Luka reached out psychically. *You did good. It's over now. The threats to you and Naomi are gone. Let her come back to me.*

The entity regarded him through narrowed eyes for long moments, then it subsided. Naomi's gray-green gaze met his, a slight daze there. And then his girl collapsed.

A telepathic voice broke into Naomi's sleep, the words muffled and rhythmic. She couldn't make them out, her thoughts too slow and cottony.

Exhaustion pooled in her mind, her limbs, her extremities, everything.

Her senses seemed dull. She was aware of low voices, of soft bedsheets, of a dark, spicy cologne, of a hand holding hers, of a thumb pressed to her pulse. But she felt somehow disconnected from it all. As if the outside world was so very far away.

She felt wiped. Drained. Psychically burned out.

It would be easy to let herself doze back off, but that telepathic voice kept moving through the fog in her brain, the words ... No, they weren't mere words, they were *lyrics*.

The person was singing. And that voice was one she recognized well.

Why are you singing? she asked.

A pause. *Because you wouldn't wake up, and it annoyed me,* clipped Lou. *I want to hear that you're fine.*

I'm fine, she assured him. *Totally out of it, but fine.*

Good. Now sleep. You need your rest.

Then why did you wake me?

Because . . . Oh, forget it. His psyche gently bumped hers, and then he was gone. That was right when all sorts of images poured into her mind. Memories of fleeing clerics, of blazing fire, of . . . Ah, shit, her demon had opened a freaking portal to hell.

The entity shrugged, unapologetic. Like Naomi, it was feeling lethargic and mentally numb right now. That display of power had zapped them both of psychic strength.

"Put that down," Tia barked. "Tobe, I swear to God if you steal anything from this house . . ."

"I said I wouldn't," he reminded her.

Tia huffed. "You're an imp. Forgive me if I don't trust your word on that."

"I wouldn't steal from Naomi's mate; it would be like stealing from her. But yeah, I'd otherwise totally pocket this watch," he unashamedly admitted.

"Why? Do you not like your fingers?"

"Belinsky wouldn't *really* cut them off. Would you?"

"Yes." A flat response from Luka—the sound of his voice seemed to bat away the rest of the fog in Naomi's brain.

"But I'm Naomi's psi-mate," said Tobe.

"That doesn't require you to have fingers," Luka told him. "You can anchor her just as well without them."

An inner smile warmed her chest. She forced her heavy eyelids partially open. Her surroundings were a huge blur. She blinked three times, clearing her vision . . . and Luka's dark gaze immediately locked with hers.

His lips kicked up, relief flaring in his eyes. "There you are." He gave her hand a little squeeze. "Feeling all right?"

"Mostly," she replied, her voice low and thick. She cleared her throat as she looked around the room. Tobe, Jolene, Tia, Alfie, Ciaran, and Beck were all staring down at her, looking both relieved and tired. Much like Luka, they had scorch marks and bloodstains on their clothes, but their injuries had either already healed or were healing well, because they seemed otherwise fine.

Alfie lifted a hand in greeting. "Hey, sweetheart."

"I didn't expect you to wake so soon," said Tia, smiling. "You recovered faster than I thought."

Naomi might have slept longer if Lou hadn't woken her.

Tobe leaned in and pressed a kiss to her forehead, ignoring the low growl that came from Luka. "It's good to see you conscious, even if you look half dead."

Snorting, she forced herself to sit upright, her movements slow and awkward due to the heaviness in her limbs. "How long was I out?"

It was Ciaran who responded. "Only about three hours."

That really wasn't long, given how much energy her demon had expended. But she would bet that three hours with these imps and Tia had felt like an eternity for Luka. They could be a trial at times.

"I take it all the clerics are dead." She couldn't imagine that her demon would have retreated otherwise.

"Dead and incinerated," Jolene confirmed. "Just as they deserved."

"As for that Kushiel guy, it looked as though your demon took care of him," added Beck.

Yeah, Naomi remembered that part. "How did you guys find me out there in that desert?" It had been in the middle of nowhere.

All eyes drifted to Tobe.

Her anchor scratched his chin. "Uh … it might have had something to do with the GPS trackers I put on your shoes."

Naomi blinked. "What?"

"Well, shoes are the only thing you *always* wear. You frequently forget your jacket, and you don't always carry a purse." He held up his hands. "I'll take them off now that the danger's over. Luckily you don't have that many pairs or I'd be here a while."

"Wait, you put them on *all* my shoes?"

"I couldn't take the chance that you'd be kidnapped when you weren't wearing shoes I'd tagged." He paused, eyeing her closely. "You mad?"

"Yep. You should have told me."

"Your demon would have taken the trackers off so that it could kill all the clerics itself."

Okay, that was true.

"While I didn't think you'd need backup, I didn't want to take the risk. Forgive me for caring."

"You're forgiven." Naomi pointed a finger at him. "You will *never* do anything like that again."

Tobe saluted her, all innocence.

"As you're clearly doing okay, we'll leave you to rest," announced Jolene.

Tia and the other imps moved toward their Prime . . . except for Tobe.

Jolene grabbed the back of his shirt. "You too, Tobe."

He frowned. "But I want to stay."

"You want to annoy Luka—that's different."

A millisecond later, the entire group disappeared from sight.

Luka opened his arms. "Come here, baby."

Gladly. Naomi edged sluggishly off the bed and eased herself onto his lap. As his arms curled around her, she sagged against him, enjoying his warmth. She never wanted to move again.

Holding her tight, he nuzzled her hair. "You definitely feeling okay?"

"Yup. Just tired and groggy."

"Not surprised. Your demon wiped you both out psychically."

"It regrets nothing."

"Again, not surprised." He brushed his lips over her temple. "So. You can open a portal to hell." A neutral statement.

"Hmm. I first learned that when I was four. I hadn't meant to do it. I'd just been annoyed with my dad about something—I can't even remember what. Anyway, a portal opened up, and he toppled right into it. He thought it was the most hilarious thing ever."

"Yes, I can imagine. Can you open portals to other places?"

"Nope, which is good. My demon is so nosy, I'm not sure I could trust that it wouldn't go wandering in places it shouldn't. Bring me up to speed on what happened after I passed out. *Again*."

"Well, I caught you before you could hit the ground. Lou sent out a wave of fire that incinerated every last trace of the clerics before disappearing into the portal and closing it behind him. He looked as though he wanted to take you with him, but then he seemed to think better of it."

"He couldn't be seen to care what happened to me just in case any of the demons there didn't know that he was my father."

Luka nodded. "Ciaran teleported us all here, since he and the others didn't want to leave your side until they were sure that you were fine." He sighed—the sound loaded with impatience—before adding, "I can't say it was a joy to have imps in our bedroom, let alone our home, but . . ."

Naomi dabbed a kiss on his throat. "Thank you for letting them stay."

"Jolene was ready to pull the 'I'm her Prime, I have a right to be here' card, so I was sure to inform her that that's no longer the case. You co-run this lair with me now."

Feeling her brows slide together, she lifted her head to meet his gaze. "I do? First I've heard of it."

"I rather thought it was obvious. Neither you nor I would want for us to be in different lairs. It goes without saying that I'd never join Jolene's, which means you'd switch to mine. Being my mate makes you co-Prime. Unless I'm wrong in believing that you wouldn't want us to belong to the same lair."

"Of course of you're not wrong."

"Then there you go."

Fair enough.

He threaded his fingers through her hair. "The illegal side of things will of course remain in my hands, however."

"Obviously." She yawned so wide it cracked her jaw.

"You didn't tell me about the deal you have with your entity."

"I never thought to mention it. I know that sounds weird, but aren't there things you haven't told me *not* because you're hiding them but merely because they haven't come up?"

"Yes."

"I *did* actually confess to you that my demon likes causing destruction and mayhem," she remembered. "I hope that seeing it in action didn't put you off, because you're stuck with me now regardless."

Luka gave her a solemn look, tucking her hair behind her ear. "Nothing about you could put me off. It doesn't work that way when you love someone."

Naomi's breath caught. "You love me?" The question came out low and shaky.

His brow furrowed. "Baby, of course I fucking do."

Emotion twined around her chest so tightly her lungs burned. "In case you aren't aware of it already, it's a two-way street."

"It had better be," he growled playfully. "I meant what I said—I'm not going anywhere, and neither are you."

"And my demon meant what *it* said—it will kill you if you hurt me, mate or not."

His lips bowed up. "Having seen what it can do, I now understand why it's so certain it can live up to that threat."

"You don't seem bothered," she observed, surprised.

"I'm not. Neither are my demons. In fact, it turns Belial on in a major way."

She did a slow blink. "I don't really know what to say to that."

Luka only smiled.

CHAPTER TWENTY-SEVEN

Naomi smiled down at the baby girl she held in her arms. "You really are super cute."

Cooing, Lilibeth grabbed at Naomi's hand, her incredible blue eyes locked on the ring there.

"She likes you," said Ella, sitting beside her on the leather sofa.

Naomi cast the redhead a quick smile. "She likes my ring."

"Oh, that too," Ella chuckled. "She took to you very quickly, though. It's unusual for her. Maybe it's because you're mated to her favorite uncle."

"He's her only uncle," said Viper from an armchair, a teasing note in his tone as his vivid blue eyes slid to where Luka stood a few feet away.

"And what am I, chopped liver?" burst out Lou in pure offense.

"Well you're *not* her uncle, so . . ." Viper shrugged his compact shoulders.

Naomi felt her lips twitch.

It was the first time she'd been to the Black Saints' compound. Several of the bikers were hanging around in the main area of their clubhouse—some leaning against the reddish-brown brick walls, others settled on the mahogany furnishings. Their focus was mostly on Lou. All seemed ready to rip out his throat if he made any overt moves toward Lilibeth.

Of course, Lou hadn't spoken to Naomi much since randomly showing up at the clubhouse—something he was prone to do, to the bikers' extreme annoyance. He rarely talked to her in front of people who didn't know that he was her father, though he would chat with her telepathically. No one here would ever suspect that they were more than merely familiar with each other, let alone that they were related.

Feeling little fingers slide over her ring again, Naomi peered down at the baby. "Sorry, you can't have it. I don't blame you for wanting it, though—it's beautiful." It was also a black diamond. A symbol of the ultimate commitment from Luka.

Feeling her lips curve, she met his eyes, finding them fixed on her. She had woken a week ago to find that he had slipped the ring on her finger while she slept. She'd tried returning the favor the next night, but he'd stirred on feeling her try to slide one onto *his* finger. He'd also fucked her stupid, smug as a motherfucker that she'd claimed him so irrevocably.

He hadn't been at all impressed when Jolene's granddaughter Heidi had tried to steal Naomi's ring. To the little girl's credit, she hadn't wilted under the weight of his radiating disapproval. She'd only given him an angelic smile.

"*Imps*," he'd merely grumbled.

"You're hogging the baby," Lou groused now, crossing to the sofa and blocking Naomi's view of Luka. "It's my turn to—"

"Told you before, Lou; sick of saying it—you do not get to hold Lilibeth," Viper stated.

Lou's voice turned whiny. "But why? You know I won't hurt her. And it's not like I'm a stranger. We're practically brothers."

Viper's brow furrowed. "No. No we're not."

"Uh, incorrect." Lou jerked his thumb toward Jester. "You consider this guy your bro. He's *my* bro. That makes you and me—"

"Totally unrelated," Viper finished.

"Wish I could say the same," grumbled Jester. Long, lean, and bronze-skinned, he appeared to have a permanent scowl.

Lou scoffed at him, a fond smile plucking at his mouth. "No you don't. You adore and look up to me. Always did."

Jester's brows snapped together. "I tried to kill you. Twice."

"I never took it to heart."

"You should've."

"You're not fooling anybody, bro. It's perfectly obvious that you've missed me all these years. *Anyone* would miss me. I touch the lives of everyone I meet."

"And they all wish you hadn't," Jester sniped.

Grinning, Lou glanced at Naomi and Ella. "Isn't he just the bestest? So hateful and grumpy and asocial. And how could he not be, when he had the perfect role model in me?"

"It makes you proud that he's so rude and mean to you?" asked Razor, a bulky, dark-skinned male who seemed almost as irritable as Jester.

Lou lifted his shoulders. "Why wouldn't it?"

Razor's brows lifted, then he just shook his head.

Lilibeth made a fussy noise, drawing everyone's attention.

Ella hummed. "Seems that *someone* is hungry." She carefully took the little girl from Naomi.

"But not sleepy," mumbled Ghost. "Never, ever sleepy." He released a tired sigh. "The bags under my eyes are so big they have pockets."

Lou gifted him a condescending look. "You're so dramatic."

"You'd know all about that," Luka quipped.

Lou ignored him, just as he'd ignored every other comment Naomi's mate had made. He hadn't glanced his way even once. It was agitating her inner entity something fierce, but Luka didn't seem to mind. If anything, it appeared to amuse him.

"Why are you acting like Luka ain't here?" Razor asked.

Lou blinked, as if confused. "Who?"

Exhaling heavily, Razor threw up a hand. "Actually, I don't wanna know."

Naomi wasn't surprised that Razor had dropped the topic. Lou was so asocial, he didn't like anyone, so there was nothing odd or suspicious about his behavior.

She was careful not to look at him as she reached out psychically. *You need to stop being an ass to Luka*, she telepathed.

Lou's mind bumped hers. *Who?*

She fought the urge to roll her eyes. *You're an idiot.*

An idiot who you love.

Yeah, she did. *I'm still gonna rip out your spine if you don't start being nice to my mate.*

That's my girl—so pitiless. I raised you well. I'd totally win Father of the Century.

The funny thing was, he wasn't joking.

Panting, Naomi let out a mewl of frustration. "Didn't I mention how I like it fast and rough?"

Fighting a smile, Luka lazily sank his cock back inside her, earning himself another soft, tortured moan. Her pussy, fuck, it was sheer heaven around him. Tight and hot and the perfect fit. "Yes, you did. Many times."

"Then why are you *still* insisting on going so slow?" she all but wailed, her eyes glazed, her face flushed, her mouth swollen.

Luka swiveled his hips, making her suck in a breath. "Because I can. Remember, *I* control when you feel good. When you get more. When you get to come. Me, Naomi." He dropped his mouth on hers as he went back to slowly fucking in and out of her.

Soft palms smoothed down his back, fingers splayed, as her hips restlessly rose to meet each sluggish thrust. He and his demons loved how she melted beneath him, giving him everything. *Taking* everything he gave her.

Possession scored his skin like blunt nails, intense and bottomless. Everything about her tantalized his senses, evoking a response from every cell in his body, making endorphins and feel-good chemicals flood his system.

Luka kissed his way down her neck and then trailed a path of suckling bites to her breast. He drew a tight nipple into his mouth, making her breath catch. He sucked it. Licked it. Nibbled on it. Rubbed it against the roof of his mouth.

She ran a demanding hand down his back and gripped his ass, her touch nothing short of possessive. "Seriously, can we not hurry things along?"

He trailed light kisses over her shoulder and up her slim neck, flooding his lungs with her intoxicating scent. "No."

She groaned in annoyance. "You're my mate. That means you're supposed to give me whatever I want."

Mirth filled him. "No, baby, it really doesn't." Breezing his lips over to her mouth, he kissed it, licked at it, nibbled its corners. "You should be a little more patient—you came three times already."

Outrage flared in her eyes. "Uh, *no*, your demons *almost* made me come. All three of them stopped just before I went over the edge."

Stifling a smile, Luka swept a hand down her front, along her side, and down her outer thigh. "Sorry. Forgot." Pushing one of her legs up higher, he fisted the hair at the top of her head and slid his cock even deeper, loving how her head shot back with a loud cry.

"Fuck," she rasped.

"Born for this," he snarled. "For me." Abraxas nudged its way to the surface, correcting, "For us." Reclaiming supremacy, Luka feasted on her mouth, plundering it with his tongue as he lazily buried his cock deep inside her over and over.

She suckled on his tongue, which of course had him imagining having her lips wrapped around his dick again. Something she well knew.

He raised a brow. "Did you think that would make me start hammering away?"

"A girl can hope." She cast him an appeasing look. "*Please*."

"Since my baby asked so very, very nicely ..." Luka began pounding into her, filling the room with louds smacks of flesh on flesh.

Her breath catching, she scratched at his back, her eyes going wide and gleaming with pure pleasure. She eagerly took everything he gave her—her tits jiggling with every brutal thrust.

Their moans and groans got louder. Their hands got grabbier. Their mouths got greedier.

"Come around my cock. Let go." He rolled her clit with his thumb, and over the edge she went, her inner walls rippling around his cock from head to base as she screamed and arched beneath him.

He powered into her, burrowing deep, his balls slapping her curvy ass over and over. And then his release crashed into him. He jammed his cock deep, snarling her name as he exploded inside her.

She sagged to the mattress, her eyes closed, her breath coming in shallow pants.

Slumping over her, Luka nuzzled her neck, utterly sated. He rolled them onto their sides and held her tight, reveling in the sheer rightness of it—her scent, warmth, weight, softness, how perfectly she fit against him.

His attention fell on the ring she wore, and emotions swelled in his chest. The feelings she brought out in him weren't soft and sweet and fluffy. They were too dark, too intense, too greedy. But they were deep and true and so fucking encompassing it almost hurt.

"I noticed that Lily kept eyeing this," he said, tapping the diamond.

Naomi opened her eyes. "It's your own fault for buying me such pretty bling." She snuggled into him like a contented cat. "She's almost unbearably cute."

"I liked seeing you hold her. It made me imagine you holding our children."

"How many do you want?"

"At least two."

A playful light shimmered in her gaze. "Hmm, children born of a legion and a half-demon half-fallen-seraphim. I wouldn't be surprised if there's a prophecy out there claiming that they'll destroy the world."

He chuckled low. "Let's hope they can't open portals to hell."

"Fingers crossed."

Sobering, he said, "If we have a son, he will not be groomed to take over this lair—or the empire I inherited—as I was. Our kids will be allowed to be children, and they'll know they're loved."

Her expression tightened. "I don't like that you never felt sure you were loved. I really don't know how I'm supposed to be nice to your father when I meet him. My demon wants to choke him."

Once Luka had made his parents aware that he'd taken a

mate, they had insisted on meeting her. On telling her that, Naomi's first response had been a hard no.

"I get why Andrey thought it best to shape you into someone who wouldn't feel he needed love and affection," she'd said, *"but I still resent the fuck out of him for it."*

Still, she'd eventually agreed to meet them. Once.

"You don't need to be nice to him, you ..." Luka trailed off on seeing that her gaze had turned inward. "Naomi?" Nothing. "Naomi?"

Her eyes sharpened on him. "Hmm?"

"Where'd you go?"

"I have not moved."

"And yet you disappeared. Now, maybe you could listen to me."

"I'm gonna hang off your every word—watch."

He nipped her jaw. "You should always hang off my every word. You should find everything I say utterly fascinating. I should have your full attention at all times."

A chuckle bubbled out of her. "You sound like Lou."

He felt his good humor fade at the mention of her father. "I swear if he randomly appears in our bedroom one more time ..."

"Once he gets over the fact that I'm mated, he'll stop dicking with you. Until that time comes, he's going to be difficult."

"'Difficult' is being stand-offish and rude. Hanging over my bed while I sleep, ensuring I wake to find him looming over me chewing on beef jerky—"

"He promised he wouldn't do that again."

"He also promised that he'd stop leaving burn marks on my suits with his joints. Guess what? He lied."

Naomi grimaced. "Yeah, he does that a lot." She pressed a kiss to his jaw. "I'm sorry that my dad's a pain in the ass. Can I make it up to you somehow?"

"You don't need to make it up to me. *He's* the issue. Not you. Never you. You bring me peace. Never had that until you."

Luka had been forced to swim in dark waters his whole life. That shit had a way of staining your soul. But Naomi had wiped those stains away, leaving her own touches behind; engraving her name right there on his soul. There would be no removing it. He wouldn't even if he could.

His father had been wrong in insisting that attachments weakened a person. She didn't make him feel weak. She made him feel stronger. And he knew that his life would be worth shit if she wasn't in it.

He curled a loose strand of hair around her ear. "Never imagined what it'd feel like to have someone who'd be your entire fucking world. That's what you are to me."

A warm smile curved her mouth. "You say some pretty nice stuff sometimes." She nuzzled his face. "Love you more than I love painting – and that says a lot. You're my person."

"Just as you're mine."

"Promise?"

"Promise."

"Always?"

"Always."

"And you'll stop subjecting me to delayed gratification?"

Luka hesitated. "No."

She let out an irritated sigh. "I was afraid you'd say that."

ACKNOWLEDGEMENTS

Writing a book is a challenge at the best of times. It turns out that writing when you're seriously burned out is next to impossible. It was only my love of these characters and this world that helped me finish. I've grown unprofessionally attached to every Dark in You character, and knowing *Legion* is the last in the series makes me honestly want to cry (I won't or it'll freak out my dog).

Thank you to everyone who took a chance on this series, whether you read one book or more. *Burn* was originally meant to be a standalone—yeah, look how that turned out—yet here we are, ten more books later ... and it boggles my mind that there are people who read every one. THANK YOU! From me and every single Dark in You character—all of whom will no doubt continue to run around my head with scissors—thank you so much to every single reader.

Thanks also to my family, my PA, my social media manager, and of course the wonderful and talented and hard-working team at Piatkus! I would go on and on but, honestly, I'm beginning to see that the not-crying-thing might just have been wishful thinking.

Love you all!

Take care,
S :)

Want more of the
Dark in You series?

Go back to the beginning
and meet Harper and Knox.

Available now at

PIATKUS

No one really knows what they are.
Only that they're the first civilization.
Aeons, they call themselves.

They're immortal. Powerful. Secretive.

Available now at

Do you love fiction with a supernatural twist?

Want the chance to hear news about your favourite authors (and the chance to win free books)?

Christine Feehan
J.R. Ward
Sherrilyn Kenyon
Charlaine Harris
Jayne Ann Krentz and Jayne Castle
P.C. Cast
Maria Lewis
Darynda Jones
Hayley Edwards
Kristen Callihan
Keri Arthur
Amanda Bouchet
Jacquelyn Frank
Larissa Ione

Then visit the *With Love* website and sign up to our romance newsletter:
www.yourswithlove.co.uk

And follow us on Facebook for book giveaways, exclusive romance news and more:
www.facebook.com/yourswithlovex

PIATKUS